'I was very impressed not only by the characters but also your command of the period. I have read many historical novels set in the same time which do not capture anything like the feel of the 19th century.'
Tim Stretton: book reviewer and author of The Dog of the North

'The Board of Editors were delighted with the unconventional plot, and were impressed with your professional and elegant writing. The Board also felt that your narrative combined with your Great-Great-Grandfather's letters made a unique and distinct manuscript.'
Austin Macauley Publishers Ltd

'In 1 Parrot in cage Steve Wylie weaves a rich tapestry of a seafaring adventure set against the background of Victorian rural England. Gentle lyricism is blended with brutal realism, giving the reader a first-hand experience. Authentic and moving.'
Anna Legat: reviewer at Bookmarked Reviews and author of the DI Gillian Marsh Mysteries

'I don't think there is an issue of whether it should be published, it should. Whether it will ever pay is another matter.'
Unicorn Publishing Group

Published by Steve Wylie 2019

ISBN: 978-0-244-17158-2

Copyright © Steve Wylie 2019

The right of Steve Wylie to be identified as the author of this work has been asserted by him in accordance with the Copyright, Designs and Patents Act 1988.

All rights reserved. No part of this publication may be reproduced, stored in a retrieval system, or transmitted, in any form or by any means, electronic, mechanical, photocopying, recording or otherwise, without the prior written permission of the publisher.

1 Parrot in cage

by

Steve Wylie

Illustrations also by Steve Wylie

Cover photographs: sunset at East Head beach, West Wittering.

For my great-great-grandfather

George William Eastland

who co-wrote this story with me

**The delicate shells lay on the shore;
The bubbles of the latest wave
Fresh pearls to their enamel gave;
And the bellowing of the savage sea
Greeted their safe escape to me.**

**I wiped away the weeds and foam,
I fetched my sea-born treasures home;
But the poor, unsightly, noisome things
Had left their beauty on the shore,
With the sun, and the sand, and the wild uproar.**

[From the poem 'Each and All' by Ralph Waldo Emerson 1803-1882]

Sunday 20th March 1842

The Bull's Head Inn, Newfishbourne, Sussex, 7.34am

Matilda Eastland.

A carpet of morning dew lies thickly atop the grass: droplets sparkling beneath the shafts of golden sunlight that pierce the canopy of branches that overhang the inn.

A blackbird fills the air with its morning song, welcoming the new day with a whistle and a trill. Aside the blackbird and the occasional rustling of leaves as a gentle breeze stirs, everything is quiet.

Until the small splutter, followed by the shrill squeal.

'Wah, wah, waaaaah.' The unmistakeable first cries of a newborn baby burst out from the crooked bedroom window that looks in the direction of the Fishbourne Channel.

We know the new arrival will be a mixed blessing but are thankful to hear the voice of Ann, our mother. Between the squeals Mother says to Grandmother, 'Thank the Lord – I'm getting too old for this.'

'I'm not sharing my bedroom with yet another sister,' I say determinedly. 'I've had to share with Martha ever since she was born, and she kept me awake with the colic for most of her first year. It's your turn this time Nancy.'

'But I'll be taking my school exams next year and I will need to be able to sleep at night, otherwise I will get my sums all wrong,' Nancy replies.

'I managed to pass my school exam at eleven despite sharing my bedroom with Martha, but I'm a barmaid now earning money and I need my sleep more than you, Nancy. I'll keep Martha but you must share with our new sister.'

Nancy can't think of a reply to this so instead just sighs.

The stairs creak as our eldest sister, Mary Ann descends before entering the scullery where Nancy and I have been talking. She says, 'Come on you two. Mother has had the baby and though it has taken all night she is well. And so is the baby as you can hear. Go and fetch

Martha and then all of you come up and see. Tell Martha to be quiet though. Mother is tired, and so is Grandma.'

A minute later and the whole family are crowded around Mother's bed, eager to see our new baby sister. Well, not quite all as Father is away at sea. He is a mariner and is away for a few days or sometimes weeks, and then comes back home for a few days, or weeks.

Mother is propped up in bed being suckled by her new baby. Grandma, who also lives with us is sitting in the chair next to the bed, looking a bit drawn from the long night with her daughter. Grandma seems unable to wipe the smile from her reddened cheeks.

We all gaze at the tiny baby: Mary Ann, aged fifteen, and I are both barmaids in the family tavern. Nancy is eight and still goes to school, and holding onto my hand is two-year-old Martha.

There had been another sister, Rosenia, but she died a year ago from the fever. Mother thinks that to have another daughter ensures there will always be one more barmaid in the making. Family barmaids are always reliable and trustworthy with the money, which is not always the case with the other casual barmaids, Mother says. It also ensures the customer tips are kept in the family - Mother says.

Mother gives an exhausted but relieved smile as she turns her baby's face towards us and says, 'Say hello to your beautiful new baby brother, George William Eastland.'

For a moment there is a stunned silence as we take in what our mother has just said. Then Nancy says, 'What, it isn't a girl?'

'No,' says Mother. 'You have got a brother – see...' And indeed we do all see as Mother briefly unwraps George from the blanket in which he lies.

'I've never been too concerned about not having a son,' Mother says. 'Healthy happy children are the most important thing. I love you all, and having girls means I have always got a good supply of barmaids for my inn, and when I'm too old one of you can run the Bull's Head. But your father is going to be speechless when he finds he has got a son.'

Mother goes on to say, 'Gran and I will rest today, but it is Sunday and the inn will be busy later. Mary is in charge of the bar with Matilda's help. Mary - make sure William works hard today and keeps the ale flowing. If I am strong enough I will come and sit behind the bar this evening to keep an eye on things.'

With that, Mother lies back against the pillow and dozes with our little brother in her arms all wrapped up under the warm counterpane. Grandma is already having forty winks in the chair, and my sisters and I run off to get on with a hundred tasks in the tavern while we get used to the idea of actually having a brother. George is going to be spoiled – for a little while.

The old English custom of naming the first-born son after his father has been followed and George is named after Father. He is also given a second name of William, after Father's Father.

My father met Mother at the inn where she worked at Emsworth when she was little more than a girl. Of all the tavern girls, Mother captured his heart, and they married seventeen years ago and moved the three miles up the road from Emsworth to Chichester. They took over the Bull's Head Inn at Fishbourne a few years later.

In many ways Mother is the head of the household. Although Father is the Licensed Victualler for the Bull's Head, Mother runs the business.

She manages the workers, keeps the ale flowing, deals with any rowdy drinkers, and pays the bills.

She knows the trade inside out and is a very good landlady - her family, the Millers having run mills and inns for years. She is also a kind but firm mother to all of us.

Our inn is on Turnpike Road at Newfishbourne, a mile and a half to the west of the town of Chichester in West Sussex.

The hazy spire of Chichester Cathedral rises above the landscape to the east like a bony grey finger pointing up to Heaven.

Behind the inn, just a stone's throw away is the Fishbourne Channel which feeds into Chichester Harbour and in turn into the English Channel.

Little Georgie sleeps through his first day in the Bull's Head. He is lulled to sleep by the constant and reassuring noises from the tavern downstairs. Just after 6 o'clock the sun sets in the distance to the west, over Bosham.

Mother also stays sleeping next to George.

Sunday 17th April 1842

Newfishbourne, 7.30am

Matilda Eastland.

A continuous curtain of rain has washed over Newfishbourne during the hours of darkness. The prevailing wind comes from the west along the English Channel, and whistles through the Solent between Portsea Island and the Isle of Wight before arriving at the door of the Bull's Head.

Having blown all the cobwebs from the eaves of the inn and rattled the masts of the boats moored in Fishbourne Harbour it flies east past Selsey Bill to clean the face of Sussex. The winds continue on past Hastings to the Straits of Dover, to play there with English and French boats passing between Folkestone and Calais, and finally off to the North Sea.

Drip drip drip, the rain leaves our roof as morning breaks. The sky is sliding from grey to blue and the countryside all around is bathed in a glittering watery sunshine. As I wash down the wooden tables in the bar I can see through the windows at the front of the inn to the roadway that links Chichester to the east, with Bosham and onto Emsworth to the west.

The Turnpike Road running in front of The Bull is still all quiet but for one passing cart driven by a man wrapped in a heavy grey cloak. He shelters under the wide brim of his brown leather hat keeping a firm grip on the horse's reins as the cartwheels slew hither and thither on the muddy road. The traveller is trailed by a puff of tobacco smoke from the pipe in his mouth, which curls past his shoulder, then vanishes.

The road may be quiet but the birds are out in great number. The blackbirds, thrush and finches are singing their hearts out as if they know the morning worship at the Church of St. Peter and St. Mary will start at ten and have to warm up their voices in readiness. With the nesting season underway the trees and hedges in Fishbourne are a riot of noise and activity. Four swans join in by flying up from the coast and over the Bull's Head, crying in time to the slow beat of their long wings.

We clean the bar in the morning because by the time the last revellers are eased out of The Bull of a night it is too late, and all we want to do is fall into our beds. Bright and early in the morning is when the tables and walls are washed down, the floors swept, and the glasses all washed using big pots of water boiled on the stove. The windows and doors are opened wide at the front and back to blow out the fug of ale, smoke and sick. We also use lemon or lavender, or whatever other fragrant wild plants are in season to freshen the air before the next day's drinkers arrive.

The cleaning mostly falls on Mary and me, as well as Emily Tur, our servant. Emily is only twelve but very hard-working and a quick learner. We also have a male servant, William Cockshott, who does the heavy work in the bar. William lives at Bosham and walks the one and a half miles to the inn each day.

Once a week, usually on a Monday the horses pulling the delivery cart from George Gale's Brewery clop up the road and stop at the front of The Bull, right next to the cellar door. The driver releases the horses from the cart and takes them round to the back of the inn to our stables to be watered and fed ready for the journey back up the steep hill to Horndean. Meanwhile William unloads the barrels of ale and rolls and carries them down to the cellar.

On the other mornings he re-stocks the bar making sure there are sufficient kegs with taps hammered into them ready for the day's business. After that he works behind the bar. Mother chose William because he is tall and wide, which puts him in good stead when a drunk needs to be shown the door, or when a fight in the bar needs to be broken up.

The Bull's Head has to be cleaned today same as any other, even though today is the occasion of little Georgie's baptism. My sisters and I had frowned at the prospect of George being lavished with extra attention as he was the first boy born to our parents. In truth this was an uncharitable thought for which I should seek forgiveness at church today. For Mother loves George just like the rest of us – no more and no less.

George's crumpled little face made Grandmother smile when she peered at his features through her tired blue eyes. And Father was cock-a-hoop when he returned home from sea to see his newest child. He could scarcely believe his eyes when he saw he had a son and did a little jig in the bar that any self-respecting mariner would have been proud of, before swiftly emptying a glass of grog.

At half past nine the bell at St. Peter and St. Mary begins to toll reminding local people from around the parish to start their walk to church. And so the people proceed past the Bull's Head on their way there. Some walk across the fields from the farms and cottages on the Bosham peninsula. A few walk the two and a half miles up from Bosham Hoe. A number come from farms to the east in the direction of Stockbridge, but most come from the farms to the north in quite a procession down Clay Lane and Black Boy Lane.

It is now clear and sunny but wet underfoot, so many of the congregation are wearing their Sunday best hats and waistcoats along with their good stout and muddy boots.

Father carries little George to the church wrapped up in a white blanket and wearing a white woollen bonnet, knitted some time in the past by Grandmother especially for baptisms. We are all at the church this morning, Grandmother, Father, Mother, Mary, Nancy, Martha and me – and of course our special little George. Although The Bull is open all day, it is not busy on a Sunday morning. We can leave it for a while in the care of the servants. But once the baptism is finished it will be back to the bar for Mother, Mary and I as there will be plenty of people drinking there today once everyone comes out of church. Sunday, the one day when people don't work is our busiest day of the week.

We have arrived a few minutes early and manage to find an empty pew halfway back on the right-hand side where we are all able to squeeze in together. Everybody knows that you have to arrive at least ten minutes before the service is due to start if you want to sit. And it is a long time to stand. Of course we youngsters have to give seats to older parishioners so I am used to standing or sitting in a corner. If the younger children are well behaved, and lucky, they might find a lap to sit on.

St. Peter and St. Mary is always dark and cold, despite the many people. I always wear lots of layers of clothes to keep me warm. But I like this old church. It somehow feels safe and it is peaceful when there are not too many people in it. In front of us, in the east wall behind the Rector is a pretty square stained-glass window. My eye is drawn to the colours in this small glass square. There is no need to light the oil lamps this morning as the sun is forcing its way through the small window, and a selection of candles enable us to see well enough. The oil can be saved for another time.

The small choir is ready, all sitting upon the two old and ornately carved wooden pews. The old stone font stands at the front of the congregation in the middle of the chancel where the Rector, William Turner is sorting his books and papers for the service. With that, he clears his throat and in his booming voice instructs the congregation to be on their knees for the opening prayer.

The Sunday service follows its usual form of prayers, hymns and the sermon, followed by the Holy Communion for all who have been confirmed, which is almost everybody. The Rector then moves onto the baptisms of which, as usual, there are several. He calls for the parents and godparents of all the children who are to be baptised to come and stand at the chancel.

He then raises his arms, looks to the heavens and starts to recite from the Baptism section in his Book of Common Prayer.

Coming to the font the Rector fills it with pure water from a large earthenware jug and says,

'**Hath this Child been already Baptized, or no?**'

The parents and godparents all respond together – a resounding 'no'.

The Rector continues with his sermon. He eventually reaches the part where he takes George into his hands and says to the godparents…

'**Name this child…**'

'George William Eastland,' they reply.

'**George William Eastland I baptise thee In the Name of the Father, and of the Son, and of the Holy Ghost. Amen.**

'**We receive this Child into the Congregation of Christ's flock** (the Rector here makes a cross upon George's forehead) **and do sign** him with the sign of the Cross, in token that hereafter he shall not be ashamed to confess the faith of Christ crucified, and manfully to fight under his banner, against sin, the world and the devil; and to continue Christ's faithful soldier and servant unto his life's end. Amen.'

This is followed by a prayer. We all kneel to say…

'Our Father, which art in heaven, Hallowed be thy Name. Thy kingdom come. Thy will be done in earth, As it is in heaven. Give us this day our daily bread. And forgive us our trespasses, As we forgive them that trespass against us. And lead us not into temptation; But deliver us from evil. Amen.'

The Rector carries on reminding the godparents to renounce the Devil, telling them that they are responsible for George attending sermon regularly, for teaching him the Creed, the Lord's Prayer, the Ten Commandments and all the other things a Christian should know. He also tells them that they are responsible for bringing George to the Bishop to be confirmed as soon as he can say the Creed, the Lord's Prayer and the Ten Commandments.

I have sat through many a baptism, yet still cannot profess to understand all those words, warnings and threats. It is, nevertheless quite clear to me that being a godparent must be a great honour, and a heavy responsibility.

Thus, having been utterly and undeniably admonished by the Rector we all emerge from the heavy gloom of the church to blink and shade our eyes from the warm and bright sunshine outside. George has been baptised and is, at least for now, sin free and under the protection of God.

We walk back to The Bull's Head to drink in celebration of this event, before getting on with a normal busy Sunday at the inn. Only God knows what path George will tread in this life, and what triumphs and trials He has in store for him.

I pray that my sweet little brother finds love and happiness.

Wednesday 31st August 1842

Woodhorn Farm, Sidlesham Lane, Birdham

Emma Collick.

She is a gorgeous baby. Twinkling little eyes, jet black hair, dimples in her cheeks, and that giggle. My little sweetheart.

As births go, that of my sixth child Sarah Jane has been quite easy. 'It's not the best time of year for a baby – right in the middle of harvest,' my husband William told me. As if he was without any responsibility for my condition!

And so I was left largely alone to get on with it. Our servant, Maria Smith stayed with me in the cottage doing household chores to be nearby when my baby started to come. I was glad of her company, but Maria is just sixteen. When I was in full labour she was to run and fetch Elizabeth Clayton, the farmer's wife from along the lane to come and help.

Apart from my two smallest children, Emily Jane aged five and Thomas Henry, two, everybody else is busy with the harvest.

Maria made her dash down the lane this morning and now I sit rocking this gorgeous baby in my arms as she sleeps.

Luckily I have never had too much trouble giving birth. It is keeping them alive afterwards which is more of a problem.

Thursday 6th October 1842

Woodhorn Farm, Birdham

Emma Collick.

My husband William Collick is a big farmer, born in the village of Bersted in Sussex, the eldest son of his father William Collick, and from a long line of farmers – and William Collicks. We were married in 1831 when I was nineteen. William, then twenty-nine, was already a well-established farmer and in need of sons to carry on the Collick family's farming line.
    I did my best.
    I gave birth to our first daughter Emma on Friday 11th January 1833. I remember it well. The Rector, William Miller came to our home to baptise Emma that very day – just before she died. Emma was buried at West Wittering the following Monday.
    Later that year I had our second daughter Charlotte. Charlotte was born on Sunday 8th December 1833. As Charlotte was born I told myself that it was Sunday – a Holy day and that the angels would be watching over her.
    They were watching – but nothing more.
    The Rector came to our home, straight after the Sunday Worship to baptise Charlotte that very day – just before she died. Charlotte was buried at West Wittering the following Wednesday.
    I wished I had died too.
    I realised I would never bear children for William and give him the son and heir he so wanted to pass his farm on to. I might as well have been dead as I could not be a wife to William. I was terrified of the promise I had made to him on our wedding day, 'With my body I thee worship.' I felt hopeless, barren and empty - like a prickly horse-chestnut shell containing no conker.
    For his part William never blamed me. He was true to his wedding vows, 'To take me... for better for worse... in sickness and in health...' He said, 'God's will shall be done and if we are not meant to

have children so be it.' At that black time it was only William's love that sustained me.

Resigned, we simply got on with our farming. I knew it would be a sin to deny William his husbandly rights but I avoided it when I could and was terrified when we did. But we found that by only lying together at the safe time of the month, and by inserting a piece of sponge into me to absorb William's release I could avoid falling.

It was therefore, to my surprise, and utter terror, that I found I was again with child, early in 1835. I was terrified that I would once again carry a baby for nine months and then murder it at birth as I had done with Emma and Charlotte. I wished I was not carrying, and thought of the pain and grief that William and I were going to have to go through once more. But William said, 'This child will be born in summer whilst the other two were born in midwinter. Have Faith.' So I relaxed and left it to God.

In late summer I gave birth to Alice Eliza, a bundle of lively energy, with fair hair, big round eyes and pink cheeks. You never did see such a picture of health. Alice was baptised at St. James' Church in Birdham on Wednesday 14th October 1835 and William and I had never prayed in church so hard as we did that day. I remember the tears running down my cheeks and the people wondering what was the matter with me. I didn't care one jot - I was so happy.

Our second daughter, Emily Jane was born two years later in autumn 1837, another bright and bouncy fair-haired girl and I was no longer worried about having babies. Except that we still didn't have a son and William was not getting any younger.

Meanwhile the farm was expanding and making us a good living, and with our growing family as well as servants we needed a bigger cottage. So whilst we lived in the old cottage William set about building us a new one – Woodhorn Farmhouse.

Woodhorn is a lovely large cottage built of red brick and grey flint and has a tiled roof, and there is a fireplace at each end of the cottage so we are not cold. Such comfort I've never known. With a kitchen and scullery and living rooms downstairs, it has six bedrooms upstairs from where you can see our fields all around. As well as the fires we have oil lamps in each room, so we can see easily even in the dark winter evenings. With three bedrooms at the front of the cottage and three more at the back we have room for plenty more children.

William has also built us a deep brick well next to the cottage so we have plentiful water and no walk to fetch it. Life is good. Woodhorn Farmhouse was completed in 1840. We are all so proud of our cottage, and William carved 'WC 1840' into a red brick and set the brick into the wall above the front door for all to see.

Moving into Woodhorn was not the only important event in 1840, as soon after I found I was again with child. In midsummer our first son, Thomas Henry Collick was born and I saw the joy and relief in William's face. It was his turn to have the glassy eyes at Thomas' baptism on 5th September at St. James' Church.

This summer brought sweet little Sarah Jane. On Sunday 23rd September William brought the horse and cart round to the lane next to our cottage and the whole family rode to St. James' in the warm autumn sunshine for Sarah's baptism. The sun streamed in through the colourful stained-glass of the church windows and the birds sung their hearts out in the churchyard. What a happy girl Sarah is sure to be.

This feels like a time to treasure. After a desolate start to our marriage our fortunes have turned. Now married for eleven years we have three beautiful young daughters and a son. Our lovely big farmhouse at Woodhorn sits amidst our many acres of arable farmland and is thriving. I am fortunate that we are able to employ our servant, Maria who helps me in the farmhouse, with the children, and with growing vegetables and looking after the chickens. The harvest went well again this year and the farm had a good crop of wheat and barley. William has two agricultural labourers William Napper and James Wollfe to help him run the farm, plus casual labourers at busy times.

Our Faith and hard work is now paying off. I thank God for helping us put all our troubles behind us.

Sunday 28th April 1844

The Bull's Head

Mary Eastland (senior).

Why has God spared me this long, I sometimes wonder? What purpose does He still have for an eighty-two year old widow?

My old bones are beginning to creak but I know God has looked down upon me favourably so many times, for which I am truly thankful.

I thought it was for the babies. I have helped many babies into this life, and most all good. The women have always shared and shared alike their time and skills in times of need and I had a knack with births. Some infants died in childbirth or came out cold while the mother lived. Some babies spared whilst the mother expired from the effort or damage of the coming. Both are harsh. In both there remain young children either without mother, or with a mother gone mad not always to recover. God has his reasons, but the pain to those remaining after a bad birth is one I shall be glad to carry no more when I am gone.

Labourers' wives have no use for doctors in childbirth. We cannot afford their rude fees for meddling with God's will. They can do nothing about a baby that won't come out, a twisted afterbirth or bleeding from inside.

I had eight births myself, and some survived. Ann has had seven and only lost one. Rosenia was born between Nancy and Martha, but died when she was little more than a toddler. Sunday 28th February three years ago – I remember that ugly day. 'Tis wicked trick of God that He should let me remember that day. Most times I can't remember what day of the week it is. It makes me so mad.

It was winter, but instead of snow there had been weeks of dreary rain. Everywhere was grey and damp and we all had coughs and colds. Rosenia was no worse nor the rest of us. Then one morning she suddenly collapsed. Mary and Matilda were busy with Ann running the inn. Nancy was at Sunday school and Martha just a babe herself, so I looked after Rosenia. I put her to bed to rest but she was very hot and clammy so I bathed her skin with cool water.

Rosenia got worse very fast. Despite my attentions her skin was hot as fire by the evening. She would not drink, and when I poured a little water into her mouth she choked and spat it out. By eight o'clock she started screaming, flailing her arms and throwing her head back, and then she fell suddenly silent. Poor Rosenia's body lay twisted and lifeless on the bed which was drenched with her sweat. A raging fever like this is almost impossible to stop.

God rest her soul.

Ann is more than forty now. I've lost count. All I know is she should stop making barmaids. I cannot tell her this – she will not be told.

George is two – a lovely boy and first son. I helped at his birth – was smooth as butter. Ann should have stopped then. But this February she had her seventh – another boy named John Onslow. I was too weak to help this time but Mary Ann and Emily Tur did the best they could. If they had asked me I would have told them what to do. But they youngsters wanted it their own way.

John Onslow has never stopped coughing or crying since the day he was born. It wears me out just listening to him. I pray this summer fills his lungs with some health.

I remember my grandmother said to me when I was a girl, 'When it comes to infants a bird in the hand is worth two in the bush.' Her name was Alice and she was born around 1710 during the reign of Queen Anne. And now we have another Queen. Veronica…or Valencia? Doesn't matter anyway does it? I sure people who talk to her just bow and curtsey and call her 'Queen.' Her blessed name will come to me, when I don't need it.

Alice taught me about childbirth. 'We do what we can to calm a mother and to ease her pain. In the end a child is born by the grace of God and nothing else – even royalty. Queen Anne had twenty babies: most died at birth. The three that survived birth died as children,' she would say. 'We be all the same in the eyes of The Lord, even royalty.'

I never believed my grandmother's old wives tale, but she were right that the birth and then life of a child is fragile in early years.

Parents have many children as they know some will be lost, but you can never tell which it is going to be. I am thankful my loss has been small. I hope Ann has no more babies.

As a girl I lived with my father, mother and siblings in a cottage just a stone's throw from Bodiam Castle in Sussex. Such a beautiful Castle you never did see with its round grey brick towers and moat all around it and teeming with fish. But ruined it was inside.

Father was a carpenter mending carts and furniture and farmers' fences, and my elder brothers worked on nearby farms. I was again lucky as I was let to go to the day school from the age of four. Many children never went to school but just laboured in the fields. I was born Mary Weaver. Weaving and hand crafts had been in our family for generations.

When I first went to school we were taught about the Bible and shown the letters of our names and shown how to count to ten. Age five I was taken to the special lace school where the Mistress taught us girls how to make lace for which we were paid. Every day around twenty-five girls from all round the village went to the Mistress's cottage where we sat in a circle in her living room. We worked from eight in the morning until three in the afternoon during which time we were lucky enough to have two ten-minute breaks to stretch our legs outside and get some air.

It got very stuffy with so many girls working hard as the room was only about twelve feet square. It was too hot in the summer but even though many girls worked in the room it was very cold in winter, and sometimes it was hard to feel your fingers. When it was very cold the Mistress's maid would put small basins of hot water called 'Dicky pots' between our feet so the steam would rise and warm our hands enough so that we could carry on working.

We were taught all kinds of lace-making and also how to make straw-plait to be made into hats and baskets. But my school mostly did pillow lace-making using bobbins, as the fine lace we produced got the best prices at nearby markets and was in high demand in London too.

We all sat on chairs each having a hard round cushion stuffed with straw upon our knees on which we created the lace. The threads were attached to the wooden or bone bobbins which had different patterns carved into them. The bobbins themselves were beautiful to see, and to hold, and clicked as we worked the threads.

The Mistress could be hard on children who couldn't work fast enough, or who made mistakes in their lace-making as she knew the price of the lace would be affected, and her 'reputation'! She would scold girls and sometimes crack their knuckles with a stick. Young fingers had to get used to pulling the threads all day long. I remember a young girl whose fingers got so sore they started bleeding onto the lace. The Mistress got angry and shouted at her, 'I can't sell bloodstained lace. Go home and don't come back till next week. You'll not be paid this week.' The girl was probably only four. She sobbed as she left the room with red and white streaks across her grubby cheeks where she had wiped her tears with the back of her hand and bleeding fingers.

In the evenings my grandmother Alice taught me ways to improve my lace-work, and how to relax my body into the best position to work for long times. She told me to look out of the window every so often to rest my eyes, and to regularly relax my shoulders and to remember 'More haste, less speed.' She said if I remembered these things I would produce more lace than most by the end of each day.

She was right.

Later when I was twelve, I started working longer hours with the other older girls and women. We worked from six in the morning till ten at night with breaks for meals, from Monday to Saturday. When it got dark a tall tallow candle was lit in the centre of the table around which we all sat. We used a 'pole-board' which is a wooden support with a hole in front of each girl. A thin glass bottle containing some water was placed in each hole which magnified the lacework below so we could see our threads and continued working into the evening.

Fine lace was in demand in the 1770s and 1780s so we were never short of work. We each had to pay a ha'penny per week which was increased to one penny in winter, to pay for the lights and thread. If we produced the required amount of lace we would be paid two pennies per day. We were paid at the end of the week on Saturday, with Sundays off to go to church. The lace was sold to the village grocer or draper who took it to market to sell to bigger agents in Hastings or Tonbridge.

I was very thankful for my time at school. I learnt skills that I have used all my life. It's a crying shame that girls don't learn these things at school today – it's all writing and 'rithmetic. I learned enough for me. I liked drawing little pictures of flowers with my mother's quill pen, and I can sign my name with a neat X and that is all I ever needed. I learn about things by listening to people talk, although most people speak too quiet these days. They should open their mouths properly. I can hear the Priest on Sundays clear enough.

In Bodiam everything, even lace-making, stops in September for hop-picking. Everybody is in the fields picking from dawn till dusk. Lots of extra pickers come down from London to help, such is the work to be done before the rains come and the cold weather of autumn. Hop-picking is hot, back-breaking work. I was very grateful to get back to my lace-making.

I thought that was my lot in life, for which I was thankful. I knew no other life until I met William Eastland who turned my head upside-down. I was fifteen at the time. My son George looks just like his father. Sometimes when I see him I think he is William.

When the Bodiam fine lace was taken to market at Tonbridge or Hastings by one of the local traders he would oft take one of the village lace-makers with him. The Mistress said, 'The lace-makers know the value of the lace, know the blood sweat and tears that went into making it, and are better able to persuade the fancy young gentlemen to buy it than is the hoary old grocer.' So she would let one of us older girls go on the pony and trap for the day, on full pay to get the best prices for our laces.

One fine spring day in 1781 I rode on the cart carrying all the village wares to market wearing my finest Sunday dress and hat. We had to leave Bodiam at six o'clock in the morning to make the twelve mile journey to Hastings. Luckily the weather had been dry for most of the previous month and the horse and cart proceeded without delays. Sometimes when it was very wet the village would not send a cart to market for fear that the wheels would get stuck in the mud on the old track and the goods would be made wet or muddy if the cart slewed off the road. It was better to wait till the next market.

We were in Hastings by mid-morning and trying, by hook or by crook, to get the best prices for our goods. It was around noon when I saw a handsome man approach our cart. It was William Eastland. I blushed and sold him a piece of lacework that I had made. It was not the best price I had ever secured but it was the best contract I ever entered into. Within two years we were married and had the first of our eight children. William had taken me away from the farming life which I had thought was the centre of existence, and shown me Hastings and many places beyond. He was a mariner and trader and told me of things I had not previously dreamt of. He said my eyes were like sapphires. God knows we were very happy.

New Fishbourne is a peaceful place. By the time William died our children had flown the nest. Thank God my son George brought me into his home at the Bull's Head. He brought all my worldly possessions on one of his barges from the port of Hastings around the coast and all the way up the Fishbourne Canal to the small jetty, just a spitting distance from the inn.

I sometimes sit in the courtyard behind The Bull in the afternoon sunshine with my knitting or sewing. I can no longer make lace as my eye-sight has gone, and my fingers are stiff and painful with arthritis. But I enjoy knitting, and I darn socks with holes in them, and make myself useful mending clothes and curtains or any other such tasks. Martha sits and watches me knit with those round brown eyes of hers, and she enjoys playing Cat's Cradle with me with a length of my wool.

If there is heaven on earth this is it. From my seat in the courtyard I can hear the meadow pipit sing and the distant cry of gulls hovering over the reeds and marshes beyond. Sometimes the heron flies over with a graceful flap of wing, his stick legs stretched out behind.

The grand Chichester Cathedral is but a mile off, though I prefer the Church of St. Peter and St. Mary just up the lane from the Bull's Head. I walk there to the 6 o'clock service of a Sunday evening when I have the strength – it's a lovely walk on a sunny evening in spring. I follow the narrow lane at the side of the Bull away from the Turnpike

Road. Three small boys run past me full of glee carrying fishing nets on their way back from the Mill Pond. A little further on the left I reach the old red brick and flint Mill House.

The house has a low red brick wall with curved bricks on top facing west and the stones absorb the heat of the afternoon sun. I often sit against this wall for a rest on my way home from church, from where I can gaze at the Mill Pond right in front of me. The still water is like glass and the flowers and trees reflect in it like a magical mirror. I am joined by the ducks and we all watch the pond glittering under the overhanging branches of the weeping willow.

My son George sails the oceans to find exotic places. If only he could see that Paradise is right here at the end of our lane, and he doesn't need to risk life and limb in storms and mountainous seas to get here. He should take more notice of what I tell him. What is the point of me living so long if nobody listens to me! I talk to the ducks – they listen to me.

Past Mill House I turn left through an old iron gate to walk the path alongside the stream. The water is shallow and slow moving and very clear. Trees overhang this path and the stream, and it is cool here whilst the trees and bushes to my right are a riot of birds singing their end-of-day songs. The robin comes and says 'hello' and I also see a sedge warbler. I don't see the chiffchaff, but I can hear his unmistakeable song – chiffchaff, chiffchaff, chiffchaff. At the end of the short path is another iron gate which I pass through. I have always loved birds. But they don't sing so loud as they used to. I expect George told the birds to be quiet just to spite his Mother – he was never interested in birds, just boats. I told him birds never killed anyone. He can't say the same about boats.

The path now turns away from the stream and heads into the grasses of the Fishbourne Meadows which criss-cross the mudflats and salt marshes along this coastline. The paths are well-trodden but inquisitive children often venture into the wrong areas and get stuck in mud up to their knees, or deeper. I don't need a walking stick to help me walk, but I use one to prod the ground to make sure it is firm.

The breeze swishes through the growing bulrushes, and the fresh-faced pink ragged robin flowers dance gaily in the wind. I see there is plenty of scorpion grass growing this year. Its lovely delicate sky-blue flowers will be opening soon. The mild sea air at the end of this creek and the south facing coastline brings all the wild flowers into bloom earlier than in other places.

I follow the path across the meadow with the woods to my left and cross another wooden bridge over a tiny trickle of water. The timber bridge gives off a comforting woody smell with the afternoon sun upon it, and the handrail warms my fingers. I think for a moment I can see a water vole at the edge of the stream. When I look again I can see only stones in the water. A reminder that my eyesight isn't what it once was.

I cross one last small field with the hedgerow now to my right and finally arrive at the gate that takes me into the churchyard. St. Peter and St. Mary is an ancient stone and grey flint church built in the thirteenth century. I walk up the grassy slope past the gravestones and enter the church through the heavy wooden doors into the quiet, cool interior and find myself a space at one of the pews on the left. I sink onto the pew to catch my breath. The walk to church is getting very hard. But if I don't come here how will I get to speak to God properly? I'll be better after I have a rest. Perhaps I will have forty winks during the sermon.

I try to arrive early as the church gets very full and some people have to stand. A seat is of course always found for an old lady but I like to sit in the peaceful church and pray for a while before all becomes busy. I like to look at the beautiful and colourful stained glass in the large arched east window. I am taken by the deep sparkling blue glass and wonder how it shines so brightly after all these years. Perhaps angels add a little more sparkle to the glass each night when everyone else sleeps? I always wonder about the many people who have gazed at these windows in the hundreds of years before me, and of those who will do the same after I am gone. Will this church still be here in six hundred years time?

The Rector, I can't remember his name, welcomes me and says the fine weather probably means the church will be full tonight. He says there are plans to build a new south aisle soon and then to extend the north transept and nave to enable the growing population of

Fishbourne to fit into the church. I tell him to be careful not to damage our beautiful church.

The Rector goes off to light a few oil lamps as more of the congregation begin to arrive. A man sits in the pew behind me and tells his wife the Rector William Turner has agreed to a date for a wedding in the summer. I don't remember that William Turner was his name. Perhaps the Rector has changed his name? Young people do odd things these days you know. Not like when I was a girl. The man in the pew behind me must have got the Rector's name wrong? I am sure it isn't Turner.

It is bright outside in the evening sun, but I like the dark and quiet in the church. I think I'll rest my eyes for a minute.

Before everyone arrives I kneel on a cushion and give thanks to God for all he has given me. I ask him to make sure the Rector, whatever his name is, speaks up so I can hear him. I also ask God why am I still here? I hope Ann has no more children. It worries me so.

Of summer 1844, Fishbourne

Matilda Eastland.

We sometimes have a strong memory of events or people, and only later realise that this cannot be for we either were not there, or were too young to have had that memory ourselves. And, that what we are in fact remembering is what someone else once told us. This is how it was for me with my gentle grandmother Mary. I have heard so many tales about her that sometimes I cannot separate the tales from my own memories.

She was the gentlest person. She had never a bad word for anybody, she had the patience of a saint and would sit with any of my sisters who wanted to borrow her ear or be comforted.

She slept more by day with her knitting and darning than by night, and people had to speak loudly for her to hear. She learnt at school that nowhere in the Bible did it say that teachers should be cruel to children, and decided that she would always be kind to them. I wish my teachers had gone to the same school as Grandmother.

Grandmother was very lean and almost bent double. She could only eat soft food as she had lost her teeth many years earlier. Her favourite was bread and dripping with hot tea. She liked slices of apple peeled, and chided Martha when she nearly threw away an apple containing a maggot hole. Grandmother said, 'Waste not, want not. Just cut out the hole. When I was a child I would have been given the strap for wasting an apple like that. Food was precious. You should thank the Lord for all the food you receive. We are so lucky these days.'

That was the nearest Grandmother got to being sharp with us.

Grandmother got quite confused in her old age. She also ate very slowly because of her lack of teeth and sometimes she fell asleep halfway through her meal. One dinner time she was still eating long after the young children had been allowed to leave the table. The adults remained at the table talking as Grandmother chewed. I had long since forgotten my dinner when I walked past the table. As I did so Grandmother fixed me with that stern 'you stand accused' glare that she gave sometimes when she wished to exert her authority. 'Matilda, have you taken away my plate?'

Having been nowhere near the dining table since being excused I was not expecting this question. I could see that Grandmother's dinner plate was before her, holding her final few pieces of cabbage and potato whilst she continued to clasp her knife and fork. I wondered whether there had been another plate which might have been cleared away. My no doubt slightly bemused expression was all that it took.

Grandmother in later life was confused and could not see or hear well. But she compensated for all these shortcomings with an instinctive observation and interpretation of the clues around her. She seemed to know what people were thinking just by their expressions and mood.

On this occasion quickly noting my apparent air of innocence, or even total ignorance in the face of her accusation, she looked down and contemplated the plate before her. 'Ah yes, I thought somebody said something about a plate. I've nearly finished, don't rush me', she said before adding, 'You should be outside in the fresh air Matilda...unless you'd prefer to come and talk to your old grandmother?'

One morning in the early autumn of 1844 Grandmother didn't get up. Nancy went to find her in bed where she found her unable to move or speak. She was able to be propped up and to sip a little water. Her eyes would follow you around the room, but she showed no expression. I sat with her awhile and she gripped my hand in hers. I'm sure I saw a flicker of a smile. Then she slept.

She slept for two days, her breathing at first wheezy. It turned into a rattle - a rhythmic rattle that could be heard from downstairs.

All of a sudden the rattle ceased and the house was filled with silence.

We realised that Grandmother had passed on to God.

She left me a wonderful patchwork quilt of every hue imaginable that she had sewn together from leftover scraps of all sorts of materials. It kept me warm for many a year.

Grandmother was buried on Monday 30th September 1844 in the churchyard at St. Peter and St. Mary and rests peacefully listening to the church bells and the birds in the trees.

Friday 20th March 1846,

The Bull's Head, Newfishbourne

George William Eastland.

Father came home last night.

His ship has been to Sunderland and back delivering timber.

My father is the Master of his ship.

I'll be the Master of my ship when I am growed up.

I am not yet old enough to go to school.

I am not yet old enough to go into the bar when The Bull is full of customers.

I am old enough to explore the inn, to play in the yard, and to look at books with pictures in them.

I am also old enough to get bored.

I like it when Father is home from sea.

He tells me stories and takes me around the world - in my head.

He tells me about the people he has met, the bad and the mad, and of places that sound so different from anywhere I have seen.

His tales include huge cities with many houses and large factories and chimneys puffing out smoke.

He tells about pretty harbours and coves and old taverns.

He speaks of snow-capped mountains in Scotland and Wales and of puffins with their brightly coloured bills, and dolphins that swim alongside his boats.

As Master of his ship, the "Sunderland", he has a very exciting life.

I am not bored when Father is home.

Father was born in Hastings and has always lived by the sea.

He loves the life sailing on all sorts of boats.

His big ship delivers grain, timber, coal and other cargoes between ports around Britain and sometimes overseas.

He is strong, wiry, as brown as a berry and very determined.

He didn't spend much time at school but is sharp as a razor from all his years as a merchant and trader, and he knows all about business.

During his travels he has met many types of people, has learnt to read and he never gets his money wrong.

And he can write well enough.

He claims to have docked at every harbour in England.

When Father was a young man I think he sailed in a large galleon to the underside of the world where he fought against pirates with his cutlass and made them walk the plank.

He dived in the blue sea searching for gold treasure and caught a whale with his fishing rod. I think.

'Happy birthday George. You are four today,' Mother says as she lifts me into the air. 'I will bake you a cake for your birthday and when Martha comes home from school we can all eat some of it.'

Father walks up behind Mother. 'Happy birthday son. While the women are all busy in the kitchen and in the tavern I will take you out on an adventure.'

A little later I walk down the lane with Father.

It is a breezy but bright day.

The white woolly clouds scud across the blue sky and the sun goes in and out.

'It is a nor' nor' westerly wind George, quite light but cold. If it blows heavy it can be treacherous at sea and blow your sails to shreds. You must get to know all the winds to survive at sea.'

We walk past Fishbourne Mill Pond and after a while Father hoists me upon his shoulders where I can see all around.

'You alright up there in the crow's nest?'

'Oh yes,' I reply.

'No son, you say - yes sir, Cap'n.'

'Yes sir, Cap'n,' I repeat proudly.

Father strides on past Saltmill House on the path that goes to the east of the Fishbourne Channel, beyond Appledram and along the coastline.

I am blown by the freshening wind up here in my crow's nest, and I wave to the gulls that swoop and hang upon the currents of air.

I look for pirates on the horizon of the channel but they daren't come near Father's ship.

Ahead I spot a red brick building.

Perhaps this is where we will fight and defeat the pirates?

We soon approach the building.

Father calls up to me, 'Able Seaman George, come down to the deck for we are about to anchor here at Dell Quay. We will refresh ourselves at the Crown and Anchor tavern.'

With that he drops me down from his shoulders.

'You are back on dry land now my lad. Come with me.'

We are soon sitting side by side on a wooden bench outside at the back of the Crown and Anchor where we are sheltered from the wind.

Here in the sun we watch a large boat unloading coal at the small dock.

Father sips from a large glass of ale and I have a lime cordial drink.

'I can see in your eyes George that you are going to be bright and quick. Soon you will go to school and you must always listen carefully and work hard, as good schooling is the key to life for a successful man. A man must not fester in a tavern all his life. A man needs to be outside breathing fresh air. A man needs to explore the world. A man needs adventures if he is to feel alive. A man must have hopes and dreams. Never let go of your hopes and dreams, George.

'On my last voyage back from Sunderland we moored for a day at the Port of Lowestoft. We were there for a few hours. While the crew unloaded timber I walked into the town and bought you a birthday present, George.'

Father puts his hand into the canvas satchel that hangs over his shoulder.

He pulls out a package wrapped in brown paper and hands it to me.

This strange package fills me with excitement.

I pull off the paper and find it hides a dark red, leather-bound book.

Father tells me the book is called 'The Life and Strange Surprizing Adventures of Robinson Crusoe, of York, Mariner', and was written by a man named Daniel Defoe.

I open the book and study the picture which is inside.

It shows a man wearing a pointed hat and a coat of animal fur.

He holds two rifles, has a cutlass on his hip but wears no shoes.

Behind him a ship is tossed by a wild sea beneath a stormy sky.

Father says, 'That is Robinson Crusoe. He was a mariner who was washed ashore on a desert island when his ship was wrecked. He was the only survivor but he never gave up hope. I'll read you a part of the story George. When you go to school and learn to read you will be able to discover the whole story of how Robinson Crusoe survived.'

Father puts his arm around my shoulder and reads...

'**And now our case was very dismal indeed, for we all saw plainly that the sea went so high that the boat could not live, and that we should be inevitably drowned. As to making sail, we had none, nor, if we had, could we ha' done anything with it: so we worked at the oar towards the land, though with heavy hearts, like men going to execution, for we all knew that when the boat came nearer the shore, she would be dashed in a thousand pieces by the breach of the sea...**

'**After we had rowed, or rather driven, about a league and a half as we reckoned it, a raging wave, mountain-like, came rolling astern of us, and plainly bade us expect the** *coup de grace.* **In a word, it took us with such a fury that it overset the boat at once, and separating us all well from the boat as from one another, gave us not time hardly to say, 'Oh God!' for we were all swallowed up in a moment.**

'**Nothing can describe the confusion of thought which I felt when I sunk into the water, for though I swam very well, yet I could not deliver myself from the waves so as to draw breath, till that wave, having driven me, or rather carried me a vast way on towards the shore, and having spent itself, went back, and left me upon the land almost dry, but half-dead with the water I took in. I** had so much presence of mind as well as breath left that seeing myself nearer the mainland than I expected, I got upon my feet and endeavoured to make on towards the land as fast as I could, before another wave should return and take me up again. But I soon found it was impossible to avoid it, for I saw the sea come after me as high as a great hill, and as furious as an enemy which I had no means or strength to contend with; my business was to hold my breath, and raise myself upon the water, if I could, and so by swimming to preserve my breathing, and pilot myself towards the shore, if possible, my greatest concern now being that the sea, as it would carry me a great way towards the shore when it came on, might not carry me back again with it when it gave back towards the sea.

'The wave that came upon me again buried me at once twenty or thirty foot deep in its own body, and I could feel myself carried with a mighty force and swiftness towards the shore a very great way, but I held my breath and assisted myself to swim still forwards with all my might. I was ready to burst with holding my breath, when, as I felt myself rising up, so to my immediate relief I found my head and hands shoot out above the surface of the water, and though it was not two seconds of time that I could keep myself so, yet it relieved me greatly, gave me breath and new courage. I was covered again with water a good while, but not so long but I held it out, and finding the water had spent itself and began to return, I struck forwards against the return of the waves, and felt ground again with my foot. I stood still a few moments to recover breath, and till the water went from me, and then took to my heels, and ran with what strength I had further towards the shore. But neither would this deliver me from the fury of the sea, which came pouring in after me again, and twice more I was lifted up by the waves and carried forwards as before, the shore being very flat.

'The last time of these two had well near been fatal to me, for the sea, having hurried me along as before landed me, or rather dashed me against a piece of rock, and that with such force as it left me senseless, and indeed helpless as to my own deliverance;

for the blow, taking my side and breast, beat the breath as it were quite out of my body, and had it returned again immediately, I must have been strangled in the water – but I recovered a little before the return of the waves, and seeing I should be covered again with the water, I resolved to hold fast by a piece of the rock, and so to hold my breath, if possible, till the wave went back. Now as the waves were not so high as at first, being nearer land, I held my hold till the wave abated, and then fetched another run, which brought me so near the shore that the next wave, though it went over me, yet did not so swallow me up as to carry me away, and the next run I took, I got to the mainland, where, to my great comfort, I clambered up the cliffs of the shore and sat me down upon the grass, free from danger and quite out of the reach of the water.'

I don't hear Father when he says, 'And that was how Robinson Crusoe came to be washed up alone on the desert island.'

I am already sitting on the grassy cliff watching the waves pound the rocks below, and sending spray high into the air.

My footprints in the sand are being washed away before my eyes, by the water that sucks at the edge of the beach.

With the salty water dripping from the strands of my hair I am ready for an adventure.

Sunday 5th April 1846

The Bull's Head, 10.30 morning

Ann Eastland.

God knows – it was a mistake. Mother would turn in her grave if she knew.

It wasn't as if I disagreed with her when she was still here. She wouldn't confront me – it wasn't her way. But when your mother-in-law drops constant hints that you should or shouldn't do something it is sometimes enough to make you obtuse and take the opposite path. That wasn't how it was. I understood her fears and I didn't want any more babies either.

I have never had any difficulty falling pregnant, nor giving birth. Compared to many I have been very lucky. With George often away at sea, and with good use of whisky we have avoided too many pregnancies.

I was forty when I had little George and I agreed with Mother that he should be the last. George was my sixth birth but it left me tired and took weeks before I felt well and able to run The Bull properly again. I knew I was fortunate to have only lost one child out of six.

My seventh-born, John Onslow just two years ago, confirmed all that I already knew. That I was too old to have more children, and that I must make sure there were no more. I tried my best to nurse him that summer but he was weak and sickly. He would cough, his nose would run and he could not settle. Neither he nor I slept well at night. He was not the healthy pink baby that George had been just two years earlier, and his grey eyes would look dolefully into mine. It was no great surprise when he slipped from us – 19th February 1845 aged barely one year. They said he died from teething – he simply didn't have the fight in him to live. I was relieved that Mother was not here to see John's demise.

He is buried in St. Peter and St. Mary churchyard where I hope he will always rest peacefully with Mary.

My bleeding comes now only occasionally, and my body is worn out. I know I can no longer have babies and I rejoice that unlike so many unfortunate mothers I have survived to old age and will watch my children grow and have babies of their own.

So why, oh why has God once again put me in the family way knowing that this can only bring strife?

George was in favour of me taking a young horse for a fast gallop to Emsworth followed by a bottle of whisky. Fearful as I am of a bad birth or another sickly baby I am more afraid to interfere with God's Will. When my time on this earth is up and I arrive at the gates of Heaven and Hell I'll have enough explaining to do about running an inn. If I take the life of one of God's children I fear there will be no hope of redemption for me.

Only God knows if this pregnancy is to be a lesson for me, or my end... or even a baby. Now I have reached this point His will must be done. I am tired but that is to be expected as I am no longer young. I did not expect a child for four weeks yet but my waters have flowed this morning. Matilda has made me rest saying the baby will come soon. I am not so sure, as apart from the waters there seems to be little movement. I fear the baby may not live if it comes this early, but Matilda tells me that many do. Though she is still young Matilda is very calm – she has helped deliver several babies, including John Onslow.

Monday 6th April 1846, 10.30 morning

Matilda Eastland.

Over a day is passed since Mother's waters came but nothing much has changed. I know the baby mustn't lie too long in there like this as that will surely bring a bad end.

I can feel the baby move – a ripple across Mother's stomach, but though she feels pains there are no regular waves. I have sent our servant Emily this morning to tell Nurse Caplin at Stockbridge that I may need help – this is not like I have seen before.

But Emily returns with the message that Nurse Caplin was not there. She is at North Mundham delivering a baby. The nurse's daughter said to come back in the late afternoon if we still need help.

Monday 6th April 1846, 6.15 evening

Matilda.

Mother has had fitful sleeps throughout the day but keeps being woken by pains. The baby seems to twist but the head is not where I would expect it to be.

Mother is hot and I have been bathing her face and chest with a cloth and cool water. She is bothered though I try to sooth her. She sips water but has not eaten since morning – and then only bread. She cries, 'Why won't this baby come? It will be the death of me.'

I need help with Mother as well as with the baby. I sent Emily at six o'clock to see if she can fetch Nurse Caplin to come and take charge. This will cost tuppence, or sixpence if she is here all night, but she will know what to do. She has seen every kind of birth.

Monday 6th April 1846, 8 o'clock evening

Matilda.

Nurse Caplin has had a busy day already. Two births; twins being born successfully in the afternoon at North Mundham. Emily arrived at Nurse Caplin's cottage at the same time as the nurse. Upon Emily's description of Mother they promptly set off on their walk to The Bull, about a mile and a half from Stockbridge.

Upon their arrival Emily is sent off to prepare plates of food for herself and Nurse Caplin. The nurse is also brought a glass of stout – we are very grateful to her for coming out immediately.

Nurse Caplin is a well-regarded midwife who works in Chichester and the surrounding villages. Probably in her forties she is firm, has kindly eyes and an optimistic outlook. I am very pleased to see her arrive.

The nurse goes straight to Mother's bed and asks her how she feels. She asks how long Mother has been in labour and has a careful feel of the baby. The nurse says to Mother, 'Mrs Eastland, your baby is a little early and is quite small, but that may be helpful. Its head is down but the baby is not lying straight and will not come out like this. You have had long enough with this pain. Matilda and I will help you get this baby out tonight – I think it's best for you and for the baby.'

The nurse goes on, 'Don't push yet, just rest. We will get clean sheets and hot water and you'll have your baby soon enough, you'll see.' She instructs Emily to continue to dampen Mother's face with the cloth and also to bring a glass of brandy to relieve Mother's pain. Mother lies there looking flushed and exhausted. 'Thank you nurse,' she says. 'Please get this baby over and done with soon – one way or another.'

Once downstairs Nurse Caplin gets a large pot of water on the stove and asks for clean linen. She says to me, 'Mrs Eastland has been in labour for well over a day and is getting worn-out. The baby's head is down and it is ready to be born but its body is twisted and it won't come out like that. The cord may be caught. I need to try to move the baby so it is straight and will come out. I'll need you to stay and help me Matilda and perhaps we will have this baby born before bedtime.'

Tuesday 7th April 1846, 12.10am

Nurse Caplin.

This birth is going to be difficult. Mrs Eastland is exhausted and desperate to the point of wanting to die due to the pain and fruitless contractions. The baby will not straighten and will not come out this way. I have tried to move the baby through Mrs Eastland's pelvis but the infant will not stay in the right position. I suspect the cord is short, or twisted somewhere.

I will have to put my hand inside and try to ease the baby's head into position. The baby still moves but time is now of the essence. I have seen births like this before – some succeed but not all. The big dangers are pain or bleeding for the mother, or strangulation of the baby by the cord.

Matilda has plenty of hot water and clean linen. She is a good helper – she listens well. Now we must proceed. But first a quick prayer……

'Please God help me to deliver this baby safe, well and swiftly, and for Mrs Eastland to be well as she has many children to support. Amen.'

With that Matilda and I roll up our sleeves and get to work. Matilda gives Mrs Eastland a sip or two of brandy for the pain and talks to her while mopping her face. I carefully insert my right hand into Mrs Eastland to try to unravel the baby.

It is of course tight and difficult trying to feel, blind. Mrs Eastland bites on a cloth to stifle a scream. For some time I struggle to make sense of what I can feel, trying repeatedly to get the baby's head in line whilst blood trickles down my lower arm to my elbow from where it drips onto the white bed sheet.

I am able to make sure the cord is not around the baby's neck but it is caught around the baby's shoulder. Despite many efforts and much sweating I cannot untwist it. I draw my bloody forearm from Mrs Eastland holding it low out of sight as Matilda wipes me clean with a damp cloth.

Mrs Eastland looks at me glazed almost beyond caring. I know she has to birth this baby now. Neither she nor the baby can take much more pain and pushing and shoving. I tell her, 'Mrs Eastland you are doing very well and your baby will soon be born. Rest for a few minutes while Matilda and I get clean water. I have straightened the baby and it will not take long.'

I take Matilda out of the room. That good girl Emily sits outside the bedroom half asleep but as always ready to help. I send her to get more hot water.

I say to Matilda, 'The baby's cord is twisted around its shoulder – I cannot get the cord free. The baby's head is now down and it will come out but the shoulder will come at an angle and will probably tear your mother. So we need small pieces of cloth and plenty of warm water. I will cut the cord quickly when the baby comes and I will pass it to you to keep warm and cradled as soon as I know it breathes. I will then work to stop any bleeding from Mrs Eastland.'

Emily brings the hot water and cloths and we all get on with it.

I once again put my hand into Mrs Eastland and catch hold of the baby by its armpits and behind its head. It is very hard to straighten. Mrs Eastland tries very hard not to scream too loudly while gripping Matilda's hand.

After what seems to be minutes of twisting and pulling the baby finally begins to shift downwards slowly. Mrs Eastland can't restrain a push and suddenly the baby's head and left shoulder bursts into sight. As expected there is a shower of blood as the rest of the baby's body begins to slide from its mother, but at last the baby is out.

I quickly untangle the baby's cord, and cut and tie it to stop the blood. The baby is a little blue but with a quick finger to clear its mouth followed by a sharp slap a healthy little scream follows, and I pass the tiny baby to Matilda who wraps it up and wipes its face of blood and mucus.

Mrs Eastland has a couple of nasty tears but she is past caring. For her the pain and the fear is far less than it was a few minutes ago. With Mrs Eastland's hips raised on some pillows I am able to control her bleeding in a few minutes, and she rests.

The baby was born at a quarter to one in the morning. It is a girl - probably a few weeks early, though in the event this is a mercy because in that position I'm not sure a fully grown baby would have survived – nor would have Mrs Eastland.

Of all my successful births this has been one of the most difficult deliveries I ever had. Mr Eastland thanks me and gives me a large and very welcome brandy in the Bull's Head bar, and a shilling for all my trouble which is very kind of him. This is double the normal sum expected for a night-time labour. He then takes me home with his horse and cart.

Sunday 3rd May 1846

Newfishbourne, Chichester

Nurse Caplin.

Mr and Mrs Eastland have done me the very great honour of inviting me to their baby's christening at St. Peter and St. Mary church at Newfishbourne.

Their daughter is baptised Fanny Caplin Eastland by the new Rector, Cecil James Greene.

Monday 21st June 1847
Woodhorn

William Collick.

A warm breeze rushes across the surface of this endless golden ocean which reaches as far as my eye can see. The yellow waves flow to and fro swishing into my ears with the current of air that also turns my cheeks and neck a dark brown colour.

A tireless lark sings merrily upon a gust so high above me I cannot see it, and the baby deer startled by my approach emerge from the barley in Sayers Meadow and career towards the far end of the meadow, where they disappear through the hedgerow into the field beyond.

It is half past five in the morning – this is the best time on a bright June day. My land is beautiful when lit up by the early morning sun. I love to see and hear the early birds and wild creatures that share this place and to smell the pungent foliage and wild flowers that grow at the foot of the hedgerow at the sides of my fields. As I walk the edge of Sayers I see purple knapweed and yellow St. John's wort, and a bit further along a mass of white stonecrop. To the north, far on the horizon I can see the spire of the great Chichester Cathedral rising as if out of my field of barley.

It is yet cool before the heat of the day and I feel strong, alert and ready for a day's labour on the land. My labourers and I have to start work early in summer because there is so much to do in the growing season, and we must not waste the light. Also on days like today it is too hot for man or beast to labour in an open field between one and three o'clock so we rest, have lunch, and work in the shade. We work hardest on the fields in the morning and early evening when the temperature is tolerable.

We are all as brown as berries. We call our labourer James who is now eighteen 'Brown Boy' as his skin is so dark in colour. He has been working in the fields since he was a toddler. James is a good worker. If all labourers were as strong and worked as hard as James my life would be much easier.

My family have been at Woodhorn for some years and the soil is becoming more productive every year from the continuous cultivation and rotation of crops. I have seventy acres of flat well-drained land divided into fields each separated by hedgerow. Since we built the new farmhouse the farming has gone well. The seasons have been mostly kind and the main harvests have been good in the last few years. If trade continues this way I may be able to expand into a couple more neighbouring fields soon.

This land is very good farming land. It is flat and even, the fields are open and wide, and the soil is rich and not prone to water-logging. This makes it good for the horses and farm machinery. Summers here are warm and long as we are on the very edge of the south coast of England. Woodhorn is in the countryside, yet not far from settlements if we need things. The small hamlet of Siddlesham with its church and inn is two miles to the east, with Pagham Harbour and the market town of Bognor just beyond.

The other way, not even a mile to the west is Birdham with St. James' Church and Manhood National School. And the grand town of Chichester is four mile due north where you can buy anything, and is where I go on the horse to do farming business.

Woodhorn homestead is one acre, and as well as the farmhouse contains the well, the vegetable gardens, and of course the privy. The next is called Barnfield. Here we store our hay and other harvested crops, farm tools and other supplies in the barn and sheds. There is a stable for our four horses, Jess, Star, Chestnut and Breeze and a paddock for them to graze in. We also keep Buttercup in this field, our black and white Friesian cow, along with our chickens. Emma or one of the girls always milk Buttercup morning and night. We also keep a pig which we will fatten up and which will provide us with many roast dinners in the winter.

I have five other fields all of a good size. The Inner Field is large and full of hay. It has grown early this year in the hot dry summer that we have had and the grasses are ripe for harvesting. We will finish with the turnips and probably start haymaking next week. I need to call in some additional casual labour and some extra horses and carts in readiness. I will speak to a couple of my neighbouring farmers,

Joseph Beale at Carthagena Farm and Matthew Cobby at Condrey. We always help each other with sharing our labourers and tools on the big tasks when we can.

Haymaking is an important time. It is the first proper harvest of the year and a good harvest earns us good money. When I look around the Inner Field I can see the meadow is ready to be mown. The grasses are in full flower and look healthy. A hay meadow is a beautiful sight in midsummer – all yellow and golden and in between those orange and scarlet poppies and the blue cornflowers dancing in the breeze.

The big challenge with haymaking is getting the hay cut, dried and stored without rain as if it gets wet the crop is destroyed and useless. So we pray for a period of warm days and no rain. I'll put word around in Siddlesham and Birdham that we want help next week to get the crop in as quick as we can. Men, women and children all play their part.

I have heard talk of newfangled mechanical reapers being pulled by horses to speed up the task of mowing the meadow. I have also heard that they are heavy and sometimes sink into the soil, as well as being expensive.

The following week is upon us scarcely before I can blink. For now we persevere with haymaking using the traditional methods. James, William and I, and the other men cut great swathes of hay with scythes, sickles and reap-hooks. The local labourers bring whatever tools they can lay their hands on to help us.

The remaining casual helpers, men women and children follow behind with the rakes, forks or other tools they have brought with them turning the hay to get the air and sun to it. The quicker the grasses dry the sooner we can get them away into the barn and safe from any rain.

The sweet smell of hay and hay-dust is everywhere like a cloud of yellow. Some people get sore red eyes and sneeze uncontrollably and have to leave the field. With the sun and all the golden hay 'tis dazzling, and makes your cheeks fair ache from squinting so hard.

Sensible women wear white hats with wide brims to keep off the glare and to prevent their faces looking like ripe strawberries!

It is too hot to work by noon so all return to my large barn to shelter in the shade and rest up for a couple of hours. With help from our neighbouring farms Emma provides all the workers with simple refreshments of bread with bacon and cold tea.

Cuts from the hay or from loose scythes or other injuries are tended. Insect bites and ankles twisted on the uneven ground are common but on very hot days heat exhaustion and heat-stroke are to be taken seriously, especially in children. The trouble is the illness often isn't seen till evening time and then the sickness starts and soft white skin can turn red like a beetroot! If it is very hot we don't return to the field after lunch until three o'clock.

The hay is left in swathes on the meadow to dry in the sun and wind. In the afternoon all return to the field with their rakes and forks to keep turning the hay. By late afternoon the hay is raked up into haycocks, small cone-shaped piles of hay, where they will be left in the field for a few days. It is crucial for the hay to be completely dry before it is stored otherwise it will turn mouldy and be useless as food for animals, or worse still damp hay can sometimes just catch fire all on its own. We continue to work through the afternoon until around seven in the evening, when the sun becomes gradually less intense. Everyone is exhausted and thirsty and thankful to go home to sleep.

As soon as I am sure the haycocks are truly dried we will get all the helpers back to finish the job. Children make straw bands by weaving long strands of hay which the women then use to bind sheaves of hay together. The men then load the sheaves onto a hay-cart by hand or with pitch-fork.

It is important to load the hay-cart evenly and as full as possible as it is a slow journey across the field to the barn. I only allow William, James and I to stand on the carts to ensure they are loaded well before driving the carts by horse. You have to take care standing on a cart-load of hay. Badly loaded carts have caused many a fall, broken back or death, even to experienced hay-makers.

At the end of each day's hay-making I pay the casual labourers – six pence per day for adults and threepence per day for children. When the final cart-load is put into the barn, in the gloom of twilight late one evening I can finally rejoice. All the helpers are brought back to the barn where they share their tales of the year's hay-making while enjoying cake and beer. A warm summer evening with beer and cake at the end of a successful haymaking is a time of satisfaction and considerable merriment in the large barn at Woodhorn.

Many of these people will be back again tomorrow and for the next few days, working in the barn with hand flails threshing the grain and sweeping it into hessian sacks. Then we can sell the grain and stack the hay ready to be used through the winter, and the haymaking task will be finally complete.

Don't be fooled into thinking farm life is always so rosy. Plenty can go wrong. Sometimes the crop is lost due to weather, disease or pests. Foxes or rats sometimes attack the chicken. If we didn't have our two dogs that live near the chicken coops most of the time, we would have more trouble with foxes.

As if there is not enough mischief from the weather, disease and pests there is also trouble from the Government men. The Tory Prime Minister Robert Peel last year abolished the Corn Laws meaning cheap corn can now be imported from abroad which threatens my income. This is a constant worry. The decision was so unpopular that Peel had to resign and I have seen no change to the price I can charge for my corn, and demand is as high as ever. So maybe this is nothing more than newspaper scare stories.

Then there are the drunks, the vagabonds and poachers. We don't get many at Woodhorn but there are always a few odd types roaming the countryside looking for free food or trouble. I've heard there are now fellows called police men in some of the bigger towns to keep the peace. In the country we look after ourselves and our neighbours.

I keep two shotguns for dealing with rabbits, fox and deer when they be too many, which I keep hidden under my bed. They come in handy too if vagabonds or runaways comes poaching on my land or causing other trouble.

One day last February William and I saw someone all dressed in black running around in Three Acres Field all waving his arms around. We'd not long ploughed the field in readiness for corn planting so with James we all went up the field to see what the fellow was doing.

When we approached and spoke to the man - he looked wild. He grunted and growled but spoke no word we could understand. He was tall though thin and suddenly ran at James wielding a large wooden branch from a tree. James dodged the branch which was swung wildly at his head and the three of us wrestled the man to the ground.

He seemed utterly mad – his eyes were red and foam came from his mouth as he tried to sink his teeth into my leg. He was all teeth and nails and kicking viciously with his legs so we pinned him down with no mercy, his face pushed into the mud. It was either he or us who was going to be hurt, and the three of us agreed which option it was going to be.

We trussed the man up and dragged him to the barns where we loaded him into the back of the cart. He was like a dead-weight – it took all three of us to heave him in. We drove him in the cart pulled by Jess up the lane to Birdham Poorhouse, but when they saw the state of the man they said they would not take him in. They only house peaceful old paupers there and have no secure cell for restraining lunatics. I realised that if we left him there he was as likely to be back in my fields again within half an hour wreaking havoc all over again.

The keeper at the Poorhouse told us we would need to take the wild man the five miles up the lanes to Westhampnett Workhouse on the outskirts of Chichester. It was a waste of an afternoon for all of us to go, but none of us wanted to take the madman on our own – he had such mad strength when he tried to lash out.

When we got to the Workhouse we helped them drag the man with his ankles, knees and wrists still lashed together to a stone cell where they keep the lunatics on their own until they either calm or die. James, William and I weren't sorry to see the back of that man and to get out of the Workhouse.

That place is a dour edifice of red brick and flint. I know it saves some of the very poor from starving but I know of no man who wants to end up there. I would rather sleep in a ditch and live on nettles and wild raspberries and water from a stream than die in Westhampnett Workhouse.

To be a successful farmer and to look after your family, livestock, labourers and servants you have to work hard every day, understand the land and animals, stay healthy, and always be planning for tomorrow, and next month, and next year. You also have to make ruthless choices sometimes.

It is a good living. I watch over my land and watch the seasons and the crops come and go with pride. I wouldn't choose any other life.

I am lucky in another way. Emma is a wonderful wife. How happy I am when she brings me lunch and tea in the barn each day. She looks after our children and runs the homestead so well that I only have to worry about the farming. Where would I be without her?

And thank God for Sundays. I see Emma and our children and we go to church, and rest, and make our plans.

Monday 21st June 1847

Woodhorn, 6am

Emma Collick.

William is a good man.

He was up with the lark and gone. I will not see him again until noon when I take sandwiches to the barn for him, and the old copper samovar full of hot tea for him and his labourers to quench their thirsts. There is so much to do on a big farm like Woodhorn that there is scarcely time to think.

But sometimes I do.

A simple farmer's wife like me probably shouldn't. Some may say that I'm getting above my station! I didn't go to school when I was a girl as often as I should of, as it was a long way to walk and the Mistress was very harsh. So my reading and writing is only basic. But I'm quick and sharp and I understand people and I came to see that whilst some can read and write better than me many of them can't think as quick. So every now and then I stop and think. And I make decisions that make things better because I have thought carefully why.

Like I decided our children must have sturdy leather boots. Although the children grow so fast and good boots cost six pennies a pair, William agreed to this because he realised that with good boots our children could still help with the milking and collecting chickens' eggs and other farm tasks, even when the ground is muddy. And he is right.

But I also thought that when the winter rains fall and the track over the fields to Birdham School is muddy and some farm children can't get there because they have no boots – well, our children won't have that excuse for missing school because they will have nice muddy boots. So they go to school and learn their writing and 'rithmetic much better than I ever did.

And I had another thought: on those wet days when our children get to school and the other children don't, the School-Master will be impressed with their keenness to get there and because there are less children in school those days he will give ours more attention and they will become better scholars. And they are, and this makes me very pleased because I know that getting schooling will give my children more chances than I had, so this is a good thing. And who would ever have thought that good boots could make you cleverer? This makes me chuckle to myself.

Before they leave for school the girls go with Mary to the paddock where our chickens roam with Buttercup the cow. They feed the chickens with grain, old bread and rough vegetable leaves and bring back whatever eggs there are in a wicker basket to the scullery. Then they start their walk to Manhood School.

Our vegetable garden is very important to the homestead. Most of the crops grown in the fields are sold. In our garden we try to grow enough to live on. We grow rows of vegetables: potatoes, cabbage, leeks, onions, parsnip, peas and beans and salad crops for the summer, and all manner of berries – raspberry canes, strawberry, blackcurrant, and gooseberry. We grow rhubarb and collect blackberries from the hedgerows in August and September. We also have two apple trees. There is always planting, hoeing, harvesting and tying up to be done. The birds clear most of the troublesome insects and slugs for us, but we have to keep the crops well watered. Without the deep brick well next to the cottage we would never manage it. Winding up the heavy water-filled bucket gives Mary and me strong arms and hands.

We have a privy at the end of the garden which William or one of our labourers usually clear out regularly, so Mary and I don't have to deal with that task. We are very pleased about that.

Mary helps the children to bed by eight o'clock and she has her own time after that while I spend time with William and find out what has happened in the fields today. Since we built the new cottage here at Woodhorn life is very comfortable. It is quite isolated here and very quiet, but Mary keeps me company, and when the house is full with the children in the evenings and at weekends all is a riot. We go to St. James' Church on Sundays, we walk in summer and go by horse and cart when the track over the fields is very wet. I feel very grateful for our wonderful children and their health, our farm and all that it gives us, and I remember this every Sunday morning when I pray.

I have had a thought. Since I had Clement two years ago I sometimes have sharp pains in my stomach. Some days I don't get them, other days I have to lie down to stop the pain. I should probably try not to have any more children and my body will get over it. We have no more bedrooms anyway.

Saturday 5th August 1848

The Bull's Head

Ann Eastland.

My husband George has been the Licensed Victualler at the Bull's Head inn since we took it on in the mid-1830s. But George is away at sea most of the time so in truth I run the inn.

As he is a mariner George knows about inns – he has drunk in many of them.

There are inns at every harbour and inlet the world over where sailors can stop, rest, drink and share their tales of the sea. Where there are inns there are also barmaids who have many a sailor to choose from to flirt with, to bed or to marry.

I was baptised Ann Miller when I was born just along the coast from here at Hermitage, Emsworth. Miller by name and by trade I come from a long family line of millers and some ran inns, so this life in a bar is very familiar to me.

George and I of course first met in the tavern at Hermitage where I was a barmaid. He entered the inn one evening with a gang of his shipmates looking for victuals having anchored their ship in the harbour. They were on their way from Mersey to Hastings, and bad weather meant they weren't going to get there that day as planned.

Some of the mariners were very loud and forward with us barmaids. But I liked the look of George straight away as he was polite, and though very handsome he did not make a play for every girl in sight like some of those other sea-scoundrels did. I had plenty of time that evening to make a good impression upon him.

Before long George found a way to sail into Emsworth regularly. In 1825 we were married at Warblington and we set up home just along the coast at Newfishbourne which is a busy harbour and trading outlet, especially at Dell Quay, and it is a good place from which George can work the sea.

Newfishbourne is at the edge of Chichester and never did one town have so many inns which are always busy due to all the passing traders and sailors. So I carry on working in taverns as it is a good living in a place like this.

Of course children came along but no difference for anyone is it? They never stopped me working. I can hold a babe in one arm and fill a pint jug with my other hand. I have had so many baby girls - Mary, Matilda, Nancy, Martha and Fanny that I will never be short of barmaids! Now we've got little George. Perhaps he will grow up to become a future landlord. Then I will be able to put my feet up and enjoy a glass of port – rather than always having to serve it to others. Of course this may not happen because his father always fills little Georgie's head with exciting tales of the sea, of white sandy beaches and coconut trees, of wild storms and mountainous seas. Time will tell which way little Georgie goes – he is but six and should have many decades to look forward to yet.

When my husband is home from the sea he prefers to drink in the tavern rather than work in it, even though it is his business. I'm not complaining, mind. George earns us a good living from his travelling and merchanting and his work can be hard and dangerous. Of course by his age he knows the dangers of the sea very well and I'm pleased to say he rarely sails beyond British waters these days.

When he was younger he sailed to wild foreign places, sometimes away for weeks at a time and I feared he'd never come home. He survived some storms and wrecks and has seen some things he won't tell me about. George was trained in all nautical skills when he left school and went into the merchant navy at fourteen. By the time we were married he was a Master Mariner and Captain George Eastland.

Early in 1830, when Mary and Matilda were just babes George took his ship to sea taking all manner of cargo to cross the Atlantic Ocean bound for Brazil. He should have come back four months later but the weeks passed and there was no word. I thought, I'm too young to be a widow at twenty-seven.

After five months George returned with his sorry tale of a violent storm and a sunken ship, and many delays waiting for passage back to England. Although there were a few men lost drowned and a number of injuries, most of the crew miraculously survived in two rowing boats and were picked up by another ship after drifting in the Atlantic for three days and nights.

Following this adventure sixty men of Chichester gave a grand dinner at the Bull's Head to celebrate the miraculous escape of Captain George Eastland from drowning. This memorable evening made such an impression on George that by the mid-1830's we had taken on the Bull's Head for our own.

I run the inn and that is just fine with me. I have it very well organised and it is much better than the alternative; and the alternative in these parts is mostly farming. Many of our regular customers are farmers and agricultural labourers. I hear their stories of working in the rain and the mud for a twelve-month, of smelly pigs and failed crops, and I would not want to work on the land for all the tea in China! Give me a nice warm tavern with beer and spirits, a crackling log fire in winter and plenty of lively company any day.

The Bull's Head sits on the main Turnpike Road, a mile to the west of Chichester. This is a very profitable position. As well as all our local farming drinkers The Bull is the first inn that travellers crossing the south coast of England come to when they arrive from the west. And very many come here from Portsea and from Southampton and from Dorset and all over the West Country. Many of those parched souls quench their thirst in The Bull before they ever get so far as the centre of Chichester with all its many ale houses. They say more ale than water is drunk in Chichester – and it's safer for your health too. A pint of India Pale Ale costs two pennies in The Bull. If a fellow drinks too many pints he might get a sore head, but at least he won't get the cholera like people do from bad water. I am keeping with ale and wine.

Saturdays are always busy. I have made sure there are plenty of us to serve in the bar today because it is summer and our customers are thirstier than ever. Matilda used to be one of my quickest and best barmaids and always right with the money. Although she still lives here she married Richard Barttelot on 27th May this year, and now she works as school mistress in the local school. William is also helping today whilst our other servant, Emily will look after little George and Fanny.

It is a long day in the tavern for we are open from nine o'clock in the morning until ten at night. I give each of the bar staff turns for a break to rest and eat so that there are always four of us serving.

This morning is keeping a steady trade with mostly traders and visitors on their way by horse or cart to or from Chichester. There is a large yard behind The Bull where horses are tethered and carts can be safely left away from the lane. We also have our regular procession of pilgrims from far and wide on their way to see Chichester Cathedral with its grey cloisters and elaborate stone monuments to all those old Bishops, to listen to the massive Hurd organ and if they are lucky, to hear the cathedral choir sing.

All these travellers are very welcome at The Bull. They stay not long, refresh themselves with a drink or two, pay without fuss and go on their way. They also bring many a tale to paint colour into our days in Fishbourne.

Today a gnarly old labourer has entered my tavern. He must be about fifty, but looks one hundred, and is desperate for a beer. He has come from the Naval Dockyard at Portsea after returning there on his ship from being at sea for five months. He comes with a tale from his recent shore leave in a Spanish port. Some sailors had got into an argument over a senorita and one of them had got so mad he shot another sailor dead on the spot and stabbed a second in the back who also died soon after.

The sailor was overpowered and tried on board ship by the Captain who found the man guilty of double murder and sentenced him to hanging. He was shackled to an iron bilbo for the remainder of the voyage. The guilty man was hung this morning in front of a large crowd in Portsea Naval Dockyard to make sure all the other sailors learnt by this example.

Our visitor also says he saw a large number of men and women being led onto one of the convict deportation ships due to sail to Australia this evening. It was a busy day in Portsea Dockyard and our traveller is pleased to be back home in Chichester for a week or two. Having earned a good wage at sea he gives us good trade in beer and before long he sleeps peacefully on the bench in a corner of the bar.

More of our local drinkers including the farm labourers are in the bar now it is evening and they have finished working for the day. With Sunday off work they are all in a merry mood. The main harvests of wheat, barley and rape are finished and by all accounts the yield is good this year, so the men are happy and more important they have money in their pockets from their haymaking labours.

The farm labourers mostly drink ale. These big men can down many pints before they fall down. Some of our old sea-dogs prefer their spirits, especially in winter – their favourites being rum and whisky. Our travelling visitors have all sorts of tastes from ale to wine, absinthe, mead and cider. Lime and other cordials are often drunk when it is very hot and dusty in the lanes in summer, especially by women and children who ride up in their carts and carriages.

'Tis now eight in the evening and many of the labourers are happily drinking and talking – some outside as it is still a warm evening. Others amuse themselves with games including toad-in-the-hole, Nine Men's Morris, and miniature bar skittles. Some sit around circular tables playing card games under an oil lamp. Of course they are all placing bets on who will win, and many coins are being swapped back and forth.

A small gaggle of farm labourers sitting together are having a keen but hushed conversation as I pass their table collecting empty tankards and glasses. They are organising a cock-fight for next Friday night in a barn up at Bethwines Farm off Black Boy Lane. Cock-fighting is perfectly legal though some say it is cruel, and they say some people are trying to stop it. Probably people in London who never saw a chicken; other than a roasted one on their dinner-plate. Cock-fights always draw a large crowd keen to wager a few pennies on which bird will win. One way or another many of those pennies will probably end up in the takings at the Bull's Head so I for one am not complaining.

Talking of fighting there is a commotion at the far end of the bar and a wooden stool crashes onto the floorboards as two men throw punches at each other. Some people shout while others back away from the two who hurl their fists at each other. One man already has a bloody nose.

'Get out of my bar,' I shout at the pair. 'Fighting is done outside, and only come back if you are to behave.' While I shout, William our giant of a barman has come behind the two men who, to their surprise find themselves both gripped by the scruff of the neck and forcefully shoved out through the pub door to the yard outside. The one with blood on his face turns round affronted, but then he sees William who fills the doorway in both directions and grins at him. The man realises that William is not a man to pick a fight with.

The pair slink away, and the bar is quieter than before. I do not tolerate the like of them in my inn. The people gradually resume their chatter and games, and the usual hum of the bar is restored. It would be nice if that was the only unpleasantness of the evening.

The trouble with too much ale is that some men get loose with their fists and others with their tongues. Luckily we have William and his friends when trouble brews, and George when he is home from the sea has a fine way of dealing with blackguards.

My daughter Nancy at fourteen has been working in the bar now for a couple of years and knows the ropes. She is slim and very pretty and some of the men will try to take advantage of her, usually when they have had more ale than is good for them.

I see everything in my bar – it is my duty, and I have noticed three young labourers looking at Nancy this evening and becoming more bold and cheeky in their comments to her as the beers have been drunk. I warned them earlier not to bother the barmaids and they said, 'Yes ma'am,' with an insolent smirk and a wink, but left off so I have said no more. But I am still keeping my eye on them. So is William who treats all our barmaids as if they were his own sisters, to be defended to the ends of the earth.

It is a little after nine and everyone in the tavern is quite merry, and some are singing songs together.

As Nancy walks past the labourers' table one of them grabs her by surprise pulling her backwards onto his lap and I see his hand clasp around her right breast as he slurs, 'Give us a kiss darlin'.' The other two labourers laugh out loud as Nancy wriggles and screams, but she cannot free herself from the man's strong grip.

It happens so fast I am barely on my feet when I see William lift the labourer by the neck bodily into the air. The man lets go of Nancy and she scampers fast as a hare round behind the bar. William fairly throws the man out of the door who lands on his back with a loud crunch. Meanwhile one of the others in the group comes up behind William wielding a glass bottle. One of our regular farmers, a friend of William's called Moffat who is also built like a haystack sees the man coming. Before the man reaches William, Moffat knocks the labourer out cold with a single sledgehammer of a punch to the side of his head. William hurls the second man out of the door where he lands on top of the first.

'I'll have no smell-smocks in my tavern. Take your scum away and do not return here again!' I shout at the third labourer, who exits the inn door faster than a ferret in a drain pipe. The first man looks seriously winded. The second is out cold. We will not see them again in a hurry. Their sort are not welcome in my tavern.

By ten o'clock the last drinkers have gone home and I can bolt the doors to the Bull's Head and turn off the lamps. We will all fall into our beds and sleep the moment our heads touch our pillows.

The day's takings are locked away safely. Cleaning the inn and counting the money can all wait until tomorrow, which will be another ordinary day running my pub, with all our extraordinary visitors. Sunday is usually as busy as Saturday. Business is good, and George will be home from sea in a few days.

Monday 25th December 1848

Woodhorn, 6am

Emily Jane Collick.

I am stirred from my dreams by a faint metallic clank downstairs. It will be Father lighting the fires.

The farmhouse will be warmer in a couple of hours, but for now there is ice inside my bedroom window pane and I am going to stay buried in my bed because it is cosy in here.

One good thing about Christmas Day is that there is no school and we are all here together. Even Father won't work today.

It is still very dark.

I doze and daydream deep inside the blankets of my bed. I can hear the rattle of pans and the soft murmur of voices downstairs which is somehow comforting. Mother and Father cannot break the farm habit of rising early – even at Christmas there are things to be done it seems.

At about half past seven there is a gentle knock on my bedroom door. I stay quiet and pretend to be asleep.

I hear the door-latch lift - Mother steps into my room and peers through the gloom towards where I lie in my bed. She listens. I lie absolutely still and hold my breath so as not to make a sound.

Right next to my ear Mother says cheerily, 'Happy Christmas Emily – 'tis time to be up to feed the chickens and clean out the horses.'

I poke my nose out from under the bedspread and say, 'Happy Christmas Mother, but how did you know I was awake – you could have scared me?'

Mother replies, 'I listened very carefully and I couldn't hear a thing. When people are asleep you can hear them breathe. So I knew you were either pretending to be asleep or had already taken yourself off to the barn to clean out the horses. I thought my first guess was the most likely,' she says with a chuckle.

'Don't be too long Emily – the animals will be hungry,' Mother says as she disappears onto the landing to go and wake the others.

I reach for my clothes which are on a nearby chair and get dressed inside the bed to save myself from freezing to death. Then I crawl out and go to the window to see what Christmas Day looks like.

It is so cold in my north-facing bedroom that I can see my breath in clouds as I breathe out. I cannot see much out of my window as it is solid white ice. Although it is not really dawn the fields and sky merge together in a grey half-light.

It has been snowing for several days and the fields as far as I can see are as if they were draped by a great white tablecloth. The hedges are also covered. Just a few bare leafless black twigs of trees stand out. Without them the landscape would be an endless white blizzard. The snow continues to fall lightly.

The farm labourers were sent home a few days before Christmas as, with so much snow on the ground there was little to do on the farm.

I go downstairs to the kitchen where we are all gathering for breakfast – Father, Mother, Alice, Sarah, Thomas and Clement are all here. The kitchen is always the warmest place to be as it is heated by the huge cast-iron range. We warm ourselves with breakfast and sip hot drinks as Father wishes us a happy Christmas and reminds us that this is a most important day because this is the day when Jesus was born.

'We should all go to Mass at St. James' Church on Christmas morning,' he says. 'But today we cannot get there even walking as the snow is too deep. We will instead say prayers here a little later this morning, but first the animals must be fed and cleaned as they get very hungry in this cold weather.'

Straight after breakfast I pull on my big boots and coat and go with Alice out into the snow to the barns to deal with our animals. In the stables with the animals is probably the next warmest place to be after the kitchen.

I cuddle up to one of the horses and feel his warmth. He turns his head and looks at me with those large brown eyes of his. 'Happy Christmas Star,' I say stroking his dark black mane.

When we get back into the kitchen we find that Mother, Thomas and Sarah have started to prepare a mound of vegetables for later – potatoes, parsnip, turnips and carrots. Father has been hanging garlands of holly threaded with ivy in the sitting room and dining room, and has lit some thick tallow candles in holders on the kitchen table.

A little later Thomas, Sarah, Clement and myself all get dressed up to go and play outside in the snow. Father says, 'Go out, keep yourselves warm and build yourselves an appetite for dinner.'

We all get dressed in our boots, coats, hats and gloves and run out into the deep soft white snow on The Common – right up to our knees. We don't run far before we just fall into the deep drifts of snow which piles very high in some places, like against the wall of the barns and alongside hedges. There is more snow for us to play in than you can ever imagine. We have a wooden sled with a rope attached and Thomas and I take turns in giving Clement and Sarah rides on it along the lane where the snow has been flattened by passing carts. Of course we throw snowballs at each other all the time.

It is great fun. We shriek and laugh and get very pink in the cheeks from our efforts, and from the cold. While we are playing the cloud begins to break as it is shovelled across the sky by the keen northerly wind.

The wind being this way carries with it peels of bells that are rung this Christmas morning in Chichester Cathedral. I look up for a moment and realise the cathedral spire is coming into sight between the clouds at the far end of our fields. I can almost imagine that I can hear the singing floating across our meadows all the way from the mouths of those grand folk in Chichester.

Later in the morning we help to decorate the sitting room. Sarah and Alice are making pretty decorations by folding different coloured pieces of paper and attaching ribbons and pieces of tinsel to them. Thomas is helping Father to make a large wreath by poking pieces of holly, ivy and mistletoe around a wire hoop till it is packed tightly together. Once it is finished they will hang it outside the front door of Woodhorn.

Soon after that Father calls us all for dinner. We stand behind our chairs, close our eyes and say Grace together. Father then carves the large roasted goose and shares it out between us all. It smells delicious. Mother dishes out the roasted and boiled vegetables and we help ourselves to the rich brown gravy, the bread sauce and cranberry sauce. Our dinner table looks like a feast fit for a king, especially with the glittering table decorations that Alice and Sarah made earlier which are now all lit up by the flickering flames of three large candles.

We gobble up our feast in no time and all help to clear the table by taking our own plates and dishes to the kitchen before returning to the dining table.

Then Father carries a heavy white dish that holds a large round Christmas pudding with blue flames swirling around it, and he sets the plate down in the middle of the dining table. I can feel the heat coming from it and smell the brandy that Father poured on to make it catch fire.

We eat the Christmas pudding biting carefully because we know that one of Mother's ingredients is silver coins and we must be sure not to bite on one. The gleaming silver thre'penny pieces are all discovered one by one. Sarah doesn't find one in her pudding but Alice has two so gives one to our sister.

Before long it is completely dark outside although the hazy moon makes the fields all around glow as if they are a purple-grey sea with its mounds of waves frozen into motionless silence. The Woodhorn curtains are drawn and we all snuggle together in the warm sitting room, our faces lit orange by the flames that lick around the wooden embers of the fire.

Father tells us that when he was a child people celebrated the turn of the New Year rather than Christmas, but that the crowning of Queen Victoria has brought this new fashion of Christmas celebrations. This includes things like Christmas stockings which we have completely forgotten until now with the day being so busy.

Father reaches from his armchair into the dark corner next to the fire and brings out seven small stockings. They are each tied at the top with a ribbon and each ribbon has one of our names embroidered on it, including William and Emma. We all untie the ribbons to our stockings and feel around inside them to see what they contain.

Each stocking holds a selection of nuts, an orange and an apple, a piece of cheese and a lump of coal. There is also a good selection of boiled sweets in each stocking and every person gets one other present – something special to them.

Father has a woollen scarf and Mother a small purple bottle of cologne. Alice has a notebook with an embroidered cover, and Thomas a pen and ink and some paper. Sarah has some pretty hair clips to put into her dark curls and Clement has a bag of colourful glass marbles.

I have a pretty and shiny lacquered round box which I shall keep my 'treasures' in. I don't have any treasures yet, apart from a silver thre'pence, but when I do... this is where I shall keep them. We are all so excited about our stockings, even Mother. And I expect she is responsible for the contents of most of them.

By seven o'clock Thomas, Sarah and Clement have all been put to bed, worn out from all the excitement. Mother then tells Alice and I as promised, how she makes her Christmas puddings. She tells me to go and fetch her old recipe book and as Alice and I sit, one on each side of her Mother flicks through the pages to the one headed Christmas Pudding.

While Mother explains all the things that have to be done to make the pudding, and in what order, my eyes float over the loopy handwriting and the long list of ingredients. There are raisins, sultanas, currants, mixed peel, dried cranberries, cherries, chopped dried apricots, dates, dried figs or dried pineapple, almonds, salt, breadcrumbs, sugar, softened butter, eggs, brandy or rum, and stout. No wonder Christmas Pudding tastes so good with all these wonderful things in it.

It is not late but Mother says she must go and lie down as she is tired. But I see her wince and hold her stomach as she stands up. I see Father notices too but he doesn't say anything.

Alice and I play patience for a while with two sets of playing cards but the light from the oil lamp is not bright and our eyes get tired. So we just sit after that talking softly and gazing into the flickering orange flames of the fire while Father sleeps in his chair.

At twenty past nine Father wakes with a jolt and declares it must be time to go to bed. As I watch the last red embers in the fire flicker I think to myself - I hope we have many more Christmases like this one.

Father makes sure the fire is going out and checks the doors are bolted for the night. He says, 'Goodnight' to Alice and I and we all go upstairs to bed.

Before I get into bed I kneel down next to it. I put my palms together and say one more prayer for Mother's stomach – just to make sure.

Monday 25th December 1848

The Bull's Head, 6.30am

Nancy Eastland.

It is dark and freezing cold.

I have not had enough sleep as it was late on Christmas Eve before we managed to clear the drinkers out of The Bull, reluctant as they were to go home. In fact it was very early today by the time the last of them had lurched out of the inn door to sing and sway their way, arm in arm along the lane.

Father brought a fir tree home yesterday and planted it in a large wooden box in the corner of the bar. Martha is now decorating the tree with small candles, ribbons, tinsel, sweets and fruit. Father says a decorated Christmas tree will be an attraction for all the pub visitors to marvel at, which will be good for business.

A little later Martha and George are sent off to St. Peter and St. Mary's Church as somebody needs to find time to pray on Christmas Day. They are told to be back by noon for lunch.

Punctually at noon Mother serves up the eagerly awaited roast beef dinner which looks and smells delicious. Martha and George skate back up the lane from church arriving just in time.

At two o'clock the inn doors are opened and the first of our Christmas Day drinkers who have been waiting outside as a few snowflakes flutter around them bundle into the inn. By four o'clock the Bull's Head is heaving with drinkers, all gabbling at the tops of their voices and slapping one another on the back.

Much beer is sold today but there is less trouble than on other busy nights. The Christmas spirit seems to have seeped into all our revellers and they remain happy and jolly. A fiddler plays lively tunes at one end of the bar and people are dancing and clapping in time to his melodies. When the fiddler plays tunes that people have asked for they throw farthings or maybe a ha'penny into the old grey cap that lies on the floor between his furiously tapping feet.

By mid-evening Father is sitting at the other end of the bar in a chair by the fire enthralling a small audience with tales of his adventures at sea. He speaks of mountainous waves and storms, of tropical islands with strange fish and colourful parrots, and of exotic native girls wearing grass skirts.

The Bull remains busy until after ten o'clock but when snow begins to fall more heavily most start to make their way home. Eventually the last few hardened drinkers are ushered out of the doors which are bolted shut at midnight.

Matilda, Richard and I collapse into armchairs in the bar. We are fit only for bed but Mother serves up a plate of hot mince pies. They are made of minced beef, raisins, sultanas, apple, pear and chopped almonds. Mixed with Demerara sugar, lemon juice, brandy, port, maraschino and noyau syrup and Silver Rays (white) rum, and encased in puff pastry - they satisfy our hunger and carry quite a kick.

Father pours us each a tumbler of brandy to wash down the pies and wishes us a "Very happy Christmas".

Monday 28th May 1849

The Bull's Head, Newfishbourne

George William Eastland.

Waking up of a morning is never difficult, especially when the bright early morning sunshine pours through my bedroom window on a spring day like today.
    I like to get up bright and early and squint through my window towards the Fishbourne Channel where I can see the glint of water and a small boat or two, unless it is misty. I can tell what the weather will be from the colour of the sky and the freshness of the wind – just by looking through my little window.
    Today looks good. Blue sky with just a few cotton wool clouds, the air is still and already warm. I quickly pull on my jersey and rough brown shorts and go to Mother's bedroom, where Fanny sleeps – or coughs, like today.
    Fanny is my youngest sister. I think Mother was around forty-three when she had Fanny though she is always a bit vague about her age. I'm not sure if she is sure herself. Fanny has always been a sickly baby. My other sisters are in their teens and beyond, are proper grown up and not that interested in Fanny and myself. So it seems only right that I do my best to look after Fanny.
    I had a brother, John Onslow. He was born when I was only two. But he was never well. He struggled and coughed on and on. He got stronger in the summer months when the warm air blew off the river. But by November he was coughing and wheezing again.
    He saw his first birthday, but only just. He didn't enjoy it and died soon after from what they called teething. That was no life. He is gone to a better place.
    I worry sometimes that Mother and Father had us late ones too late - with the death of John Onslow and with Fanny being so sickly. But Fanny has a twinkle in her eye and determination, and I am strong as an ox. So I try not to worry any more and just get on with looking after Fanny.

I collect her from her bed today, like I do most mornings. She is wrapped in a shawl and I carry her downstairs to the kitchen. Being now upright, Fanny has stopped coughing. Staring at me with her blue eyes she pokes her wicked little finger into my ear.

Today is a school day. Only Martha and I go to school now. It is about a mile and a half for me to the National School at St Pancras. Martha doesn't have to go so far. She goes to the Central National School which is at the Cathedral Churchyard in the centre of Chichester.

I think that one of the best things about being a child is that your nose is nearer to the ground. The lane from the Bull's Head towards Chichester runs between large fields and passes just a few cottages. The fields are filled with crops or animals grazing.

At this time of year the lane bursts with the many scents of cow parsley, yellow ragwort and nettles which assault my nostrils in a most wonderful way. In between the greenery bright yellow dandelions and scarlet and orange poppies wave their flapping heads in the breeze. The hedges are full of the song of all the world's birds – blackbirds, thrush, starlings and wrens.

Our route along Portsmouth Road takes us past Laurel Cottages and Fishbourne Lodge, and we cross the railway line on the way to the Tannery and then onto Westgate. As Westgate turns into West Street we leave the fields behind. Instead there are tall brick town houses where the wealthy people live.

The grand Westgate House towers above West Street on the north side, and opposite sits the ugly Prebendal Boys School. There are horrible little boys everywhere wearing their fancy uniforms, and I do not stop here.

I leave Martha at the Cathedral Churchyard where the schoolmistress Miss Mercy Coote makes the girls line up. I find this an interesting name for a teacher. The masters at my school never show us boys much mercy. But I must not daydream and make myself late. No good ever came of that.

I run through the town centre with its inns and hotels, along East Street, and past the Corn Exchange to Eastgate. I pass St. Pancras

Church and continue to run along St. Pancras Stane Street until I reach the gates of St. Pancras National School.

I see John and Matthew and go to join them. We have a few minutes to run about and keep warm before the bell on the school roof rings at nine o'clock to call us in. It is warmer in the sun in the playground than it will be inside the school.

At the sound of the bell we quickly line up at the door under the watchful glare of one of the Monitors. The school has two or three assistants called Monitors who help the teachers. They are older boys aged twelve or thirteen.

When the Monitor decides we are completely quiet and still, he leads us through the doorway. We go into the large room where we are lined up once again - the smallest boys at the front and tallest at the back.

We all sing the morning hymn as loudly as we can, partly to keep warm and partly as anyone seen not singing heartily will be pulled out and added to the new line of pupils at the front – those who will be caned later.

The nastiest Monitors are looking for the tiniest lack of attention during the morning assembly to justify dragging a pupil out. I surmise that it must be because they were viciously caned when they were younger and now they want to get their revenge.

I have quickly learnt how to put an expression of concentration upon my face, and how to avoid looking in the eyes of the Monitors. Most of the time this seems to keep me out of trouble. Nevertheless, every now and then a vindictive Monitor pulls a boy out for punishment no matter how innocent the boy might look.

After the morning assembly we are required to stand still behind our small wooden desks until Mr Cawthorne has finished calling the register. If a pupil is not here we are required to answer 'absent', but it is not advisable to offer suggestions as to why absent pupils are not here.

Today's register is called.
'Anderson' – 'Yes Sir.'
'Birch' – 'Yes Sir.'

The Master raises his eye to observe Birch. 'Never has a name been more apt for a scallywag than is yours, Birch. Wouldn't it be a pleasant experience, mainly for you, if you could go a week without providing me with the necessity to apply the birch to your rear-end?'

We all, especially Birch, know how important it is not to smile, snigger or even twitch our faces at this comment from the Master. Matthew Birch has a naughty streak which is very funny but gets him into lots of trouble.

Last week on his way to school he caught a bullfrog and put it in his pocket. Between the morning assembly and the register he had put the frog onto the Master's chair. The Master soon identified Birch as the culprit which led to ten lashes of the cane.

'Burfoot' – 'Yes Sir.'
'Clark' – 'Yes Sir.'
'Dall' – 'Yes Sir.'
'Eagles' – 'Yes Sir.'
'Eastland' – 'Yes Sir,' I reply firmly.
'Farrell' – 'Yes Sir.'
'Forsyth' – 'Yes Sir.'
'Hammond' – 'Yes Sir.'

The Master pauses and looks up again. 'You arrived late to this morning's assembly Hammond. I saw the door open which let in the sunshine during the first hymn when you tried to sneak in at the back.'

'Yes Sir,' comes Hammond's reply. The master goes on – 'If you don't get yourself organised in life, Hammond, you will be a failure and you will end up in Westhampnett Workhouse. You need discipline and focus Hammond. You must be set a challenge to achieve and maybe you will find redemption.'

The Master continues. 'On Friday Hammond, you will be caned once for every day that you are late to school this week. Let's see if you can achieve just the one lash on Friday.' 'Yes Sir,' replies Hammond.

'Harrison' – 'Yes Sir.'
'Hayler' – 'Yes Sir.'
'Hull' – 'Yes Sir.'
'Lane' – 'Absent Sir,' we all reply.

The Master doesn't bother to raise his face this time. He knows that on a sunny day like today Lane will be somewhere else – probably lying on a grassy bank and day-dreaming at Bosham Harbour, watching clouds float by as his feet dangle in the cool water, while trying to catch a crab on a baited hook. The Master marks the 'reason for non-attendance' column in the register accordingly.

'Moir' – 'Yes Sir.'
'Offord' – 'Yes Sir.'
'Roberts' – 'Yes Sir.'
'Smith' – 'Yes Sir.'
'Stretton' – 'Yes Sir.'
'Wood' – Yes Sir.'
'Sit. We begin with scripture.'
We always begin with scripture.

The school day always follows the same daily timetable. After the school assembly we have scripture, followed by arithmetic and then a short break when we are sent out to play and to eat what lunch we have brought to school. Writing and reading follow in the afternoon.

I find the sums involving money easy – probably because I help with the money in the Bull's Head. First thing in the morning I help count the cash that was taken the day before. We sort the coins into piles to make them easy to count: 12 pennies to a shilling, 20 shillings to a pound. There are plenty of farthings, halfpennies, sixpences, half crowns and crowns, and a few groats.

George lll copper Cartwheel pennies and tuppences are common, but are very heavy and we get rid of them in change whenever possible. If I get a gold sovereign I bite it between my teeth to make sure it is gold. I'm not sure that I would know if it wasn't, but the biting makes me feel grown-up.

Sometimes I find arithmetic at school difficult. They set us questions like - bring 4 years, 36 weeks, 6 days, 16 hours, and 53 minutes to minutes. Write your answer in words. Stretton is the best at this. God only knows how he gets the answer so quickly. I get there in the end after lots of sums and crossings out.

Reading and writing is what I love about school. We read from a small selection of English text books. Sometimes the Master brings in a new book. Most of us like this as it relieves the boredom of studying the same old stories every day. We read the same books so often that some of the poor readers just memorise the words.

When they are told to read out loud they hold the book open but speak from memory. Sometimes they get it wrong and the Master realises they aren't reading which leads to a caning.

The day continues in its usual routine. We all look forward to being let out into the fresh air at four o'clock, but we must follow the rules until the end of school, otherwise our escape may be delayed – sometimes for a long time.

At ten to four the Master snaps his books closed. He calls the register again to make sure that no child has sneaked out early, and at this time each Monday he collects one penny from every pupil – the amount of the weekly school fee. Anderson and Burfoot don't have their fee today so they have to stay after school to sweep the classrooms and to clean the offices.

Before we finish school any caning due today is carried out. The Master says it is important that all the caning is done in front of all the children to make sure we all learn the lessons. Today it is just Smith for daring to blame his mother for his untidy clothing. 'If you blame other people for your own failings you will never achieve anything in life. If you are not honest with yourself you lie to God. Bend forward, trousers down Smith.'

With that the Master delivers three sharp strokes of his cane to Smith's bottom. Smith then pulls his trousers up and limps back to his desk, trying hard not to screw up his face from the pain.

The school day ends with a prayer……….

> **'God be in my head, and in my understanding;**
> **God be in my eyes, and in my looking;**
> **God be in my mouth, and in my speaking;**
> **God be in my heart, and in my thinking;**
> **God be at mine end, and at my departing.'**

A Monitor then opens the door and we file out one by one in total silence. If there is any running, pushing, speaking or even a disobedient look we will all be ordered back to our desks to contemplate our sins for a further five minutes. We will then be given another chance to leave the school in a 'civilised' manner.

Some of the children go straight home where there are younger brothers and sisters to be fed and looked after. The children of farmers have many jobs to do all year round including sewing crops, mending fences, haymaking, milking cows, and lots of other things that I do not know about. They usually go home quickly.

Living in The Bull provides plenty of little tasks for me but not the same back-breaking labour that the farm children have to endure every day, whatever the weather. Eagles is busy kicking a large pebble around the playground. We leave him to his pebble and wander up the pathway out of the school gates. I am a crack-shot at marbles and enjoy playing in the lanes with Farrell and Harrison on our way home.

Martha doesn't wait for me at the end of the school day. She walks home on her own, not wanting to waste time with us 'urchins' - as she calls me and my friends.

Girls are silly.

Thursday 29th November 1849

Woodhorn, 7.30am

Sarah Jane Collick.

**Red sky at night; shepherd's delight,
Red sky in the morning; shepherd's warning.**

If I think about it I realise Mother and Father use a lot of these funny old sayings in their everyday speech: 'a stitch in time saves nine', 'don't look a gift horse in the mouth', 'a bird in the hand is worth two in the bush'.

I don't understand some of these sayings. I don't see what use it would be to have a bird in my hand. It would probably peck me and make my fingers bleed.

But if there are two in the bush they can eat the greenfly and help to look after the fruit and vegetables in our garden, and I can enjoy listening to them sing.

But I do understand the 'Red sky' saying. This morning the early gloom is lit with a strange pink glow.

We kiss goodbye to Mother, and then Thomas and I bundle Clement out of the farm door to start our walk to school. Clement is only four and Thomas will carry him most of the way.

We are captivated by the strange pink colour in the high fluffy clouds as we walk along the lane in the direction of Hill-land Farm.

Each side of the lane high beech and hawthorne bushes grow and hang over the way. Their trunks are tangled in a mass of brambles. I watch the spiky dark branches from the bushes and trees try to poke the pink clouds as we walk.

After a couple of hundred yards, just before the corner to Mapsons Lane we turn off the lane and go onto the path to our right that leads across the fields to Birdham. The view opens here across the wide flat fields on both sides of the path, the cold west wind hits us full in the face and we have to lean forward into it to stop ourselves being blown backwards.

The sun is not quite up yet from behind the trees but it shines on the edges of some of the high puffy grey clouds giving them a golden edge. This makes the clouds look just like the ashes of burnt paper in the fireplace, dark but with glowing golden edges flickering and shimmering.

A flurry of birds fly up out of the tree tops to our left; a twirling, looping, swooping, fluttering swarm of black shapes against the pale pink and blue sky.

They look for a moment like a heap of dried autumn leaves thrown into the air by a gust of wind and then abandoned by the currents to fly and float wherever they will go.

As we walk further across the fields the perfect golden sun at last peeps up from behind the tree-tops over my left shoulder, and I start to notice that the grey landscape is turning to a dull olive green colour.

The path bends to the right where there are deep water-filled ditches on both sides. The ditches are lined with brambles and other bushes, and somewhere deep in the leaves a field bird cheeps sharply at us as we pass as if to say 'good morning'.

Puddles of water lie in patches on the fields with small ripples on them made by the wind that whips across the land. To our left a fresh new green crop shoots like grass from the soil, as far as my eyes can see to the furthest sides of the field.

The edges of our path are lined with the dying remains of the summer's wild plants and flowers. Old dry brown burr-heads sway in the breeze, waving alongside the broken skeletal remains of other tall flower stems, their flowers and petals blown away long ago.

The crisp brown and grey stems cling together, shivering in the wind and waiting for the winter frosts and gales to finally blow them away. The last few yellow and white flower heads bloom hopefully, unaware that they will soon also be ripped away by the wind, or frozen solid.

The flowers are not alone in trying to hold on to the autumn. I am sure that I hear a skylark twittering, somewhere high up in the wild winds and twists of air above my head. Perhaps I am still dreaming?

A little further along the path I do not imagine the four stray seagulls that float by overhead with their caw-cawing cry that breaks the constant twittering of the field birds that are always foraging for food in the crops and hedgerows.

Suddenly I see three grey shapes halfway across the field to my right.

One of them stands, and I realise they are deer. Clement points and shrieks. All three deer now stand and stare at us. They stand dead still and so do we. We stare at them and they stare back. Suddenly the three creatures turn and bound away to the far side of the field, their white tails bobbing up and down as they run into the distance before springing straight over the hedge – and gone.

A crowd of black crows cover the next field to the left of the path, nestling amongst the red and brown stubble of an old crop. Just after this we come to Whitestone Farm with all its wooden chicken coops at the back, and the noise of clucking and squawking birds fills the morning air.

This is where we meet Mary and James Clayton who have walked across the field from their farmhouse at Belchamber. James and Thomas are friends, and James takes a turn carrying Clement to give Thomas a rest.

Mary is three years older than me. She talks to Thomas and James but not to me. I think she thinks I am too young and silly for her to bother with. I'll be darned if I care – she has a fancy pony-tail and a turned up nose. I don't want to be like her.

Soon we get to Birdham Lane where we turn left along it. Back over the fields that we have just crossed the sun is beginning to rise higher. I think it has nearly reached my shoulder. Perhaps I imagine it, but I think I can feel a little warmth from the sun as it glows softly yellow through the cloak of hazy white cloud. A spot of rain lands on my nose. And then suddenly the rain starts to pour.

We hurry the last hundred yards alongside the iron railings that mark the school boundary next to the lane that goes to Chichester. The entrance to the Manhood National School is on the right, through a black iron gate into the boy's playground.

The school building appears through the rain - red brick and grey flints under the red tile roof. The door is to the left just inside the gate, and we hurry into the shelter as quickly as we can.

We would normally stay in the playground until the bell is rung at nine o'clock, but when the weather is like it is today we are allowed to take shelter in the cloakrooms until school begins. Provided we are quiet and well-behaved. Boys and girls are kept separate at all times except when we are in the classroom. There are separate playgrounds, separate cloakrooms and separate offices (toilets).

With Thomas and James gone Mary goes away to find her grown-up friends with their pony-tails. When the hand-bell is rung by one of the Monitors at nine o'clock we all get into a straight line inside the cloakroom and wait to be allowed into the main school hall.

When the Monitor is happy that we are all quiet and well-behaved we are led into the hall where we stand in lines facing the end of the hall where our teacher, Mr Laurence stands facing us. Mr Laurence has been the teacher at the school forever; certainly for as far back as any children can remember. The school has been here since 1817 according to a notice on the classroom wall, which would mean Mr Laurence must be very old.

Mr Laurence lives in the large two-storey cottage which is attached to the rest of the school building. At lunchtime he goes back to his cottage for some dinner, or maybe a sleep. Old people always sleep a lot, don't they?

The main school building is on one level but the hall has a very high ceiling with two skylights. This means we can see our work, even in the middle of winter, although it does get very dark on some winter afternoons and the Master has to light oil lamps so we can see what we are doing.

There are over two hundred children at my school, although not always at the same time. Illness, bad weather, and 'more important things to do' means there are always plenty of reasons why some children are not here.

Some country children do not see much need for schooling and neither do their parents, especially when their children can earn money scaring birds from newly sown seeds, picking fruit or helping to get in the harvest. The children come from all around Birdham including from Earnley, the Witterings, Itchenor and Sidlesham.

Thursday begins like every other school day. Mr Laurence leads us in saying The Lord's Prayer, followed by a hymn. Then we sit down on the rows of wooden chairs to listen to a lesson from the Bible read by one of the Monitors.

The Master sits at the front in his chair with his face either pointed to the high ceiling, or down towards his feet. Either way his eyes are closed and there is no way of telling if he is awake, or just taking a nap.

However, if there is any kind of disturbance, or even a sneeze during the school assembly the Master always opens one eye to fix it immediately upon the culprit, before directing the pupil to stand at the front of the hall to await his or her punishment.

After the assembly the hall is divided into our separate classes. Thomas, James and Mary go to the other end of the hall. At nine and ten years old they are all in their last year at school and trying to learn well so they can pass their Standard V School Examinations next summer.

I am only seven so I go with my friends in our class towards the middle of the large hall. A good thing is that my class have one of the fires in our area which makes the English lesson seem better to me.

The Master rings the bell at eleven o'clock for our play time and after lining up quietly at the classroom door we are all allowed out to the playground. I am pleased to see the rain has stopped and the dark cloud in the sky is now streaked with blue flashes as the rains seem to be blown away to the north.

But we have to watch out for the large puddles on the ground. Over in the boys' playground some of them are shouting and jumping in the puddles trying to splash each other.

One of my friends, Jessie has brought a long skipping rope to school today, so with Harriet we are taking turns to skip while the other two swing the rope from each end.

We came out with our coats on but we soon take them off and hang them on the fence between the boys' and girls' playgrounds as we are getting hot from our skipping. This is the fastest fifteen minutes of the day.

The next lesson is arithmetic and we share abacus to help us with our sums. We sit in rows at our wooden desks and write our numbers on our slates using chalk, which is easy to rub out if I get something wrong.

I can do adding and subtracting without too much difficulty but today we are doing short division which makes me screw up my face, and think very hard. I am pleased when the bell rings again at one o'clock for lunchtime as my head needs a rest.

I have brought my lunch to school like most of us do. Some of the children who live very near the school in and around Birdham go home each day for their lunches.

Before I came to school today I put some bread and ham, and an apple into my bag and I am very hungry now. I am always surprised how I get just as hungry at school when all I am doing is using my brain, as I do when I am at home working hard in the house or garden.

Although it is winter and the sun is quite low, the sky has turned blue and the sun shines on most of the playground, and after eating we are pleased to go outside to play. The boys run around their playground making as much noise as they can, chasing and fighting each other with pretend swords.

Some others race each other with hoops and sticks, and others play leapfrog. The last few conkers of the autumn are being smashed to pieces on their strings, whilst some boys play with colourful glass marbles.

The girls' playground is much quieter. Skipping and hopscotch are popular and other girls just talk or walk in groups. Some of the little ones run in circles playing chase. A group of my friends have found a thick scarf and we decide to go to a nice sunny area to play blind man's buff, well away from the fence by the boys' playground and all their silly taunts.

Caroline goes first. We tie the scarf over her eyes so she cannot see a thing and then the rest of us stand in a circle around her. Caroline then walks with outstretched arms until she finds one of us. She is allowed to feel the person she finds: their face, their hair, and their clothes, and then has to say the name of the person she thinks she has found.

If she guesses the right person they have to take over the blindfold. If she gets it wrong we all move places and she has to try again. Caroline guesses right that she has found me. 'That was too easy – you could feel my long curls,' I tell her.

I put on the blindfold and move forward with my arms outstretched. I soon feel skin at the end of my fingertips. It is a hand and I reach higher and find I am touching the woollen hat upon Harriet's head as only she has one like it. When I take the scarf off my eyes I find that Jessie stands in front of me, and is wearing Harriet's hat. 'You cheaters!' I squeal as my *friends* all laugh.

'There's no rule about hats - you must have another go Sarah,' Jessie laughs as she pulls the scarf back over my eyes and tightens it again. I can hear them giggling and all moving around. So I reach out again and soon find another warm face.

This time I ignore the hats, scarves and coats that they have probably all swapped. I also ignore Jessie's skipping rope that I find in the hand of my captive. I can feel that this girl is a couple of inches taller than me, has straight hair but only as long as her neck, and has very long thin fingers. I am pretty sure this must be Emily, who is a year older than me.

I'm right this time!

Before long the bell rings and we get back into line before being allowed into the school room. This afternoon we are having a needlework lesson under the eye of some of the older girls.

Being late November the sun sets early and although some oil lamps are lit it starts to hurt my eyes sewing in the darkening classroom. I enjoy sewing letters and small pictures but today I am quite pleased when the bell rings to end this lesson because it has become hard to see what we are doing.

At a quarter to four all the children put their chairs on top of their desks in the hall and the class screens are put away by the Monitors. We all stand in lines again in front of Mr Laurence. The school fires are dying down and the hall is nearly dark apart from the few oil lamps.

The day ends with three prayers before we are dismissed from school. A few children who have misbehaved today are kept back when the rest of us leave.

Some sit at desks writing the details of their errors fifty or one hundred times, while others put away desks, sweep the floors and carry out other tasks as directed by the Monitors as punishment for their miserable sins.

Thomas and I collect Clement and make sure he is dressed up warmly ready for our walk home, and that he hasn't left his hat or gloves behind in the cloakroom. We must walk quickly now to get across the gloomy fields beyond Whitestone while we can still see where the path ends and the mud begins.

Wednesday 21st August 1850

Woodhorn Farm

Emma Collick.

I am starting to think there is something really wrong with my stomach.

It has been playing me up for so long that I can't even remember when it started. I have a few bad days and then I don't notice it for a while. When everyone is here and wanting things I don't have time to feel unwell, but today everyone except Clement is in the fields making hay. I am here on my own making butter and thinking about all manner of things. So I have time to notice that I have stomach pain once more. Of course, I could hardly fail to notice. Yet again I am inflicted with the bloody flux and I have to hurry down the garden to the privy.

The privy is not a nice place to have to spend so much time, especially during this hot weather. Where do all these flies come from? I squat here not a moment longer than I need to.

For as long as I can remember I have developed hiccups in the afternoon and then a stomach ache. I have a hearty lunch at noon for I find it hard to eat anything in the evening. By bed-time it is such a blessing to lie down as my stomach hurts so much and swells into a solid ball.

I hide my pains from William as he will say I mustn't suffer and he will send for a doctor. And that would be a fate worse than death. In fact for most people who call in the doctor it is an occasion leading to death – and it has to be paid for too! When my aunt had severe headaches the doctor was called and he said the only hope was to drain blood from her body to release the illness. Auntie was dead within two days. I would rather die with dignity than call in those blood-suckers.

I have tried many remedies. I always boil our drinking water in case there are any diseases in the well, but that has made no difference. I tried drinking William's beer instead of tea, but that just made me hiccup more, and William teased me if I was tipsy when he came in from the farm saying I was a 'wench of loose morals', and he pinched my bottom. It was quite amusing but it didn't help my stomach.

I told Mrs Clayton who said her mother had suffered similar stomach pains. She brewed up a bottle of herbal waters and told me to take two spoonfuls after lunch each day. I tried it for three days and stopped. It tasted horrible and made no difference to me. When I poured it onto a strawberry plant in the garden to make it grow, the plant turned brown. When Sarah asked me if I knew what had happened to the plant I said the dog had weed on it before I could stop him. I mustn't tell my children about my stomach because I am afraid they might say something to William.

I have tried resting, and I avoid going out after dark and breathing in the night air. I even bought a small green bottle of cordial from a travelling salesman at Siddlesham. He said if I took a spoonful every morning my stomach would be cured after two weeks. I persevered every morning for three weeks. The little bottle cost me three pennies. The cordial tasted worse than Mrs Clayton's herbal elixir.

By the third week I was having diarrhoea every lunchtime, so I stopped taking it and cursed the rogue salesman. Had he still been anywhere in the neighbourhood I would have told him he was a cheat and asked for my money back. He was long gone. I poured the rest of that poison onto some weeds. They flourished!

I have such cramps and wind it is terrible. I don't know what else to try. At least the beer is pleasant to taste.

Clement is happy playing in the kitchen. It is three o'clock and the girls won't be home from the haymaking till at least five. I'll go and lie down as this will reduce the pain under my ribs, if only for a little while. I don't have the energy to go and get a drink. I'll just put my feet up and pray to God to ease my stomach. It can do no harm to pray.

I'm sure this will pass.

Saturday 19th October 1850

Woodhorn Farm, 6.00am

Thomas Henry Collick.

We eat our breakfast in silence by candlelight in the kitchen. It is dark and still outside. There is no school today. I am helping Father on the farm.

By the time we pull on our boots and coats and step out from the cottage door a few crimson wisps stretch across the sky to the far-east. Dark shadows of trees and hedges can be seen.

We close the door gently so as not to wake the women. We step out into the fresh morning chill and walk towards Barnfield.

There is no frost this morning but a stiff wind rushes across our cheeks to blow away any remaining sleepiness.

A slow flap of wings breaks the air. A barn owl flies past on an arching swoop. A last hunting flight before daylight chases it back to the deep woodland.

While the horses feed in the stables Father and I take two carts into the yard and load them with well rotted manure. We soon warm up and by the time the carts are loaded high the horses are well-fed.

We put a collar and harness as well as a bridle onto each of the two horses, Chestnut and Breeze. Then we back them in between the wooden shafts of the two carts.

Having strapped them in we climb aboard and drive slowly out of the yard and into Barnfield. We drive carefully round the edge of Barnfield before passing through the gate at the far side into The Common.

We stop here and with the two horses resting side by side Father and I begin our task of spreading the muck each side of the carts.

The autumn sun sits low in the sky. Fluffy clouds gallop past pushed along by the fresh breeze, and a few brown curled leaves flutter into my face as I toil with the fork.

It is turning into a nice autumn day – perfect for hard labour as it is dry but not too hot. The ground is firm as the winter rains have not yet started.

Father works hard, but with few words. Apart from a few instructions we have hardly passed a word today.

We have all the time in the world to think, under this huge patchwork sky – broken only by a passing rook or crow.

I am thinking about Mother.

Being at school all day I don't see very much of her, but recently she hasn't seemed to me as lively and cheerful as she used to. I often see her lying down and resting when I come home from school while Alice cooks the dinner.

I suppose old people get tired and need more rest. But Mother is not as old as Father and he is shovelling muck right now like he is as strong as an ox. And I know he can do this all day.

I hope Mother is alright. Perhaps I should ask Father if Mother is not well, though he might tell me off for being forward? I'm not sure what to do. I hope Mother is not unwell.

Half way through the morning we stop work for a few minutes to rest. Father reaches into the box in his cart and brings out a bottle of cordial and some bread for us to share. We sit on his cart as we eat and watch the crows hanging on the wind over our field, hunting for their lunch.

We have nearly finished our bread and soon we will go back to work. I finally pluck up enough courage to ask, 'Father? Is Mother not well? She seems to spend more time sleeping than she used to?'

Father looks at me with no expression. It is as if he hasn't heard me, or understood my question at all? He looks thoughtful for a moment and then says, while shaking his head, 'No. Mother is fine. We, none of us are getting any younger. Do not worry yourself Thomas.'

We sit quietly for a few moments watching the clouds move. I am relieved by Father's reassurance and start to think about what I can do this afternoon. Father will not expect me to work after lunch.

William Collick.

Thomas and I return to the barn with the empty carts. We fill them with another load of muck while Breeze and Chestnut drink from the old iron trough. As we drive the carts slowly back up the field my mind goes back to Thomas' strange question.

'Tis funny how sometimes things change so slowly you don't notice them – until someone else mentions them.

Now I think of it I have noticed that Emma goes up to bed earlier than she used to. I often find myself in the sitting room in front of the fire at the end of the day talking to Alice instead of Emma. And many times lately when I've gone up to bed Emma has already been fast asleep.

It is also true that more often than not Alice now serves up the dinner when I come into the farmhouse at the end of a day. It is a good thing that Alice is becoming so competent in the kitchen. Perhaps Emma is doing less in the house than I think?

Emma has also become thinner, which is odd considering all the fresh food on our table. Perhaps Thomas is right? Perhaps Emma is not well? Illness is a terrible worry especially in big towns where I hear hundreds of people die from consumption, smallpox, or typhus. I am glad we live in the country where the air is clean and there are less of these diseases. I will talk to Emma to see if she needs a doctor.

When Thomas and I have emptied our carts of manure we return them to Barnfield. We say little as we concentrate on keeping the cartwheels in the well-worn tracks, to ensure a smooth ride and no damage to the wheels.

We release Breeze and Chestnut when we reach the barn. 'That was a good morning's work,' I say to Thomas as I leave him to feed the horses.

I head towards the farmhouse to find Emma.

November 1850

Woodhorn Farm

Alice Eliza Collick.

Mother has made me promise not to say anything to anybody else about her stomach.

She says it's just 'woman's troubles' which will pass in time. 'If your father finds out he will send for the doctor and I don't want no doctor poking my stomach... or worse. They don't know what they are doing. Please be obliged to keep it to yourself, Alice.'

What do I know about 'woman's troubles'? I bleed most months and get a frightful pain down there and am certain to tell no-one. So I shan't tell of Mother's troubles either.

Mother rests in the sitting room in the afternoons, or sometimes in bed. She says it stops the pains. I usually prepare and cook the dinner for her while she rests and talks to Sarah and Clement when they come in from school.

It makes me feel quite grown-up, like a mother. I have always liked being in the kitchen and helping Mother with the food. And it's often the warmest room in the cottage so that is another good thing, especially in winter, like now. I ask Mother when I am not sure about something and I am now quite expert in cooking a chicken and roast meat, as well as making pastry and cakes.

I cooked a large mince and leek pie one day last week and wondered if I had done something wrong as Mother just picked at her meal and hardly ate any. She took herself to bed straight after dinner saying she had a bad head. The dinner was all eaten and Father was looking for more so I decided there was nothing wrong with the pie.

One day back in the summer Emily was helping me prepare the meal. I was plucking a chicken in the garden while she skinned potatoes. She said to me, 'I think Mother has taken to the bottle. She drunk beer at lunchtime and now is fast asleep in bed. Father is going to wonder where his beer is gone.'

Alarmed that Emily might say something to Father I took a deep breath and spoke to her quietly. I put on my most grown-up face, puffed out my chest and said, 'Mother is having 'woman's problems'. She told me it is nothing to worry about and will go away in time. She just needs rest, and the ale is a kind of medicine to clean her innards. She doesn't want us to say anything to Father as he will worry himself.'

Emily looked disbelieving. 'What are 'woman's problems?' she asked.

'I dare say we will find out when we turn eighteen,' I replied, becoming increasingly annoyed by Emily's persistent questions that I couldn't properly answer.

'But I do know that Mother's 'troubles' mean we can do more cooking, so you should be grateful for that,' I added, knowing Emily has always liked being in the kitchen, even more than me. To my relief that, at last, brought an end to Emily's questions.

Nobody else notices Mother's afternoon rests, and the fact that she seems to be eating less at dinner each day, to rest her stomach, and that she seems to be getting gradually thinner. By the time the others come in from school and from working in the fields, Mother is usually up again and doing her normal things.

One Saturday lunchtime a few weeks ago, Father came in from the fields and sat on a kitchen chair while Mother and Emily were making some lunch. It was odd because Father doesn't usually arrive until someone calls him in. Even more unusual he didn't go back into the fields after lunch. He stayed sitting in the kitchen drinking beer and talking to Mother all afternoon.

He asked her if she was well, and if she needed any more help in the farmhouse. Mother looked puzzled, as if she was wondering why he was asking these questions and not going to work in the fields even though the weather was dry. She probably wanted to go and lie down as she normally would. I saw her hold her stomach but she stayed in the kitchen and even did a little sewing.

That evening after another dinner that Mother had eaten very little of, she complained of a headache. She blamed it on sewing when the light was too dim and took herself off to bed.

After Mother had gone up Father asked me if I thought there was anything wrong with her lately as she seemed more tired than usual. I told him Mother had said it was just 'women's troubles' and nothing to worry about, but Father persisted with his questions.

I was no longer sure what to think. Mother was right to say if Father found out he would worry and start talking about doctors. But at the same time Mother's stomach pains and tiredness hadn't passed yet, several months after I first noticed them.

I wasn't confused for long. This month events are rapidly taking their own course.

In the first week of November Mother is confined to bed. Her tiredness and headaches become severe and she also runs a mild fever. A persistent cough follows and I can see she has pains in her stomach by the way she supports herself there. Mother says her stomach is just tired from all the coughing. Then she starts a nosebleed. We manage to stop it by bending her forward with her nose pointing downwards, but not before she has bled all over the bed.

The following week Mother is weaker. One minute she is calm and the next she seems agitated. She still has the fever and I help her to wash to cool her down. That is when I see the red spots across her chest and stomach. I also notice that although she is thin her stomach is very swollen on the right side. Mother is constantly using the wooden commode, which Father or I have to empty into the privy before cleaning it thoroughly again.

Despite Mother's protests Father sends Thomas with the horse and trap to fetch the doctor. The doctor sends a note back saying…

From Thomas' description of the illness Mrs Collick has a contagious fever. There is little I can do. Give her boiled water, cordial or ale, or mix her a caudle. Keep her cool with a wet cloth. I will not attend her as she is now for I cannot risk infecting other patients. Have only one person attend her and keep a window open in her room for fresh air. Give Mrs

Collick beef and wine, and one tea-spoonful three times daily from the bottle of Quinine that I am sending back to you with Thomas. The fever may pass in a week or two. Pray for Mrs Collick's deliverance from the fever.

Dr Melling, Physician

Father is beside himself. He hasn't worked in days and now paces up and down unsure what to do.

Mother's deliverance, however is swift.

In the early hours of Wednesday 20th November, delirious with the fever she screams and makes an odd gurgling sound.

I light a candle and hurry from my bedroom to where Mother sleeps to find her lower body and bed covered with blood as well as from her mouth. Her eyes are fixed wide open looking at the bedroom ceiling - but she is already gone.

Father bursts into the room behind me and falls to his knees at the sight before him. 'Oh my God – why has it come to this,' he sobs.

'Why must you take my Emma – she is not yet forty? Why why…and what am I to do with a farm and five children, and no wife and mother? Do you not have enough wives and mothers in Heaven to be able to spare my Emma?'

At this moment Emily's shocked face appears at the bedroom doorway. I leave Father sobbing by the side of the bed, clinging to Mother's hand, and I tell Emily what has happened. Emily goes quietly to check that the rest of our siblings still sleep. Fortunately they do, so we decide to leave them this way. I go back to Father.

What am I to say to Father? I have no idea. He continues to cry as he lies slumped on the floor next to the bed holding Mother's thin white hand. I sit on the bedroom chair and cry. I stay here just in case there is something I can do for Father.

Wednesday 20th November 1850

Woodhorn Farm, 5.00am

Alice Eliza Collick.

I have a pain through my neck to my shoulder as I almost slip off the chair. I am momentarily confused in the darkened bedroom before the horror of the night returns to me. The candle must have burned out.

I hear breathing coming from the bed. If the images from the night were not so vivid in my eye I could imagine that it was all a dream and that now I can hear Mother sleeping peacefully in the bed. But my memories are not dreams and the breathing is not soft enough to be Mother. The breathing belongs to Father.

'Alice – are you awake? I've not slept – how could I. I have cried myself dry. I thought Mother would recover from the fever – she is only young. Emma came to me in the night and told me for all my grief I must not be selfish. She told me she needed me to look after our children now she is gone. I have much to do today. Will you help me Alice? I'm sorry – you are very young to suffer all this…'

'Of course, Father.' I am relieved to hear that Father is now calmer, and thinking. I was scared when his grief was uncontrollable and I didn't know what to do at all.

Father lights a candle and puts a cloth over the bedroom mirror. He says this is to ensure Mother's reflection isn't seen in the mirror and her spirit thereby trapped in the room. With that done we leave the bedroom and Father closes the door. He places a heavy chair outside the door to prevent anyone going in there. It is still dark and all is quiet in the cottage. We stop the clocks at the time Mother died, and make sure all the curtains remain closed before going down to the kitchen where we sit until dawn.

A little later I wake up Emily, Thomas, Sarah and Clement and bring them downstairs. At the kitchen table Father tells them of Mother's passing, and leads us in saying a prayer for her. Sarah and

Clement cry, but are comforted by Emily. Everybody around the table has red eyes and streaky cheeks, including Father.

'Your Mother is in Heaven watching over us and she wants us all to look after each other…I must get you breakfast?...'

Father suddenly looks lost. Emily and I realise this is where our help begins. We know about breakfast for children better than Father as he would normally be in the fields by this time.

When our servant James Green arrives, Father sends him on our horse, Star, to Aldwick to fetch the undertaker. Once the undertaker has been, the bedroom where Mother died is clean again, and Father takes the bloodied bedding to Barnfield and burns it all. The window is open and yellow scented candles burn in the room where Mother's body lies.

At last Mother looks peaceful, sleeping quietly… no longer holding her stomach.

Tuesday 26th November 1850

St. Peter and St. Paul's Church, West Wittering, 11.30am

Emily Jane Collick.

It is raining. Everything is grey – the road, the trees, the sky and all the mourner's faces.

Father drives us all in the cart pulled by Jess, following the funeral cart. Jess is a 'grey'. I'd normally describe her as white but today in all this rain and mist even Jess is a murky, miserable, dirty grey.

Father says the journey from Woodhorn to West Wittering is about three miles. As Jess clops along the road behind Mother in her wooden cot, through the rain and wind it feels more like three hundred miles.

People at the roadside stop as we pass, take off their hats and look down to their feet.

Clement and Sarah hold hands and cry quietly together. Thomas is biting his lip, his eyes a puffy red as he tries hard not to cry like his younger brother and sister. In this rain it is hard to tell who is and isn't crying.

We are all soaking wet – I can see large drops of water forming and falling from the tip of Father's nose. Alice and I are still trying to be strong and reassuring for Father and for our younger siblings.

We eventually arrive at West Wittering and Father stops the cart and tethers Jess to a sturdy wooden post outside St. Peter and St. Paul's Church. We get down from the cart, walk through the entrance to the churchyard and stand underneath the old oak and maple trees as the undertakers untie the coffin from their cart.

Large droplets of water drip onto my shoulders from the branches overhead. Not that I care. I can't get any wetter. What does it matter how wet I get? Mother is dead.

The church path bends to the right in front of me, past the grey stone tower with its black pointy cap, to the entrance porch just beyond on the left. The dull churchyard is inhabited by the ghostly black shadows of gravestones and bushes that blur together in the dark drizzle.

We enter the porch and then go through the grey stone arch doorway into the back of the church which is dark and cold, but I am thankful to at least be out of the freezing cold wind and rain. My fingers are red from the cold. We pass down the aisle and sit huddled together in the front pew waiting for Mother's arrival.

Despite the foul weather many have come to Mother's funeral. Her family, the Symonds have come along the coast from nearby Earnley as well as others from there who Mother knew as a child.

We all cower together, huddled in the old wooden pews for warmth and comfort. When everyone is settled the heavy wooden church doors close with a bang - the wind, rain and shadows all banished from the building. Just the soft glow from the thick cream-coloured candles remains to flicker on the stone and wooden interior of this dark place. Some people kneel and pray quietly.

Alice and I sit arm-in-arm as the Reverend Charles Gaunt stands before us and raises his arms to the Heavens to begin Mother's funeral service...

'We brought nothing into this world, and it is certain we can carry nothing out. The Lord gave, and the Lord hath taken away; blessed be the Name of the Lord...'

The Reverend's words wash over me, the harsh and vivid images twisting in my mind like daggers. Alice is inconsolable, sobbing into my shoulder, and I find the tears also run from my eyes so I cannot see clearly. It is as if I am back out in the rain.

Alice and I have been so busy in the last seven days since Mother died looking after everybody else we have had no time to cry for her. Now the Reverend's words are piercing our hearts and we empty our eyes together, clinging to each other.

The funeral proceeds, and after the lesson the congregation all leave through the porch at the back of the church. We go to stand by Mother's grave and some of us are ushered to cast earth upon Mother's body as it is lowered into the ground.

I notice that the rain has stopped and light has banished the grey swirl from the churchyard which now has some colour and life restored to its cheeks.

We say our own goodbyes to Mother, then move away from the grave. Alice and I are still clinging to each other.

'It's all my fault Mother has died. I should have told Father that I thought she was unwell,' Alice sniffles as she wipes her blotchy red cheeks.

'But Mother made you promise not to tell. You couldn't have gone against her will. You can't blame yourself for that Alice, and you did all you could have done to try to nurse her back to health.'

'But perhaps I should have just told Father…?'

'And what could Father have done? You know what the death certificate said, Alice. Mother's death was caused by 'inflammation of the bowels'. As Mother knew only too well doctors can't do anything for infections and complicated illnesses inside the body. No-one did more than you to try to help her.'

At this very moment a small but almost perfectly square blue patch of sky appears immediately above our heads amongst the white and grey mass of clouds to catch our eyes. It is as if the door to heaven has opened momentarily to let Mother's spirit in.

'I suppose you are right Emily. Mother always seemed to know what was right and how could I go against her at my age. God takes us all when He is ready and cannot be defied. I must not dwell on regrets. You and I must continue to look after each other for we have to support Father and our younger brothers and sister.'

'At least Mother no longer has a pain in her stomach.'

The blue square of sky has already been washed away with all our tears.

Through my damp eyes the sky now looks a bit like the sea. The white tips of waves rush sideways in a great urgency, with the deep blue and grey ocean churning beneath them.

Sunday 6th July 1851

The Bull's Head, Newfishbourne, 4.30am

George William Eastland.

I cannot sleep.

The night was hot and sticky even with my window wide open. And now, through my window bursts the dawn birdsong from the tree right outside. It has already been light for a while although gloomy grey, and though the sun is not yet seen it feels as if the heavy air is warming again even before it properly cooled.

I lie awhile listening to the thrush and to the flick of the curtain against my bedroom wall, pushed by the breeze through my window.

Before long the breeze turns into a stiff wind that ruffles my hair and cools my cheeks, and the gulls hovering on the wind currents give their insistent cry from upon high, whilst the bright white sails flap and the rigging clanks insistently. I turn my head to watch the waves breaking on the starboard side of the prow of our boat and find myself looking at... my bedroom chair.

I must have dozed off to sleep again.

The sun is now up and glints golden off the leaves upon the tree outside. I can feel the heat rising even though it is early and all is still quiet. I remember it is Sunday – no school today.

I leap from my bed, dress quickly and head out of my bedroom door and down the stairs. I find Mother in the kitchen. I also find a loaf of bread and tear off a chunk as I head out of the door calling to Mother, 'I'm going down to the creek – back later.' I am gone before Mother can utter a word.

It is still early – I noticed the clock on the shelf in the kitchen said it was a quarter to seven but the sun is now shining low and bright from the east as is rises up above Chichester. As I glance back at the Bull's Head the four red brick chimney stacks point into the deep blue sky. There is not a cloud to be seen – I can already tell today is going to be a very hot summer's day.

I skip down the lane past flowering blackberry bushes to the mill pond where the ducks lie sleeping on the grass under the willow tree, and on past the mill to my left. I follow the footpath that goes behind the mill pond before emerging at the neck of Fishbourne Creek.

Lush vegetation overflows onto the path from both sides including healthy crops of nettles, and thankfully dock leaves in equal numbers. I pick my way carefully through, picking two large dock leaves as I go… just in case.

The path quickly enters the dense and open expanse of reeds that are the salt-marsh. As long as I keep to the raised path through the reeds my feet will stay dry. The strong reeds are already about six feet high and I can see nothing but their golden heads waving in the deep blue sky, and hear little above their rustling as they sway in the breeze. It sounds like the swish of silk skirts in a never-ending dance.

Before long I am past the reed beds and onto the raised bank that runs along the western edge of Fishbourne Creek from where I can see the channel opening before me. A white dove flies over the path, whilst all sorts of birds chirrup and warble in the trees and the hedgerow to my right. In the field beyond a small herd of brown and cream coloured cows graze in the shade of some trees.

There is a fresh breeze blowing off the water but the sun is more powerful and is beginning to warm the air. I continue along the path, with the creek to my left and a line of hawthorne with their vicious spikes on my right. A seagull passes silently overhead.

I can smell the mud before I see it – the tide is out. Straight ahead in the distance I get my first glimpse of Dell Quay on the opposite bank of the creek. Dell Quay is a small but busy trading harbour. I go there sometimes to watch the ships come and go, loading and unloading all manner of goods including crops and grain from the nearby farms, flour and coal. I like to fish for crabs and eels at Dell Quay and to watch the weather-beaten sailors and listen to some of their strange accents. I imagine the exotic lands they have sailed to and the wild and beautiful oceans that they have crossed.

Small birds constantly dart back and forth across the path in front of me – these are the warblers and reed buntings. Occasionally I catch a flash of gold or green feather and know I have seen a bird I recognise – a goldfinch or greenfinch. Most - I cannot tell the difference.

If Grandmother Mary had still been here she would have known all the birds by sight, and by the sound of their song. The white sea-birds fly differently. They hang motionless on the breeze above the path and then suddenly dive down to the mud, or soar up into the blue.

I stop and look around. Over my left shoulder Chichester Cathedral rises above the distant trees pointing to the early sun which is climbing steadily. Away from the creek to my right lie grasslands. As I walk further along the path the smell of mud is turning into the smell of the sea, and the cries of seabirds and waders are taking over from the warblings of the field birds. A number of small boats sit beached on the mud waiting for their release when the tide rises.

I push through some longer grass in a shady patch on the path, and two surprised moths fly up from the undergrowth startled from their sleep in the long cool grasses by my unexpected arrival. Just here my head also passes through a cloud of tiny flies glittering silver in the sunlight as they flock around me, but I soon leave them behind.

The path at this part of the embankment is a little wider and there is a large array of weeds and wild plants growing. I notice in particular the deep heady aroma coming from clumps of tight white daisies that insists its way into my nostrils.

The only sounds in this place are the cries of sea-birds and the wind in my ears.

Water is draining from the marshes back into the creek – I hear it trickling onto the mudflats from under the bank along which I walk. A dark bird sits on the top of a post that protrudes from the green weed-draped rocks and mud. He is focused intently on the mud and pools – presumably expecting that his breakfast will crawl out soon, whatever it might be. The time must now be around half past seven.

I have stepped down from the raised bank onto the path nearer the creek where it dries out at high tide. Long grass grows on each side of this path and waves to me as I pass by. I soon enter a small glade of oak trees which are beginning to display tiny acorns. It is shady and cool under the trees where the wind blows through.

Behind this small wood is an equally small pond. The pond is home to sleeping ducks and purple and mauve dragonflies that dart to and fro across the water. The pond is covered with tiny ripples like miniature waves whipped up by the steady breeze.

I walk on.

I am back into the open again and have turned inland and away from the creek. The sun is beating down upon an ocean of cream and yellow barley that stretches to the north, with the hills of the South Downs rising in the distance. Orange and red butterflies flutter over the barley.

To my left a hedgerow runs alongside the field. A pale pink wild rose scrambles through the trees and the hedgerow to capture moisture at its feet and sunshine on its heads. I also spot a row of sloe berry bushes. The fruits are forming though too small and bitter yet to pick. I will remember to come back in a few weeks with a sack to harvest them. That will earn me some money from Mother as she can use them to make sloe gin and earn the Bull a good profit. I will drag as full a sack of sloe berries as I can manage back to The Bull, as my reward will depend upon the weight of my harvest.

A sudden disturbance deep under the hedge right in front of me makes me start. Then all falls quiet again. I can see giant thistles that are about to flower at the base of this hedge but nothing else. There is probably a deer in there somewhere, or a badger. Either way I do not want to meet it.

The sun is getting hot and I can feel droplets of sweat running down my back. I decide to go back. It is too hot to walk to Bosham today – in another hour the sun will be unbearable out in the open. I return the way I have come, back a few hundred yards to the clump of oak trees. The lower branches of one of the bigger trees are perhaps six feet off the ground and lie level with it. I climb up there and lie upon the branch enjoying the shade from the canopy of leaves and the cool breeze blowing through. This is the best place to be.

From my perch in the tree I gaze upwards to see specks of blue moving between the leaves and branches above my head, and somewhere up there I can hear the skylarks. Or I can look to the east at Fishbourne Channel where the water sparkles and dances in the sunlight, and where one or two boats now begin to move on the waves as the tide starts to come back in and the water starts to lap against their hulls. In the distance I hear a farmer fire his gun.

My eyes are drawn involuntarily to the gleaming sparkling silver water in the creek and to a small rowing boat that bobs up and down with the rising tide. I imagine picking my way through the mud and rocks and wading out to the boat and clambering aboard, untying it from its mooring and gently taking up the oars.

With the sun to my port side I row backwards against the incoming tide, down river and soon passing Dell Quay on my right. I presently pass Birdham Pool, then take the bend in the river to the right at Longmore Point and glide silently past Bosham Hoe before anyone even notices my going.

Some old fishermen sit mending their nets at the small harbour of Itchenor and look up at me as I pass, and I wave at them cheekily. I soon round the corner opposite Cobnor Point and head into the wider canal heading straight forward towards Chichester Harbour.

Although this is a sheltered harbour my small craft feels the rolling motion from small waves which are picked up by the wind across this larger expanse of water. The sound of water laps rhythmically against the timbers of my small boat. With gulls flying on the breeze above and making their gull cries my voyage has now begun.

Ahead of me a grand clipper with three tall masts is moored, and I set my course towards it for this is to be the start of my great sea adventures. When I reach the side of the clipper with its great hull towering above me a sailor drops a rope ladder down the side of the ship for me to climb up. I tie my little rowing boat to the hull with a bowline knot that Father has taught me, and I am welcomed aboard the ship.

The captain agrees to take me into his crew, to feed me and train me in the ways of the sea in exchange for my labour as a Ship's Boy, but he says he will not keep the rowing boat as it was stolen, and so it is left tied to the mooring to be discovered whenever it will.

Within the hour our ship raises its sails and catching the breeze edges out of the mouth of Chichester Harbour, and cruises for a while alongside Bracklesham Bay before passing Selsey Bill and then plunges into the great English Channel. Before long we are in a huge ocean and all I can see in all directions as far as the horizon is blue sea, and surrounded by the crash of the waves and the cries of gulls flying around the masts, and the wind puffing up our sails far above my head.

I am taught how to navigate using the sun and a compass and maps and am told of the evil ways of privateers, as well as those of other wild natives in faraway islands where we might sail to deliver our cargoes and to trade in new ones. I must have dozed off whilst swinging in a hammock in the shade because I am suddenly awoken by the sound of two cannon shots. I nearly fall out of my hammock in panic at what must be certain attack from the French or Spanish Armada, but just manage to prevent my fall by hanging on tight to the branch of an oak tree.

With my heart pounding I blink at the sun flickering onto my face between the branches and leaves of the tree in which I am sitting, and remind myself that I am in Fishbourne and must have been dreaming.

I hear two more gunshots in the distance – the farmer after the rabbits or the fox. I lie in my tree hammock and it takes me a few moments to re-gather my wits and for my heartbeat to slow down as my dream was so vivid.

The sun is well up in the sky now and it must be mid-morning. Out from the trees it is hot and I am thirsty so I start to make my way back to the Bull's Head for a drink and shelter from the heat. Perhaps I shall while away some time during the midday heat by reading some of my favourite book, Robinson Crusoe.

I walk back to the Bull, the full glare of the sun burning the back of my neck as there is no shelter alongside the creek. Not a soul have I seen all morning, except Mother when I fled with my bread.

Sunday 5th September 1852

Woodhorn, 3pm

Sarah Jane Collick.

I can't make up my mind whether I am supposed to feel happy or sad?

Some days I really miss Mother and I wonder if she is happy up in heaven. Father misses her and some days he looks so sad that it makes me cry just to look at him. I wish people didn't have to die because it makes other people so sad.

Nobody knew what to do when Mother died. Father was crying one day and shouting the next. Clement and I would just cry. Clement was only five and Father sent him away to be looked after by an aunt saying it was plenty enough for Alice and Emily to manage the farmhouse, without having to look after a young child as well.

Mother's friend, Mrs Clayton from the farm along the lane, came to Woodhorn for a few days to show Alice and Emily how to keep the farm from falling into 'rack and ruin'. She explained some of Mother's recipes and made sure my older sisters knew how to do the washing without burning themselves.

She told Father that some of the work, like lifting buckets of water from the well and tasks in the garden were too heavy for us girls. Father arranged for our servant, James Green to help with heavy tasks in the homestead. James is twenty-three and is very strong. He lifts the heavy wet washing and does most tending of the crops and fruit in Woodhorn garden. At Father's specific instruction he also attends to the privy at the end of the garden every week.

Father thought he should send me away to live with my aunt as well, but I made a huge fuss saying I had lost my mother and I would be heartbroken if I was torn from my older sisters as well. I also reminded Father that I am very good at looking after the chickens and know all about peeling potatoes, shelling peas, and picking fruit and I told him Woodhorn would go to rack and ruin without me! He said he would give me a chance and see how we all managed. He has not mentioned that silly idea again!

Mrs Clayton calls in at Woodhorn occasionally to check all is well but she can't stay long as she has her own busy farmhouse to run. It is hard to believe that it is nearly two years since Mother died, but Alice, Emily and I can now run the farmhouse quite expertly. Alice does most of the cooking, Emily is in charge of washing and drying the clothes and bed sheets, and I help tend the garden, look after the chickens and prepare vegetables for the meals. We all clean the house together.

Today I feel happy. On Sundays we all have a rest – even Father.

I made a pitcher of Natural Lemonade this morning, ready to drink with lunch. It will be very refreshing on a hot day like today. It was the first of Mother's recipes that I learnt. I do not need to follow the recipe any more – lemonade is very easy to make. But sometimes I just like reading Mother's loopy handwriting…

Natural Lemonade

Take one large lemon, two tablespoonfuls of Demerera sugar, one and a half pint of boiling water. A popular way of making this is to slice the lemon, but it often produced a bitter taste. A much better way is to peel the lemon very thinly using the yellow part only a Lancashire potato peeler, costing sixpence, is the quickest and most effective knife to use for this purpose. Put the peel and sugar into a jug, over the jug place a strainer. The lemon should be cut in half and the juice squeezed from it with a lemon squeezer or small wooden spoon through the strainer in a jug leaving all the pips behind. Pour the boiling water over it let it stand for half an hour and it is ready for use or in hot weather half boiling water stirring well to dissolve sugar then add the remaining cold water.

Mother used to make us lemonade on hot summer days. A tear squeezes from the corner of my eye as I am reminded of her.

I am ten now and just starting my last year at school. What with Mother, and work to do at the farm I missed some school days last year. I must try harder to go to school regularly this year and pass my school exams, as I know Mother would have wanted me to read and write as well as I can. She always said it is important for girls to do well at school, as well as boys. Now that Alice and Emily have Woodhorn so well organised, and with James Green helping them I must try to go to school every day.

Saturday 13th November 1852

The Bull's Head

Fanny Caplin Eastland.

I hate Father!

He is sending George away to London and I will never see him again.

It is not fair.

George left school in the summer when he passed the annual examinations – he is clever.

Since then he has helped Mother in The Bull.

George has always looked after me. He walks with me to school sometimes.

He picks me up when I fall over: which is quite often. George is my only real friend in the world.

My sisters are so old they creak – like creaky old chairs. Mary and Matilda are married and gone and Nancy will also be married next year.

Martha is all 'airs and graces' with the men in the bar. I am invisible to my sisters.

Only George sits with me, and listens to the very important things I have to say.

And Father thinks he is so clever to send George away to become a mariner so he can sail around the world. He says it is a rare privilege to go to the Royal Hospital School to learn to be a mariner.

How can a hospital be a school?

I don't think Father is clever. I think he is stupid.

If George goes in a boat into a great big storm with thunder and lightning and is drowned then everyone will see how stupid Father is.

But that will be too late for George. And for me.

If George drowns I shall run away and never speak to Father again.

Mother doesn't want George to go either.

She told Father that George should stay here and learn how to run The Bull.

He could be in charge of the inn when she gets too old.

She told Father, 'You are only here by some divine miracle – you should have drowned a dozen times. George may not be so lucky.' She shouted at him and sobbed.

But Father would not change his mind. Because he is STUPID.

Father said, 'George must see the world and taste the freedom of the oceans. It's no good for a boy to mope about in a tavern all his life surrounded by women. He has always dreamed of being a mariner.'

And what is wrong with 'women'? What does Father know?

He is never in the tavern. He is always at sea.

George is only ten and too young to be drowned or captured by pirates.

I ask George not to go to London.

He tells me he has always wanted to go to sea and to explore the world and have adventures.

   He says, 'Father sailed with me in a schooner around the Isle of Wight in the summer. I love feeling the salty spray on my face and the sound of the wind in the sails and in my ears.
   'Anyway Fanny, I won't be going to sea yet as I will probably be sitting in a classroom for years learning how to sail ships. And merchant ships are now built with iron hulls and steam engines and are much safer than when Father went to sea. You have no need to worry. It is my dream coming true.'

I can see George's heart is set on it. He dreams of blue seas, whales and parrots.

I shall worry if I want to – George can't stop me. I still hate Father and his silly old boats – it's all his fault!

Saturday 26th March 1853

Chichester Railway Station, 6.15am

George William Eastland.

At 6.15am a shrill blast on the stationmaster's whistle sends this huge hulking black train into a loud shunting frenzy. I have never been on a train before – its raw, dirty black power excites me. Clouds of steam and smoke swirl through the station and around the carriages, and also invade my eyes and nostrils as I stand next to the open window in the carriage door.

With a grinding sound as the metal wheels begin to turn, and clanking as the carriages tighten together the train slowly moves forward. As the train edges out of Chichester Station I can see Father standing on the cart and waving. I wave back at him, my arm out of the carriage door as he disappears inside a huge black puff of smoke and flying ash.

By the time the ash cloud clears Father is out of sight and I am at last beginning the most exciting journey of my life so far. For as long as I can remember I have wanted to become a mariner and to go to sea and travel the world. Today I am going on this great big steam engine to Greenwich in London to learn to be a mariner. It is my first real step towards a life of adventures upon the seven seas. I cannot wait for the adventures to begin.

Father spent weeks through the winter organising my place at the Royal Hospital School at Greenwich, the school where they train boys to become mariners and future ship's Masters in the navy. Father had to obtain all sorts of documents and authorisations, and he had to write a long application form to get permission for me to go to Greenwich.

Some evenings with papers spread out before him on the table under the candle-light he would scratch his head and curse. But he would not give up until all the papers were completed. I helped him with the writing.

Father walked to the Church of St. Peter and St. Mary at Fishbourne to see the Rector, Stair Douglas to obtain a copy of the Parish Register for the date of my baptism.

Father rode a horse to Warblington on a bitterly cold frosty day to see the Rector William Norris, where he got a copy of the papers for his and Mother's marriage. Father somehow forgot to send his marriage papers to Greenwich along with the application which caused a further delay and he cursed all over again, before sending it with a very apologetic letter.

Father also rode his horse all the way to the Custom House at Arundel to see the Customs Collector Mr Daniel Gill. Mr Gill wrote a long statement in his small curly handwriting stating all the ships that Father had sailed on and been Master of. Father said that Mr Gill bent over a huge Book of the Registry of Vessels belonging to the late Port of Chichester (before it became reduced to a creek and then attached to the Port of Arundel).

Father showed me the long list of vessels that included "Britannia" of Chichester, "Stephen and Elizabeth" of Chichester, "Flying Fish", "Ruffrell", "Waterloo" and several others. Father's maritime history had to be detailed and confirmed in writing by the Customs Officer of the Port from which he sailed, because only the sons of mariners, alive or now dead can be considered for entry to the Royal Hospital School.

One fine sunny day early in January Father got me dressed up warmly and took me around the coast path to Dell Quay where we got on a sloop loaded with timber. The sky was blue but the sea choppy although the sloop didn't venture far from the shore.

I was terribly sick, but Father said this was good training for a mariner and before long I would get used to the sea and not feel sick any more. I felt sick all the way to Brighton where we docked and got off the sloop. I was very glad when Father took me into a warm tavern near the sea-front where I rediscovered my frozen fingers.

In the tavern we met an old mariner friend of Father's called Charles Edwards. Father told Mr Edwards that I was very lucky to be going to Greenwich to learn to become a mariner and following in his footsteps to go on adventures at sea.

Whilst drinking their ale the two men poured over my application form for the Upper School of the Royal Hospital at Greenwich. I half-listened to their earnest discussion while I sipped my own beer.

Father read, '…**no Boy shall be admitted who is not possessed of the requisite attainments; which are, - To read fluently - write small text well – perform the rules of addition, subtraction, and multiplication, with facility and accuracy; and to be free from any infirmity of body or mind.**'

There was some tutting and sucking in of cheeks as Mr Edwards said, 'Well if he takes after his Father it might be touch and go…' The two men laughed and drank more of their ale and Father read on.

'**The age of admission is from 10 to 11 years of age.**

Not more than one Child of the same Father is admitted, unless under special circumstances, by order of the Board of Admiralty.

At the time of Admission, two respectable Housekeepers (of whom the Father, if qualified, should be one) are to be jointly bound in the sum of Fifty Pounds, that the Boy shall not abscond from the School, nor embezzle or injure any of the Clothes, Books, Instruments, or other Property of the Institution, and to remove him from the School when required to do so, if no opportunity offers of placing him at Sea.'

At this Father and Mr Edwards began choking on their ale and slapping each other on their backs. Mr Edwards splutters, with tears running down his cheeks … 'Since when were you and I respectable housekeepers? We wouldn't know a house if one crept up behind us and bit us on the backside! We have spent most of our lives away at sea and nowhere near our houses and when it comes to respectable, well…'

They carried on laughing as they supped more of their ale.

Father went on, 'Do not worry Charles, if George falls foul of the School for any reason and the fifty pounds becomes due I will not expect you to pay any of it, but I will be eternally grateful if you will countersign the application form as co-guarantor so George can go to Greenwich.'

'I am sure George will be an excellent student, and if he turns out to be half as good a mariner as his father you will have no worries,'

Mr Edwards winked at me as he said this. 'Added to that, you can rest assured George that if you ever need fifty pounds you can always come to your old friend Charles. After all the times you have saved my skin on the high seas that is the least I can do.'

With the form signed and rolled up in Father's coat pocket and a glass of rum inside Father and Mr Edwards, we all stumbled out of the warm fug of the tavern and into the biting January wind outside. Father and I were taken by cart to Hove where Mr Edwards lives, where we were well fed and slept the night before our return home the next day by the same route that we had come. For the return journey the sloop was loaded with dusty black coal.

A few days after we returned from Hove Father took the now completed application form once again to Fishbourne Church where the Rector, Stair Douglas as well as two of the Churchwardens, Mr Howard and Mr Osborne all signed it. On 19th January Father rode into the town and after waiting for hours he was able to secure the signature on the application of Mr George Irving, the Magistrate of the City of Chichester.

Father breathed a sigh of relief when the long application form was finally sent off in the post to London. 'That was harder than sailing across the Bay of Biscay!' he declared as he sank into his chair with a tankard of ale. And when another letter was received in the post telling Father he had omitted to send the proof of his marriage to Mother, the air turned the colour brown from all Father's cursing.

My long wait was concluded at the end of February when a letter arrived to say that I was to be admitted to the Greenwich Hospital School, and that as I was already nearly eleven years old I should start at Easter. My pupil number was to be 1515 and I was to start at Greenwich on 26th March when I would be eleven years and six days old. The day could not come quickly enough for me.

When we arrived at Chichester Railway Station very early this morning Father paid the man seven shillings exactly for my third class ticket to London. He tucked it into the top pocket of my jacket and told me to be very careful not to lose it.

'Only take it out if a Railway man needs to see it, and put it straight back into your pocket afterwards. Keep your wits about you and make some friends as soon as you can when you get to the School. It is always good to have friends in a big place like London – you can look out for each other.' That was Father's advice. And very good advice it was too.

I soon get over the novelty of the noisy smoky train. I look into the third class carriages and find an equally noisy, smelly mass of men, women and children all jammed onto the benches. I decide instead to stand in the corridor where there is more air, and with the window slightly open I can watch the green fields rush past.

As soon as I look at a tree or a farmer with his horse they are gone into the distance. I soon realise that it is best to look at things that are further away and then my head doesn't get so dizzy.

Every time the train starts to get a bit of speed it begins to slow and huff and puff out smoke and steam and we stop at another station. It seems as if we are stopping at every village and town on our way to London – first Drayton, then Woodgate, Yapton and Ford. I think it will take all day to get to Greenwich if we stop at every station, and I wonder how many people can get on this train before it will be too heavy to move.

I continue to daydream as the trees and fields roll past my eyes, along with more station names, Angmering, Lancing, Kingston, Southwick, and then Hove. I remember Hove.

It took most of the day to get there on the boat with Father back in January and now I have come here by train in perhaps an hour and a half! A few minutes later the train pulls into a large and busy station and stops with a loud swoosh of steam. The train doors are opened and I and my heavy bag are pushed out onto the wide platform by the swarm of passengers from behind me. I am barged and buffeted by men with walking sticks, and by women with large packages and screaming babies and swept along the platform by the crowd.

I remember now that Father told me I would have to get onto a different train at Brighton to take me to London. I wish now that I had listened more carefully to him. I had imagined that I would get off one train and there next to it would be another train bound for London. But it is not like that.

There are people everywhere, shouting, waving their arms, bustling hurriedly along, intent on getting somewhere. There are lots of trains and the noise from their engines is deafening, and everywhere steam and smoke is swirling into the high rafters of the huge station roof. I have no idea which way I should be going.

In a moment I see a railway man pushing a trolley along the platform towards me, stacked high with heavy looking packages. 'Hey mister, please can you tell me which is the train to go to Greenwich?'

He stops his trolley and rests his arms. 'Well sonny Jim, I dare say I could tell yer that. And why would yer want to be goin to Greenwich? And all on yer own are yer?'

'I'm going there to become a mariner, and I need to catch the right train.'

'Well me lad, and mariner. Sailors always have a crock of gold stashed away somewheres so if you give me a thruppence I'm sure I can point yer in the right direction for the train to the seaside.'

I begin to realise that scallywags like this are the reason Father has told me to keep my wits about me. I have seen peddlers before with that shifty glint in their eyes just like this man, before they try to trick you out of your money so I start to walk away from him. He tries to cuff me with his fist, but I am far too quick for him, even with my bag and dart behind his back and into the crowd before he knows where I have gone.

A little further along the platform I see an older man wearing a railway uniform and holding a watch on a chain in his hand, and decide to try again to ask where I should go to catch the Greenwich train.

He focuses me with his grey eyes and points a few yards over to the right. 'Platform one young sir, where that train is blowing out all that steam right as we speak. It's about an hour and a half to London. Be warned young sir, there is no station at Greenwich, but if you look out for New Cross station and get off there you will be able to walk to Greenwich. Now get yourself on that train and as soon as I see you in the door I will blow my whistle and you will be on your way.'

We soon leave Brighton behind and head inland into more green countryside, but now the train stops at places that I have never before heard of: Hassock's Gate, Burgess Hill, Hayward's Heath, Reigate. Gradually the countryside is replaced by large buildings, tall smoking chimneys, and rows of red brick houses. I realise that London seems to be covered in smoke – and it is not all coming out of the chimney of my train but comes instead out of hundreds of brick chimneys as far as my eyes can see.

The train puffs on. London seems to go on for ever. And then the train lets off steam and the brakes begin to squeal as metal rubs on metal and we enter a station. I look out for the sign New Cross but instead see Forest Hill. A few passengers get off here but many more cram onto the train forcing me back away from the door where I have been standing.

'Is it far to Greenwich?' I ask a man who comes in the carriage door but he ignores me, or doesn't hear me and shoves on past, dropping ash on my sleeve from a pipe that hangs from the corner of his mouth.

The train door slams closed and soon we shunt out of the station. Before long I feel the train slowing again. I have learnt to tell the difference between slowing for a corner or a tunnel, and approaching a station to stop. I push my way, dragging my bag towards the door straining to see through the grubby glass for a glimpse of a station name. It is New Cross at last.

When the train finally stops moving I scramble out of the door, leap from the carriage and over the big black chasm that separates the platform from the train. I quickly move across the platform out of the way of all the disembarking passengers that follow me and sit down on my bag and catch my breath.

Finally I am in London.

I have never seen anywhere like this place. I could not have imagined how big this city is. The train has passed street after street of houses and factories. London must be a hundred times bigger than Chichester which I had always thought was the grandest of towns. How easy it would be to get lost here.

I feel a bit lost now. I am still sitting on my bag with my back to the brick wall on the station watching people rushing on and off the train. There are porters moving bags and crates on trolleys on wheels and there is a constant din from the steam engines and from so many people talking and shouting at the same time.

I tell myself I just need to be calm and work out which way to go to get to Greenwich. There is a large clock with a white face and black hands and numerals hanging down above the platform. The time is ten o'clock in the morning. I remind myself that I have all day to find Greenwich. It won't be dark yet for hours. When Father showed me on a crumpled map back home how to get to Greenwich from the railway station it was less than two miles, which is no further than when I used to walk to school in Chichester every day.

Some of these people in London look wild and fearsome and I realise I must not draw attention to myself or look lost. When the train pulls out and most of the people have gone on their way I spot an old railwayman sitting on a trolley with a steaming drink. I decide to ask him which way I need to go to find Greenwich.

'Well me lad. Yer must go up them steps and go left dan the old New Cross 'igh street. Afta abaht a mile yer goes left agen. Blimey - do yew know yer left from yer right?'

I lifted my left arm to show him.

'Nuff said then sunshine. So as I was sayin', yer turns left agen, this time dan the old Gren'ich 'igh Road and the Gren'ich 'ospital an all the other buildin's is right in front of yer. If yer can't find em yer not fit ta nav'gate a ship Captin. Off to the Navy School are yer me lad?'

'What makes you think that?' I ask.

'Stan's ta reasin dunnit me boy. Boy on 'is own with a big bag. Two mile from Gren'ich and don't know where it is? Yer too young ta be a pensioner an' anyways yer doesn't have a wooden leg.' He chuckles at his own joke. 'Yer just follows the road, an' don't yer go stopping at no pubs or knockin'-shops along the way, cos I knows what yon sailors are like with ale and wenches.'

Despite his teasing I can see by this man's eyes that he means well, so I thank him kindly and head for the steps out of the station. Just before I get through the gate a uniformed rail man shoves out his hand before me and says, 'Ticket?'

I feel in my jacket pocket and to my relief my fingers find the ticket which the man takes from me as he steps aside to let me through the gate. That was another bit of good advice Father gave me. I remind myself of the other things Father told me – to keep my wits about me and to make some friends here in London as soon as I can.

The railway man was right in saying Greenwich was easy to find. Forty-five minutes after leaving New Cross the huge white stone buildings of the Royal Hospital rise before me. As I come closer I realise there are a number of these great white palaces gleaming like giant diamonds in the bright spring sunshine.

Already in my short time in London I have seen such contrasts: from the squalid dark streets with houses jammed on top of each other and washing hanging out of dingy small windows, to the huge gleaming palace which I am going to work and live inside. I stare speechless.

After asking for more directions I am pointed to the building called the King's House. A number of boys of my age are waiting on the grass outside the building. One of them, John, tells me we are to be called together this afternoon and that we are to wait here on the grass until that time.

John tells me he comes from Chatham. His father is dead – he was crushed when unloading cargo at the docks there. John wants to be a mariner because all his father ever talked about was life on the ocean under a mast full of white sails.

I am pleased to lie down on the grass in the warm spring sunshine and just watch the wispy clouds float quietly across the sky above my head. It has been a long journey. Soon I am asleep.

I awake later with a twisted neck and a dreadful thirst. In the early afternoon about fifteen of us new boys are taken inside the King's House where we are lined up and introduced into the School. One by one we are stood in front of a desk and asked to answer questions, beginning with our names and birth dates.

I am passed on to another man who measures how tall I am and how much I weigh, and then he puts a comb through my hair looking for nits. After all this inspection is completed we are led into another room where we are issued with our uniforms and are told we will wear this uniform all the time we are at the School.

I am handed a pea jacket, a waistcoat and trousers and a glengarry cap. I am also given an ordinary white shirt with a soft turned-down collar to be fastened at the throat with a black ribbon tied in a bow knot, and a pair of hose which will all be changed once a week. I am given a pillow case and a towel. I can't remember how often the man said these will be changed.

Loaded up with all my clothing, and also still carrying my bag I and the other boys are led off to our dormitory in the Stuart Building where we are to sleep at night. Our dormitory is a large room with rows of hammocks slung all the way along each side in two levels – upper and lower hammocks.

I count the rows and calculate that there are about two hundred hammocks in this dormitory. I wonder if I will get any sleep here at all? John and I have stuck together and quickly find two empty hammocks – one above the other.

'I'll 'ave the top one,' John says as he slings his towel and pillow case up there.

'I'm happy down here,' I reply. 'Heat rises. I'll be nice and cool down here.'

'Yep, and you'll be nearer to any rats dan there,' John replies. We snigger.

We are told to report in the dining hall at six o'clock sharp dressed in our uniforms for supper. I will certainly be ready for supper. After five o'clock some of the existing resident boys come into the dormitory. Boys are apparently allowed to spend Saturday afternoons in town and they have come back in high spirits. Two of the tall boys decide to pick on some of the new pupils and chase them around the dormitory, until a Pupil Teacher thunders into the room and orders the two boys out delivering a clip round the ear as they go.

By six o'clock all the boys have returned to the School and our dormitory is full of voices before we all swarm downstairs to the dining hall for supper. The hall is lit by a few gas lamps suspended above our heads. We line up to collect a hunk of bread and a knob of butter and a large mug of tea with sugar and milk. To my despair this is all we get.

We take our supper and sit down on wooden benches at each side of great long tables that run the length of the very long hall.

'Is there no more food?' I ask one of the older boys.

'Bread and drink for breakfast, and bread and drink for supper. The main meal of the day is the dinner at one o'clock sharp. Miss that and you go hungry. Did you arrive too late?' he replies.

'No, but nobody told us about dinner. We were told to wait out on the grass.'

'You'll enjoy tomorrow's dinner all the better then – Sunday roast!'

My stomach clenches into a knot at the thought of a hot roast dinner. I think I will starve before tomorrow's dinner time arrives and I grimace in desperation.

After supper we have free time until half past eight, but it becomes dark soon after supper is over and many boys go back to the dormitory where they can play games or just lie in their hammocks. John and I decide not to go back there straight after supper but to explore the buildings and grounds while the last remnants of daylight lurk before the sun finally goes down for the night.

John leads me away from the other boys and around the corner of one of the buildings, from where we can see the Thames flowing past in silent orange ripples with the last of the evening sun. 'So now we know not to expect much at suppertime, George. You still 'ungry?'

'Blimey yes. I could eat a horse,' I reply.

'Sorry I ain't got no spare 'orse,' he jokes. I would laugh if I weren't so hungry.

'How 'bout an apple?' John pulls two red apples from his jacket pocket.

'Where did you get those from?'

'Me Mam made sure as I brought supplies 'cos she knows I'm always 'ungry. 'Ere – 'ave one,' he says as he thrusts one into my hand. Apple never tasted this good to me before, and I eat every last bit of it except for the little black pips which I spit gaily into the now black night air.

'I got toffees too. We can split 'em between us and eat 'em on our way back to the dormit'ry. There's ain't no rush – must be an hour till bedtime yet.'

'Thank you John – I feel so much better with a bit of food in my stomach. How can I ever repay you?'

'I'm sure you'll find a way. Anyways it was me Mam's doin really. An that's what friends is for ain't it?'

To my surprise I sleep like a log, exhausted by the long day and my strange new surroundings.

Easter Sunday begins when we are woken at six by a bugle and drums. John and I stick together and follow all the others as we make up our hammocks, get ourselves washed, dressed, and clean our shoes before having some time to play before breakfast at eight in the dining hall. As promised breakfast comprises another lump of bread and three-quarters of a pint of cocoa with another measure of milk and sugar. I wipe every last drop of the cocoa out of my mug with the last pieces of my bread until it gleams as if it was brand new.

As it is Easter day all the boys are taken off straight after breakfast. We are marched in lines to the school chapel in the west wing where the full Easter service lasts for most of the morning. The chapel is a huge hall. All us boys, perhaps eight hundred of us sit, some on the floor and others on low benches with our hats on the ground in front of us. Any boy who forgets to remove his hat on the way in receives a slap from one of the Pupil Teachers. The Masters sit spread out in the balcony which stretches the full width of the massive chapel, up there high above the boys from where they look down upon us.

The Easter Service is like any other church service. But with so many people in this chapel I am not cold, and due to my hunger I have little energy. I am content enough today to sit, stand, kneel and rest.

Dinner eventually comes. Along with the bread comes roast beef, suet pudding, potatoes, oatmeal, carrots, onion, peas, parsley and thyme. The boy next to me doesn't want his onions – I get there first!

I don't know yet what to make of Greenwich. The food and the accommodation seem good, and what a grand place it is to live. Just like any school I know I must work hard and follow the rules otherwise the punishments will be harsh. Some of the older boys are very big and intent on trouble. I can understand why Father told me to keep my wits about me and to make friends. John and I will definitely look out for each other.

I am here to learn the skills to become a real mariner, just like Father. Father is a Master Mariner and survivor of many perils at sea. My work has not yet started. I think of my school friends back at Chichester – and think to myself what a grand and exciting opportunity I have to travel the world. Many of those people in Chichester will never even get to see London.

My wanderlust continues to burn brightly.

Friday 1st July 1853

The Bull's Head, Newfishbourne 5.00am

Martha Caroline Eastland.

This is quite early to wake up, I know.

In fact, I don't know if I did wake up because I'm not sure I really went to sleep. It doesn't help that those birds decided to start singing as soon as the sun came up – which was at about four o'clock this morning.

I am going to make today last as long as I can because today my older sister Nancy is to marry George Cox, and I am to be the main bridesmaid. Fanny is also going to be a bridesmaid.

I do not remember much about my other sisters' weddings when I was younger, but this time I have been involved in all the preparations and after waiting for this day to come it has finally arrived. I am excited.

I faintly remember that Mary married William Pescod when she was eighteen. I don't remember the wedding. I think they got married in Hampshire – I don't know why?

William worked as a teacher in Chichester when Mary met him. Trust Mary to marry a teacher – she was always the clever one. They lived here for a couple of years and had their daughters Rosina and Georgina, and then they moved into a huge house at Petworth called Worlds End!

When they got there Mary gave birth to her two boys William and George and they set up a Dame school to educate all the local children. Mary taught as well as William.

Father sent my brother George and me to William and Mary's Dame school in autumn 1850. Father said, 'Why waste money on the local schools when we have the best teachers in our own family?' I went there for a year and George for two, and we both did well in our end of school tests.

As well as attending the school at Worlds End George and I also lived there during term-time. We came back to Fishbourne to the

Bull's Head for the holidays. I think Mary does most of the teaching now as William says he is a Professor of Education. I'm not exactly sure what that means but he looks very pleased with himself, so I am sure it must be a very important position.

My other older sister Matilda married Richard Goff Barttelot when I was nine. I think it was a small wedding in Portsea. I was not at that wedding either.

Richard is a mariner so he is often away at sea. Matilda is another school teacher. She works in Chichester. I asked her why she doesn't have any children yet as she and Richard have been married for a few years now. Matilda said, 'I have more than enough children at school and can scarce do with any more at home.'

I think it is because Richard is always at sea. Matilda tells me I know nothing of such things as I am only a child myself.

Anyway, all the Pescods are going to be here at Nancy's wedding today, and so will the Barttelots – even Richard has found his way home from sea for this occasion. And I am going to enjoy the first proper family wedding that I have ever been to.

The only person who is missing out is George. He will be taking his mariners' exams in a few days which are really important if he is to do well in the merchant navy.

After all the trouble and expense to get him into the Royal Hospital School at Greenwich he can't possibly miss the exams, but it does mean he has to miss Nancy and George's wedding which is a great shame. I will make sure to keep him a large slice of wedding cake.

The marriage service is to be at noon at St. Peter and St. Mary's and this will be followed by the wedding breakfast back here at the Bull. Mother, Father and the servants spend the morning preparing food and decorating the bar ready for the celebrations to come this afternoon. I have never seen so many flowers, horse-shoes and wish-bones all hanging up in the Bull. The tavern will open to our regular customers later on.

Meanwhile Mary and I spend the morning in Nancy's bedroom brushing her dark hair, before plaiting it with blue and yellow ribbons and silk flowers and hairpins into the most elaborate style you can imagine.

Nancy's dress is made of pure white and very shiny organdie, and is decorated with lace with thin blue ribbons woven in. The tightly fitting bodice sits above full skirts with so many layers that I lose count, and has a proud bustle hooked up at the back and a long train behind. Nancy must not sit on the bustle so she will put the dress on as late in the morning as she dares.

As we dress her we recite the rhyme, 'Something old, something new, something borrowed, something blue, and a silver sixpence in her shoe.' Nancy wears a silver necklace which came from Grandmother Mary, while her dress is new and stays hanging on the wardrobe for now. Her veil has also been passed down through the generations – a delicate tulle mesh that Mother wore at her wedding.

Nancy will wear a fancy blue lace and elastic garter that I have made, and of course she will carry a tiny silver sixpence. Nancy is also wearing white embroidered silk stockings with yellow ribbons at the tops, and white gloves. The sixpence is tucked into her flat white shoes which are decorated with fine blue ribbon bows at the instep. She has all of this on except for her wedding dress. 'Tis a good thing that George Cox is not here to see her now as we would all blush.

Father bangs on the bedroom door. 'It is just past eleven. I hope you ladies are nearly ready? The horses and cart are all at the door.' Mary calls back, 'We are doing very nicely Father. I trust the Father-of-the-Bride is looking like the smartest man in town today?'

The door handle starts to turn and Father begins to push it open as Nancy squeals. Mary moves smartly to the door. 'You can't enter yet Father. No men are allowed in Nancy's boudoir. I shall inspect your attire in the hallway,' She says as she hustles Father backwards and closes the door behind her.

Eventually Nancy has her dress and veils on. Mary has also neatly pinned veils onto Fanny and me and we are all ready to go to the church. It would normally be a task for a boy to hold Nancy's train and, had he been here, the responsibility would undoubtedly have fallen to George. But he is not here and Mary's boys are too young. Fanny is taking charge of the train for now, but at the church George Cox's nephew William Sowter who is now eight will hold it, leaving Fanny to enjoy the wedding.

I have never seen Father looking this smartly dressed before. He is wearing a dark blue frock coat over a white waistcoat as well as an expansive dark blue silk bow tie. The finishing touch is the white carnation pinned to his coat.

Father waits next to two large grey horses that stand in front of Nancy's carriage which is all covered with white and yellow flowers. 'Come on you three, we haven't got all day. Let's get you into the carriage and off to the church. You don't be wanting George to think you've changed your mind now, do you Nancy?'

St. Peter and St. Mary's Church is only a few hundred yards along the lane so the ride takes little more than five minutes. One or two carts pass the other way, the occupants waving and calling to us, Father acknowledges them with a salute and Fanny and I wave excitedly. The bell at the church tolls as our carriage rolls as close as it can to the doors. All is quiet and peaceful in the churchyard. Everyone is already inside.

As we enter through the arched entrance at the west end of the church the bell stops ringing and a hush falls upon the congregation. We walk slowly up the aisle towards the chancel whilst everyone in the congregation turns to look and see how pretty Nancy looks, and how unaccustomedly smart Father is looking today. As we pass along our way I see George Cox's sister, Ann Sowter and her other son Stephen who is little more than a baby and looks restless.

Nearer the front are Mary and William and my four cousins, and next to them Matilda and Richard. Also here are many old family friends including Charles Edwards and Ann Farne, and George's father William Cox sits right at the front of the church.

And of course there are many other local people here on this sunny summer's day to witness the marriage of Nancy and George. The inside of the church is draped with flowers of all colours and all the women are wearing their best bonnets. The rainbow of colours is almost like being in a meadow of wild blooms on a breezy spring day, where all the flower heads wave and merge together like an ocean of coloured splashes.

Fanny and I clutch our posies of white and yellow blooms and enjoy every moment of this walk. As we get near to the front of the church I see George Cox standing there, smiling at Nancy and dressed very similarly to Father. George is the miller at Newfishbourne, living in Mill House, just along the lane from the Bull's Head. He is normally covered from head to toe in dust and sweat when I see him so I scarcely recognise him today in his fine frock coat and bow tie.

As we reach the chancel, Reverend Stair Douglas welcomes Nancy and Father to the church. Nancy stands between the two Georges and the Reverend begins the proceedings.

Fanny and I sit next to each other in the positions specially reserved for us on the front pew, feeling very important. We steal furtive glances around to see if anybody is looking at us in our fine bridesmaids' dresses. Most people have their eyes firmly fixed on Reverend Douglas.

The Reverend first addresses George asking if he will take Nancy for his wife, and he then addresses Nancy in the same way. They then repeat all the correct words and promises to each other before the Best Man presents the wedding ring to the Reverend and the Parish Clerk upon a bible.

The Reverend passes the ring to George to put upon the third finger of Nancy's left hand. Nancy has had a slit cut in that finger of her glove so that the ring can be slid onto her finger without her glove having to be taken off. The ring goes on smoothly and I can see her smile at George through her sheer white veil.

The Reverend bids the congregation to kneel and pray. On the way down Fanny whispers to me, 'I thought somebody was supposed to drop the ring during the ceremony to make sure any evil spirits were shaken out, but nobody did?'

'I know,' I reply. 'We had better pray a bit harder for good luck for Nancy and George.' I pray extra hard for children for the newlyweds seeing as the wedding ring wasn't dropped in the church, and seeing as Matilda and Richard haven't had any children yet either.

The church choir sings and the bell chimes as the pair make their way out through the doors, out from the cool stone church and into the hot summer sunshine. Our parents, George and Ann are next out of the church followed slowly by the rest of the congregation. George's best man has to wait until everybody else has left so that he can quietly pay Reverend Douglas for all his wedding duties.

Once outside the church Nancy lifts her veil from her face and we all gather round to shower the happy couple with a mixture of rice, grain and birdseed. I thought this was just a bit of wedding fun, until I hear one of the old ladies from the congregation telling a little girl that this is an old custom to encourage the newly married couple's fertility. The little girl looks a little perplexed at that, then asks the old lady, 'What is fertility?' I don't catch the answer she gives.

There is a lot of milling around and chatter in the church grounds before George and Nancy climb carefully up onto their carriage again pulled by the two white horses.

The carriage sets off slowly down the long path away from the church and we all wave and cheer as George and Nancy wave back at us. We then take the more direct walk across the water-meadows to the Bull's Head where we are to be served the wedding breakfast by the servants there.

I wonder why it is called 'breakfast' because the food served is nothing like what I normally eat for breakfast? There are many types of cold meat and later there are cakes. There is also much ale and wine, and cordials of green and red colours and other shades in between. And as the afternoon merges into the evening there is more ale and more wine and all the usual customers of the Bull turn up and join in with the noisy wedding celebration.

I don't know why the grown-ups always have to descend into such a loud drunken mass after a wedding? I leave them to it in the Bull and wander down the lane to the millpond where I sit on the wooden bench as the last gleams of golden sunlight flicker between the treetop branches. It is cool and peaceful here as I sit with the ducks that doze quietly next to the silent, motionless pond.

This has been one of the best days of my life. Fanny and I loved being bridesmaids, getting all dressed up and feeling important, and it was lovely to see Nancy and George smiling and laughing. It was exactly how I always imagined weddings should be. I hope they live happily ever after, and have many children.

I look at the darkening reflections in the pond and see the sky is turning from golden to an ever-darker red and think about my brother George. The only pity about today is that my brother had to miss the wedding as he is studying at Greenwich. I understand Greenwich also sits on a river. I wonder to myself if George is right now sitting by his big river at Greenwich, and if he is watching the same red sunset rippling in the water as I am?

Perhaps if I look hard enough into the deep dark waters of Fishbourne Millpond I may be able to see George looking back at me from the banks of his big river in London?

Saturday 3rd December 1853

Greenwich, London 4.00pm

George William Eastland.

We work hard in the Upper Nautical School.

After washing and making our beds, followed by breakfast we work in the classroom from nine o'clock till noon. Then we are taken out for forty minutes of drill – marching up and down in straight lines and small groups.

The older boys also march with sticks and cutlasses, and there is gun drill on board the training ship "Fame" and furling of the sails. On Wednesdays and Saturdays, instead of drill we do gymnastics. For this there are climbing bars and ropes suspended over a trench which is about a hundred yards long. The trench is filled with wood and bark shavings in case anyone falls – which they do sometimes.

Dinner at one o'clock is followed by a short playtime and then more lessons in the classroom between two and five o'clock. The rest of the day is made up of play and supper and prayers. On Sundays we are free to play and rest and go to church. Boys who have relatives living nearby are allowed out until seven in the evening. The rest of us stay within the School grounds.

On my first day in School all the new pupils were given a sheet of paper that listed what we were to be taught whilst at Greenwich. We were told that once we had completed all the objectives we would be ready to go into the navy. The sheet said...

A person, properly qualified, shall be appointed by the Board of Directors as Schoolmaster to the Boys...to teach them writing, arithmetick, and Navigation in the following manner:-

1) The four first fundamental rules in arithmetick, with the rule of three, practice, and the extraction of the square and cube roots.

2) Plain trigonometry, geometrically and instrumentally in all the various cases of rectangles and oblique triangles.

3) Plain sailing, namely, the working of traverses and the application of plain triangles to oblique sailing, and the doctrine of currents, together with sailing by middle lattitude.
4) Mercator's sailing.
5) The usual methods for finding the golden number, epact, and moon's age, the time of southing; as also the times of high water at any port.

Our classrooms are large with high ceilings and there are tall windows containing many small oblong glass panes. About sixty boys sit in rows around the sides of the room with the Master sitting at a high desk in the centre where we can all see him. We all have the luxury of our own desk, with paper, an ink well and a quill pen to write with.

Several Pupil Teachers walk around our class to watch what we are doing and to help any pupil who is struggling with the lesson. The classroom has large diagrams and maps on the walls showing the whole world and all its seas, and there are also globes that we can use in our studies.

Best of all I like the lessons away from our desks. We regularly have lessons in other workshops where we are taught about all sorts of equipment and instruments and steam engines, and where we can touch and investigate these things.

We are regularly taken along by the Thames to practice surveying using sextants and here we also do our drawing practice. It is very important for mariners to be able to draw well to record the places they visit. We are told that it is normal for a crew member to draw a picture of every port a ship visits, recording the layout of the harbour and any particular geography or hazards. Such a picture might save a ship on a future visit arriving in the dark or in bad weather when there is poor visibility.

On Wednesdays and Saturdays two hundred boys are taken up to Blackheath, high above Greenwich to run and play cricket, whilst others are taken onto the Thames in boats for rowing practice. I like getting onto the river to row but I often wish I was rowing on the Fishbourne Channel, breathing in the smell of Sussex mud and wildflowers instead of the stench of the human and other waste that attacks my nostrils on this stinking open sewer.

While rowing here we often see putrified remains of large black rats at the water's edge, lying on their backs with their legs in the air, poisoned by this rancid river. The best days for rowing are when there is a stiff breeze to blow away the fetor of decay.

Sometimes boys get hurt – occasionally seriously. We all know that a life at sea can be dangerous, from storms, drowning, pirates and other conflicts. I for one would rather take my chances on the beautiful ocean travelling the world, in preference to working in a dark stinking factory and breathing in smoke every day. Since coming to London and seeing the filth and squalor that so many people live in whilst crammed into this big city, I am all the more certain that, like Father, I shall spend my life at sea.

So, like most of the boys in the Upper School I work hard at my studies as well as at the physical activities to make me strong and well-educated and ready for the challenges of being a mariner. I am a good swimmer and a fast runner, and I pull hard on the ropes and climb to the top of the gymnastic bars and to the top of the masts on the "Fame".

A few weeks ago one of the boys fell from near the top of the rigging on the training ship and landed on his back on a hard area below. It was a cold day. I remember I was finding it difficult to keep my fingers warm in the cold wind. The boy's fingers could probably no longer hold onto the rope ladder when he plunged to the ground. He was not dead, but he could not move his arms or legs. He left the school. The talk was that he would become the youngest Royal Hospital pensioner. I don't know if he lived.

As well as proving to us boys in a most horrific fashion that we are all mortal, the incident had other consequences.

There is another school just up the Greenwich road, the Collegiate School. Fee-paying boys there get a naval education. They are a well-to-do lot, all airs and graces and they wear a pretentious uniform of yellow stockings, buckled shoes, knee-breeches with green coats and hats. Most of them never go to sea. These lickers are known as

Boreman Boys – named after the school's founder Sir William Boreman.

There has long been bad blood between the pupils of the Royal Hospital School and the Boreman Boys and the accident on the "Fame" set off a bad phase. Hearing of the accident, the Boreman Boys had been taunting Nautical School boys for a few weeks, including the frequent singing of a bastardised rhyme whenever they saw us...

'Oh dear, what can the matter be?
Dear, dear, what can the matter be?
Fell off a toy boat and bashed in his brains, did he?
Silly boys best stay ashore.'

One of the best friends of the injured boy was so angered by the Boreman Boys and their singing of this rhyme that last Saturday he dealt out some of his own justice. He is a big boy and strengthened by his anger he went into town looking for some Boreman Boys. He found three of them together down near the river and single-handedly beat them all badly, ripping their uniforms and bloodying their faces. He was of course flogged severely on Monday after a complaint was received at our School from the Boreman School.

This Saturday there is no excursion to Blackheath for the boys and all rowing has been cancelled due to the bad weather. Many boys have stayed in the dormitories and others have gone swimming in the Hospital Baths. John and I decided it was too cold to go swimming and have dressed up warmly to spend some time in the town this afternoon. The town is always lively and it makes a change from the school rules and discipline. We take in the life and atmosphere of the busy streets as we stroll past the shops and the ladies dressed in their smart frilly dresses and coats.

The market is always crowded and you can buy a bag of crisp apples there for a farthing. In the smaller lanes and the back-alleys the dollymops hang around waiting for Greenwich Hospital pensioners, or other men to totter out from the taverns and pay for their services. John and I are intrigued and shocked at the same time at what we see in these squalid back-alleys.

As John and I walk down the alleyway that runs behind Trafalgar Tavern one of these glossy strumpets with red lips, a false black spot on her cheek and a large overflowing cleavage flashes her long black lashes at me.

'You bin a sailor in trainin' I'll bet me lover? Do ya 'ave a spare shillin' me lad? For a shillin' I'll teach ya wot they doesn't teach ya in that school o' yours, darlin'. I'll teach ya proper wot all good self-respectin' sailors needs ta know. Come 'ere – ya a good-lookin' boy…'

As she puckers her bright red lips into a kiss and grasps for my arm I take flight further into the dark alleyway with John hard on my heels and the dollymop's shrill laughter echoing behind us.

And that is when our trouble really begins.

It is one of those depressing damp dismal winter days. Fog sits heavily upon the Thames and envelopes most of Greenwich in its wet grey blanket. There is no breeze today to disperse the fetid stink of the river which is clogged with the accumulated waste from London. It is one of those dank days when daylight never truly comes.

With dusk now descending, the half-light blends with a glow from the occasional gas lamp, to provide the day's final dim embers in place of the winter sunset that is absent today. The long narrow alley into which John and I have entered links Park Row with Eastney Street which we will walk along, then back around to the school in time for our supper at six o'clock.

We can hear laughter and the clink of glasses from the high open windows at the back of the Trafalgar, and we smell the ale and burning wood from the fires inside. Towards the far end of the alley it becomes quiet and the shadows deepen. Before we reach Eastney Street several figures emerge from the side walls of the corridor before us as if to block our way. John and I pause before a voice in front of us says, 'And look what we have here Richard. I do believe we have found a couple of those Greycoat 'Scallies' who have clearly got themselves lost in the fog.'

'I think you are right, Frederick. It was one of those bastard Greycoats who beat up our brothers last week and I think these Scallies must be taught a lesson.' I see the glint of a metal blade in the hand of the one called Frederick, caught momentarily in the lamplight, and so does John.

We instantly turn back the way we have come. I am running. Hard.

My heart is pounding in my chest as if it wants to leap out and my mouth has gone dry. John and I are both quick on our feet which is just as well with at least three Boreman Boys chasing us hard along the alley.

One of them whistles and then we see two more figures at the end of the alley in front of us. A voice behind us shouts, 'Greycoat bastards,' and the two shadowy figures in front turn to face us.

'Keep runnin' George an' stick together. Three behind with a knife an' bad intentions is worse than what is ahead. Just run through 'em and 'ead for the school quick as ya can.'

We are upon the two boys in front almost before they know it but they are clearly as ready for a fight as the boys that chase us. I manage to swerve just before I reach the one on my side of the alley. There is little room and I bounce off another body.

The moment that dirty bony fist flashes into my nose I feel hot blood squirt down my chin. I inhale that odd smell you always get in your nostrils when you are punched hard in the face. My swerve has taken me between and past the two assailants however, and my speed sent one of them off balance and toppling onto his back against the wall at the back of the Trafalgar.

John has been halted squarely by a punch in his stomach as he was not able to jink past the pair as I have. But John is quick and sharp and seizes his opportunity to twist and bury his shoulder into the chest of his attacker which sends him towards the first boy sprawled on the ground behind. The second boy promptly falls backwards over the first losing his grip on John, who wrenches himself free and stumbles over the two of them to join me just before the other three who were following catch up. The Boreman bastards all get in each others' way in a dark foggy tangle of cursing bad temper. John and I keep running - fast. We do not look back.

John and I fly along Park Row and into the Greenwich Hospital grounds and mercifully vanish into the dark night and thick fog in an instant. We finally stop running when we draw near to the building where our dormitory is. My heart is still pounding, though not quite so wildly as before, and my hair and skin are soaked with the putrid black foggy air - and with my sweat and blood.

I may have a bloodied nose and John's ribs are black and blue but we know our fate could have been much worse, and we also know our friendship has helped us survive this assault. We vow to have a quiet day in the dormitory tomorrow.

I also look forward to getting back on that train to Chichester in two weeks' time for the Christmas holidays.

Thursday 15th December 1853

Woodhorn Farm, Birdham, 6.00am

Emily Jane Collick.

I awaken. It is dark so must be still early. It is nice and warm here under my eiderdown, but I must not dally in bed today.

I peep out of my bedroom window to check the weather. I can't see much it is so dark, but I can see the ground is dry and I can see stars, which means there are no clouds. That is good.

I hear a bump downstairs and Father's cough. It is cold but I know Father will not light the fires this morning like he usually does for there is something different about today.

The day begins like any other. After a small breakfast Father takes Thomas and Clement off to Barnfield to feed and muck out the horses. Meanwhile Alice, Sarah and I tidy up the kitchen and feed the chickens before we all head to Alice's bedroom – the only room with a fire burning.

Today my big sister is getting married.

Alice is just eighteen – only two years older than me. I wonder if I'll be married at eighteen?

Alice has a gorgeous dress made of pale blue cotton covered with layers of fine white tulle netting and white ribbons. Beneath the dress are a multitude of hoops and petticoats creating a big dome effect and emphasising how narrow her waist is above the skirts. She has white gloves, 'To keep me warm,' she says, and white silk stockings.

Sarah and I have dresses made of white cotton with pale blue laces and ribbons. Our dresses are calf-length and of a simpler cut, and without so many lace and ribbon decorations as are on Alice's dress.

I feel very proud today as Alice has chosen me to be her First Bridesmaid, which sounds very grand, but it also means that I have certain responsibilities. I am not sure what they all are but I expect it will be simple enough. I continue with my responsible and important attitude by looking outside the window now that it is light to find that the weather is still dry, though a little cloudy. What frost there was is thawing and it looks promising for our ride to church in the carriage.

December weddings are more popular than might be expected especially in the countryside. Sometimes winter weddings are arranged because the bride is expecting a child, but that is not the case with Alice; at least not as far as I know. And Alice says not, and she is very honest. It is very busy on the farm right through from February to November, what with working the land, and the succession of crops and harvests. Whereas in December when the soil is wet and dormant, and the days are wet and short there is little to be done except cook, enjoy Christmas, and get married. With both our families running busy farms a December wedding suits everybody.

We have quite a long journey by carriage to St. Giles Church at Merston, which is where Alice and John Jacob are to be married. They will be living at Park Farm House at Merston from today which is why the wedding is happening in that village.

It turns out to be a lovely carriage ride. I love hearing the clip clop of the horses' hooves along the lanes, while the birds sing in the hedgerows as we pass by. From Woodhorn we turn left at Mapsons Farm, past Fletchers before turning left towards Sidlesham Common. Before long we take the right fork onto the path across the field at Marblebridge and pass Hatcher's Farm to our right.

We soon return to a wider road and then pass Kipstonbank Windmill on the way to Hunston village. After the village we pass Pages Farm and then we come to the Chichester and Arundel Canal. We follow the path along the south side of the canal and I watch the dark smooth waters flowing silently just a stone's throw from the cart.

At last our carriages wind their way up the hill towards the small village of Merston. After a short while the low squat church of St. Giles, with its tiny grey stone belfry comes into view on the right hand side of the lane. As our carriages draw near the church bell begins to ring. Somebody must have seen us coming up the lane.

We enter the church to the chiming bell and after a few steps turn right to walk up the short central aisle. There can only be five or six pews on each side of the aisle and the Rector, Eustace Cornwall waits at the end of the aisle standing just in front of the small altar table at the east end of the church.

As the Rector launches into his welcome to St. Giles and other preliminaries to the wedding ceremony I find my eyes wandering round this tiny little church. I have never been here before – it is almost like a doll's house of a church. The white ceiling is vaulted with old dark timbers and the roof is supported by three thick round pillars towards the north side of the building. There are beautiful stained-glass windows at the east and west ends of the church which light up even on this winter's day.

The ends of the pews and the deep stone window sills are festooned with winter decorations – including shiny green holly leaves, sprigs of mistletoe, trails of ivy and large fir cones. There are red and white ribbons and the red berries of the holly stand out against the white stone walls of the church.

The wedding service proceeds in the usual way, the promises and declarations are made, the wedding ring is slipped onto Alice's finger and the Rector pronounces John and Alice to be man and wife.

With the deepening dusk outside my eyes are drawn to the orange flickering candles that light the church. There are large candlesticks on the deep window sills at the front and on the south side. At the end of each pew on the darker northern aisle I now notice there are tall floor-standing candle holders each holding seven long candles so the people can see their hymnbooks.

When the Rector eventually dismisses the congregation we tumble out of the cosy candle-lit church into a semi-dark world where the wind is whipping up. There are droplets of rain carried by the wind and everybody heads up the lane as quickly as possible in search of Park Farm House, the next sanctuary from this rough winter weather.

When we arrive at the farm and alight from our carriage Alice and John are welcomed by a crowd of children. Then John picks Alice up and she screams as he carries her across the farmhouse threshold, which is apparently done to bring good luck to the marriage.

Servants have been preparing the wedding breakfast while we were all in the church, and before long the wedding guests are helping themselves to a glorious farmers' winter feast set out on the large oak dining table.

There is roast ham, beef, chicken and pheasant, with roast potatoes, parsnips, carrots, swede, Brussels sprouts and cabbage all laid out on great white plates, as well as bread sauce, cranberry sauce and gravy. The servants are pouring jugs and glasses of ale and wine; the talk is loud and the laughter louder still.

Flames leap, and sparks crackle in the roaring fireplace that heats the large dining room. I can no longer hear the winter gale that blows outside.

I think this merry breakfast will continue long past lunchtime, dinner-time and supper-time.

Wednesday 5th September 1855

The North Sea, off Cromer Point, 7.00pm

George William Eastland.

Over to starboard the large fiery orb rests its red chin on the horizon, from where it continues to warm my right cheek at the end of this gorgeous late summer's day.

There is only a light southerly breeze and the green sea swells, gently rising and falling without breaking to white foam. We sail close to the shoreline, though far enough away to avoid the sand shallows. We are accompanied by the constant cries of a flock of gulls on high as they dip and soar playfully in the currents above our heads.

The air is clear but salty and leaves my long hair dry and tangled. I fill my lungs in the fresh clean breeze, close my eyes, listen to the water splash against the keel, feel the throbbing engine vibrating through the timbers of this ship, and enjoy the sun's last warmth on my arms.

This is the paradise of the sea that I have always sought.

It was for these huge blue and orange skies, the endless seas sparkling silver and gold all the way to the horizon and beyond, for the winds – sometimes gentle and at other times a ferocious roar, and for the endless freedom and space of the oceans that I studied so hard at Greenwich. I endured the dismal grey, the cold blanketing fog and the stench of the Thames, and I grew sharp and shrewd as I learnt to fend for myself away from home.

I made a good friend in John, though I don't know if I will see him again. I will write to him and tell him of my voyages at sea and encourage him to complete his studies as quickly as he can. John is not a great writer so it remains to be seen if he sends me a reply. But still I hope to inspire him to reach out into the world for his own adventures.

I completed my studies at the Upper Nautical School last summer. I attended a presentation ceremony in the sumptuous Painted Hall with all the other boys who were leaving. Such a grand affair I have never seen before. We had to make sure our uniforms were freshly cleaned, our jacket buttons shining and our shoes gleaming with polish.

The Painted Hall itself is like a palace with carvings and statues and paintings all over the walls as well as all across the ceiling, which must have been fifty feet above our heads. The huge painting on the ceiling is like some vision from Heaven. As I gazed upwards my eyes were drawn around the endless trail of bodies, creatures, angels, a ship and all manner of life. It seemed as if they would all pour out of the ceiling at any moment. A golden light as if straight from the sun did pour from the ceiling and I suddenly felt giddy and had to lower my eyes to the floor.

A long inscription runs all around the edge of the ceiling,

Pietas augusta ut habitent et publice atlanter, qui publico securitati invigilarunt regia Grenovici MARIAE auspiciis sublevandis destinata regnantibus Gulielmo Maria MDCXCIV.

I marvelled at the strange Roman lettering. Of course I couldn't understand the words but we were told they confirmed the gift of Greenwich Palace by the King and Queen of England, to help old sailors who had served the nation at sea and who had fallen on hard times.

The Painted Hall was filled for the presentation ceremony with boys, the Masters and other staff, and also many of the old pensioners with their wooden legs and crutches and other injuries. Some of their tales of adventure and storms and faraway places were re-told to inspire us boys to follow in their footsteps and commit ourselves to the sea. I needed no more encouragement.

I was presented with my 'Nelson Medal' for good conduct whilst at the School, as well as my Upper School certificate. It is a very smart affair and I am very proud of my achievement. On the front of the certificate it says…

THE ROYAL HOSPITAL SCHOOLS,
The Reward of Industry, Application and general Good Conduct,
To George Wm. Eastland
Given at the Annual Examination.
Midsummer 1854
Greenwich

On the other side of the certificate is written...
Second Class
Upper School
with signatures and the red wax seal.

Some boys stay at the Nautical School for three or even four years. I was able to complete my studies in a little over two. This was mainly because my reading, writing and arithmetick were very good when I arrived at Greenwich. Some boys take two years just to learn to write well enough. My school education in Chichester and Petworth was good which enabled me to spend most of my time at Greenwich concentrating on learning sailing and navigation skills.

Another reason some boys stay on at Greenwich is because it is becoming more difficult to find places on boats for ship's boys, so they carry on studying while trying to find a ship that will take them. I didn't have that problem because Father is a ship's Master and he knows many other masters of ships. The School wanted me to stay on to be a Pupil Teacher for sixpence a week plus full-board accommodation. I wanted only to go to sea.

During the time when I was living and studying in London my parents moved out of the Bull's Head at Fishbourne and went to live at the small harbour at Dell Quay, not two miles along the river. With my sisters Mary, Nancy and Matilda all getting wed and moving away from home Father no longer needed the large tavern. Father got himself the job of wharfinger and miller at Dell Quay which means he needs to live there if he is to control the shipments at the small harbour.

In the end Matilda and Richard stayed. They took over the Crown and Anchor, the old tavern overlooking the harbour at Dell Quay. This inn is even bigger than the Bull's Head. As yet Richard and Matilda have no children of their own but they fill the tavern by letting out spare rooms to other boarders - agricultural labourers and the like. There is also plenty of accommodation in the Crown for Father, Mother, Martha and Fanny to live in comfort. As well as me - now that I have returned from Greenwich.

Father says he is getting too old now to be sailing. But as wharfinger he can watch ships come and go and still be involved in the world of mariners that has been his life, all from the safety of dry land. It also means he can get me passage to work on lots of vessels while he stays at Dell Quay milling and supervising the landings at the harbour. This arrangement suits us both perfectly.

Last weekend this great wide barge on which I now sail was loaded at the quay with oysters bound for Brighton and with leather, timber and grain for Sunderland. After unloading our cargoes at the end of our voyage at a busy yard called Shields, just outside the mouth of the Tyne, work began straight away to reload our vessel – this time with dusty black coal from the local mines. A large wooden chute was positioned over the boat and the coal just pours straight in. It will be much harder work when we get back to Dell Quay shovelling the coal out of the barge and moving it into one of the three large coal pounds that stand on the quay.

When our barge had finished being loaded our crew took a break to rest, eat and drink before our departure. I also took the opportunity to walk round the shipyard in search of an old shipmate of Father's. Father wrote a letter for me to pass onto Old Jock. I asked after him and was soon pointed in the direction of an old man sitting in the sun surrounded by fishing nets that he seemed to be repairing with a large clasp-knife and some coarse twine.

'Are you Old Jock?' I asked as I approached the man.

'Mebee, mebees not. An' who might ye be young me'lad?'

'I am George William Eastland, ship's boy and son of George Eastland, Master Mariner of Fishbourne. Father instructed me to give you this letter,' I said as I pulled the folded sheet of paper from my jacket pocket and offered it to the man.

A wide beam immediately crossed his weather-beaten red face as he put down his nets, stood up and shook my hand vigorously. 'Well ahm most pleased te meet ye young man. An' noo, ah can see yer face - ah can see ye has thee fatha's chin an' eyes. Howay an' I cannot tell ye how grateful I am te hev served alongside yer fatha on the oceans o' this world an' of the time he saved us from a certain drowning when ah was knocked off a boot by a falling timber.

'Ahm tee old fre the sea noo, but ah don't regret me adventures at sea, not fre one minute. They wez wonderful times on the seas – an' in the taverns o' the world.' The old man winked at me as he remembered his past exploits and conquests.

'How is aad George?' he went on.

'Father is well and working now as miller and wharfinger at Dell Quay. Like you it seems, he is enjoying living by the sea but no longer keen to be on it. I expect he has told you more in his letter?'

'Yer fatha always wez the clever one. Me reading wez nivvor as canny good as his, an' me eyes aren't tha' good any more eether. Perhaps ye could read the letter to us?' So of course I did, and Old Jock seemed very pleased to tuck the letter signed by Captain George Eastland safely into his jacket pocket even though he couldn't read it himself.

Old Jock fetched us each an ale which we enjoyed drinking whilst sitting on the quay in the warm sunshine. He also handed me an old-looking wooden box.

'This is fre ye. A present frem a git grateful aad sea-dog. Git grateful te hev sailed wi' yer fatha an' te hev noo met wi' his laddie. Follow in yer fatha's wake, explore the world an' enjoy aal its wonderful places, an' cherish yer memories. Is this yer forst sailing te Sunlun?'

'Yes, that is why Father asked me to deliver the letter to you.'

'Ye gie me greatest respects te yer fatha an' tell him te come on the boot sometime up te Shields te see us. Aa'd myek him git welcome. He be always welcome te stay a few neets wi' us an' the missus at me hoose an' te share some jars. This box is fre ye, me lad – te remember yer forst voyage te Sunlun an' meeting aad Jock. One of those sailing memories fre ye te keep.'

I thanked Jock and returned to my barge. It was reloaded and ready to make the return sailing down the east coast of England, and around the corner into the English Channel, and eventually back to Dell Quay. I could see that with the weight of the coal the barge was now lying much lower in the water than it was with our earlier cargo.

We slipped out of Shields shipyard some while ago. Now, as our barge drifts slowly towards Scarborough and its sheltered harbour where we will berth tonight, I take a peek inside the box that Old Jock has given me. It contains something wrapped up in layers of brown paper. I push my fingers in between the papers to reveal a large cream jug with a big handle and a wide spout for pouring. The jug is covered in gaily painted pink, green and golden strokes and its smooth glazed finish glints in the orange sunlight. On one side is a painting of the cast iron bridge over the River Wear at Sunderland, which was built in the 1790s.

On the other side of the jug is a painting of three great galleons sailing in choppy waters, their canvases all bursting with the squalls and with the following rhyme underneath…

Majestically slow before the breeze
The tall Ship marches on the azure seas
In silent pomp she cleaves the watery plain.
The pride and wonder of the billowy main.

I feel like a proper mariner with a fair treasure. I pack my Sunderland jug carefully away once more, safely into the layers of brown paper and the wooden box, and I wedge the box carefully under my bunk.

Tuesday 1st September 1857

Willswood Farm, Woodlands Road, Netley Marsh, the New Forest
8.00pm

Nancy Cox.

I love it here at Willswood Farm.

My husband, George and I moved here not long after we were wed. Our modest cottage has very plentiful land. George says we have fifty acres.

George was miller at Fishbourne before we married but his Father, William is a farmer as were many before him. It is no surprise that we have ended up with our own farm as this is what business George knows best. I didn't expect to be quite so far from Mother and Father though.

It is so peaceful here at Willswood. I can go for days and hardly see a soul. George and his labourers toil with the livestock and in the pastures from dawn to dusk.

My companions are our dog Bessie, the birds and the bees, the rabbits and hares, and at dusk the hedgehogs. Sometimes I do not see them - they are very shy. But I leave them water to drink, and the next morning I know they have visited by the thin tarry streaks they leave behind on the grass.

The birdsong at dawn and dusk is ten times louder and more merry than ever it was at Fishbourne. George and I are woken early in summer by the joyous chorus which sets us to work with a happy smile. The best time to work on the farm is early and late to miss the heat.

I tend our cottage garden, growing fruit and vegetables from seed for our table. In the middle of the day when it is too hot for garden tasks or even for churning butter I sit quietly under a shady tree. Then I make or mend clothes, or write letters.

I am so grateful I learned to read and write well at school so that I can write to Mother and Father and to my sisters. So many older people, and some younger ones, cannot write at all.

Sometimes I miss the life and laughter in The Bull's Head inn. Sometimes, when they are very thirsty, the men go to The White Horse Inn on the road to Totton. My husband says taverns are not places for women, but he forgets there is nothing I do not know about taverns and what goes on inside them.

I miss my sisters. We are all so spread out and busy we only seem to meet at weddings and baptisms these days. That is an exaggeration, but sometimes it feels that way.

Mary is busy teaching hundreds of children at Petworth. Matilda and Martha work many hours in the tavern and Fanny is growing so fast she will soon leave school. Occasionally Martha, who is now eighteen brings Fanny to stay at our farm.

In the summer we love walking in Busketts Wood or even into Lyndhurst which is barely a mile away, and has the best butcher and greengrocer in the whole of the New Forest. I don't know why it is called the New Forest - the trees are very old? Martha and Fanny came to stay not long ago in the school holidays. I miss their chatter already.

They told me about Mother, and the inn, and the barmaids and all the gossip. When Fanny was gone to bed Martha and I drank my Red Current Wine and Cherry Wine, and Martha told me about all the handsome men she serves in the tavern. The Red Current Wine is particularly good this year and I have quite a number of bottles stored in the cool pantry.

There is little news of Father and my brother George. Since George passed his examinations at Greenwich he spends most of his time away at sea while Father stays at Dell Quay.

Father's last ship was called "Stephen and Elizabeth". I think father's other ships had much more ship-like names – "Flying Fish", "Waterloo", "Britannia". The "Stephen and Elizabeth" sounds more like the King and Queen of England than like a ship.

Martha doesn't take much notice of what Father and George get up to. She says she has more important things to do. She did tell me the ships sail out of Dell Quay harbour loaded with coal and grain and other things. She says they mostly sail to London and to the north of England to places like Newcastle and Dover and – I don't know where else. Faraway places I'll never see. My brother, George was always the one who was set on exploring the whole wide world. I am happy here in peaceful Netley Marsh.

I would love to see my little brother. But now he has gone to sea, which was all he ever wanted to do, who knows when he will return to dry land?

When she was here in the summer Martha said Father has grown weary of the sea – he is nearly sixty. She said he now spends his days trading in coal and running the mill at Dell Quay. I am sure my brother will be sailing for many years yet.

I do not know what I am doing wrong.

George and I married four years ago and I have always wanted children. I think I am doing all the right things, but who ever knows really? It is not the sort of thing you can talk about is it? And even if you could, what could anyone else do?

I know it is one of God's games of chance. Mother had many babies and my older sister Mary has had four in five years – as easy as shelling peas. Whilst Matilda and Richard were wed – must be ten years ago now – yet nothing.

I am starting to get old for children now. I will be twenty-four years next birthday, in October. I am beginning to fear that to be barren may be my lot in life. This is my biggest anguish and regret.

But regrets do no good. There are many others who live in harsh stinking towns with no space or green fields, and others who are ill and impoverished. I must be thankful for my peaceful farm and loving husband... and for the sweet nightingale that sings outside my window as the darkness falls, whilst I ponder my fortunes in this life.

Saturday 28th May 1859

West Wittering, Sussex, 11.30am

Sarah Jane Collick.

The first signs that something was amiss with Emily were at Christmas. Emily always loved Christmas: making Christmas stockings, decorating the farmhouse with holly and mistletoe and most of all preparing the food, especially the Christmas pudding.

But she was out of sorts last Christmas. She went down with influenza the day before Christmas Eve and though she tried to carry on with the preparation of food and decorations she couldn't stop sneezing and shivering and I put her to bed on 24th December and told her she must stay there, keep warm and sleep.

Emily had a terrible cold and she said her head and limbs ached terribly too. She had no strength and stayed in bed for days. She filled her bed sheets with sweat and completely lost her appetite. Every morning she would sit in her chair huddled in a thick blanket clutching the bed warmer I had brought her while I flung her window open to get in some fresh air and changed her sheets.

With the dull damp weather and short days it was the devil's own job to get so many sheets washed and dried. Every evening for days I would have the next day's sheets hanging in the sitting room near the fire to dry and air ready for the next morning. I regularly brewed up a hot posset for Emily made of curdled milk, wine, sugar and spices to help rid her of that terrible fever.

When Emily finally stopped sneezing in January the cold went to her chest and her cough would prevent her from sleeping at night. Her appetite returned a little and she had hot soups and as much drink as I could give her, but by the end of January she was stick thin.

By the longer days at the end of February Emily improved a little and managed to walk a short way in the garden on fine days. Her fevers and sweats had thankfully passed so I no longer had the daily bed-washing to do. But Emily's cough persisted despite the onions, garlic, brandy and other assorted elixirs we gave her to try to shift it.

Jane Parsons, our servant worked tirelessly in the kitchen and garden to help keep Woodhorn going and William and Thomas properly fed, while I was spending so much time nursing Emily. Jane was happy to work herself very hard but would not go near Emily or the clothes and linen washing. She did make sure I always had plenty of boiling water for the washing. Jane said she had a weak chest and feared the fever, but I knew she was worried Emily might have consumption.

Father, Thomas and the other labourers used all the daylight hours in March and April to sow wheat, peas and beans, and to prepare the land ready for sowing barley, clover, mangold-wurzels and grass. Father would return weary to the farmhouse when it got dark and sit heavily on his chair at the kitchen table for his dinner. Thomas arrived soon after having fed and watered the horses at the end of the day's work.

Father, Thomas, Emily and I ate dinner together around the kitchen table and shared the events of the day. It was noticeable that Emily had not put any weight back on. She picked at her food like a sparrow and her clothes hung loose on her body.

Father asked me quietly one evening when we were alone if I thought Emily was recovering from her illness and he said, 'She looks pale as a ghost and her wrists are as thin as two pencils.' He asked me to take her into the fresh air more now it was getting warmer to clear her lungs. We thought it might even be a good idea to take her in the cart to the coast at Wittering to breathe some salty sea air if there was a warm Sunday. I did my best to do what Father had asked but May began with cold winds blowing from the north which kept Emily indoors, and her cough became more persistent again.

Three weeks ago on Sunday Father got up early and filled in the privy before digging a new one at the other end of the garden. He was worried the privy might have caused Emily's illness, and blamed himself for not making time to do this before. I told him not to be silly as no-one else was ill.

Emily suddenly got worse. Her cough became constant and raked her body. The fever returned and she went to bed and just slept. She had no strength left to fight the illness. Her eyes were surrounded by black rings. Her chest hurt when she coughed. She never complained but I saw her wince as she coughed whilst holding a blanket tight to her chest.

Emily knew she wasn't recovering this time. I would hold her hand as she lay, half-asleep in her darkened room – the bright light hurt her eyes. She said to me, 'I'm going to find Mother and we will make the best Christmas puddings together and they will contain gold sovereigns instead of silver thre'pences. Please look after Father. I know he blames himself but it wasn't his fault. He is a good man.'

Emily's death came suddenly. She slept all day and didn't wake up. Instead she coughed blood all over her bed and died instantly. A friend, Phebe Barnet was sitting with Emily at the time while I was out in the garden collecting vegetables. She came running to me as white as a sheet but there was nothing to be done. It was a blessed relief for Emily in the end. That was last Sunday 22nd May.

Emily and I were very dear sisters to each other. Tears roll down my cheeks until my eyes run dry. I have lost three sisters, Charlotte, Emma and now Emily. And Mother. Only Alice remains.

Alice and I cling to each other today at Emily's funeral in the church of St. Peter and St. Paul at West Wittering. Father, Thomas and Clement stand in their grim dark suits, their heads bowed. Alice and I stand in the nave looking into the chancel at the eastern end of the Church. With its grey stone floor, white stone walls, and dark wooden rafters high above I feel as cold as dead stone. This unchanging, wretched place returns my memory in an instant to Mother's funeral day nearly ten years ago now. How many times will He drag me back to this scene to remind me of my precarious mortality?

The Reverend Charles Gaunt delivers his words in that quivering drone to squeeze every last tear from our eyes. The words wash over me – to listen to them would be like torture. My mind drifts off to remember Emily and me running, laughing and playing in fields of poppies and cornflowers and making daisy chain necklaces for each other.

Every now and then the drone of the Rector cuts back in…

In the morning it is green, and groweth up: but in the evening it is cut down, dried up, and withered…

Man that is born of a woman hath but a short time to live, and is full of misery. He cometh up, and is cut down, like a flower; he fleeth as it were a shadow, and never continueth in one stay…'

We leave the dark church to stand by the gaping grave that awaits Emily's coffin. The sun shines under a blue sky and birds sing in the trees. Why has the sun waited for Emily to die before coming out to shine? Her last weeks were so cold and grey. She did not deserve the gloom.

I pray silently to God…

I wish funerals didn't have to be so long, twisting the knife into those sad souls who remain on this Earth. Isn't it punishment and pain enough to expect us to continue to live without our loved ones? Amen.

Autumn 1859

Woodhorn

Sarah Jane Collick.

It has taken Father months to come to terms with my older sister Emily's death. His mind isn't on his work and he seems to have lost his physical strength. In June he cut his leg with an axe and had to rest with his leg up for a week. Fortunately Clement, who has been working away from the farm has been able to come back to Woodhorn for a while to help Thomas keep the farm going at this busy time of sowing maincrops and preparing for the harvest.

Meanwhile Father blames himself for the deaths of his wife and three daughters. He says after Charlotte and Emma died at birth he and Mother shouldn't have had more babies. He says, 'The deaths were a warning from God that I didn't heed – I just wanted children to pass Woodhorn on to. I should have listened to God and just looked after Emma. But I was too stupid and now God is punishing me by taking Emma and my children and letting me grow old so I must see the results of my stupidity.'

Alice and John bring their children over from their farm at Merston as often as they can to remind Father that good has come from his marriage, and this helps Thomas and me, who see the most of Father's pain and anguish.

Little Alice Eliza Jacob was born in September a year ago and she came to Woodhorn with the rest of the family on her first birthday. I baked a birthday cake for her. It cheered Father no end to see his daughter Alice and Granddaughter Little Alice both in his kitchen together laughing and enjoying the cake.

It is only now that Father's melancholy subsides a little, and he starts to work and sleep properly again. Jane Parsons helps to fill the gaps left by Emily by working longer days at Woodhorn and spending time talking to Father. They seem to talk easily together about farming and other things and this company has helped Father. Jane's son Thomas, aged eleven has also come to work at the farm as an agricultural labourer which means Father can spend more time in the farmhouse garden and leave the heavy work to the younger men.

Jane's presence and help at Woodhorn is also helping to free me. I try to remind myself that I am not a trapped farmer's wife. Although much responsibility has come early to me I am still only seventeen. The young men are starting to run Woodhorn and Jane is happy to work in the homestead for Father.

Perhaps I can spread my wings a little?

Tuesday 4th October 1859

Dell Quay

George William Eastland.

'Hey George, what you doing?'

'Oh hello Matthew. Well I'm working, same as you. Though I daresay I'm working harder than you – just like when we were at school.'

'What a scurrilous thing to say George. I always worked very hard at school, though I'll grant you I was not necessarily always employed upon the same task as that which the Master intended!

'You given up sailing George, now you are at Dell Quay?'

'Not completely. I sometimes sail with a cargo to one of the local ports to ensure its safe delivery, or to collect a payment. But you are not altogether incorrect Matthew. I mostly stay here – I've plenty to do at the Mill, and trading in coal and other cargoes. I seen plenty of seas and plenty of storms when I was in the navy.'

'Must have been exciting sailing around the world. I envied you travelling far and wide while I stayed rooted in Chichester. Don't you miss it, George?'

'I miss the beauty of a sunset on a calm sea, the power of the wind in the sails whipping the ship across the sea, and the excitement of arriving at a new port and hearing a different speech and seeing the colourful clothes. The storms and the sickness I am happy to do without.'

'What of the women, George? I hear say the women in those foreign places are tanned and very beautiful, and are falling over themselves to spend a nice time with a sailor. Am I right, George? I would love to meet an exotic European lady in some foreign place. It would make a change from the pale grey Sussex milk-maids!'

'Become a mariner then, Matthew. The world is your oyster.'

'Nah. I've got the family carpentry business to run, which is why I'm here today – delivering timber to be shipped to Southampton.

Anyway, if I go in a boat I usually feel ill. I'll have to continue to make do with the milk-maids.

'Which reminds me, George... are you coming to the Birdham Harvest Celebrations on Saturday?'

'No, I don't think so. I've been to them before and the old people just get drunk and, the dancing... well as you say Matthew, some of those milk-maids couldn't skip if they were barefoot on pine needles, let alone dance.'

'Oh come on George. The Harvest Celebration is one of the high points of the year around here. It will be much more fun if you come along with me. There will be plenty of good food and ale and you don't have to dance with the dowdy milk-maids. I am sure there will be a few comely wenches we can find some fun with. After all... what else are you going to do on Saturday evening? Sit at Dell Quay and watch the sun go down over the water?'

'All right Matthew – I suppose I could come and keep you company. Where is it to be held this year?'

'It is going to be in the big barn at Manhoodend Farm on the main road to Chichester. Meet me at the barn at five o'clock and we'll have a good supper and plenty of ale before the dancing starts. The ale is sure to make the girls look prettier too!'

Once all Matthew's timber has been loaded onto a barge he climbs onto his cart and tells his horse to get on. He raises his arm to me as he leaves the quay and calls out, 'Remember George, Saturday at five o'clock. We'll have some fun, you'll see.'

I'm not convinced. I'm not sure I should have agreed to go. It will as likely be just a lot of simple farm folk drunk and falling over. But Matthew is a good friend and I've said I will go so I won't let him down. I have to admit those farmers know how to lay on a feast so I'll enjoy the Harvest fare if nothing else.

Matthew and I will create ourselves some fun somehow. We'll probably wager two shillings on which of us can dance with the ugliest milk-maid, or the oldest hag with whiskers on her chin, or some such nonsense so I might come home a little richer. You never know.

Saturday 8th October 1859

Manhoodend Farm, Birdham, 5pm

George William Eastland.

I left the Crown and Anchor and strolled along the lane with little enthusiasm. But I promised Matthew, and I won't break a promise. At least it wasn't raining, though it was gloomy and grey. This had less to do with the weather than the fact that autumn is now closing in, and the sun is setting a little earlier every day.

At the end of the lane I reached the Chichester road where I turned right towards Birdham. It is only a couple of miles to Manhoodend Farm. I soon passed Croucher's Farm where there was lots of activity – no doubt the people there also getting themselves ready to go to the Harvest Celebration. Next I passed the Black Horse tavern and was tempted to go in and forget the whole evening. But why pay for ale there when I can get plenty at the Harvest dance, as well as at the Crown and Anchor?

I continue to trudge along the road, around the right-hand bend and over the Chichester Canal that connects the town to the Chichester Channel just a mile south of Dell Quay. I carry on walking along the dead straight road and past old Coomber's Barn, until I reach Manhoodend Farm on the right-hand side of the road. There are quite a few people walking along the road now in both directions, all heading for the farm before the light fades to darkness.

I arrive to find Matthew standing outside the barn with a tankard of ale and already looking cheery. 'Hello George. I thought you were never coming. I've nearly drunk all the ale – it is strong stuff.' Matthew slaps me on the back and we stumble into the noisy barn.

Matthew may have already had a beer or two but the casks are not going to run dry for some hours yet. There are a stack of wooden beer kegs as well as bottles of wine, cider and assorted cordials.

Farmers being farmers, the air is full of the scent of roasting beef, hams and chickens turning slowly on large spits. There are also tables laid out with sausages, gingerbreads, oranges, pear tarts, apple pies, sweet biscuits and sweetmeat. The children in particular enjoy sucking boiled sweets into their cheeks. We are certainly going to be well fed this evening.

It is hard to tell how many people are here – perhaps one or two hundred, but with more arriving all the time. The large barn is dimly lit by the fires over which the spits turn, and by several hurricane lamps hanging from wooden joists above our heads.

As the meat is roasting people gather in groups talking about the important business of the day and the even more important local gossip: who has died, whose son has been sent to gaol for poaching, and whose under-age single daughter is in the family way.

All the people here are farmers along with their families, friends and acquaintances from Birdham and the surrounding settlements. I know many of them by sight especially those from Birdham and the villages to the north including Appledram, Donnington and Hunston. Whereas I don't know the people who have come up from places like Highleigh, Somerley or Sidlesham.

A band plays merry tunes to entertain us and a few people near them are already dancing. There are several musicians playing two fiddles, a mandolin, drums, a wind instrument – possibly a flute or clarinet, and a girl dancing with a tambourine and ribbons. They are a jolly bunch.

Matthew and I enjoy the ale and some apple pie as we watch the crowd swell in the barn. We scan the crowd to see if we can spot a pretty girl lit up by a flickering light who we might dance with later. Neither of us are yet experienced with the ladies, but with a few ales inside us and with our seventeen-year-old hopes and dreams we are becoming bolder.

Matthew nudges my arm. 'Who are they?' I follow his eye and see a group of four young ladies across the barn, two of whom are looking in our direction. As our eyes meet theirs they quickly turn away amidst a flurry of giggling and chatter.

'They were looking at us. I like the look of that one with the long fair hair,' he tells me excitedly, slopping some of his ale onto my sleeve.

'That one I know – the others I don't. She is Mary Clayton – her brother James is just over there. They live on a farm, Belchamber I think it is, just down the main road. Mary is no milk-maid. I don't know what she does to be honest. Looking at her white fingers I'd guess she plays piano! She must be twenty by now. She's too old for you Matthew. Anyhow, they are starting to serve up the roast meats and you don't want to miss out on that. You can think about the girls later. Come on, let's fill our bellies.'

The feasting is a grand affair. Even the band stops playing while the musicians tuck into their plates of food. The meats and roasted vegetables are followed by the fruit tarts, plum pudding and cakes, and all the time amply washed down by the free-flowing drink. Such a merry affair has not been seen in Birdham – at least, not since the summer village feast in August after the hay-making was completed.

Once the feasting is done the band starts playing again. The spits and tables of food, as well as the lingering children are all cleared away and the serious business of the evening gets underway. For many this means drinking themselves into a stupor, followed by a contented slumber in a dark corner of the barn, invariably clutching a tankard or a bottle tightly in hand.

For the rest it means dancing, singing, a bit of flirting and perhaps more. There are many dark corners in the barn where couples might sit and entertain each other.

Despite being distracted by the comely Mary Clayton, Matthew has of course challenged me to a wager – one that I shall inevitably win. The wager relates to the Cushion Dance. This dance is a favourite in Birdham, and I daresay throughout the land. The fiddler plays a tune while a man walks amongst the crowd holding a cushion. When the music stops, which it does frequently, the man drops the cushion in front of the nearest lady so that she can kneel on it and kiss him. Many young ladies are too shy to kiss the men, and if they do not they must forfeit a penny – to the fiddler.

Matthew is becoming ambitious. He has bet me half a crown that more ladies will kiss him than me. This is not likely to happen as Matthew is of course less handsome than me, and in any case I shall make sure I place my cushion at the feet of the slightly older ladies –

those who are less shy about kissing a man and less willing to waste a penny on the old fiddler. Matthew is certain to drop his cushion at the feet of all the prettiest young ladies, many of whom will likely prefer to pay the fiddler a penny than kiss a young scallywag like Matthew. This wager is as good as won already.

With the dancing well underway Matthew and I have found a few pretty girls to dance with. Most scuttle away shyly with scarcely a word the moment the dance finishes, happier to point and chatter with their friends. I have identified a few of the women in their twenties who I will try to get close to with my cushion when that time arrives. I can see Matthew is trying to edge his way nearer to Mary Clayton for a dance, but I know she has eyes for me. We have danced together previously on one of these occasions and although she is a handsome woman I find her forward and try to keep a distance from her.

Mary however, has outflanked me and puts her hands over my eyes from behind. 'George, I think it is time we had a dance,' she breathes into my neck, and I feel her firm bosom pressed into my back.

I turn and find her rosy cheeks beaming into my face as she clasps my hands and heads me into the dance. There is no harm in dancing.

'How are you, Mary?'

'I feel fine now, George,' she says as she holds her body close to mine making sure that I can feel her every move. Mary is nearly as tall as I am and is a very fulsome woman with full red lips and strong curvaceous hips.

I see Matthew out of the corner of my eye glaring at me. I wink at him and think to myself all will be well. I will steer Mary towards Matthew at the end of this dance and thrust them together ready for the next one. They will both surely be very happy.

All is going to plan until Mary clutches me tight at the end of the dance, catching me by surprise as she thrusts her generous thigh into my groin and spins me straight into the next dance.

'You didn't think I'd let you go as soon as I had got a hold of you did you, George?'

'Of course not, Mary,' I reply, as I consider what manoeuvre I will carry out just before the end of this dance to deliver her into the very willing arms of Matthew.

And then I see her.

Sitting on a wooden bench, her dark lashes flickering in the fluttering light from the fires. She is a Vision such as I have never seen before. A silver diamond sparkles in each of her eyes and her long curly black hair drapes over her shoulders, so fine and white that they could be made of porcelain.

She sits upright with a delicate elegance, her slender arm resting on a table. She is slim and willowy – I cannot tell her age. I care not – she looks simply divine. Her face is also white, perhaps too pale, and she appears sorrowful. I wonder what causes her to look so sad?

I realise I have not taken my eyes from this troubled beauty throughout the course of the dance. It is confirmed when Mary coughs in my face, 'What sort of a gentleman dances with a lady whilst ogling some dowdy peasant woman? She looks thin and weedy as a dandelion. What a fool you are George, to waste your time looking at a dandelion when you could immerse yourself in a passionate rose such as myself?'

As Mary thrusts herself away from me she almost knocks Matthew over, but he manages to ask her for the pleasure of the next dance. 'First I need a drink,' she huffs as she makes a beeline towards the bottles of wine.

Before I have a moment to collect my thoughts it is announced that the Cushion Dance is about to commence. A cream-coloured cushion is thrust into my hands as the music begins. Before I have gathered my wits the music stops and all I can see is farmers. I manage to drop my cushion at the feet of a nearby woman who promptly kneels on it and turns her face to look up at me with a grin. I can see, despite the gloom that she is middle-aged and as she moves her face towards me for the kiss I also see that she has no front teeth. Argh…argh!

I collect two more kisses on my way across the barn as the fiddler starts and stops his music, but I no longer have a care for Matthew's wager. My mind is only on the Vision who sits in the shadows – now just a few feet in front of me. The fiddler is animatedly sawing once more, with his fingers flying across the four strings of his violin, and loose horse hairs from his bow flicking through the air whilst he taps his feet. When the music suddenly stops I place my cushion carefully at the feet of my Vision, and look into her delicate face.

A total stranger and, as I can now see, pretty, young and unblemished. I am expecting her to push a penny into my hand. When I instead feel a soft, almost imperceptible brush of her lips against mine I feel a tingle jolt through the entire length of my body.

My look of total surprise seems to amuse this beauty as a glimmer momentarily adds a crease to the corner of her mouth and lights up her face into a beguiling smile. I stand next to her and continue to look into her eyes as the music plays...and stops.

After a while she says to me, 'Young sir, should you not be collecting more kisses?'

Though I am transfixed by her beauty, my mind is more alert than it has ever been before and I answer, 'Why yes you rarest of beauties, how amiss of me,' and before she can as much as blink I plant a delicate kiss of my own upon her satin red lips.

My Vision seems surprised and amused but is not indignant; the reaction that I might have anticipated had I thought about it for even one moment. But I am not thinking. This is pure instinct.

'You have an unusual way of performing the Cushion Dance, young sir?'

'I am more than content. I have enjoyed the only kiss that I wanted,' I reply.

'And do you refer to the first, or the last kiss that you have collected during the dance, sir?'

I am sure my face colours, not that anyone can see in this gloom. 'The last two kisses were equally wonderful. The earlier ones an irrelevance, and the first kiss of all was a misfortune that befell me entirely as a consequence of you.'

'And how can that be?' she says.

'Because having set my eyes upon you I was so entranced that I had no idea which woman stood before me when the music first stopped.

'I was going to ask why such a beautiful face as yours is set so sad, but I am pleased to have now already seen a twinkling smile spread across it.'

'And why should a total stranger expect me to answer such an impertinent question?' she responds, but with such a lightness of tone that I know it bears no malice.

'My apologies. I am George. George William Eastland – mariner, miller and merchant of Dell Quay. And very pleased to make your acquaintance, as well as…spellbound.'

'You certainly have a way with words, George. You are clearly a busy man – far too busy I am sure to bother yourself with me. I am Sarah. Sarah Jane Collick. A simple farm girl from Birdham.'

'You are far from simple, Sarah. You are very pretty and a sharp-witted treasure trove – I can tell that already. What makes you think I am so busy?'

'Well George, most men seem to struggle to cope with one job. And you – well, you have three. You are a mariner, a miller, and a merchant. Do you find time even to sleep?'

I am not sure how I have done it but I am delighted to see that Sarah, who looked so melancholy when I first saw her, now has a smile in her eyes and dimples in her cheeks that make her face sparkle like a star. She is wearing a well-fitting white muslin dress above multi-layered and frilled skirts that fall to her ankles. She wears white boots and gloves with a trail of white and yellow silk flowers running through her dark locks. We delight in just talking.

It is as if we have always known each other. Even when we pause quietly for a moment, we do not feel awkward. We talk and dance and the evening simply melts away. Later, hungry we find delicious toffee apples and I watch Sarah's sweet lips suck the crusted toffee from the fruit. I am utterly spellbound watching her.

Eventually Sarah explains the reasons for her apparent gloom at the start of the evening. She tells me of her mother's young death. Also the shattering blow when her older sister, Emily died earlier this year from consumption, and of the burden of responsibility Sarah now feels running Woodhorn Farmhouse for her father.

Sarah introduces me to her older brother, Thomas – a fine looking and strong young man who also works at their farm. He checks if Sarah would like him to walk her home when the dancing finishes. I have already offered and Sarah tells Thomas this. He seems quite happy about that as he has promised to walk a young lady he has been dancing with to Courtbarn Farm, which he says is on the opposite side of Birdham, over near Birdham Pool.

The time is well past ten. With the evening drawing to a close I go and find Matthew. I pay him the half-crown I owe him for collecting sixteen kisses during the Cushion Dance compared to my five. I have no regrets at losing the wager, for the two kisses I shared with Sarah were more wonderful than ten thousand others could have been.

Matthew is also rather pleased with himself, happily dancing with Mary Clayton and now better-off by two and sixpence. We bid each other good-night.

After a final dance Sarah and I bundle ourselves up in our coats and tumble out of the barn door into the dark night. It is a cold, clear night with a sky full of shimmering stars and a bright three-quarters moon to light our way. I wrap my arm around Sarah's shoulder to keep her warm and we walk back along Chichester road for nearly a mile towards Birdham. A couple of carts pass by on the road spilling whoops and laughter into the night – more Harvest revellers on their way back to Birdham.

After a while we turn left into Siddlesham Lane where all is quiet but for the hooting of an owl and the sly fox, his eyes sparkling, lurking on the lane fifty yards in front of us. He hears our footsteps and vanishes.

We soon reach Woodhorn, and stand at the gate and plan when and where next we shall meet. It is too cold to loiter for long. 'Just before we part there is one thing I have been meaning to ask you, Sarah. I must confess that when I placed that cushion at your feet I thought that you would pay a penny rather than kiss a man you had never met before. Of course it was a most pleasant surprise when you kissed me.'

'Why George, how could I possibly have passed on the opportunity to kiss the handsomest man at the dance? 'Tis true,' her eyes sparkle at me in the moonlight.

''Tis also true that when I went to Manhoodend Farm this evening I was scarcely in a dancing mood. But after the events of this year I did not want to stay at home alone with Father feeling miserable, so I agreed to go with Thomas to the Harvest Celebration. The last thing I had on my mind was being kissed by a handsome man – with three jobs! So I didn't have one penny on me, and therefore had very little choice when you dropped your cushion in front of me.'

We both laugh and kiss once more before Sarah enters Woodhorn Cottage and closes the door quietly behind her. I turn, head out of the gate and start my walk up the lane back towards Dell Quay.

Above me the stars twinkle in the sky along with the silver angels who sing in tune with my whistling.

Sunday 15th July 1860

Woodhorn, 6am

Sarah Jane Collick.

I awake to a heavy blue-sky summer day.

I lie on my bed and watch the tiniest breeze flap my curtain through the open window. The bright heat tells me it is to be one of those endless hot days and that I should get done what I can while there is still a cool lick to the air. Woodhorn is presently surrounded by a sea of golden barley and the sky is filled daily with the swooping, looping airborne display of the swifts and swallows with their forked tails.

At the same time the blackest, gloomiest cloud remains stubbornly anchored over Woodhorn to darken our hearts and make us blind to the golden sea of barley. Father was heartbroken at Mother's early death, blaming himself with all sorts of wild self-accusations to try to explain her untimely end.

It was a great shock to us all, but my sisters and brothers helped each other and took on new tasks to carry on day-to-day life on the farm. Woodhorn thus continued, and the new tasks and responsibilities kept Alice, Emily, Thomas, Clement and me busy and helped dull the shock in our hearts from the sudden loss of Mother.

Father had no new tasks to fill his black void. The only new thing he could see was a new loneliness at those times when he would have been with Mother: sitting with her, quietly talking in the kitchen at the end of a long day on the farm, or walking hand-in-hand with her across the meadows on a sunny spring morning on their way home from church. My sisters and I did our best to comfort him but none of us could replace the hole left by his darling Emma.

By the time Alice married John Jacob and moved out to set up their home at Park Farm House at Merston, Woodhorn was once again running more smoothly. Emily was sixteen and I was eleven, both of us having left school and working all the time on the farm. With our housekeeper Jane Parsons we carried on without Alice and continued to get everything done by just working a little faster than before.

Knowing this, Father was able to smile at the wedding of Alice and John and before long he took pleasure in becoming a grandfather following the births of their children John, Emma Jane, and a new tiny Alice Eliza Jacob. Father enjoys playing with his grandchildren, and lying on the grass in our garden while they climb on his back and sit on him. At last he re-discovered some joy and his own black cloud began to disperse.

Until last year.

There was some warning, and in the end we knew what was going to happen. But that didn't make it any less painful or unfair. It is not right that a pretty twenty-one-year-old girl should be taken to her grave by consumption before she has tasted love and had a chance at her life.

I miss my older sister dreadfully. Father is once again inconsolable.

Alice visits when she is able to and does all she can to help, as does Jane Parsons. But at night, once Jane goes home it is all down to Thomas and me to manage. I think Father has taken Emily's death even harder than Mother's. Partly as she was so young but also due to the angst the accumulated deaths are causing him.

Father is approaching sixty and sometimes seeks solace in drink. The years of hard labour are taking their toll on his body. Some nights he just rails at God demanding to know what he, William Collick has done to be forced to live and just watch helplessly, while his wife and three of his daughters have all died far too young.

Thomas and I do our best for Father. We love him very much and we share in his pain, but sometimes we know we have to get away from the farm for a while – for our own balance. Today is my turn.

Sunday is good as the farm is less busy. The farm labourers are not here, and Father will rest, sit in the garden under the shade of a tree, read a book or just doze in his chair.

I prepare lunch which is easy today. It is too hot to cook so a meal of cold ham, hard boiled eggs provided by our chickens, and fresh salad from the garden washed down with home-made ale goes down well. There are only three of us now most Sundays.

Earlier this year Clement, now fourteen went to work and lodge as a servant with the Eastlands in the Crown and Anchor inn. It is good that Clement has found some life away from the sadness at Woodhorn and to earn some money of his own. My dear George helped to arrange this.

With lunch over and father peaceful I am free to go and find my darling George. I wash quickly, change into a yellow patterned dress and pack a picnic basket for later. Thomas takes me in the cart pulled by Jess along Sidlesham Lane, and onto the main Chichester road as far as the bend before Appledram at Rock Cottage. It is now mid-afternoon and the sun is beating down relentlessly.

I hop down from the cart, give Jess a hug round her neck and with that Thomas turns around for the return to Woodhorn. I skip down the narrow lane with my picnic basket seeking what shade I can from a few trees along the way. I am pleased to get some air, to stretch my legs and to enjoy a little freedom.

The lane takes me straight to the Crown and Anchor, the large rambling sixteenth century inn at Dell Quay overlooking the Fishbourne Channel. All the windows and doors at the front and back of the inn are wide open which allows a cooling breeze off the water to blow through the bars. I step into the cool hubbub of the inn where I find Ann Eastland, Martha and Fanny busy serving customers. Martha smiles at me and points me towards the next lounge where I find my brother Clement moving a beer keg.

Clement is looking well – carrying casks of ale is making him strong, and the sun and sea air has put colour into his cheeks since he came to the Crown and Anchor. He cannot stop to talk for long as the inn is busy on a hot Sunday afternoon like this. He tells me he will likely have a break later when it is cooler and the inn is quieter, and may walk along the coast path to Birdham or Itchenor and take in the evening sun. Clement then goes back to moving his casks and tells me I can find George out on the terrace.

Sure enough George is lazing on a bench, sunning himself with a beer glass, and gazing at the silver lights dancing on the surface of the estuary which is disturbed only by a few passing small boats. He is doubtless day-dreaming of pirates, shipwrecks and treasure chests brimming with gold coins and sparkling gemstones. How I love my dreamer George.

I sneak up behind him, put my hands over his eyes and say, 'I've caught a pirate!'

Recognising my voice George leaps up and turns quick as a flash taking me in his strong arms and plants a firm kiss on my lips before saying, 'Do you not know that creeping up behind a Captain is a serious offence punishable by...'

He hesitates before adding – 'Punishment to be decided later. Good conduct may assist you in this matter but you will have to be *very* good, to be sure.'

It seems too hot to get up and do anything so George and I sit together on the terrace talking as we watch the boats come and go, while the oyster-catchers with their orange-red bills swoop over the water with their busy little cries.

'I've brought us a picnic George – perhaps we could go for a walk in a while?' I suggest.

George ponders this. 'It's still very hot,' he says. 'I know – let's go out in the sloop and sail down river. It will be cooler on the water and then we'll have the picnic.'

'Oh yes,' I say. I am very excited. I have only been on the boat once before and it had been a bit cold, but today a cool breeze upon the sparkling water will be a relief from the fierce sun. George goes into the inn to let his father know we are taking the boat and returns with two blankets, and four bottles of ale to add to the picnic.

'Why do we need blankets, George – it is so hot?' I ask.

George replies with a grin, 'The blankets will make the wooden seats in the boat more comfortable Sarah, and they may come in handy if it gets cool later on.

'It's just gone four o'clock which gives us plenty of time for an adventure and we'll still be back before sundown,' George says as we get ourselves and our supplies into the boat. He then unties the rope holding the small sloop to the Dell Quay jetty and cries, 'Ahoy there deck-hand Sarah – we are now cast-off.'

The sloop is twelve feet long and made of a lovely deep orange-coloured wood. It has a single wooden mast and two sails and George sits at the back and steers using the hand rudder. I notice there are two paddles lying in the bottom of the sloop – 'Just in case the wind doesn't blow,' he says.

I sit in the middle of the boat and smile at George as the breeze off the water sends my long black hair in all directions. I feel such freedom upon this little boat with the glinting water all around, the wind in my face, the bump of the water under the hull, and a fine splash of cool spray flicked up by the sloop onto my hand. I feel my shoulders relax as the troubles of Woodhorn seem to fade into the shrinking fields of Birdham as we slip away down river.

I watch George, sitting before me looking tanned in his crisp white shirt that flutters in the breeze, his brown arm upon the tiller. His eyes squint into the sun as he keeps an eye on the sails, and his long hair is tied behind his neck. He seems hardly to move and I am surprised how quickly the Crown and Anchor disappears behind us into the distance, and out of sight when we turn the bend at what George says is Longmore Point. George tells me, 'The tide is going out and we will pick up speed now as we sail before the wind.'

I trail my hand in the water and splash some onto my face and chest; it feels so lovely and refreshing. I also flick droplets at George and giggle when he smiles at me. 'Remember I'm still considering your punishment for earlier misdemeanours,' he says with a wicked grin.

Our sloop passes a few others – people enjoying the perfect sailing weather as we are. But there are not many boats – it is gloriously tranquil out here with the wind and the occasional gull. I think of Father on the hot farm and wish I can bring him out here on this boat on the river one day. I'm sure the warm breeze and sound of the water splashing against the sides of the boat would help to blow some of his sadness away. Poor Father.

All of a sudden we run into a little cluster of sailing sloops as well as a fisherman's boat which is much larger than ours. George steers expertly past them all as we rush by West Itchenor on the left and round the head into a larger expanse of water.

Our boat begins to pitch slightly as some gently rolling waves meet us sideways and for a moment I panic as I am not a strong swimmer.

'Where are we going George?' I ask as I grip the wooden seat to retain my balance.

George replies with a dark look in his eye, 'I be taking the lady across the Seven Seas to a wild faraway land where there are tigers and palm trees with coconuts. I have a map that will lead us to a cave full of gold moidores washed up from the wreck of a Portuguese man-o'-war. We will be married in a white chapel with a bell on the roof, make love on a sandy beach under a red tropical sun and live happily ever after.'

I can't help but laugh at my silly romantic George. 'Where did I find you?' I ask him.

"I was tottering at the end of the plank with a dagger between my teeth and the sharks swimming below…when you came and rescued me Sarah,' he replies.

The pair of us can hardly stop ourselves laughing as we sail on towards the big wide sea.

'If you put your telescope to your eye,' George demonstrates by putting his index finger and thumb together to form a circle, 'and look ahead, you will see our sandy desert island approaching on the horizon in front of us.'

I turn and look behind me, and sure enough an expanse of flat sand topped by fluffy hills of sand and grasses lies just a few hundred yards ahead.

'This lovely desert island of ours is called East Head,' George tells me as he adjusts the sails to take the wind out of them to slow the sloop down. A minute later George beaches our boat on the sand flats at the north-west tip of East Head securing it with the small black metal anchor for when the tide turns.

The flat sands stretch before us in rippling patterns dissected by little channels of sea-water all glinting and winking and gurgling in the sun. I take off my shoes as I won't be needing them on the soft beach. Clutching our picnic basket in one hand and George's hand in the other I step out of the boat and dig my burning toes into the cool damp sand. We walk across the wet sand flats towards the dunes, the sun still hot on our backs and the wind in our hair. This place is deserted – it really is our own desert island beach.

When we reach the dunes I find they are higher than I expected, and all covered in tall yellow grasses, their stems and seed heads waving and rustling together in the breeze. We sit down amongst the dunes and look west into the lowering sun above Hayling and lean back against the soft sandy slope.

I close my eyes and listen. I can feel the evening summer sun warm on my face and body, and also the beads of perspiration that run cool along the small of my back. I feel the fine sand blow across my forehead and bare arms covering me in the finest white dust. I keep my mouth and eyes closed.

I can hear only the wind in my ears and the swishing of the long grasses all around. I cannot hear the sea. It is quite calm and some way off across the expanse of rippled yellow sand and shallows that George and I walked across.

I gradually become aware of the cries of birds. There are two types – the long wailing cries of gulls as they float and hover upon the wind currents somewhere above my head, sometimes near, sometimes far. And there is also the peeping and piping of pipits and warblers: very busy, always busy darting and chasing each other in and out of the long grasses. They flit about over our heads, here and there – I imagine their feathered wings brush my cheek as they flutter past on their endless, tireless business.

I can feel George's hot strong hand in mine as he lies quietly next to me and I can hear my heart pumping in my chest. I open one eye to look at him. George is gazing up at the few wispy white clouds that skid faraway across the blue heavens whilst he sucks on a golden stem of grass. He is tanned, has hair to his shoulders tied at the back and a strong jaw line beneath his cheek bones. He has removed his shirt to lie in the late afternoon sun and soak up its warm rays and I see lines of sweat criss-crossing the side of his chest.

His mouth seems set in a permanent grin. I feel so lucky to have found George – he is so handsome and gentle. And to think he has lived all my life just two or three miles away and we'd never set eyes upon each other until the Harvest dance last year. 'Tis true that he's been away for most of the last five years. What a funny world of chance and luck we live in.

If I could lie on this beach with George forever with no worries and no trials I would need nothing more. I am eighteen and in love with the most wonderful and handsome man in the whole world. I am in Paradise!

Well, I suppose I am only seventeen years and nearly eleven months, but that is as good as eighteen isn't it?

I roll towards George and put my arm over his chest covering him in a cloud of fine white sand that makes him splutter and laugh.

'I love you George,' I tell him as I look into those blue eyes that blink with the tiny grains of sand.

'I love you too, Sarah,' he says and runs his fingers through my long black curls. 'Especially when you don't throw sand in my eyes…'

With that George flips me over onto my back and pins me with his firm body as he kisses my lips and face. How I love George's kisses. I rub my fingers over the muscles of his back and feel his bony spine from his neck all the way down his back.

Our ravenous mouths feed upon each other and I feel George's hand squeezing my thigh through my skirts before hopelessly pulling up the layers of material to rub my bare skin. I shudder with uncontrollable desire as George's fingers part my legs and I feel his hard body arrive at the edge of my wetness.

George kisses me again hungrily, long and hard as our bodies move together and merge into the soft sand in a swell of passion that flows like an endless tide until we come to a shuddering finale. We lie like this, forever inseparable as my heart gradually returns to its usual beat and the sound of the birds and the breeze return. I tickle George's ear with a blade of grass and he continues to rub my lower back with his strong hands.

Eventually our appetite for food overtakes us and we dust off the sand and sit ourselves up. We dive into the basket for our picnic and the bottles of ale. How love makes you hungry I think as we devour the hunks of bread and cheese, boiled eggs, apples and cherries. And how much better love makes these simple things taste.

After our food we lie in each others' arms once more and watch the wading birds poking the sand at the water's edge with their long bills searching for crabs or ragworms. A little egret stands on the flat sand not far from us enjoying the sunset. It flicks its thin white pony-tail as it turns its head from side to side, keeping an eye out for trouble. George tells me the pretty white sea-bird is well to be wary as many egrets are caught locally and sold to milliners who put the white feathers into fancy hats.

With the sun sinking lower George presently says, 'It must be past seven and the tide has now turned to flow back upstream. If we leave now we will reach Dell Quay before dusk.' We pick ourselves up, shake the sand from our clothes and walk hand-in-hand through the cool shallow waters back to the sloop to cast-off once more.

With the sun now behind us George raises the sails and our boat picks up speed and scuttles up river. I cuddle into George's warm body. There is a gentle breeze, though not so strong as earlier. But that which there is, along with the inflowing tide takes our little craft steadily back upstream.

The lowering sun, deepening red behind us still lights up our sails and provides a little warmth on our backs. I am grateful now that George brought the blankets as I snuggle inside one of them next to him. A few lights twinkle as we pass Itchenor harbour and other occasional cottages, and the grass-hoppers or crickets can be heard scratching their legs together in amongst the long grasses along the river banks.

A graceful heron swoops low across the Fishbourne Channel in search of his supper and soon George lights an oil lamp and places it at the front of the sloop. The light is very pretty as it flickers in front of us, and draws to it a few moths and other fluttering insects.

The sun is going down but there is still dusky warm daylight at around nine o'clock as our sloop gently nudges against the jetty at Dell Quay and George once again ties it to a metal ring with a fancy knot. George says, 'It is a round turn and two half hitches, and won't come undone.'

I tell George, 'If you give me a round turn and two half hitches I'm sure to come undone.' George laughs as he picks me up, puts me over his shoulder and carries me up to the Crown and Anchor.

I will stay here tonight with dear George – it's too late to go back to Woodhorn. I probably won't sleep a wink. I'll just lie in bed, look at the ceiling and remember as many details as I can about our wonderful voyage to the tropical sandy island.

Sunday 9th September 1860

Birdham, West Sussex, 11.20am

George William Eastland.

I walk across the fields collecting wild flowers for Sarah as I go. It was her eighteenth birthday last week.

I'm not normally nervous when I come to Woodhorn, but today is not a normal day. Sarah thinks she is with child – it must have been our boat trip to East Head. It is a surprise to have happened so soon, but we love each other so we will marry as soon as we can.

I find Sarah in Woodhorn garden picking beans and hand her my posy of flowers as I take her in my arms. 'Hello George. What gorgeous flowers.'

'Not nearly as gorgeous as you,' I reply.

I get down on one knee and say, 'Sarah, will you marry me?'

'Of course I will, George,' and she laughs. 'There is nothing in this world I would rather do.' We kiss, then talk for a while in the garden.

'I am going to ask your father for permission to marry you, Sarah. How is he today?'

'I hope Father is fine today... Since Emily's death last year he has his days when he doesn't say much. I think he still blames himself – I wish he could find a way to be happier. When the farm was full of people and full of noise Father was happy. With Mother and Emily gone, and Alice and Clement elsewhere it is quiet now. When Thomas is out and I am busy in the kitchen Father sometimes says all he can hear is time passing.'

'How can you hear time passing?' I ask.

'Father just means it is so quiet he can hear nothing but the tick of the clock.'

At that moment William Collick steps out of the farmhouse holding his pipe. 'Hello George. Did I hear my name mentioned?'

'I was just telling George how it is sometimes so quiet here that we can hear nothing but the clock ticking; except for when Alice and the children come to visit.'

Mr Collick grins at the thought of his noisy but happy grandchildren. 'Are they coming today?' he asks.

'Yes, I think they will all be over this afternoon,' Sarah replies.

Lunch is a quiet affair with Sarah serving up a cold meat pie followed by plum pudding for William, Thomas and myself. Afterwards Mr Collick lights his pipe and gazes absent-mindedly out of the window.

I clear my throat. 'Mr Collick, there is something I must ask you. I wish to ask your permission for Sarah's hand in marriage. We are very much in love.'

Mr Collick says nothing and just continues to look out of the kitchen window, puffing smoke from his pipe. I glance at Sarah who shrugs her shoulders and looks nervous.

'Mr Collick, did you hear what I said? I wish to ask your…'

'No,' he thunders, his face tightening.

'W-what do you mean?' I stammer.

His face reddening, Mr Collick roars, 'Yes – I heard you, I am not deaf. And no, I do not give my permission. Sarah is needed here at Woodhorn. There is no other woman to look after me and to run the farmhouse – they have all gone!'

Sarah blurts, 'You can't expect me to stay at Woodhorn forever Father – just because I am your youngest daughter. You have Mrs Parsons – she is pleased to run Woodhorn Farmhouse and could easily manage for just you and Thomas.'

'You will not marry a good-for-nothing sailor. He will go to sea and leave you all alone while he gets drunk on rum and frolics with wenches in faraway taverns. No… you need to marry a solid, honest farmer who owns land and who will come home and sleep in your bed at night. Anyway, Sarah, you are too young to be married.'

'Alice was eighteen when she was married,' Sarah blurts out.

With his face growing an ever darker red, Mr Collick's voice is growing louder. 'Alice married a reliable farmer. Do not argue with me, Sarah. I will not agree to you marrying this…this…'

I raise my voice to say, 'You cannot talk to us like this. Sarah and I love only each other and I will be honourable and true to her. Sarah carries my child and we must be married. Where would you be if Sarah hadn't looked after you? How can you be so ungrateful?'

'Get out of my cottage,' Mr Collick shouts, his eyes wild with rage. 'You will not tell me what I can do in my own home. You sailors are all scallywags – and you have put my girl in the family way already? It just proves my point. Anyway, Sarah cannot be married before she is twenty-one without my permission. And I shall not give it. By the time she is twenty-one I am sure you will be long-gone.'

Before I can get out Sarah hurls a pottery dish she is holding onto the flagstone floor of the kitchen and it shatters into a hundred pieces. In floods of tears she runs from the cottage screaming, 'I hate you Father!'

I run after her through the garden and she is away up the lane. She runs blind, her mind in turmoil. Fortunately John sees her running wildly towards him and he slows then stops his horse and cart. Alice jumps from the seat next to him and smothers Sarah as she hurls herself into her sister's arms, sobbing and wailing with tears all over her face.

'What on earth is the matter, Sarah?'

Between her sobs Sarah can only say, 'I hate him.' Alice looks at me horrified and confused. I explain to John what has just happened.

Alice comforts Sarah and presently says, 'Do not worry, I will speak to the silly old fool and show him the error of his ways. I expect he is just scared to be on his own, as you are his last daughter. But Jane Parsons will have to run the farmhouse and look after Father. And they get on well. He just needs to see some sense.'

Sarah hugged Alice and smiled a watery smile at her. 'I'm not going back at the moment – Father said such horrible things to George.'

'We'll go back to the Crown and have a quiet afternoon,' I say before taking Sarah by the hand. I can feel her trembling, like an injured little bird.

'We'll see you both soon,' says Alice. 'Once Father spends some time playing with his grandchildren I'm sure he will see things differently. And they will love to play with a new cousin. I am so pleased for you,' she twinkles. Sarah can't help but raise a smile at this thought.

Alice turns and lifts her eldest son John down from the cart. 'Go and find your silly old grandfather!'

Sunday 16th September 1860

Park Farm House, Merston

Alice Eliza Jacob.

'After you left last Sunday, John and I spoke to Father. He can be a stubborn old mule sometimes. I told him George is a good man, that the two of you love each other, and that he should consent to your marriage. He listened, but he seems stuck in his rut at the moment.'

Sarah replies, 'I've not said a word to him this week – he was so horrible to George. I've a good mind to leave the farm and leave Father to stew on it. Why is he being so unfair?'

'I think Father is just getting old, scared and confused. He is afraid that he might not be able to manage if you leave the farmhouse. You and I both know that Mrs Parsons would look after him well, but he seems to be scared at the thought of his youngest daughter leaving Woodhorn,' I reply.

'Father was also taken by surprise when you told him you are with child. In his eyes you are still his little girl, and he needs more time to realise you are growing up now. He spends all day in his fields where nothing much changes, and he sometimes doesn't seem to notice that the rest of the world is moving along.'

John says, 'I think your father will come to accept everything in his own time. The trouble is that his time may not be quick enough for you two. You have to do something.'

Sarah sighs, 'But what can we do? I don't want to have a bastard child, but without our parents' consent we cannot be married.'

'If you were both twenty-one you wouldn't need your parents' consent.'

'But we are only eighteen. By the time we are twenty-one our baby will be nearly three years old. A three-year-old bastard!' Sarah looks dejected.

John perseveres. 'What I meant was if you told the Rector you are of age he will not require your parents' consent to marry you.'

Sarah replies, 'But that would mean lying. Anyway the Rector and everyone around here knows George and I aren't twenty-one.'

'You would have to go to be married in a parish where nobody knows you. Many people do that.'

There is a silent pause while we all think.

I break the silence. 'Doesn't the bride have to live in the parish in which she is married?'

'The bride has to give an address in the parish in which she is married, but what Rector ever checks it? When we married, you gave your address as Merston Farm even though you were still living at Woodhorn. It meant we could be married at St. Giles Church here in Merston, and after the wedding we all walked a few yards along the lane to our farm for our wedding feast.'

John continues, 'I hear under-age weddings happen all the time in the big towns. People come and go and if they are happy to pay for their wedding licence Rectors are usually happy to take the money for the church coffers, and not ask too many questions. If you go to Littlehampton or Portsea and say you are twenty-one I think you could be married by licence tomorrow!'

'But I don't know anyone in such places,' chokes Sarah, her eyes turning watery in despair. 'I've only ever lived in Birdham.'

'I do,' says George. All eyes, including Sarah's damp ones, turn to look at him.

'I know a man called Sam. Sam Weller. I talk to him most weeks when he comes on his ship to Dell Quay delivering coal. He is around twenty-five and married with two boys. I was telling him about us this week and he said we should go to Portsea – he says anyone can get married there.

'Sam told me a story. He said the busy port sees many travellers and many strangers arrive in town from all the places in the world. The chapels marry anyone willing to pay the licence fee. There was a sailor by the name of John who married a Portsea girl called Mary. They told the chapel he was twenty-eight and she twenty-one. No questions were asked. He was thirty-six and she fourteen. Mary was a big girl and very wifely to John. Mary now lives in Southsea with her twin girls and John is somewhere sailing the seven seas. He has not been seen in Portsmouth for over two years now.'

'You wouldn't be like John and sail away and leave me would you George?'

'Of course not Sarah. We would only go to Portsea for the day to be married. We will live together at Dell Quay. But the point is that we could get married at Portsea with no questions asked, and I can ask my friend Sam if you could use his home address to register our marriage. I can ask him when he next docks at Dell Quay.'

'And John and I will be very pleased to come to your wedding and be the two witnesses. We will tell the Rector that I am your older sister and that our mother is dead. That is no lie.'

For the first time in a week that heavy black cloud of despair hanging over Sarah begins to lift. I see a flicker of hope return to her tired hazel eyes as she sees the impossibility of her marriage to George at last turning into a possibility.

Saturday 15th December 1860

Park Farm House, Merston, 5.30am

Sarah Jane Collick.

I believe it is not uncommon for brides to be denied sleep on the night before their wedding – just when they want to look bright and fresh God plays one of His little games. For most it is probably their own excitement or fear that causes this sleeplessness. This is not the case for me, as although I am overjoyed to marry George I am too tired for the excitement to keep me awake.

Nevertheless I am awoken early and prevented from sleeping any more by a pain and gurglings in my tummy made by my unborn child. Just like its father, my baby seems to be always moving and always busy – I wish it would rest.

I have stayed this night with my sister Alice and John at their farm and we are preparing for an early start. Alice helps me get ready – I am to wear her wedding dress for my special day. Alice has been busy adjusting the dress to fit my expanding waistline, and removing the train which we decided would get in the way and be impossible to keep clean on our long journey. George has made the arrangements and we are at last going to be married at Portsea Island.

I expect George is drinking ale for his wedding breakfast at the Crown and Anchor. I do hope he is sober when we are wed this morning. My brother Clement is to drive George from Dell Quay to Merston in a cart, collect Alice, John and I and take us straight to Chichester railway station to catch the 9.50am train to Portsea. We have lots of shawls and blankets ready to keep us warm on the cart, and even now in the early morning gloom I can see the frost on the grass and bushes, and stars twinkling in the sky which is now beginning to grow pale as the night slips away. I am very happy to have a fresh, crisp winter's day for my wedding rather than a wet, grey miserable one.

Alice's children John, Emma and Alice, are too young to come all the way to Portsea so they are to stay at Park Farm today where the servant Emm White will look after them. Alice, John and I are all ready to go, and I am starting to wonder where George has got to as it is past 8.30am which is when he was supposed to be here. And then I hear the clip-clopping of horse hooves and look out of the door to see Clement driving the large cart with George beaming next to him.

'Good morning my dear Sarah. Are you ready for me to make an honest woman of you?' George calls down from his seat.

'It's a bit too late for that I think, dearest George.' George looks happy and his face is flushed pink, but probably this is due as much to the cool morning air as to any alcohol that he may have already drunk early on our wedding day.

'Come on,' calls Clement without getting down from the cart. 'We are in good time at present, but if you are all ready we should go because you do not want to miss the train.'

Alice replies, 'You are right Clement because if we miss it the next train is too late for the wedding. Let's get tucked into the blankets and be on our way.'

We wave goodbye to Emm and the children and our cart soon trundles carefully along the frosty lane through Merston. We clip-clop past Tapner's Barn and cross Merston Common till we reach the Bognor road. There we turn left onto the road and with the sun behind us head west towards Chichester. Water droplets in the hedges and trees glisten like gold as if set alight by the yellow early morning dawn. Soon we pass the King's Head pub on the left before Drayton, and then on past the brickworks before we reach the crossroads.

We continue straight ahead on the Bognor Road for about half a mile till we get to Wickham, on past the Roundabout House tavern on the right and before long we reach the Hornet. It remains fresh and cold as the sun rises reluctantly into the sky, but thankfully there is no wind to freeze us nor all the other cart drivers and horsemen making their way into the town on their Saturday business. We follow the road west into town until we rumble along East Street.

We are drawing ever closer to the towering cathedral spire which reaches far into the now blue sky. As we near the cathedral a bell chimes and the echoes resonate around the old town walls. We turn left at The Cross in the centre of the town and head down South Street.

Soon after, Clement brings the horses to a halt outside the railway station. He wishes us luck and we say our goodbyes. Alice reminds Clement to be back at the station at six-forty-five this evening to collect us, which is the time we are due to arrive on the last train.

We hurry into the station office to purchase our tickets and to warm ourselves in the shelter of the building. George approaches the counter and asks for four first class return tickets to Portsea. The ticket-master raises an inquisitive eye-brow at him and says, 'First-class tickets cost three shillings and fourpence sir. That will come to a total of one pound six shillings and eight pence?'

George pulls a gold sovereign and some other coins from his pocket saying – 'And the train ride will be worth every penny. It is not every day that a man marries the girl of his dreams.' As the tickets are handed over I feel the ground under my feet shake, and hissing and shunting noises from outside the station building become steadily louder.

Alice and I squeal at each other with delight. I have never been this close to a steam train before. We walk out onto the platform and are confronted by the huge black steam engine coming to a halt right in front of us. My ears are blasted by a metallic scream as the giant engine finally stops moving, and there are jets of steam and smoke pouring from the funnels and up onto the platform from underneath the engine, along with loud swooshing noises. I grab hold of George's arm tightly in fright.

'I had no idea the train would be so big and noisy. Is it going to take us all the way to Portsea?'

Just then a large man climbs down from the engine with an equally large beam across his face. His round cheeks are smeared black with soot and sweat and he wipes his forehead with the black sleeve of his shirt. He is clutching a china mug in his other hand as he heads for a small door along the platform which has a sign saying 'STAFF'. The station is full of the noise of the engine and the smell of coal smoke which blows into the sky, but which also at times puffs back along the platform and into our faces and hair. As well as the commotion of the train the platform is busy with porters wheeling trolleys, and passengers getting on and off the train. There are boxes and crates, people coming to Chichester's market and shops, and others like us heading the other way to the big town of Portsea.

We make our way along the platform clinging onto each other and when John spots the sign 'First Class' we head for a narrow carriage door. As we approach the carriage a station porter appears in front of us to open the door. 'Mind the gap,' he says as I follow John. John is standing just inside the carriage door as I come face to face with the large black chasm right underneath the train where clouds of smoke and steam swirls. Before I lose my nerve John grabs my hand and hauls me up into the train as I take a step over the wide gap. Alice, and then George follow and the carriage door closes behind us.

Suddenly the noise fades into the background as does the stinging smoky air, and we walk along a narrow wooden corridor before opening a door to a small passenger compartment. George closes the door behind us and we all collapse onto the plush firm upholstery. The small carriage is like a miniature palace – as well as the comfy seats it is furnished with strips of wood and metal, there are racks for luggage and even a mirror on the wall.

A few minutes later I think I hear a whistle, but I think nothing of it as I am still spellbound by this gleaming Alladin's Cave of a train compartment. I can smell the wood and the seats – everything seems so new and sparkly. Just then the train starts to make a loud shunt, shunt shunting sound and the carriage jolts with a great clank. I am looking at George and then I see the platform is moving - before I realise that it is the train that is moving.

We watch out of the window and marvel at the countryside passing before our eyes. No sooner do I see a cottage or a tree and it is gone. All the time the train goes shunty-shunt, shunty-shunt and our carriage vibrates as it passes over the fields. We pass the small villages of Bosham, Southbourne and Emsworth and I look out at the bays and sea as the train makes its way along the coastline. Sometimes the smoke from the engine comes down and blots out the view from our window. The train stops again at Havant where lots more people clamber aboard. There are trunks and boxes, and blasts of steam and whistles before the train suddenly moves off again with a jolt and a shunt and a clanking of the carriages.

After a while the train seems to turn a little towards the sea and slows down. I clutch George's arm as I realise there is water on both sides of the train. 'Are we going straight into the sea?' I ask in terror.

'It's all right Sarah. The train is going slowly over the bridge at Portcreek and taking us onto Portsea Island. It won't be much longer before we arrive in the town centre,' George replies holding my hand to reassure me. The train trundles more slowly now. I have not been to Portsea before, although when we meet the Registrar I have to remember that officially I live here with an aunt. As we go deeper into the town green fields gradually give way to red brick houses and factories, the buildings getting closer and closer together until I can see almost no grass at all. I wouldn't want to live here with all this smoke and no fields and horses, I think to myself. I feel sorry for my aunt.

The train gets slower and slower and then the red brick station buildings emerge through a cloud of swirling engine smoke. The wheels screech, the shunt-shunting sounds stop and the carriages finally come to a clanking, grinding metallic jolt as the train comes to a halt, followed by the loudest whoosh of steam that I have ever heard. The sign on the platform says Portsmouth Station. We find our way out of our carriage, step over the gap and down onto the platform. I realise now that Chichester station was quiet by comparison with Portsmouth. Here there are ten times more people, mothers with children, sailors in uniform carryings large bags of luggage – all sorts of people hurrying and scurrying in every direction.

A large clock hanging above the platform says the time is ten-forty. 'We must be going. Everybody is walking this way, so it must be the way out,' George cries over the din of the station. He grabs my hand and we all follow him. George shows our train tickets to the man at the exit, and we tumble out onto the street and turn right along Commercial Road in the heart of the town. George has a small paper map that his friend Sam has drawn for him to help us find our way to the Registrar's office at Fratton.

'We will get there in time, won't we George?' I ask. 'We must be there before noon or the Registrar won't marry us.'

'Don't fret Sarah,' George replies. 'We have plenty of time. Sam says it will only take twenty minutes to walk there. Let's follow the map.' I don't like to tell George I am feeling a bit tired and sick. It was probably the train journey and all that smoke we breathed in. We walk past the tightly packed red-brick terrace houses along Bow Street, and at the end turn left along Dorset Street which has more terraces on both sides of the road. Hundreds of people must live here, all crammed together in these buildings. I see a few faces peering from the dark windows of the small houses. Meanwhile little girls are skipping and singing in the streets and boys run around with hoops. They all seem happy enough.

We turn into Surrey Street and soon after that we go left along Upper Arundel Street. There are fewer properties here and between some of them are small fields and paddocks. I can hear the birds sing now the noise and smoke of the railway station has faded behind us, and walking on this crisp sunny morning I begin to feel much better.

Alice is holding my hand as we walk, and she asks George, 'How much further is it now?'

George glancing at his scrap of paper replies, 'We are just turning onto Fratton Street and we are probably about halfway there now.'

Fratton Street is a wide avenue with large fields on each side and occasional cottages with interesting names like Cornwall Cottage, Ebeneezer Place and the Meander Cottages. We also pass several taverns including the Lamb and Flag, and the Spreadeagle. A drink would be welcome, but I know I must wait until after we are wed as we cannot risk arriving too late to be married.

Before long we arrive at Fratton Road where we turn left. Fratton Road is an imposing street with large buildings and grounds, but with smaller roads and more of those red-brick terraced houses running from it. We come to the Trafalgar Brewery on the corner of Stamford Street, at which point George takes us across Fratton Road and into a side street called Clive Road. A few yards further and we turn into Trafalgar Place and quickly find house number one, which is where the Registrar Mr William Hatch lives, and where he also carries out all his official duties in his office.

George rings the doorbell and we are shown into the house. As we walk along a hallway an ornate black marble clock chimes once and tells us the time is a quarter past eleven. We are shown into the Registrar's office where we are invited to be seated alongside several other people who are evidently also here to be married. The room is filled with rows of books in tall bookcases and the air is warm and stuffy, a considerable contrast to the sharp temperature outside. We remove our outer clothing and then sit down quickly so as not to cause any more disturbance to the proceedings.

William Hatch sits at his desk holding a quill pen over a large register, opposite a man and women who he has evidently just married. A bible sits on the large leather-topped desk, and the bride and groom are stealing furtive glances at each other as Mr Hatch writes carefully and neatly upon the register. When all the writing is complete Mr Hatch gives the couple a copy of their marriage certificate, bids them good day and sends them on their way.

We observe two more wedding ceremonies while we await our turn. In truth I can hardly describe these weddings as 'ceremonies', and it makes me a little sad that George and I will not have a church wedding in the summer with all our family and friends present. But as George and I are both only eighteen, and with my father not prepared to give his consent to our marriage we have no other choice. We must be wed before our child is born.

It is a quarter to twelve and we are the last people left in the Registrar's Office when Mr Hatch beckons George and I to come and sit in the two chairs facing the desk at which he presides. I am concentrating hard on the things George and Alice reminded me on the train journey that I have to say. I am concentrating so hard that Mr Hatch says, 'Come now Miss Collick, there is no need to look so serious. This is your wedding day and you are permitted to smile.' Of course this makes me smile, as well as blush.

'Let me check I have your details all proper and correct. You are George William Eastland, a bachelor and miller by profession living in the parish of Appledram in Sussex?'

'That is so,' replies George.

'And what is your age?'

'I am twenty-one, sir.'

The Registrar then turns his gaze upon me and I feel my hands trembling as I clutch them together tightly in my lap.

'And you are Sarah Jane Collick, spinster living at Castle Road here in Portsea?'

'Yes, I am,' I reply, quickly averting my eyes to the floor.

'And a very nice street Castle Road is - as I'm sure you will agree,' the Registrar adds. I nod my head hoping he will not ask me any more questions about Portsea.

'Please confirm your age Miss Collick.'

'I am also twenty-one, sir.' This is a lie that I have no difficulty remembering - I have been having bad dreams about it for days. My father's attitude means I have no choice. Our son must have parents who are married, and I will ask God's forgiveness for my sin of lying about my age next time I go to church, which is bound to be soon as it is nearly Christmas.

'There are no parents here present today?' Mr Hatch comments in an enquiring tone and raises his eyes from his paperwork.

George answers first. 'My father is a mariner and away from home much of the time, and my mother runs a tavern near Chichester, sir.'

Before I can reply Alice adds, 'And our mother is dead and our father runs a farm at Woodhorn and the animals need tending every day – and I am Sarah's older sister if you please. My husband John and I are here to be witnesses to the wedding.'

'Well thank you very much madam.' And looking back at me Mr Hatch asks, 'And please can you tell me your sister's full name, and that of her husband?'

'They are Alice Eliza Jacob, and John Jacob,' I reply.

Mr Hatch asks for the full names of my father and George's father and continues to write all these details on a sheet of paper. He pauses, reads through all his notes, takes a deep breath and sits himself upright.

'I do believe that I have all the facts that I require, and I note also that Mr Eastland recently paid one pound and ten shillings to this office for a licence for the marriage meaning that no banns were required to be read in the local church. So I shall now proceed with your marriage. Would you both please stand and repeat your lines after me.'

'**I, George William Eastland, do take thee Sarah Jane Collick, to be thy lawful wedded wife.**' George repeats these words carefully.

'**And I, Sarah Jane Collick, do take thee George William Eastland, to be thy lawful wedded husband.**' I say my words clearly and without any mistakes. I have dreamt about this moment and I can hardly believe this time has come. I am so relieved.

Mr Hatch then addresses Alice and John as he says, 'Unless I am advised to the contrary I declare that there is no impediment to this marriage and I call upon those present to witness that George William Eastland and Sarah Jane Collick have indeed taken the other to be their lawful wedded spouse.'

Alice and John both eagerly agree to this.

'I declare, George and Sarah, that you are therefore now husband and wife and I would ask you, Mr and Mrs Eastland to be seated for a few minutes whilst I write up the marriage register and prepare your marriage certificate.'

'Hello Mrs Eastland,' George says as he takes my hand and kisses me. How strange to be Mrs Sarah Eastland after so many years of being Miss Sarah Collick, I think to myself.

The paperwork is soon completed. I expect Mr Hatch is pleased to see us leave so that he can rest after a busy Saturday morning. He bids us good afternoon as we get up to leave his office, and as he ushers us through the door, and with just the hint of a grin he says, 'And good luck with the baby.'

The four of us re-emerge onto Trafalgar Place which is still bathed in bright sunlight. 'How did he know you are with child?' George blurts out.

Alice replies, 'Well apart from the bump which shows clearly now when Sarah is standing, I expect that registrar sees lots of couples getting married for precisely the same reason as you, especially when they pay for a licence and happen to be twenty-one years old! I think Mr Hatch was very kind. Come on, it is time to go and celebrate the marriage of Mr and Mrs George and Sarah Eastland.'

I take George's hand and Alice takes John's, and we all hurry round the corner back onto Fratton Road where we head straight into the warm cosy interior of the Trafalgar Arms where John orders drinks for us all. Before long Sam Weller and his wife join us in the pub and we spend a merry afternoon of drinking, talking and laughing.

At last I am married to George and I think all my troubles in the world can now go away.

Sam seems to know everyone in the tavern which fills to bursting during the course of the afternoon. Sam says it is because everyone has finished work and there are plenty of ships in the port, so all the pubs in Portsea will be busy today. As the Trafalgar fills up I can hardly hear what anyone says over the din of talking, laughter and singing. One thing sticks in my mind no matter how loud and raucous the tavern gets as I hold on to George's warm hand – I am no longer Sarah Jane Collick. I am now Mrs Sarah Jane Eastland.

George, John and Sam are all enjoying their ale when sometime later Alice pipes up, 'John, John I've just realised it is dark outside. What is the time?'

Sam calls back, 'There is a clock above the bar which I can just see if I stretch up – ah yes, it's just gone twenty past five.'

'The last train leaves at a quarter past six, and we still have to walk back to the station in the dark,' says Alice.

'Oh I'm sure there is plenty of time for us to finish our last ale,' says George. But I see him wink at Sam and realise he is teasing me.

Sam leads us all the way back to Portsmouth station – he knows the quickest ways and we arrive there with ten minutes to spare. Fortunately Alice has looked after the train tickets, as judging by the number of beers George and John have drunk I'm not sure they could have been relied upon today.

The train journey back to Chichester is just as exciting as this morning even though I can't see much out of the windows. I enjoy the now familiar shunty-shunt of the engine and the rhythmic noises as the carriage is pulled along the line. In the dark it feels as if we are going even faster than this morning. We stop at Havant, then Emsworth and after that Bosham. Those homely-looking brick stations burn dim flickering lights which illuminate the platforms and guide the way for the people who get off the train on their journeys back home. The train eventually comes to a halt at Chichester station. As we jump out of the carriage over the black gap and onto the platform I feel the cold night bite my face and fingers. I look up to see the stars are shining brightly.

We are pleased to find Clement and the horses waiting for us, and he takes us first to Dell Quay where tonight I will sleep for the first time with my husband.

I hug and kiss Alice and John and wave them on their way. Clement will take them back to Merston now and stay with them tonight as it is getting late. He will return to the Crown and Anchor in the morning.

What a perfect and wonderful day this has been. I shall treasure it for the rest of my life.

Sunday 16th December 1860

Crown & Anchor, Dell Quay, 9.40am

Ann Eastland.

BANG BANG BANG.

'Someone is banging on the door,' calls Martha from the bar where she is washing down tables.

'Ignore it, Martha. We are not opening until ten. Whoever it is will have to be patient until then,' I call back.

That's one of the troubles with running a tavern. There are always a few drunks that won't abide by the opening times and try to get in early or stay after time at the end of the day. There aren't many men that manage to achieve both antics on the same day. Although I have known one or two who have managed the feat ... albeit with the help of a few hours sleep in the yard or in a nearby ditch during the middle of the day to separate the two drinking sessions.

BANG BANG BANG.

This one is clearly persistent. I put my head out of a nearby window facing the front of the Crown. I first see a horse and small cart standing outside the inn, and then I see a large and rather dishevelled-looking labourer outside of the door. His fist is raised as he is about to hammer on the wooden door again.

'You can give your knuckles a rest, and my door. We don't open until ten and then you will be very welcome to come in.' With the window open I feel the biting chill outside. The ground is white with frost and the nearby trees look like they are frozen solid. 'I'm closing the window – it's freezing out there. Come into the warm bar at ten.'

BANG BANG BANG.

The traveller shouts from outside the door – 'I'm not here for no drink. I'm here to see my daughter. Open up...' and he bangs loudly on the door again.

My husband George has by this time come into the bar rubbing his head. 'What is the commotion about Ann? Can a hard-working man not get some sleep on a Sunday morning? It is only just daylight?'

'Don't worry yourself George. It's probably some passing traveller who doesn't know what time the inn opens. I'll soon get rid of him. At least the trouble-makers are generally sober at this time of the day.' George wanders off towards the scullery to find himself a hot drink, still rubbing his head.

I shoot the bolts on the heavy door to the Crown and swing it open. I come face to face with a red-faced man all wrapped up in brown sacking clothes, dark leather boots and gloves and with a battered old hat with a wide brim covering his head and shoulders.

'Did you not hear me sir? The Crown does not…'

Before I can finish my sentence the sack man thunders, 'Did you not hear me woman? I demand to see my daughter.' Face to face with this man, and without the distorted glass of the window between us I can see a rage in his face as well as hear it in his voice.

The penny drops and now, despite the man's anger I can see some likeness in his face to that of Sarah. 'And what makes you think your daughter is here, who is your daughter, and for that matter who exactly are you to come here making all this fuss early on a Sunday morning?'

'You know damn well who I am woman. I am William Collick and I demand to see Sarah. I presume you are Mrs Eastland? My daughter has gone off behind my back and wed your damned son. I daresay you knew all about this. You probably all planned it together, didn't you? Quite a catch I expect my beautiful daughter is for your wayward son. Was it a good wedding? What a thing it is when a man isn't even invited to his own daughter's wedding.'

William glares over my head trying to see into the inn, but he can't get past as I am standing in the doorway. He shouts, 'Sarah, Sarah can you hear me. Come out and speak to your father.'

My husband George comes to the doorway and steps in front of me to face Mr Collick. 'Good morning, Mr Collick. If you calm yourself and stop shouting you will be welcome to come inside and talk to us and I'm sure that Sarah will join us. Ann and I also did not go to the wedding. It was a very small affair. That was what George and Sarah thought best under the circumstances.'

'Circumstances? Bloody circumstances,' thunders William. 'If your bloody son hadn't got my daughter into the family way outside of wedlock none of this would have happened. I tell her not to get involved with a bloody scallywag sailor. I told Sarah, sailors are only interested in ale and wenches, and with a sailor's moll in every port. She should have married a bloody farmer – a decent sort who would stay at home and look after her. As soon as Sarah has her baby no doubt George will be off to sea again wenching, and leaving Sarah to look after the child.'

George puffs out his chest and leans towards Mr Collick staring right into his eyes. 'As a Master Mariner, and as Captain of numerous vessels, and furthermore as a loyal servant in the Queen's merchant navy I refute your disrespectful slurs upon mariners. My son George has done the honourable thing and married your daughter, because he loves her and because it is the right thing to do by the child. And George is a miller now, not a mariner so he will not be going off to sea at all. If you loved your daughter as you should and had supported her marriage they would not have had to run off on their own to get wed, and both our families could instead have celebrated the wedding together.'

I can see over George's shoulder that Mr Collick's eyes are blazing and his cheeks are red with rage. He looks like he is about to explode with anger. He huffs and puffs and stamps his heavy boots on the flagstone in the doorway. George doesn't move a muscle. With his own steely determination I know his fearsome eyes are glaring unblinkingly into Mr Collick's face. Having looked death in the eye at sea many times in his life one angry farmer will not for one moment intimidate George.

'And you are not coming into my home shouting and blaspheming like you have been, and on a Sunday of all days. Shame on you Sir,' George adds.

Mr Collick seems to be lost for words. 'Hell. You haven't seen the last of me. I'll see my daughter...' He seems to run out of steam.

George stands firm. 'You go and calm down and think about it. The way I see it I have gained a lovely daughter and before long will also have a bright new grandchild. I have heard a lot of good things about you Mr Collick and I would like to welcome my son's new father-in-law into my home. But I will not have anger and coarse language under my roof. God knows family must stick together – there are enough enemies out there without us fighting each other. Sarah and George will live here as man and wife and we will look after them. All friends are welcome here at all times.'

Mr Collick turns away, and spits on the ground as he does so. He climbs onto the seat of his cart and slaps his whip at his horse which sets off swiftly up the icy lane. As the horse's hooves disappear from earshot the trill of a single blackbird high on a frosty branch breaks the awkward silence.

Sunday 16th December 1860

The lane to Birdham

William Collick.

George Eastland's words spin around my head as I drive the cart away from Dell Quay. I was so mad at the thought of Sarah and George and all his family going behind my back over the wedding. I thought I must go and tell Sarah off for betraying me and leaving me on my own like that – leaving her old father in a big farm while she went off with a drunken irresponsible sailor like George.

But where has this anger got me?

I still haven't seen my daughter. And can I blame her for not coming out of that tavern? She is only young and carrying her first child. Why would she want to come out into this freezing winter's day to face an angry old man shouting and swearing at her?

If I am honest I cannot say George has ever seemed irresponsible towards Sarah – he has always been loving with her. Nor have I ever seen him drunk. I got drunk last night after dinner when Thomas had gone out, and when Jane Parsons and her son Thomas were busying themselves.

Is it fair that I expect Sarah to stay and look after me in my big farm at Woodhorn? The farm has been my life and now I am getting old and must face it – I cannot run it any more. I must pass it onto Thomas.

It is not Sarah's fault that I am getting old. It is not Sarah's fault that her mother and sister died, and that Alice married and moved to Merston. Sarah and her sisters did so much after my wife died to keep me, the farm and our family going. I should be eternally grateful to Sarah for all she has done for me.

I must not be a selfish old sod, trying to deny Sarah her own youth, love and happiness. She is eighteen and in love with a good man who comes from what seems like a good family. I had not met George and Ann before today but if I opened my eyes and looked beyond my loud self-righteous pride, before me stood two sober, sensible and upstanding people, man and wife, running their business and trying to look after their own family…and Sarah.

And who am I trying to convince that I am on my own? Sarah knows full well, as do I if I am honest with myself, that Thomas is already more or less running Woodhorn. If I stop meddling and let him get on with it he will do a good job. I just find it hard to let go after all these years of being in charge of my farm.

And Jane keeps house for me, attending to the meals and washing, and all those other tasks of which I know little, in exchange for a roof over her head and work for her son, and we are friends as well and enjoy each other's company at the fireside of an evening. And Alice and John come up from Merston when they can with the grandchildren to see me, which I enjoy greatly.

George Eastland is right. I should embrace my new son-in-law, and the rest of his family instead of pushing away my youngest daughter – before it is too late. Before long I will have more grandchildren and I should be very happy.

I must stop being a selfish old fool and go back to the Eastland's before Christmas, act like a gentleman and make amends. Mr Eastland even said he had heard good things about me when I was shouting obscenities in his face. I should be ashamed of myself.

By the time I drive the horse and cart back through the gate of Woodhorn Farm I can see that I really do need to put things right with the Eastlands.

Monday 24th December 1860

Crown & Anchor, Dell Quay, 11am

William Collick.

As my cart draws up at the front of the inn everything is different from the last time I came here.

Today I have brought the large cart as I collected Alice, John, Emma and little Alice from Merston on my way to Dell Quay. It is not as cold as last time I came here as it started snowing early this morning. We have driven through fresh fluffy snow a couple of inches deep while all around the large flakes float gently down upon us. The children looked with wonderment at the white landscape as the cart drove along the lanes.

Today I have not arrived too early and the Crown is open and already busy. We are shown into a parlour where there is a lovely log fire and I hug Sarah and George and greet the rest of George's family. Alice and Sarah are so pleased to see each other and hug each other and start their incessant chattering.

I shake George senior's hand. 'Please accept my apologies for my dreadful behaviour last time I was here. I was upset and angry and not thinking straight. I am most grateful for your calmness and for the sense that you talked despite my rudeness. I can see now that it was selfish and wrong of me not to support the marriage of George and Sarah, and I would like to apologise for my insults to sailors in general, and to George in particular.

'I would like to start again, and I intend to be a better father to Sarah and father-in-law to George if they will let me, and to do what I can to help them in their married life. I do hope you will all forgive me, and to help me to make some amends to you I hope you will accept the gifts that I have brought with me today. This time of year is very good on the farm as the animals have been fattened up, and good fresh meat is aplenty. So I have brought with me a side of the best ham, two large chicken, and three rabbit caught early this morning for you to enjoy this Christmas.'

George shakes my hand vigorously. 'That is very kind of you William, and you must all stay with us this afternoon, warm yourselves by the fire and join us for a grand Christmas Eve roast later this afternoon. But far more than that I am pleased that you have come to your senses about George and Sarah, and I now look forward to getting to know you properly.'

'Thank you for your words and the offer to stay for dinner. I fear we should leave before dark though, and before the snow lays too thickly, as it is very cold and Alice's children are very young. I wouldn't want them to catch their death of the cold.'

George replies, 'Of course you shall not travel in the dark on Christmas Eve. The Crown is large with many bedrooms. You shall all stay for dinner, and a good glass of wine, or the best ale of your choice and please, sleep tonight in the tavern and tomorrow night if you wish. We will need help to eat all this wonderful meat you have brought us William. Happy Christmas.'

And so indeed it is. Thomas is looking after Woodhorn Farm perfectly well without interference from me. God knows, there is little to be done on a farm at Christmas, with the ground frozen hard and snow on the fields. And because I have at last swallowed my pride and my silly selfishness the Collicks and the Eastlands have come together, and George and Sarah are happy and sharing the first of what I hope will be many happy Christmases together.

Sunday 31st March 1861

Crown & Anchor, Dell Quay, 9pm

George William Eastland.

I gaze into the reddened depths of my glass of ale. It is as if alive, reflecting the flickering orange embers in the fireplace beyond the table. Father dozes, his head resting against the back of his old chair, a contented snore resonating from deep in his throat.

It has been a long and eventful winter – the bad half and the good half. Until Christmas everything was difficult. The difficulty arranging our wedding and the dreadful conflict with Sarah's father weighed heavily on Sarah and me. All the time Sarah was trying to keep Woodhorn homestead going whilst being ill with our unborn baby. Sarah would laugh, scream, and cry in equal measures – some days I did not know what to do for the best.

Thank God for Alice.

We were so relieved to be married at Portsea, but at the same time unsettled by Sarah's father. He has suffered, but I know he is a good man. I did not want to go against him, but Sarah and I love each other and nothing could be allowed to prevent us from being wed – not even William Collick.

Life is just like an ocean. Behind every towering wave is a trough followed by another wall of water and then another trough. And then there is a calm. If it wasn't for these desperate storms a mariner may not embrace the peace and beauty of the calms. And I have come to realise that life is just the same.

Following the storm of the autumn Sarah and I were wed just days before Christmas, and the final storm of William Collick's anger also blew itself out. Our families have grown together, Sarah's sickness passed, and on the 5th March she gave birth to our first child. He is the most wonderful little boy you could ever imagine. He has a strong voice already and pink cheeks. The cold winter snows have passed, and the sun rises higher and gains strength. The river reflects the blue sky. The weather is calm. Life at last is calm. I rejoice.

Today is Easter Sunday. The sun shone brightly and yellow daffodils swayed gently in the spring breeze. Our son was christened today in St. Mary's Church at Appledram – George William Eastland, just like me. The church was bursting. We knew it would be on Easter Sunday and Curate Henry Smith was rushed off his feet. Mother and Father presented little George to the Curate for baptism –we thought it best in the circumstances of our rushed wedding outside the parish.

As he baptised little George the Curate raised an eyebrow at Father who pierced him straight back with his own razor sharp blue eyes. As the wharfinger at Dell Quay and Master Mariner now of many decades Father is very well respected in this community. The Curate was too busy to contemplate any verbal admonishment, nor did he wish to cross Father in public.

Little George was duly baptised.

Sarah was nonetheless keen to see George christened for herself, so we sat at the back of the church along with William Collick and Alice who also wanted to be there. Little George squealed from time to time probably wanting milk, but Mother is so good with babies that he cried remarkably little.

Sarah and I still feel remorse at having had to lie about our ages when we were married at Portsea, and I have worried that God might look harshly upon little George's birth as a consequence. I took the opportunity in church today to pray very hard for forgiveness for that lie.

During the baptism the Curate uttered the following words, along with all the others –

'Give thy holy Spirit to this Infant, that he may be born again, and be made an heir of everlasting salvation; through our Lord Jesus Christ, who liveth and reigneth with thee and the Holy Spirit, now and forever. Amen.'

I felt myself breathe a sigh of relief. I somehow felt that however the lies and misdeeds of Sarah and myself with our runaway wedding may have tarnished God's view of little George, by his baptism he is now washed clean of our sins. George is now one of God's innocent children, and God will look after him.

After the church service we all returned to the Crown in William's large cart where Matilda provided us with a lunch of bread fresh from the oven, with cheese and pickled onions. After lunch Sarah and I, along with her father and Alice walked a little way along the coastal path in the direction of Fishbourne.

I watched the fluffy white clouds race across the blue sky borne on a brisk westerly current. William seemed happy to breathe the fresh air rushing off the water, to feel the wind on his cheeks, and to think his long thoughts as he gazed over the Fishbourne Channel towards Hook Farm on the Bosham peninsula. Sarah and Alice walked behind us, arm-in-arm chattering and giggling.

The day is now nearly done. Sarah and the baby sleep. So does Father in his chair opposite me. Mother and my sisters Matilda, Martha and Fanny are still busy in the bar.

I continue to look into my red flickering ale. I dearly hope this calm lasts for a very long time.

Thursday 18th September 1862

Dell Quay, 3.30pm

Sarah Jane Eastland.

Life could not be more perfect. George and I are like an old married couple. We are comfortable just sitting quietly together, enjoying each other's company, feeling the warmth from our bodies as we touch, without the need always to say anything. Peace and quiet is sometimes blessed.

I sit now in the warm sunshine behind the inn facing the river nursing Henry. Henry was born on the 27th June. I remember the date well as the birth was not nearly as easy as little George's was last year. Henry's birth was very painful, I bled heavily and I was very tired for weeks afterwards. I prefer to forget it – Henry is well now. I am still tired.

The summer is drawing to a close. The shadows over the river become longer and the leaves on the trees are beginning to turn orange and golden. It is as if the trees want a rest after a long summer, and no longer have the strength to hold onto their leaves. So they just let them go, one by one. I feel the same – the birth of Henry has worn me out. I feel as if I want to curl up under a deep bush, like a hedgehog and sleep all the way through to next spring.

I couldn't even face going to Appledram for Henry's baptism. George waited a few weeks to see if I would get stronger but by August we felt Henry should not wait any longer. In the end Henry's grandparents presented him for his baptism at St. Mary's just like they did for little George.

Last summer seemed so easy with our first son. He was born in the spring when it was cooler and George and I loved making a fuss of him all summer as we watched him grow so quickly. We would go for walks along the paths by the Fishbourne Channel where we picked samphire, and we watched goldfinches dart in and out of the hedgerows that grow near to the sparkling blue river. George and I, along with Fanny also took little George in the cart along the dusty summer lanes all the way to Bracklesham Bay, where we dipped our toes in the sea and delighted as we watched the waves wash up onto the sandy beach. I remember the seagulls squealed in the breeze over our heads.

This year has been much harder. I was sick again as I was when I carried George, and I found the early summer heat very uncomfortable. Fanny was an angel to look after little George as much as she was able when she could be spared from the inn, which allowed me to rest. How my mother and George's managed to bring up so many children I'll never know. I have not had the energy to go to the beach this summer, but George and Fanny took little Georgie a couple of times while I rested here at Dell Quay with Henry.

George is working hard in the mill and with the ships and their cargoes of coal, timber and grain at the quay. I am always very pleased when he returns home to spend time with me and our sons. I love to see the three of them together. George lies on his back with little George and Henry on top of him laughing and tumbling together.

The busy-ness is set to continue. Martha is going to wed George Garwood in November. George is a carpenter, which I am sure will be very useful as we could do with some new furniture. The wedding is to be at Appledram so I must try to be well enough to enjoy it, though at the present time I am still too exhausted to join in with anything.

I wish I didn't feel so tired as it puts me in a bad mood, and I know I am sometimes short with people who are only trying to help me. Little George is asleep in his bed and now Henry has dropped off in my arms as we sit in this warm sunshine. I will take the chance to rest my eyes and try to be rid of my weariness.

I awake with a jolt and a bad taste in my mouth. I suddenly realise Henry is not in my lap and squeal for fear that I have dropped him onto the grey flagstones.

'It's all right Sarah. I have Henry all safe.' As my eyes adjust to the bright sun I now see Fanny sitting on a nearby seat in the shade, with Henry lying fast asleep in her lap.

'Thank God Fanny. I was afraid I had dropped Henry - it gave me such a start. I had no idea I had fallen off to sleep.'

'The bar went quiet so I thought I would come out and join you in the sunshine for a little while, and there I found you both fast asleep. So I decided to have a cuddle with Henry and let you rest. You do look tired Sarah, and your eyes are dark. Are you sleeping at night?' Fanny asks.

'As much as any mother does with a young baby. I am sure my tiredness will pass in a few weeks when Henry sleeps for longer.'

Fanny's observations, however, have made me think. It is nearly three months since Henry was born and he sleeps now most nights. Yet I feel more tired than ever, and Fanny is right – my eyes are black with tiredness. If I look in the mirror my face seems thinner than before. I expected to lose some weight after the baby but I seem to be getting thinner than I was before I carried Henry. I seem to have lost my appetite recently too – I thought it was just the hot weather that took away my hunger. With the autumn nights getting colder I had better try to eat a bit more to stop me from wasting away.

The sun is starting to set much earlier now and the shadow that has fallen across my legs feels surprisingly cold. I shiver suddenly, and cough. It pricks in my chest. I have had this annoying cough since August. I should not have a tickly cough like this in the summer months.

Perhaps I have swallowed a feather from out of a pillow sometime this summer, while I have been sleeping so much!

Saturday 11th October 1862

Crown & Anchor

George William Eastland.

    Something is not right with Sarah. She has not been herself since before Henry was born. His birth seemed to take all her energy and spirit in a way that wasn't so with little George.
    Sarah is not one to complain or to call the doctor, but I know she is not herself. She has lost her spark and enthusiasm for life. Sarah - who always has a twinkle in her eye and a bounce in her step. And I know that she also thinks she should have got over Henry's birth by now.
    There is something else. She has been afflicted with a persistent little cough for weeks – I cannot even place exactly when it started. Despite Sarah's protest I call in the doctor to examine her. He comes and listens to her chest and back. He says there is some congestion and that he can give her a linctus to try to soothe her tickly cough. He also says her skin is a little clammy and that she should get plenty of rest as well as take the air whenever she is able. The doctor also does some head-shaking. I don't know what this means, but it bothers me no end.
    Sarah has moved herself into the small room in the attic – with the window facing the sea – to get the fresh air, she says. She says she doesn't want the boys to come up there until she is better as she doesn't want to pass them the nasty cough. I don't want her to move up there alone but I can see in her eyes that she is absolutely determined. Still I know she will be back down soon. I am sure that in less than a week of rest she will be as right as rain. She is healthy and has always had boundless energy and she is only twenty after all. Mother is to nurse her and take her food in bed. Sarah just needs rest.

Sunday 30th November 1862

Crown and Anchor

George William Eastland.

I don't understand why Sarah is not getting well again. Mother takes good food to her bedroom and Sarah is getting plenty of sleep. In fact she seems to sleep more than she wakes. No member of the Eastland family has ever been this ill in the prime of life.

It seems like it is Henry's fault. Ever since that terrible birth Sarah has been weak and tired. Henry is only a baby of course so he cannot be held responsible. It must be my fault as I put Sarah into that state. But having babies is as natural as breathing. Why is God punishing Sarah and I like this? Surely it is not because we lied about our ages in order to be wed?

Sarah was not born an Eastland. Her mother passed early and her sister Emily also of consumption. But that was years ago now, and Sarah and her sister Alice have always been full of vigour. And William Collick must be sixty or more. I will not harbour the idea that this can be anything but a nasty cough and perhaps a mild fever.

Sarah looks so thin. She tells me she is sweating the illness away. She won't let me stay in her bedroom too long, and always tells me to go out into the fresh air on the quayside before I go near our boys to make sure I don't pass them any illness. Sarah says she must get better soon for George and Henry.

I am pleased that Sarah is thinking positively. I mustn't show her that I am worried. She looks so thin and her skin is almost grey. Of course she will get better soon – there is still that magical twinkle deep in her eyes. It is just the fever. I want to hold her in my arms but she won't let me. She says, 'I must get better first. You will be able to hold me at Christmas I am sure.'

Sunday 4th January 1863

Crown and Anchor, 3.20pm

George William Eastland.

'Why does Sarah not accept that she is ill, Mother? I am so worried about her. You see her every day. What can we do?'

'Sarah knows she is ill. Remember she nursed her older sister? Sarah knows what it is to be ill, and she knows that the illness can be beaten if you don't give in to it. She will never stop fighting. She wants nothing more than to get better for you and George and Henry.

'She also knows the fever can be passed to other people and she will not let herself be anywhere near to your boys. Nor does she want to pass the illness to you or even to me. She is such a brave little girl.

'Go to her George. Tell her you love her and your boys. Give her hope and something to fight for. Your strength and God's Will are what Sarah needs now to get her through this.'

I go up the stairs to the attic room and tap on Sarah's door. All is quiet. I open the door gingerly. The room is very dark, but the stench of vomit invades my nostrils. 'Is that you George?' Sarah coughs from her bed in the gloom.

'Yes,' I reply as I light the lamp on the small table.

I can see Sarah has been sick in the basin next to her bed and there is a reddish smear on the sheet next to her. She looks gaunt and sweaty and is struggling hard to stop herself from coughing. 'I shall take this away and clean up,' I say as I move towards Sarah's bed.

'No,' she says. 'Fetch your mother. She knows how to deal with this. I don't want you getting close to me as our sons will want to be close to their father. They must not catch this fever – we must protect them from it.'

'Please get better Sarah. I can't bear to see you suffering like this. You don't deserve this. Why couldn't it have been me? It should have been me. What can I do to help you Sarah?'

'You must go away George and keep yourself well. Let me rest. I just need to sweat the fever out. Go and look after our boys George. Always look after our boys. Remember I will always love you.

'But go out into the fresh air first and fill your lungs. And send Mother to clean up for me.'

'I love you Sarah.'

I stumble down the stairs, my heart like stone and my eyes watery. I call for Mother before bursting out into the fresh gale blowing across Dell Quay. I look up at the black clouds and pray for a miracle.

Friday 23rd January 1863

St. Mary the Virgin, Appledram, 2.25pm

George Eastland.

Our dear Sarah is dead…

Just twenty.

With two baby boys.

The doctor confirmed. Consumption.

What the Hell is God thinking of?

It feels like everyone in our family has died with her.

My daughters, Fanny, Nancy, Matilda and Mary look stony and bereft. Their pretty, gay, generous new sister has been stolen from them no sooner has she become an Eastland. Yet already they loved her dearly.

William Collick is beside himself. Having lost his wife and now four daughters he believes he has cursed his family. His only remaining daughter is Alice. Alice is terrified that she will be next – to be wrenched from the arms of her young family.

My wife Ann is very strong in mind. Working the tavern she could not be otherwise. Whilst nursing Sarah in her last weeks Ann came to know and love her even more deeply. Although Ann knew Sarah might succumb to the fever she didn't really believe she would as Sarah never complained.

Ann couldn't believe Sarah was dead when she took tea into her room last Friday morning. She opened the bedroom door to find George kneeling next to Sarah's bed in the early winter morning gloom. 'What are you doing here George? I am surprised Sarah has not shooed you away.'

George said nothing.

Ann reached for Sarah's hand to wake her and found it to be as cold as stone. Sarah had not cried out in the night – she had just quietly slipped off into her final long sleep. It was so like her – to make no fuss.

I can scarcely describe George. He is like a mariner whose legs have just been blown off by cannon fire. He stares blankly. His eyes are open and he is breathing. He is here, and yet he is not here. I fear his full terror is still to come.

Little George and Henry are as yet the least distraught – such is the oblivion of infancy – too young to comprehend. They have stayed at home today with our servant Fanny Smith. This foul weather and fouler burial is not for those two sweet boys. Of course those two poor mites may well ultimately suffer the most. They will have to go through life without their mother and will need all the love and protection that I and my family can give them.

I have toiled hard all my life and I am growing old. The burdens I now face seem harder to bear than any hard labour, or any wild storm at sea. Just when my creaking body tells me it is time for me to rest I am called to take on new responsibilities – to support my younger family members, not with shelter or money but with love. God give me strength.

I don't know where to begin. My family all sit in the front pew on this God-forsaken day. My arms are around George on my left and Ann to my right. George's head faces down to the red tiled floor – his head in his hands. Ann is quiet – tears running in rivulets down her cheeks. I'm not sure when I last saw her cry.

My four daughters huddle together and sob behind me. Martha has not been able to come to Sarah's funeral, all the way from Brighton in this filthy weather. She may know not how blessed she is to miss this sickening scene. Amidst all this desolation the thought that I am fortunate to have my daughters unexpectedly forces its way into my consciousness and catches me unprepared, like an easterly wind. If there is anything I can do to ease William's pain I must do it.

William and his children, Alice, Thomas and Clement also sit on the front pew – a quivering mass of despair and mourning.

I look around this church where God is supposed to reside and try to feel his presence. I know he has been with me at sea many a time but where the Hell is he now? I wish I understood.

St. Mary's is a small ancient church with grey stone walls and dark brown wooden beams arching over our heads for the full length of the building. The church is dark, the faces of the congregation even darker. The only light comes from flickering orange flames in the curling metal candle holders mounted on the walls, and from the tall candle stands in front of the altar.

Today I cannot see the arched windows, the coloured glass, the patterned floor tiles, and the ancient stone font. Today I see little. I only feel. I feel despair.

I hear the words delivered by the Curate Henry Smith and yet they do not stay with me. Perhaps they are blown hither by the winds that buffet the tiled church roof and determinedly enter as draughts amongst the rafters above our heads. The church feels cold. As cold as death.

Perhaps his words are washed away and drowned by the tears that flow from my eyes and those of all who loved Sarah. The tears of all of Appledram pour down the outside of the narrow grey church windows distorting the glass into a dark green tangled blur like sodden seaweed.

When the service is finished the casket bearers carry Sarah through the door at the south of the church. In this foulest of storms most people remain in the shelter of the church.

Henry Smith leads the casket bearers. George follows behind clutching his Mother's arm and I follow them with William Collick. We each support the other.

The coffin is carried out through the porch and into the teeming rain and wind. Once out of the door the men turn to the right and follow the path around to the back of the church where a black hole looms right next to the north-west corner of the church building. A gaping chasm in our lives.

We stand aside the grave and the Curate says his words. Most of what he says is flung away by the wind and washed along with the rain and the mud into Sarah's grave.

'Earth to earth, ashes to ashes, dust to dust.'

The casket is lowered into the ground and George falls onto his knees into the mud. William and I grab him by the arms to prevent him from falling into the hole on top of the coffin. George sobs and weeps, though all our faces flow with rainwater and tears.

Henry Smith nods to the grave-digger to fill the grave before it fills with rain. He leads us back around the side of the church to the porch where he shakes my hand and that of William.

Our families come out of the church and follow behind William and I, along the narrow church pathway which is flooded to its full width. Even in my heavy boots I can feel the cold dark water seep through the leather and in between my toes.

On the lane it is worse. Rainwater washes from the fields. The ditches on both sides of the lane can no longer be seen. They have joined with the lane to form a single stream flowing to the east towards Fishbourne, and south to Dell Quay. Our procession trudges south in the wintry gloom. We are all speechless, our faces clenched against the rain – buried in our own thoughts, memories and pain.

There are no birds. They are all dead.

All I can hear is the persistent downpour of rain and the splashing of our feet. It is scarcely light. God has made it dark all day. Without Sarah it may remain dark forever more.

The Eastlands and Collicks paddle arm-in-arm along the waterlogged lane, drowned as we are in this stream of desolation.

Friday 13th February 1863

Appledram marshes, early morning

George William Eastland.

Above my face the sky is black as night – even though it is day.

I would wish to be hung on a rough gibbet, so my blood could gush forth to release me from this stench of misery. It would be a blessed relief if I were granted a sudden catalepsy with which to lurch with one final spasm into eternal sleep. But no – for all my prayers such blissful escape is denied me.

The wind howls in my ear like the Devil. My other ear is submerged in stinking slimy water.

I force myself to keep my eyes wide open into the teeming splinters of freezing rain and hail in the vain hope that treacherous demon God will make a mistake and allow a large hailstone to blind me.

I lie in the marshes near Appledram Common, almost entirely under water. A wicked storm rages with deafening thunder overhead and lightning forks all around. I have come to die in this frozen watery coffin as my life is ended.

'God I hate you.' My screams are stolen by the gale, just like He stole my soul. I may as well not be here. I am invisible, like a worthless, pitiful maggot in the mud.

'I may as well not be here,' I shout at God, whilst spluttering on rain and putrid marsh water. 'You are no God. The moment you give happiness to us mere mortals you take it away. There is no life on earth, no joy, no purpose, no beauty. Just pain and suffering. I hate you.

'Yours is treachery and deceit and lies. Yours is the most foul torture and misery. I have seen the light. There is no earth, no salvation and no Heaven. We are already here in Hell where you are the Devil, weaving your web of lies about Earth and Heaven before burying us in despair and squalor for your entertainment. You play with men as you please. No sooner do you give a man a scrap of happiness and purpose in life than you snatch it away from him and laugh. You are the most hateful, treacherous demon, passing yourself off as some God. You deceive and punish men for their sins, whilst their sins are as nothing compared to your vile evil.

'I no longer seek happiness as you will steal it and replace it with misery. I no longer seek love as you will tear it away and replace it with numbness and despair. I no longer want life as you will fill it with pain.

'I ask you to blind me with hail and strike me down with a lightning bolt. But I know you will not do it for this is Hell and you will not allow me a quick end as any just God would. You will make me suffer slowly as you are the Devil exuding only hate, bile and misery.

'But I will defy you Judas and just lie in my wet rotting coffin until I drown or freeze. You cannot keep me alive against my will for you are no God. You cannot heal, you cannot create love, you cannot hurt me any more. I have nothing left for you to take. I will go – go to somewhere better than this Hell in which I now rot.'

I scream again, and my cry is instantly blown into the mud where it is buried with the worms and the beetles and the sludge of centuries of dead weeds. My limbs are so cold I cannot feel them. My filthy remains are merging in with the rest of the marshy muck that has come to rest in this sodden silted sluice.

Earth to earth, ashes to ashes, dust to dust.

My mind becomes calmer as I am slowly released from my earthly torment. I dream of worms crawling into my brain, of water rats chewing on my intestines, and of crows plucking my cold dead eyes from their slimy bone sockets.

Water slugs slide through my ears and into my brain. I dream a watery dream of Little George and Henry calling 'Daddy.' I sleep. My sons will be better off without me.

I dream of Father. He is saying something to me. 'George, George – you cannot leave your boys. They are too young. They need their father.' I shrug my shoulders up against the rotten roots of the putrid marsh weeds.

'You cannot leave them. You owe it to Sarah. She had to go – she was given no choice. Sarah needs you to look after her boys. You mustn't fail her. You mustn't fail Sarah. George, George!'

'GEORGE, GEORGE!'

Father is shouting. 'What are you doing? Get up. You will catch your death of cold.'

Father tries to pull me out of the mud, but he slips and falls in shoulder-first next to me. He is covered in filth and has fear etched across his face. I have never seen fear in Father's eyes before.

My brain is numb from the cold but I cannot let Father suffer like this. I must get up and help him, but I can't feel my body.

Father hauls himself up and grabs me under my armpits and drags me little by little towards the path. I manage to push a little with my boots to help him. Clement has followed Father and between them they manage to get me to my feet. Together, like three drunken vagabonds caked in mud and the faeces of a million dead creatures we lurch arm-in-arm back along the path beside the river towards the Crown and Anchor.

Later Father and I sit by the fireside with glasses of rum. 'I'll shout at you no more. Nobody said life was easy. We can only enjoy what we can. Life brings with it responsibilities and one of them is to love and bring up your children as best you are able.

'I will always love you George and will do what I can to help you, as will your mother. We will help you to bring up George and Henry, but we are old – we will not be here forever. George and Henry need their father, even more with Sarah gone. You owe it to Sarah to do your best to look after these two precious lives that you created together through love, and you must tell them about their mother so they do not forget her.

'Think less about yourself. Instead think of George and Henry and do what you can for them. Only you can do this George.

'But remember, God knows, I will do all I can to help you George.'

Summer 1863

Crown & Anchor, Dell Quay

Ann Eastland.

Consumption is a curse. Almost none survive it.

Once I realised that Sarah's tickly cough was turning into that persistent rasping hacking I feared for all our family, for the dreaded disease spreads so readily.

Sarah, bless her, realised first. Having nursed her older sister Emily to her consumption-riddled demise, Sarah recognised the cursed affliction quicker than any of us and took swift action. She made the smallest bedroom in the attic hers, closed the door and opened wide the small bedroom windows facing the sea. She said that until she got better, food and drink should be left outside her bedroom door and that one person only should attend her. She said her boys must come nowhere near her. How that must have torn her – knowing she might never hold her boys again?

Our brave Sarah.

Nor would she see her father or her sister Alice. Alice came to visit one day but Sarah locked herself inside her room. Sarah shouted through the door, 'I will not pass any illness to you dear Alice, or to your children. Go home and do not come back here until George tells you I am well again.' Alice was dreadfully upset yet she knew that Sarah was right. Hard-bitten old landlady I may be but I gave Alice a bottle of whisky I felt so sad looking at her crumpled face and red eyes. How these Collicks get inside your heart.

I realised that it would be best if I attended Sarah, for so many reasons. At my age I know plenty about nursing people through illness – nursing their spirits as well as their bodies. And we could not risk Sarah's boys or Fanny catching the infection. I could attend Sarah quickly and hope to avoid the illness. If I should fall to the cursed cough… well, I am old. I have had my children, my life and my threescore years on this earth. I would not complain in the face of the longest sleep.

So it was that I took Sarah what she needed and attended to her toilet in what became her last weeks and days. I watched her cheeks turn hollow and her eye-sockets become black. It was not a sight for young people. Of course I couldn't stop George from visiting his wife. I could hear Sarah talking to him. She soon shooed him out of her room and sent him straight down the stairs and out of the inn to take in the sea air on the quay before he came anywhere near their boys, or the rest of us.

Sarah wouldn't even let me stay in her room a moment longer than I needed to. She'd say, 'I need you well Mother for you may soon have three Georges and a Henry to look after.'

I saw then that Sarah was so far in front of me. While I was still fretting, worrying about her illness and hoping yet to nurse her to recovery, she knew her death was likely to come soon and was planning for it.

Sarah told me, 'If I am gone, George probably won't know what to do, but he will find himself eventually. He is only young. I won't begrudge him finding a new wife in time. He must not mourn forever. Perhaps… Mary Clayton always had a soft spot for George? She is yet unmarried. George is too good a man to be alone.'

'Mary Clayton? Not over my dead body!' I retorted.

Sarah and I laughed, but that started her coughing again and she pointed me out of her room once more.

When I visited Sarah again later that day she returned to the subject. 'If I am gone please help George to be a good father. Look after little George and Henry for me, and make sure they go to school and learn to read and write.'

'Of course I will look after them,' I tell her. 'But you are far from gone Sarah. Your fighting spirit can scare this illness away. Don't you give up. Come spring you will be out in the sunshine with your boys.' I hoped against hope that this could yet pass.

One day when I visited Sarah in her high bedroom she asked me to wrap George and Henry up well because it was winter, and to take them onto the quay in front of the Crown and Anchor to watch the boats coming and going. It meant she could drag herself to her small bedroom window to look out at her boys. She told me she wouldn't wave because she didn't want them getting excited and coming up to her bedroom.

I told Sarah off for that. I said, 'George, Henry and I will all wave to you until our arms drop off and you must wave back. You must trust me to look after your boys.'

So George, Henry and I went to the quay, looked up and waved at Sarah. The two boys laughed and shrieked they were so happy to see their mummy waving to them. They didn't see the tears running down her cheeks...and mine.

Sarah inevitably lost the fight.

My son George lost his mind. He wailed, sobbed and cursed. He could not settle his head to work. He wanted to fight someone but didn't know who. He would take himself out early in the morning whatever the weather and come home late. We all wanted to help but he was beyond reason. The best place for him then was out, away from people. We thought he would thrash his temper away in the great outdoors but spring then summer came and he was still as wild and unsettled. He became thin, his hair long and matted, and a scruffy beard grew on his face.

So now I sit down with my husband, and Matilda and Fanny to discuss what we should do.

'George has no interest in his boys at the moment. He has no interest in anything. His mind is still scattered. If you can look after the inn Matilda, I shall take Henry and George in hand. I can play with them and keep them occupied in the kitchen,' I say.

'And I will help wherever I'm most needed, either in the bar with you Matilda or with Mother and the boys,' Fanny chips in.

'I think our son needs more time and space to clear his pain and anguish. I think he needs to get away from this place and all its painful memories. I'll send him on the boats with some of our coal deliveries to Portsmouth and Brighton. It will give him something to do and a change of landscape. It also means George won't be shouting at his old Father for a little while!'

Today is Monday 17th August. The Crown will be quiet today, but more important is that a year ago today Henry was baptised. With Sarah gone and George in the state he is I feel drawn back to St. Mary the Virgin at Appledram. George and I have brought our two grandsons here. God knows, if any child needs His love and encouragement so early in this treacherous life it is poor Henry.

I am glad we have come here. The quiet peace of the church seeps into my mind, and I hope Henry's also. When we emerge again from the cool church and its sun-dappled windows into the quiet green churchyard of this sunny August day, George places a posy of wild summer flowers on his mother's grave which lies in the shade behind the building.

All is quiet here… even little Henry and George. The only sound is the chirping of a blackbird deep in the shady branches. This sunny day under the rustling trees in the churchyard seems a hundred years from the dismal grey tragedy of January. If only Sarah could have survived that damp, grey winter gloom she could have been here with Henry today, feeling the warm sun on her back.

A bright green leaf flutters down from the trees above and lands on Henry as I carry him along the grassy church path. I look up to the rustling branches above with the triangles of blue darting between them.

Perhaps these dancing, shining skylights between the leaves are Sarah's sparkling eyes looking down upon her beloved Henry and George?

Thursday 8th December 1864

Port of Southampton

George William Eastland.

I am tortured with guilt. But what else can I do?

I love my boys, but I am not their mother. I know not the first thing to do with two boys aged two and three, nor how to answer their impossible questions.

I shout at Father and Mother, and even Fanny. My temper is shorter than my finger nails and knows no bounds. The anger inside me burns so I can't control it. My head is full of rage. I walk for hours in the sun and the rain – I notice not whether I am burnt or drenched. I don't care.

I look at the clouds in the sky and all that space up there. Sometimes I think I can see Sarah's face in those clouds. Most days my mind wanders aimlessly – like I do, up and down the coast from Fishbourne to Wittering, to Bosham, and to Hell. I can't sit still. My brain won't rest, especially when I sleep. Neither is it any relief when I wake as I know I face another day just the same.

I don't care for anything or anyone.

Sarah has gone and I am worthless. If I could will myself dead I would, for I cannot find peace from this torment anywhere on this Earth.

Fanny cries when I raise my voice at her, 'Go away – I want to be on my own.' It's best if I am on my own because I can't stop myself from shouting at people. Shouting at my family. It is not right, I know. I should love them, but I don't love anything any more. Especially not myself. This is all my fault.

What is the point of loving anything or anyone anyway? Everything is taken away sooner or later. The more you love the more you lose. I've given up loving. Mother now looks after little George, and Matilda cares for Henry.

It is better for everybody if I take my temper away and leave them all in peace. If George and Henry can forget me it will be one less source of heartache for them. If I manage to die and go to join Sarah up in the clouds they won't need to feel sad if they can forget about me. I have already caused them enough trouble.

Of course, Sarah may not want me in her cloud. If it wasn't for me she would still live. If I hadn't dropped my damned cushion at her feet and forced her away from her father and her farm, married her and given her two babies she would have become a happy farmer's wife, spending her days making butter and milking cows. I have been a Jonah to the Eastlands, to Sarah and our boys, and they are all better off if I take my leave out of their lives.

As God won't let me just drop down and die I have done the only thing I can, the only thing I know, the only thing that might give me some purpose. I now seek the only place where I can be invisible to this family to whom I am nothing but a sore – a cause of grief and pain.

Father shouted at me. 'It's been hard on you George, I know. But so it has for us all – especially little George and Henry. You are no good to them boys with your vile and bitter temper.'

Father's tone softened. 'You need time and space, and something to do to recover your senses, George. The best place for you now is to go to sea. There you can find all the space in the world to clear your head. Work hard, make yourself busy. With the Fishbourne Channel silting up we don't get the big ships at Dell Quay any more, which means less work in the mill and fewer visitors to the Crown & Anchor. Business is slack. You can earn good money on long voyages, plenty for you and your boys. That is the best way you can help them now. After a few weeks or months at sea you will come home a good father again. You'll see.'

And he added, 'And when you go, besure to write – at least occasionally. Else Mother will worry.'

So, early today I packed a bag, and got on a train from Chichester to Southampton to find myself a ship.

All sorts of merchant shipping passes in and out of big ports like Southampton, so I am hopeful that with my mariner's training I should be able to secure a posting in a few days. Meantime I will find somewhere cheap to lodge.

I know Father has berthed at Southampton many times transporting coal, timber, grain and all manner of other cargoes between the large ports of England, Wales, Scotland and Ireland. If I am lucky, I think to myself, I might even get on a ship going to France or Spain and get a longer voyage. The further away from home the better, and the longer the voyage the better too. That way you don't have to keep trying to secure a new posting, and the pay is more on longer sailings. More time to forget Sussex.

When I arrive at the quay in Southampton I find a long queue of men outside an office. They say there is work to be had on a Royal Mail ship. So I join the back of the queue. It is just after four o'clock in the afternoon when I finally reach the front of the queue and am called into the dimly lit office. However, once inside the office has a bright amber warmth compared to the grey drizzle of the quayside. It is now pitch black outside where I have been standing and shuffling forward slowly during the last three hours. I am saturated to my skin.

Two weather-beaten old sea-dogs sit behind a heavy wooden desk which is covered with papers. They tell me the Royal Mail Ship the "Mersey" is due to sail tomorrow, but that most of the mariner's positions have been filled. They ask after my name, age and sailing experience.

I see their ears prick up when I tell them I have been trained in mathematics and navigation at the Royal Hospital School in Greenwich, and that I have served on many merchant ships with my father. They tell me all the navigation crew are already appointed, but the man on the right starts running his pencil up and down a long paper list.

He asks me if I have done any other work so I tell them about milling, trading in grain and coal, and of living and working in taverns most of my life. That is when the first man's pencil stops moving and he looks at the other man who nods.

'So Mr George Eastland, I take it that you are well practised in moving beer kegs and know how much rum goes into a tot?'

'Of course, I reply. I have spent many hours getting stronger by shifting kegs of ale to the cellar, and back out again at the Crown and Anchor... and a tot of rum is an eighth of a pint, served neat for

Officers, and mixed with two-eighths of a pint of water to make three-eighths of a pint of grog for ordinary seamen, sir.'

The first sea-dog looks at me and says, 'Well then, Mr George William Eastland, how would you like to be the most nautically qualified Barman and Pantryman the Royal Mail has ever had?'

We agree on pay and I accept the position straight away. When they tell me the posting will be for a whole year delivering the mail to Rio de Janeiro and Buenos Aires in the River Plate I can't believe my luck. This feels like the first piece of good fortune that has come my way since before I can remember.

I am instructed to board the RMS "Mersey" immediately. There is much to be done in the stores before we set off to sea tomorrow.

Tuesday 20th December 1864

Crown & Anchor, Dell Quay

George William Eastland (junior).

Mummy went to Heaven.
That was a long time ago.
Heaven must be a very long way away.
Grandfather says Mummy won't come home again?
I don't think I believe him?
I hope Mummy isn't lost.
I'm sure Mummy will come home.
Everybody has a mummy.
Even Daddy has a mummy.
She is Grandmother.
I like Grandmother.
She makes my breakfast and tells me stories.
Henry is my brother.
We play together.
Henry is two.
Henry doesn't remember Mummy.
That is how I know Mummy has been gone a very long time.
Father also went away…weeks ago now.
Grandfather says Father won't be here for Christmas.
What is Christmas?

Grandfather says Henry and I have to wait patiently to find out.

Father is big and strong.

I think Father has gone to find Heaven – to bring Mummy home.

I think that Heaven must be even further away than Chichester.

I went there once with Grandfather on the cart.

That was a long way away.

I hope Father doesn't get lost like Mummy did.

…George sobs.

Friday 8th September 1865

Crown & Anchor, Dell Quay

Fanny Caplin Eastland.

I dread to think what is becoming of my brother. The death of Sarah loosed his soul – it was as if he went mad.

It was understandable. It was awful to see the beautiful Sarah decay before our eyes – that hacking cough that shook the life out of her with no mercy.

The boys are too young to understand. That has its good side. They missed their mother at first, though Henry doesn't remember Sarah now. He was only six months old when she was taken.

They both cried when George went off to sea last Christmas. Being young they have all but forgotten him. It is sad to see, but young children need peace around them which George and Henry have here now. When I am not working in the bar I like to play with the boys. We play games, like marbles, and I read to them. Little George so reminds me of my brother when we were young. He has the same bright blue eyes and lively imagination, and he looks after Henry, just like George looked after me when I was small.

It was probably the right thing for George to go to sea. He needed something to do to take his mind off losing Sarah. He didn't know what to do with himself here. He tortured himself with guilt and recriminations. None of us could reason with him. He just shouted and walked, and shouted and walked again.

Father sent George to sea. It is what he went to London to train for. It's all he ever really wanted to do. Father says the sound of the wind in the sails and an orange and red sunset on a dark motionless sea will calm George's anguish. I pray for this at St. Mary the Virgin Church, along the lane at Appledram.

I wrote a letter to George in June. He didn't reply. He probably never received it. Writing to a ship on a faraway ocean seems a strange thing to me. They tell us to send letters to Southampton to be forwarded. I imagine a Southampton seagull flying with my letter all the way to George on his ship. A Royal Mail seagull of course!

The seagull brought a letter back from George addressed to Father and Mother last week. It was not a long letter but said, along with the usual pleasantries, that George was in Lisbon and expects to be home for Christmas. George also sent money to help Father and Mother, and so they can buy things for little George and Henry.

I am so pleased that George is thinking of George and Henry - and also of Father and Mother. The death of Sarah and its effects on George have also taken their toll on my parents. Over the last two years they have both suddenly started to look old and tired. Running the mill and helping Matilda with the tavern, as well as looking after two toddlers is too much for them now they are in their sixties.

Father no longer goes to sea but watches wistfully as boats set off from Dell Quay piled high with their cargoes. He puffs on his old pipe and imagines the places they are sailing to.

Matilda and Richard are continuing the family tradition and getting a tavern of their own. In a few weeks they will be moving into the White Hart in Littlehampton. Mother will take charge again of the Crown and Anchor when Matilda and Richard leave. Mother will employ outside barmaids now all her daughters except me have left home. But with Matilda gone, Father and Mother will not be able to cope with two small and energetic boys. With my help they are going to try to look after George, and Matilda will take Henry with her to Littlehampton. She has been mostly looking after him since Sarah passed, and they have become close.

I have been to Littlehampton. I think little Henry will like it there. Littlehampton is by the sea and Matilda tells me the White Hart is a stone's throw from the long sandy beach. Littlehampton is not really that far away, but too far to go to regularly especially when the weather is bad in winter.

My only worry is how George and Henry will feel about being separated?

Autumn 1865

Dell Quay

George Eastland.

Your little boy is always your little boy – when he is three, and still also when he is twenty-three.

He is bigger and stronger and better schooled than I, but he does not yet possess the wisdom of years and, as do all fathers, I worry he may make unwise choices in life.

In truth I feel much responsibility for George going back to sea as I encouraged him strongly to go. Though I still feel there was no better option. He was scaring little George and Henry and even the usually spirited Fanny with his temper and his tantrums, fuelled by self-pity and despair. I understood, but sought a way to help George get past his rage, and the sea is what he has always loved.

I didn't think he'd be away for a whole year. It's hard to tell if his long posting with the Royal Mail is helping him. He has only written me two letters. I told George to write often so his mother would not worry. The first letter arrived in the spring to tell us he was on the Royal Mail Ship "Mersey" bound for Rio de Janeiro. The second arrived in the post from Chichester a week or two back saying all is well, he has the ship's stores all shipshape and Bristol fashion, and that his ship is due in Southampton before Christmas. It wasn't much to inform me, and yet his tone seems more cheerful.

I can't help but worry. I'll worry more than most mariners' fathers will as, having been a Merchant Navy Captain all my life, I know the dangers of the sea only too well. Many of them are in the hands only of God.

There are other man-made perils – among them being too much drink, diseases caused by too much wenching, and injury from too much fighting. Loners, gowks and slubberdegullions may get picked on by gangs and beaten or otherwise tormented and made miserable.

When George left here he was talking to no man. I hope his duties on board ship have tempered his rages and that he sits, plays cards, and talks to his ship-mates. I hope I didn't send him off to sea too soon. Although he was unsettled here, at least we knew where he was and that he came home all safe each night.

I had such a dreadful nightmare last night about George in a violent storm on his ship. He was at the top of the mast in the crow's nest and his ship was being rolled by a wild black sea, with the screams of mariners coming from far below on the deck.

I was shouting at George not to try to climb down from the crow's nest but he couldn't hear me over the deafening roar of the storm. Then a wave as high as the sky and as wide as Chichester rose to tower over the ship. It was about to fall down upon us and crush us to the ocean floor never to surface again when I awoke in a cold sweat.

It took me a full five minutes after I awoke to convince myself it had just been a dream. Trouble is, it takes so long to get word back from ships the other side of the world that George could have been in a storm in Australia two weeks ago and I would be none the wiser.

I'll hold onto my hope. George's letter says little but it isn't despairing in any way as he was before he left. He talks about 'his' stores so perhaps his usual pride in his work has returned. He also sent a money order for us to buy George and Henry some new clothes, which means he is at last thinking of his boys.

I do hope his ship is not delayed and that George comes home for Christmas. I look forward to looking into his face to see for myself how he fares.

Saturday 9th December 1865

The English Channel

George William Eastland.

I hold tight to the fiferail against the force five sou'westerly that howls over the sea. The keen wind whistles in my ears and the salty spray hangs in the air like mist. This weather refreshes me.

Our ship tumbles across the Channel, dipping between the rolling grey waves with their frothing white summits. The sky and the sea blend as one and I cannot see far ahead through the veil of water, but our ship flies on unperturbed by this moderate swell.

A year ago I would have been as sick as a parrot on a ship lurching like this but I soon regained my sea-legs from sailing every day. I can scarcely believe I have been back at sea for a year now. What I do believe is that the sea has been my saviour.

When I got work on a mail ship in Southampton last December I hoped it would sail into a wild storm in the middle of a large ocean, where I could jump from the deck into the black thunderous sea below and be freed from the misery of this life.

Much to my surprise however, my views on life gradually changed. After the first few days of sea-sickness had passed my feelings of despair at the loss of Sarah also began to recede. This was not because my mind was taken over by fear of the sea, the wind and the storms for I have sailed in them many times before. If anything I was disappointed the weather was not wilder as I wanted only to drown at that time.

Nor was it because my memory or love for Sarah was fading. My memory of Sarah will never fade. She was my love and my light. The pictures in my mind of how lovely my Sarah was and how dreadfully, painfully and rapidly was her demise and how cruelly short was our love together – all these memories are burnt into my soul forever. No storm, no matter how fierce, will ever wash away these memories of mine.

But my self-pity diminished a little. The agony I had felt from the twisting of that knife when Sarah became ill, and the final stabbing of that merciless blade when Sarah was taken from me retreated a fraction. This was mainly because being Barman and Pantryman is a busy occupation, allowing my mind no spare time to wander off and to dwell upon my former troubles.

My days are filled with serving and recording tots of rum to all the crew, washing glasses, cleaning the bar, checking supplies, recording stocks and preparing orders for victuals. Of course, with all the bottles of rum and casks of ale under my keep I could easily have drowned my sorrows. But I did not see that as any escape from my torment. You still dream when you are fuddled or asleep, and sometimes those alcohol-soaked nightmares are more colourful and dreadful than normal dreams. I have seen too many drunken fools wasting their lives away in the Bull and the Crown for me to want to follow that path.

I still have my pride and integrity. As Barman and Pantryman I must account for every drop of alcohol, and I would be rightly dismissed from this ship quicker than a black rat if I was caught drunk on duty.

The crew all come to my bar every day for their rum and their ale. They try to persuade me to pour them an extra measure and they entertain me with their banter and their tales. When I first joined the ship I had no conversation and was still buried deep in my own thoughts. But gradually the tales and the troubles of the other men took over some space in my mind and I began to enjoy listening to them and they would want to know about me. So I began to unburden myself of my own tale of woe.

I take pride in my work, and before long my pantry and stores and all my inventories were straight and neat and all ship-shape. The Master commended me on the job I was doing and for the first time in a long while I felt I was doing something of worth, and doing it well.

In my rest time I like to sit on the deck on a fine day and gaze at the blue ocean, and bluer sky, to listen to the splash of the sea against the timbers and to feel the wind on my face. These last twelve months I have sailed back and forth from Southampton to Brazil, calling at the Madeiras, Tenerife and other places. My skin has turned brown and I have put on a little weight from the food on board and at the ports where we berth.

I think of everyone back home, in particular little Georgie and Henry. I hope they are well and happy.

I feel guilty that I behaved so badly towards Father and Mother and my sisters after Sarah's death. They were all trying so hard to help me and they looked after my boys when all I could do was shout and scream at them. I was so rude, so utterly self-possessed and a useless father to my sons. Thank God Father sent me to Southampton. I feel sure they are all much better off without me.

When I first came to sea I couldn't bear to think of home or my family. I just wanted to forget everything. But once I had settled my brain I increasingly thought of home, the Fishbourne Channel, and of George and Henry.

I hope to make amends for my bad behaviour. At Easter I wrote my first letter to Father and Mother since going to Southampton last December. I also sent them a money order for all that I had earned and saved so far. I told Father to buy something for George and Henry, and also to buy something useful for himself and for Mother.

I started to write home more regularly after that telling Father and Mother of the places I had sailed to, and always sending home a money order. I spent as little on myself as I could. I do not deserve luxuries – I would rather my wages go to Father and Mother and my boys. In July I wrote a long letter to my dear sister Fanny. I sent her a money order and told her to buy herself a pretty summer dress or something else that would please her. The wages on board ship are good and I have little need to spend much on myself as I do not drink or smoke. I can send most of my money home. I feel a little less guilty now for my dreadful behaviour.

By the summer my love of the wild seas returned. I once again marvel at the multi-hued skies from heavy dark turquoise-grey stormy heavens, to fiery streaked red and blue sunsets, to the calm blue of a quiet summer dawn where the rising sun sets light to a thousand twinkling silver candles on the flat plain of blue water before me. I know this is why I studied so hard at Greenwich. I remember my childhood dreams of Robinson Crusoe as I lay on the banks of the

Fishbourne Channel watching the boats come and go. I know this is where I am meant to be.

I wrote and told Father and Mother I would come home at Christmas. I desperately wonder what they think of me now? I hope the money orders I sent home all arrived? I hope I will be forgiven for my bad behaviour? I wonder how much my boys have grown? George is now four and Henry is three.

The ship I am on is bound for Southampton. When I get there I will buy presents for Father and Mother and for Fanny and my other sisters. I will then go by train to Chichester.

It is odd that I am feeling a little nervous now to go home after so long at sea. I know my memories of Sarah's demise will return when I enter The Crown and Anchor, but I am also longing to see my boy's faces again and the rest of my family. I hope to enjoy Christmas with them all.

I am no longer broken. I am once again a mariner. Next year I plan to sail more in faraway seas as I like the warm weather and the excitement of foreign people and exotic foods. The colour and warmth provides such a lift after the grey damp of an English December.

When George and Henry are older maybe I will one day take them to see the sun and blue skies of Spain.

MARINE DEPARTMT
COM. OF COUNCIL FOR TRADE

SANCTIONED BY THE BOARD OF TRADE MAY 1855. IN PURSUANCE OF 17 &18 VICT. C. 104.   **76**

(E-1) CERTIFICATE OF DISCHARGE.
For Seaman discharged before a Shipping Master.

Name of Ship.	*Mersey*
Official Number.	*27.224*
Port of Registry.	*London*
Registered Tonnage.	*729*
Description of Voyage or Employment.	*Mail Service*
Name of Seaman.	*George W Eastland*
Place of Birth.	*Chichester*
Date of Birth.	
Capacity.	*Barman & Pantryman*
Date of Entry.	*9th Decr 1864*
Date of Discharge.	*9th Decr 1865*
Place of Discharge.	*South'ton*

I Certify that the above particulars are correct and that the above Seaman was discharged accordingly.

Dated this *9th* day of *Decr* 186*5*

Signed *J. Thoraithis* Master of the Ship.

A. Naidej Shipping Master.

NOTE. –One of these Certificates must be filled up and delivered to every Seaman who is discharged whenever the discharge takes place before a Shipping Master.
Printed by Authority of the Board of Trade.

241

MARINE DEPARTMT

COM. OF COUNCIL FOR TRADE

SANCTIONED BY THE BOARD OF TRADE MAY 1855. IN PURSUANCE OF 17 &18 VICT. C. 104.   **76**

(E-1) CERTIFICATE OF CHARACTER.

Character for ability in whatever capacity............*V.G*............

Character for conduct...............................*V.G*............

I Certify the above to be a true copy of so much of the Report of Character, made by the said Master on the termination of the said Voyage, as concerns the said Seaman.

Dated at *South'ton* this *9th* day of *Decr.* 186*5*

Signed *J. Thorailhis* Master of the Ship.

A. Naidoj Shipping Master.

For Signature of Seaman see back.

NOTE. Any Person who fraudulently forges or alters a Certificate of Character or makes use of one which does not belong to him may either be prosecuted for a Misdemeanour or may be summarily punished by a Penalty not exceeding £100 or imprisonment with hard labour not exceeding six months.

Printed by Authority of the Board of Trade.

Monday 11th December 1865

Crown & Anchor, Dell Quay

George William Eastland (junior).

It will be Christmas soon. Grandfather says he will put a big fir tree in the big bay window in the bar facing the sea, and that it will be decorated with sparkly things, sweets and tiny candles. I am excited about Christmas.

I am a big boy now – four and a half years old and I go to school. My Aunt Fanny holds my hand and takes me to school. Some children think Aunt Fanny is my mother. We don't say anything.

I like school. There are lots of boys to play with. A few weeks ago Henry went with Aunt Matilda and Uncle Richard to live with them and their new baby Ann Elizabeth Barttelot. That name is hard to say, and I can't spell it. They are teaching me spelling at school.

Grandmother told me that Matilda has taken over the White Hart Inn at Littlehampton. Our family like living in taverns. They are full of people and always warm. Not like my school – it is so cold there I have to wear two jumpers to keep warm.

I like to go to school to play with the other children. But I miss Henry. Aunt Fanny tells me I will see Henry at Christmas. She is going to take me to Littlehampton on Boxing Day in a cart and we will stay with Henry for a few days.

Grandfather says my Father is also going to come home for Christmas.

I am looking forward to playing with Henry again. I miss him. I have never been to Littlehampton. I hope Aunt Matilda will read some stories to me and Henry when I'm there. Aunt Matilda tells really good stories. She reads them out of books. Aunt Fanny tells me this is because Aunt Matilda used to be a School Mistress in Chichester.

Aunt Fanny also reads to me and she says if I keep working hard at school I shall be able to read lots of stories all by myself out of books.

Thursday 28th December 1865

The White Hart, Littlehampton, 6.30pm

Matilda Barttelot

'The wind is howling in the ship's sails, the white canvas wet through with the salty spray, and flapping noisily in the gale. The great ship is half-way across the English Channel on its way back to Southampton when this frightful storm blows up out of no-where. The god of the sea, King Neptune has developed indigestion after a huge lunch and as a result all the oceans have gone into turmoil.

'The sky suddenly turns an inky black and as Captain George looks into the heavens he realises darkness is about to fall upon his ship early this evening. His ship rises and falls between the ever-growing waves. It rises upon the peak of a mountainous white crest only to be plunged ever downwards, deeper and deeper into the hollow between the high cliffs of waves, as deep as the deepest and darkest cave.

'Captain George can no longer see the sky and begins to fear that he may never see a blue summer's day again, or the smiling faces of his two sons George and Henry, or the face of his beautiful sister Matilda.

'The mariners gasp from fear and the timbers of the great wooden ship creak desperately from the strain that the sea is putting upon them. George clings to the wheel of the ship and prays that his vessel will not be broken into a thousand pieces by the thunderous seas.

'As if by a miracle George's prayer is answered, and a beautiful fairy with a slim face, twinkling eyes and silver wings appears and hovers in the sky high above George's ship. The fairy, although only small, has great magical powers but the gods only permit her to use them when lives are in danger.

'Clearly the lives of all the mariners in the stricken ship far below the fairy are in the very greatest of danger as the ship is flung between the monstrous waves, so the fairy takes action.

'She holds her arms aloft as she casts her spell...
That silly King Neptune has whipped up a breeze,

**By huffing and puffing to stir up the seas,
But now that this storm is blowing so strong,
Those innocent sailors will drown before long,
The sea must return to its former calm state,
And Neptune must halve what he puts on his plate.**

'With that the seas miraculously level and the howling winds reduce to a gentle southerly breeze. The sun comes out again as the grey clouds fly away to the east to reveal a deep blue sky that reaches all the way to the distant horizon, even as far away as Littlehampton. The fairy, named Fanny, satisfied with her work flutters away on the warm summer breeze.'

There is a gentle tapping on the bedroom door and a head looks into the darkened bedroom, lit by the single candle.

'Matilda – it's only me. Have you got the boys to sleep yet?'

'Yes Fanny. I've just finished one of my little bed-time stories and they are fast asleep now. I will tuck them up and come down presently. You go on Fanny.'

I sit in the cosy gloom of the bedroom watching the candle-light flicker, sending darting shadows across the walls as the two boys breathe quietly, and I think about the year that is now coming to an end.

For me it has been a year of many changes – mostly for the good. After the terrible trouble when Sarah died from consumption and left George bewildered and desperate, this last twelve months has seen some calm return to our family. With George gone to sea a year ago his two boys have been able to settle a little, though God knows it is hard for them with no mother and their father away at sea all the time.

Mother and Father and Fanny and I have been able to restore some order to their lives and a daily routine in The Crown & Anchor, and little George has also started school which keeps him busy and gives him things to think about, and other children to spend time with.

In February a miracle happened. I gave birth to my first child, Ann Elizabeth Barttelot. My precious daughter who I thought would never be born. Richard and I were married seventeen years ago and had long since given up any hope that we would have children. Ours was to work and to look after other people's children. I loved being a teacher and spending time with children in Chichester when we lived in The Bull at Fishbourne, but at Dell Quay I was needed to work in the tavern.

When I first fell with Ann I was afraid I had some dreadful illness as I had pains in my stomach and was sick every morning for weeks. I had no thought that I could have a baby growing in there. Then a local midwife came and put me straight, and I was so overjoyed but still never believed the baby would be born safely.

She nearly wasn't. The pains and the birth seemed to go on for hours and when Ann finally came I bled like a fish on the quay, and swore never to have another baby as long as I shall live. But Ann is beautiful and I can't now imagine any life without her, even though it was weeks before I felt truly well again. Fortunately I had Mother and Fanny to help me recover, and to help look after Ann in our first weeks together. Little George and Henry were fascinated by this new tiny girl in our midst – someone even smaller than them, and so pink and delicate.

The unexpected birth of Ann led to the next change in our lives. We realised that in time we would need more living space than was possible in The Crown. Also Richard's health has not been so good and he decided to give up his life as a mariner and concentrate on running the tavern. So now he is home with us all of the time. We managed to get ourselves the White Hart tavern in Littlehampton and we moved here in November.

I like it here just a stone's throw from the sea but it has been very hard this last two months trying to get ourselves settled in, making repairs to the tavern and looking after our customers and our living. I am looking forward to the warmer weather next summer when being by the sea will be a treat. At the moment the cold wind blows through all the doors and windows, and we have to keep the children warm by the fires so they don't catch their deaths of cold.

Mother and Father aren't getting any younger, and before Richard, Ann and I moved to Littlehampton our family all sat down together to decide what to do with little George and Henry. Mother and Father felt they could not manage both boys any more and Fanny is flat out running The Crown now Mother is past helping much in the bar. But with our new business to settle at Littlehampton and our young baby, Richard and I were concerned about trying to look after George and Henry as well.

After heart-wrenching considerations we eventually decided the best way would be for George to stay with his grandparents at Dell Quay and for Henry to come and live with us at Littlehampton, and for us to all get together whenever we can. Henry hated being without his older brother when we came to Littlehampton, but when his father and Auntie Fanny brought Georgie to visit us in the cart today Henry's face beamed. I hope it will work out.

George started out with the cart from Dell Quay this morning. It is about ten miles away. The lanes are normally quite good and the weather today was windy but mainly dry. Of course the tracks are wet and muddy in places from the winter rains, and George and Fanny were very pleased when they stabled the horse and got inside the White Hart, and in front of the big crackling fire before darkness fell.

The sea has done my brother good. His face was not the gaunt ashen grey that it was when last I saw him a year ago. Sarah's untimely death left our whole family bereft - such a lovely, lively girl was she. It was no wonder to me that George and his boys were like lost sheep and I cried and prayed for them all. This is the first time George has come back to Chichester since he went to sea and I can tell that being at Dell Quay brought back painful memories for him.

I hope George can relax more now he is here at Littlehampton with my family. He has enjoyed being with his two boys today, and Henry was beside himself with joy to see his father. A year away is a lifetime for a three-year-old. I hope George is able to get home from sea to see his sons more often in future.

Children are only young once.

Crown & Anchor
Dell Quay
Thursday 27th June 1867

My Dearest George,

Father told me that if I wrote to you and sent the letter to the Port Office in Southampton they might be able to forward it to you?

Little George is growing fast. I take him to school and he seems quick to learn and the Master says he works hard. He is six and when you see him next you will not believe how tall he is. He looks just like you did when we were both small.

I haven't seen Henry since Christmas. Matilda and Richard have their hands full running the White Hart at Littlehampton, but I know they do their best with Henry. Matilda and Richard have had no more children since Ann Elizabeth was born. I can hardly believe that Ann is two years old already. She is like a little sister for Henry — someone for him to play with.

It is a pity that little George doesn't have any brothers or sisters here to play with. I remember I always had you to stop me being lonely when I was a small child. When I am not working in the tavern I spend as much time as I can playing with George, talking to him and reading him stories.

I decided to write to you today because it is Henry's fifth birthday. I have all the important birthdays listed in the back of my bible so I don't forget any of them. I wish I could visit him today but I cannot get time from work at the moment as the Crown is busier with the extra farm hands helping with the harvest, and I cannot leave the new barmaids on their own as they cannot yet work quickly enough without me. I will take Henry some boiled sweets when I next visit him — I hope it will be quite soon.

When will you be coming home? Little George misses you and so do I. He tells me he is the only boy at school who doesn't have a father. I told him that is not true. There is at least one boy at George's school whose father, a farmer, was killed by a mad bull. I also tell him he has a father — a brave, handsome mariner, sailing on the blue oceans in a grand ship with tall masts and white sails earning a fortune of gold and silver for his sons.

Please come home to see George and Henry soon before they forget who you are!

My Dear George,

I think Father is becoming worn out. I tell him to rest but he is so stubborn. He is becoming stooped and the arthritis in his hands is worse now. He is still Wharfinger at Dell Quay but earlier this year he gave up the mill.

Mother put me in charge of the daily running of The Crown & Anchor last year although Father is still the Licensed Victualler. Mother has also grown tired and she doesn't work in the bar so much now.

Mother and Father put little George to bed in the evening when I am working in the bar. When I finish work George is fast asleep in his bed and Father and Mother are wrapped up in their blankets and snoring in their chairs by the fireside.

I could probably earn more money if I worked somewhere else but it has come to me to look after Father and Mother and little Georgie who is such a lovely boy. Father still earns a little as Wharfinger from the trade in coal and other cargoes though the harbour is not busy like it once was. The channel is silted up and only smaller barges can get here. Most ships go to Arundel or Portsea now.

Please do come home to visit us soon George. Or better still, come home and stay. Have you not by now found enough gold and treasure?

Your ever loving sister,

Fanny

Saturday 11th January 1868

Crown & Anchor, Dell Quay, 3.30pm

George Eastland.

The old clock chimes once to signal the half hour. With some effort I raise my scraggy eyebrow and force my eye open to squint at the clock face to determine which half hour has just passed.

It is only half past three. Not that it makes much difference to me any more. I usually have a nap in my chair by the fire after lunch these days for an hour, or maybe two while Ann helps Fanny for a while in the tavern. Thankfully we can burn the fire all day while it is this cold. The money George sends us from his ship means we can remain warm. He is a good boy. Today, being Saturday and not a school day means Ann is playing with little George.

It is raining hard and there is little going on at the harbour, and even less reason for me to go out. I light my old pipe and let the tobacco smoke curl around my head, as I gaze quietly at the orange flames licking around the blackened logs in the fireplace. The fire occasionally crackles and pops. With my eyes half closed I can see the whole world in that fireplace. The flames and the charred lumps of timber dance and shift into new shapes to reveal ships, and places, and the faces of people that I have known in my long life.

It is comfortable here in my warm chair by the fire with my memories. As comfortable as an old man with arthritis and worries can be. I will soon be seventy. This is a very old age and this last year I have started to feel *very* old.

For years I was strong and sharp and able to overcome any man. Nor was I afraid of any storm. But now my strength has gone. I find it hard to lift heavy things due to the pains in my fingers and arms, and sometimes I fairly lose my balance in a strong wind out on the quay.

I never used to worry like this. I worry about how Ann will cope when I am gone. Little George is only six and hardly sees his brother. I will be long gone before he is a man – who will bring him up? It is a lot to ask of poor Fanny. She has a huge heart but she has never been physically strong. She struggles to run the tavern and look after little George at the same time. And Mother and I are not getting any younger. We rely on the income from the Crown and the money that George earns at sea and sends home to us.

I feel sorry for Fanny having to shoulder such responsibility so young, before she has had a life of her own.

Then there is George. Was it right to send him to sea or would it have been better if he'd stayed at home? Life can change so much on a single decision.

If George was here running the Crown perhaps it would be easier, and he could bring up his two boys together instead of them being forever separated. He might have even been able to carry on with the mill. And Fanny would have more freedom to go and find a husband, and have some time for herself.

As it is George has gone to sea. He always dreamt of sailing the world as a boy and I encouraged him as I loved being a mariner too. And now he is there he doesn't want to come home. He has been back at sea now for three years since he first reported to Southampton. He earns good money as a mariner, because it can be a dangerous life. He earns more in three months at sea than he could here in a tavern or as a miller in a whole year, and he is generous giving all his spare wages to Mother and I to keep us comfortable and to pay for the little Georgie and Henry.

George was here for a few days at Christmas and, although he was pleased to see George and Fanny and Mother and me he was keen to get back to his ship. I can see that George loves the sea – it is in his blood, just as it was for me. He is still a young man – only twenty-five, with years of adventures on the oceans in front of him.

I fear George will not know his sons, especially Henry, as he is away so much. I was away at sea for many years but Ann was always here to bring up our children. With no wife George's two boys are like castaways. It is dreadful how poor Sarah's death has changed the lives of so many people – George, their sons, Mother and I, Fanny and Matilda and Richard.

I worry about Richard. He is not in good health. He also used to be a mariner but he can no longer go to sea as he has no strength. Matilda runs the White Hart tavern at Littlehampton and looks after her daughter Ann as well as Henry. I know Matilda finds it hard. She is not having any more children. I think she is taking in lodgers to get more money. I worry what will become of them if Richard doesn't get well again.

I draw deeply on my pipe. Do all parents worry about their children until their dying day?

I wonder if my parents worried about me? When I was a young man I wouldn't have wanted my parents to worry about me. I was happy working hard, sailing the seas, taking my chances, having my adventures. I loved the sound of the wind in the sails and the rigging, putting a smile on a tavern girl's face, and seeing a golden dawn in the sky and upon the sea in front of my ship. Had I drowned in a storm or been killed by a pirate I wouldn't have wanted my parents to be worried. I was enjoying my adventures. Perhaps that was selfish? Perhaps I shouldn't worry so much about George?

When George was here at Christmas he was talking of trying to get passage to the Americas or the Caribbean. He likes the warmer climates, and I think still holds his dreams of Robinson Crusoe on a desert island of fine white sands and green swaying palm trees. I worry about these places as they have fearsome storms and diseases. I know the ships today are bigger and stronger. In my days it was mostly sailing ships, but now George tells me of the powerful steam engines that can send his vessels against the strongest tides.

I have seen seas with which no steam engine could contend. In the end survival at sea relies only upon luck, and God's Will. In his young life George has already had more than his fair share of misfortune. I continue to pray for good luck for him.

I worry that George's dreams may yet be scuppered. If Mother and I depart this life George may have to leave off the sea for a while to look after his boys.

Perhaps worrying is futile. If only I could see into the future.

I have heard it said that God looks down and laughs at men who are foolish enough to try to make plans for the future.

I will try not to worry so much.

[*Price, 3d.*]   487 — 4   A.9.

CERTIFICATE OF DISCHARGE.

NAME OF SHIP.	Rakaia
OFFICIAL NO.	54 660
PORT OF REGISTRY.	London
REGISTERED TONNAGE.	907
DESCRIPTION OF VOYAGE OR EMPLOYMENT.	Mail Service
NAME OF SEAMAN	Geo Wm Eastland
PLACE OF BIRTH	Chichester
DATE OF BIRTH	1843
CAPACITY.	Cf Steward
DATE OF ENTRY.	17 April/66
DATE OF DISCHARGE.	2 March/68
PLACE OF DISCHARGE.	Sydney

I CERTIFY that the above particulars are correct, and that the above Seaman was discharged accordingly.

DATED this   5   day of   March   186 8

Witness--   A H R Shorter   (Signed)   F Harry Wright

                                          Master of the Ship.

s m 15---67

Conduct……..VG…………………………..
Character……….VG……………………….
Qualification…… VG………………………
Master declines as to………………………..

       J W M Shorter   Shipping Master.

Panama, New Zealand & Australian Royal Mail Co
("LIMITED")
Sydney Melbourne & New Zealand

31ˢᵗ March 1868

Mr George Eastland joined this Company's Steamer "Rakaia" in Glasgow in April 1866 and up to the present has held the position of Chief Steward under me during the vessels various passages from Sydney to Panama and back; he has conducted his duties in such a manner as to give entire satisfaction to the passengers, and now leaves at his own wish with the view of advancing his position in the Intercolonial Branch of this Company's service. I have every confidence in recommending him as a thoroughly sober steady & persevering man, besides being a good pen man & accountant.

C P Farnfield

Purser R M S "Rakaia"

This is to certify that Mr G.W. Eastland served on board the R.M.S. "Rakaia" as storekeeper for a period of 3 months & 21 months as Chief Steward making a period of two years service. He has faithfully & efficiently fulfilled his duties and conducted himself with strict standards & sobriety. I can strongly recommend him.

He leaves this ship on promotion to purser.

F Harry Wright

Com R= R.M.S
"Rakaia"

Wellington N.Z.

April 7/68

Panama, New Zealand & Australian Royal Mail Company, Limited

Sydney and New Zealand

Wellington 8th Dec 18 68

I hereby certify that Mr G.W. Eastland served with me as Purser on board the Panama Companys S.S. "Lord Ashley" for a period of eight months, from May 68. to Decr. 68. during which time I feel great pleasure in stating that Mr G.W. Eastland conducted himself to my entire satisfaction with the greatest sobriety perseverance and zeal.

J V Nicols
Commander S.S. "Ld Ashley"

Conduct V.G.

Ability V.G.

CC.5. See paragraph 18. Colonial Officers Instructions.

MARINE DEPARTMT
COM. OF COUNCIL FOR TRADE

Sobriety V.G.

SANCTIONED BY THE BOARD OF TRADE, In pursuance of The Merchant Shipping Act, 1854.

CERTIFICATE OF DISCHARGE.
For Seamen discharged before a duly appointed Officer in a British Possession abroad.

Name and Official Number of Ship.	Lord Ashley
Port of Registry.	Grimsby
Tonnage.	296
Description of Voyage or Employment.	Coasting
Name of Seaman.	Geo Wm Eastland
Place of Birth.	Chichester
Date of Birth.	1842
Number of Fund Ticket (if any).	------
Capacity.	Purser
Date of Entry.	28/5/68
Date of Discharge.	9/12/68
Place of Discharge.	Wellington

I certify, That the above particulars are correct, and that the above-named Seaman was discharged accordingly.

Dated this 9th day of Decr 18 68

(Signed) A M Crisps Master.

(Countersigned) _____ Seaman.
Dated at Wellington, and given to the above-named Seaman in my presence, this 9th day of Decr 18 68

M N Grant & Com Signature and Title of Officer.

NOTE. –If the Seaman discharged was possessed of a certificate of competency or service, and it is held by the Master, the Officer before whom the Seaman is discharged will see that it is restored to him.

LONDON: Printed by GEORGE E. EYRE and WILLIAM SPOTTISWOODE, Printers to the Queen's most Excellent Majesty.

Panama, New Zealand & Australian Royal Mail Company, Limited

Sydney and New Zealand

Wellington 1st March 1869.

This is to certify, that Mr George William Eastland, served this Company, as Purser of their Steam Ships, "Lord Ashley", "Airedale", & "Egmont", from April 1868, until February 1869, & discharged his duties in a zealous, faithful manner, to my entire satisfaction, that of the Co's Superintendent Purser, & the Commanders under whom he sailed.

The dissolution of the Company is the cause of his leaving.

H McPherson

General Manager

P.N.Z. & A.R.M. Co LIMITED

Sydney 15th March 1869

This is to certify that Mr Geor Wm Eastland has been employed in the Panama & New Zealand Royal Mail Company's service for a period of two years & ten months — the first two years he was Chief Steward on board the S.S. "Rakaia" running our Panama route - & the remaining ten months he was Purser on board steamers employed on Interprovincial routes - during the whole of the above time he uniformly conducted himself with the greatest sobriety & propriety & gave the Commanders under whom he served every reason to be satisfied with the manner in which he performed his various duties — & from my own observation I believe him to be an efficient & trustworthy servant.

Mrn Frouds

Marine Superintendent

ROYAL MAIL S.P.COMPY SOUTHAMPTON

CERTIFICATE OF DISCHARGE

FOR SEAMEN DISCHARGED BEFORE THE SUPERINTENDENT OF A MERCANTILE MARINE OFFICE IN THE UNITED KINGDOM, A BRITISH CONSUL, OR A SHIPPPING OFFICER IN BRITISH POSSESSION ABROAD.

Name of Ship.	Ruahine
Officl Number.	52749
Port of Registry	London
Registd Tonnage	1018
Horse Power of Engines (if any)	350
Description of Voyage or Employment	Mail Service
Name of Seaman.	G. Eastland
Age.	26
Place of Birth.	Chichester
N4 of R.N.R. Commissn. or Certif.	—
Capacity. If Mate or Engineer No. of Certif. (if any)	Chief Steward
Date of Engagement.	18 Mch. 69
Place of Engagement.	Sydney
Date of Discharge.	3 June. 69
Place of Discharge.	Southampton

I certify that the above particulars are correct, and that the above named Seaman was discharged accordingly*, and that the character described on the other side hereof is a true copy of the Report concerning the said Seaman.

Dated this 3 day of June 1869.   AUTHENTICATED BY Standy

JHCB Barhe   MASTER   SIGNATURE OF SUPERT. CONSUL. OR SHIPPING OFFICER

NOTE. Any person who makes, assists in making or procures to be made any false Certificate or Report of the Service, Qualifications, Conduct, or Character of any Seaman, or who forges, assists in forging, or procures to be forged, or fraudulently alters, assists in fraudulently altering, or procures to be fraudulently altered, any such Certificate or Report, or who fraudulently makes use of any Certificate or Report, or of any Copy of any Certificate or Report which is forged or altered or does not belong to him, shall for each such offence be deemed guilty of a misdemeanour and may be fined or imprisoned.

Character for Ability in whatever Capacity engaged.   VG

Character for Conduct.   VG

Saturday 5th June 1869

Harvest celebration in a large barn near Birdham, 7pm

George William Eastland.

On the ship I know not to drink. My livelihood, and that of my sons, depends on me staying sober. Although I am no longer Barman or Pantryman and in charge of the ship's liquor, I am now of more senior rank and it is even more important that I remain sober and reliable at all times. During the last year or two I have been either Purser or Chief Steward on the ships upon which I have served. I am more or less teetotal when at sea.

Perhaps that is why the strong punch at this Harvest celebration is affecting me. I have grown unaccustomed to alcohol. With a week or two from the sea I am back home at Dell Quay with my family. I decided to join in the merriment this evening and for a change to have a drink, or two.

I do not know what the farmers' wives put into this punch in these large jugs but it has a kick. I feel light and gay, and perhaps I shall dance to the fiddler's bright tunes on this sticky, sultry evening.

There is quite a crowd of people, young and old. The ale and the punch is flowing. Some of the young farm girls look quite comely. Some are dancing, with a flash of their brown legs as their white dresses flick up and their milky white chests ripple with the dance. I recognise one of them – a pretty young girl who I remember coming to Dell Quay and into the Crown and Anchor. This was some years ago now, when Father and I were running the mill. I remember that pretty face but her name escapes me – perhaps it was Hazel, or Heather or something similar?

I fill myself another jug of the deep red punch and find myself next to Mary Clayton who I have not seen since I went back to sea.

'Hello George,' she says with an uncertain smile. 'I was sorry to hear...' We both fall silent.

Mary hasn't changed. Her long blond hair tumbles over her shoulders into her full pink bosom which seems fuller than when I last saw her.

'Mary, have a drink,' I say and pour her a jug of the punch. We sit on a wooden bench and drink from our jugs. A smile crosses Mary's rosy cheeks as the warming liquid flows through both our bodies. Mary's ample bosom is turning red even before my eyes.

'We should dance, George. It has been a long time since you took me in your arms.'

It has been a long time since I have taken any woman in my arms, I think to myself.

'Are you still at the farm?' I ask. 'I am, and still awaiting my lost mariner to come and sweep me away.'

I see Mary still has no rings on her fingers even though she must by now be around thirty.

Mary and I dance, and in between dances we quench our thirsts with more of the punch. We hold onto each other as we sway to the music, a little more intoxicated with each jar of punch as the evening proceeds. I like the feel of Mary's hips as they push into mine and the smell of her hair against my cheek. It is so long since I felt the touch of a woman that I am starting to ache. Mary pushes her tongue into my mouth and grins up at me, those light blue eyes of hers twinkling through her lashes.

At the end of a hot and sticky dance we each collect another refill of the punch. Mary takes my hand and leads me from the barn into the now thankfully cooler evening air outside. The late red sun hangs over the horizon and our long shadows stretch all the way along the path in front of us.

Mary leads me by the hand through the farmyard to a smaller barn. We enter to find this barn contains some farm machinery and a loose stack of sweet-smelling hay into which the pair of us tumble with our drinks. We soon empty our glasses and attend to more pressing matters.

Mary pulls the ribbon bows holding the top of her white cloth dress together and rolls towards me, kissing me greedily upon my mouth. Her sleeve slips from her shoulder and her very full milky breast finds its way into my hand, her swollen brown nipple pressing into my palm.

We tumble a little deeper into the hay and feel the warmth of each others' bodies as we lie facing one another. Mary's hand travels downwards into my breeches and her hot grip makes me gasp.

I reach behind Mary with my left hand and fumble through countless layers of fabric until I feel her cool smooth skin. My fingers glide over Mary's generous bottom and down still further. My fingertips edge into her coarse mass of hair and become wet with her juices. Mary's thighs part as she slides smoothly onto me.

I remember little else of the evening. I must have slept for some time. I am woken by a young lady who says her name is Hellen. Her face seems familiar, though I can't place her. Perhaps we were at school together? Mary is gone.

It is dark. Hellen carries a lantern and has a shawl over her head and shoulders. 'You must leave, George. You must not be found here like this.' The young lady helps me to my feet and takes away the empty punch jugs.

A little shaky at first I stumble along. Hellen leads me through the darkest trees and behind a hedge to the road, by which time I am steadier on my feet. She bids me farewell and I feel her warm hand brush my arm, before she disappears back into the shadows in the direction of the farmhouse. The road is well lit by the nearly full moon and I walk along its edge.

A while along the lane I am startled by the flap of wings as a large barn owl swoops low upon its prey, but I see or hear nothing of the mouse that the owl slaughters.

I am slowly revived by the cool night air by the time I reach the Crown and Anchor. All is dark and quiet. I do not know what time it is. I sit on the doorstep and remove my boots, before entering and climbing the stairs as quietly as I can. I fall onto my bed and in moments I am asleep.

Sunday 6th June 1869

Crown & Anchor, Dell Quay, 10.25am

George William Eastland.

I am lying in this deep, soft mound of hay when I become aware of a sharp prod in my chest. I try to sleep on but the prodding continues and becomes more insistent.

I open my eyes and realise Mary is sitting naked astride me, her large breasts swaying as she pokes her thumb into my chest. I don't remember her breasts being quite this heavy and swollen before.

'Why won't you marry me George, why...?' Mary glares at me as she stabs her thumb into my flesh.

'You have had your way with me and now you must marry me. I carry your child...'

The prodding continues and I cry, 'No,' and try to push Mary from me.

This is when I awake to find little George lying upon me and pushing me with his finger, and with Henry and Fanny just behind him in my bedroom.

'Good morning George. I think you must have been dreaming. Did you enjoy the Harvest celebration?' Fanny looks at me with an inquisitive grin. I take a deep breath and try to calm my racing heart as I recover my senses.

'Daddy, Daddy get up,' George squeals in my ear.

'Time to be up, sleepy head,' Fanny adds. 'Come and play with your sons. Matilda has come over from Littlehampton so you must come downstairs to see everybody.'

'What time is it?' I blink.

'It's gone half past ten and high time even for a drunken sailor to shake a leg.'

George and Henry start to pull my arms.

I spend some time on the quay with my boys. They each dangle twine with a hook and bread attached into the water hoping to catch a fish. I sit and watch them as the sun burns hot on my arm. George is now eight and Henry seven. They have grown so fast and it feels like I hardly know them. Apart from a few visits home in the last few years I have been away at sea for much of their short lives.

Intent on their fishing the boys stand apart and hardly talk to each other. It dawns on me that they scarcely know each other – I don't even know when they were last together?

A little later we all sit around the table for the lunch prepared by Mother and Fanny. It reminds me of my childhood with all my sisters at the table at mealtimes. Of course Mary, Nancy and Martha are not here today but Father is here, unlike during my childhood when he was frequently at sea. When I was a boy family meals were mostly shared with Mother and my five sisters. Today seems strange to me as the males outnumber the females.

Father raises his glass, 'To George – back with his sons on dry land.'

'To George and his sons.'

George and Henry are hungry for their food and say nothing. The adults have endless questions and news to share.

'So how is the White Hart, Matilda?'

'Business is good and we have three lodgers so we can afford to eat well, but it is hard running the inn with Richard so ill.'

'Is he getting any better?'

'No. If anything the pains are worse. Sometimes he cannot even get out of bed to help in the tavern.'

'How do you manage with Ann and Henry, Matilda?'

'I get very tired but our barmaids work hard, and I can get some time away from the bar to cook the children dinner. We also have a lodger – Isaac. He is a gasfitter but he is such a help. He moves the kegs and stocks the bar when Richard cannot, and all for a tankard of ale. I couldn't manage without him. Isaac is a very good man.'

'Is trade good in The Crown, Mother?'

'Not very. It's not like it used to be when I was younger. But it is enough to keep Fanny busy, and with her having to look after George as well as us two old crocks. It is just as well we don't have the crowds we used to have when the harbour was busier.'

Fanny nudges me in the ribs. 'I'll bet the bar on your ship is busier isn't it George, with all those thirsty mariners clamouring for ale?'

'Plenty of ale and rum is drunk aboard ship, 'tis true. You can't trust the water in many overseas places and milk is scarce, so ale is the safest thing to drink for mariners if you want to avoid a bad stomach.'

'So why did you give up the Dell Quay mill, Father?'

'Age is catching up on me, son. I no longer have the strength to run the mill, and all the lifting was hard on my back. Running the harbour and the tavern is enough for me now.'

Father pierces me with his blue eyes. 'How are you finding life as a mariner, George?'

'I love being at sea, Father, and I do a good job. I am hoping to be promoted so I can earn more money."

'Where have you sailed to, George?'

'I have been to all the UK harbours and Ireland. In the last three years I have been working for the Panama, New Zealand and Australian Royal Mail Company as Chief Steward and Purser. The mail ships sail through the wonderful blue seas around the coast of the two islands of New Zealand – the South and North Islands. We call regularly at Wellington, Auckland, Lyttelton and Bluff Bay.

'New Zealand is a wonderfully pretty place with blue rocky coves and rushing waterfalls, while inland from the beaches rise high purple mountains capped with dazzling white snow. It was such a pity the Panama Mail Company was wound up, as delivering the Mails in New Zealand and Australia was a wonderful life.

'I have heard the Royal Mail Steam Package contracts out of Southampton are growing. I know someone who might be able to get me onto one of the routes.'

'Where might that take you?' Mother asks.

'The Caribbean. I have always dreamt of sailing to tropical islands like Robinson Crusoe did.'

Fanny chuckles, 'I hope you don't get shipwrecked and have to live in a mud hut with a parrot!'

'Those tropical places can be dangerous.' Father looks concerned, and adds, 'I have heard the dangers from pirates, tropical storms and diseases are worse in those islands.'

'I have heard these tales as well, Father. But the big iron hull steam ships can ride the storms better these days, and the pay on the long tropical routes is very good. I miss my boys and I know you and Mother and Matilda cannot look after them forever. No, I plan to have myself a well paid job for a couple of years to save lots of money. There is a ship due to sail out of Southampton on 10th July for Australia. From there I may be able to find a ship to the Caribbean.

'Once I have made my fortune I will come back to Chichester and buy a cottage with a piece of land to farm, and I will settle down with George and Henry.'

'And perhaps it is time for you to find another wife, George?' Mother watches my face intently.

'Maybe you are right, Mother. There will never be another Sarah, but maybe you are right. But there's no good me looking for a wife while I'm sailing far and wide. When I come home to Chichester that may be the time to find me a wife.'

'I hear Mary Clayton could use a good husband...' Fanny flashes a mischievous grin in my direction.

Mother retorts, 'Off you go Fanny and wash the dishes. I never liked that one. I can't put my finger on it.'

'I'll help,' says Matilda, and calling to George and Henry, 'Come on boys, you can help to dry the plates and put them away before you go out to play.'

I have never really understood why Mother is so against Mary. The Claytons are a good family and Mary has always had a liking for me. But the memory of my dream reminds me what I have always known in my heart – that Mary isn't the wife for me.

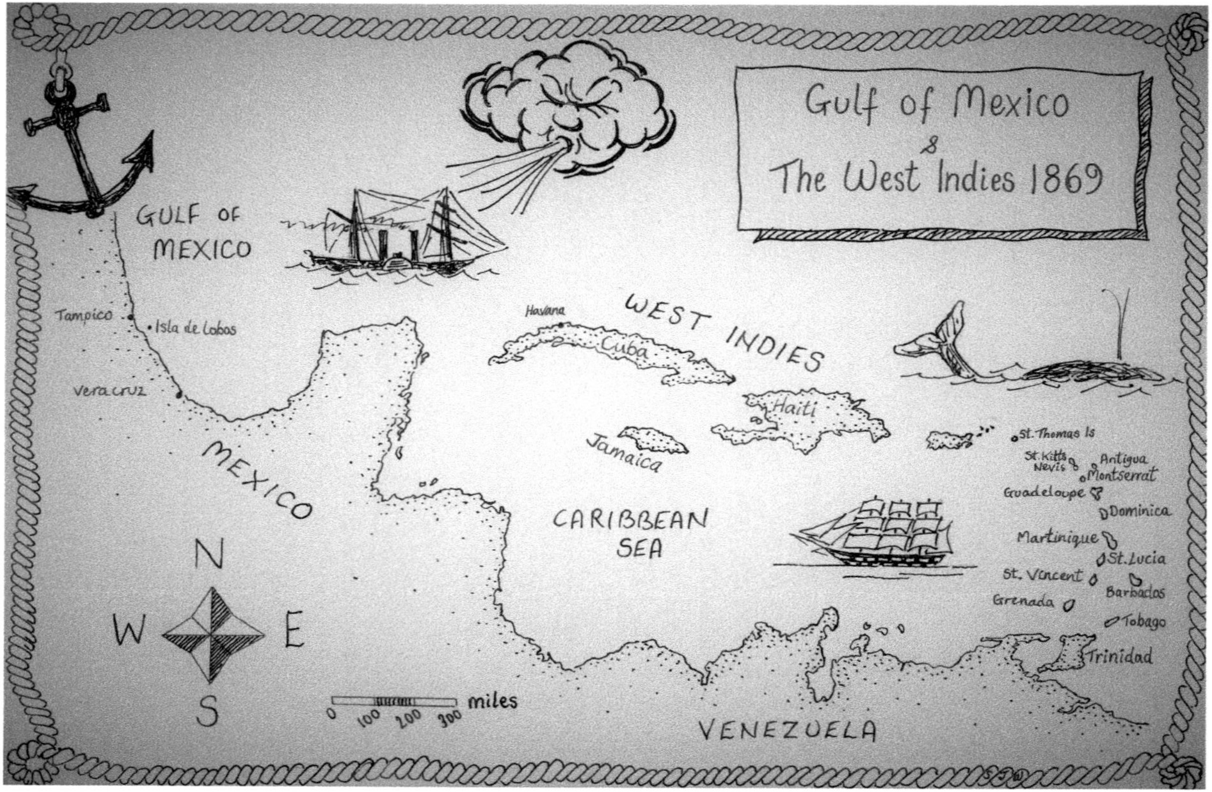
Gulf of Mexico
&
The West Indies 1869
GULF OF
MEXICO
Tampico
Isla de Lobos
Veracruz
MEXICO
Havana
WEST INDIES
Cuba
Haiti
Jamaica
CARIBBEAN
SEA
St. Thomas Is
St. Kitts
Nevis
Antigua
Montserrat
Guadeloupe
Dominica
Martinique
St. Lucia
St. Vincent
Barbados
Grenada
Tobago
Trinidad
VENEZUELA
N
W
E
S
0 100 200 300 miles

Saturday 17th July 1869

Mail Ship "Egmont", Adelaide, Australia 8.00pm

George William Eastland.

I am lying in my cabin having been appointed Purser on this Intercolonial Mail Steamer, resting at last after many weeks of sailing.

When I left Dell Quay on the other side of the world some six weeks ago I was both happy and sad. I was full of anticipation for a long posting in the exotic Caribbean if I could get it, as I fully intend to enjoy a year or two in the tropical sun to make my fortune. I will then take extended shore leave, buy a cottage near Chichester and look after my boys now that Father and Mother are getting too old.

I also left Dell Quay with a heavy heart knowing I will not see George and Henry for a year or more. Early one June morning I set off for Chichester carrying my large sacks of belongings, and caught the train to Southampton where I reported straight away to the Royal Mail Provedore Department for work.

Southampton was busy with traders, mariners and passengers converging on the town for the weekend sailings. The wealthiest passengers and their servants stay at one of the grand hotels adjoining the quay and custom-house, including the Royal George, the Sun, the Castle, the Dolphin, the Star and Radley's New Hotel near the railway terminus.

Poorer passengers stay at one of the many less endowed establishments in the old town. In advance of a sailing some passengers and mariners indulge in the many pleasures and casual distractions of the lower town, sometimes delighting in them so much that they miss their sailing. Woe betide any such loafer who attempts to demand that his fare be refunded on account of one hundred tales of misfortune. The regulations clearly state that any passenger missing his ship will forfeit half the passage-money. The ticket sellers will not back down and are not the sort to pick a fight with. For a start they are part of an army of very strong and hardy port workers.

Before I boarded my ship I had an hour or two to myself. I have never previously explored the town so decided to look around, and to my surprise I found it to be quite as historic as Chichester. There are old town walls where it was once enclosed, and other remains all built using large grey stones. God's House Tower stands near the sea and in the middle of the town is the Bargate. It is an old gate of curious structure, its north front being a kind of semi-octagon, with semi-circular turrets, towers and battlements.

There were few mariners at the Bargate. Most were in the town's many ale-houses. I stumbled upon Lankesters iron works at the Holy Rood Foundry, and remembered I may need a proper secure safe for this long voyage in which to keep my money, my gun and other valuables. If I cannot find one at a favourable price I may need to ask Father to send me one from Chichester.

Once our sea-voyage was underway we worked our way southwards experiencing the usual variable European weather. Once upon the ocean I somehow feel more alive with the power, the grandeur and the delicious fresh air of the seas. It is another world – a wonderful world that most men will never experience.

The westerly winds fly in from the wide Atlantic driving the long swell of deep blue water, and the ship groans and creaks through the whole of her mighty frame as she plunges through these great rolling watery hills. Everyone aboard sways and staggers – there is no rest on deck – the sick retreat to their beds. And then comes another day and another night followed by the Bay of Biscay.

Here the waves rise with a power beyond all imagination. They are not like the waves in The Channel which heave - discoloured, broken and bothered by the many obstructions. These are like deep-blue cliffs of water which reach to the sky to tower above our ship, coming on with unfathomable force and with never a break, swooping down as if to engulf us. The third wave is the largest yet. It hangs over us for an instant, with its crest curled, as if it will surely swallow us in its briny depths. We rise to meet it as it comes bearing the heavy ship high on its back, and rushing up to the nettings at our feet - before slowly subsiding and receding at the other side, only to rise again and again.

And the ship glides on faster than before in the trough left by the receding wave.

I stand as far aft as I can, my back to the taffrail and look forward to the bowsprit, from where I marvel at the long beautiful line of the deck. How gracefully the ship glides with the surge of the wild seas. She bends and sways and rides over all that rushes beneath her brave timbers allowing not a drop of green water to wash over her deck.

Another night and we reached the latitude of Lisbon. The weather which was till now squally with rain became pleasant and warm and the sun shone out with gratitude. Fires were no longer needed, cloaks were discarded and crowds were upon the decks – crowds that had previously cowered invisibly in the quarters below. Sea-birds flew past, or hung on the sea-drafts as they accompanied our ship.

Appetites returned. The sea was now smooth, the air warm, and the moon, though young, shed a bright glow. It shimmered so high above us that it hardly cast our shadows upon the deck.

Our voyaging continued down into the southern hemisphere and the weeks sailed by. As the skies became bluer so did the seas. And my skin once again turned browner - and dry as old canvas.

Once we rounded the Cape of Good Hope at the southernmost tip of Africa we caught the eastern trade winds and fairly flew across the Indian Ocean to Australia. This part of the world feels like home territory to me as I have been working here on various intercolonial mail routes for most of the last three years, plying the seas between Australia and New Zealand,.

I feel quite safe out here. The seas are clean and fresh with usually a healthy breeze to blow away the mosquitos and other diseases. Privateers were a big threat twenty or thirty years ago but they and other pirate ships are rare these days, and the modern ships I sail on are well prepared with guns of all sorts to deal with any foe. The Aborigine tribes are also more settled now. A few years ago they too would sometimes attack white men, but all now seem to live side by side in Australia with only occasional disturbance.

I have mostly sailed in and out of Sydney, which is a place that has seen a huge influx of new settlers in recent years. It is a place where people come from all over the world to seek their fortunes in gold and diamond mining. The Queensland Gold Rush of 1859 is long past and they say the gold is getting scarcer to find. But even on our ship there were several gold prospectors bright eyed and keen to make their fortunes, all loaded with their pans and picks, and their gold-miner's cradles. I would rather do an honest day's work for an honest wage than scrabble in the streams and the dust, baked under the high Australian sun in the uncertain pursuit of a lucky strike.

Of course many more people have come to live in Australia this century on the convict ships. They say the ship that unloaded its cargo of two hundred and seventy-nine convicts from England last year will be the last such ship to come to Australia. I'll be surprised if that is the case. There are always more convicts in England to deal with.

At this time of year the days are quite short. The sun is up at seven in the morning but down again by five o'clock in the afternoon. When I first came out here it struck me how suddenly night comes in this part of the world. The afternoon passes and the large fiery sun sinks all at once onto the line of the horizon, then down and darkness comes all of an instant. But the stars are bigger and brighter than in England under the clear night skies, so it is never truly dark as it is back home.

Today we approached land along the southern coast of Australia where the Indian and the Southern Oceans meet. The sight of land after days at sea is always a pleasure. Beyond the blue waters I saw slopes of lush green vegetation rise from the sea, and behind them the hazy purple peaks of mountain ridges. Our ship was accompanied by countless sea creatures including long-tailed rays, octopus and playful dolphins that love to leap out of the waves alongside our ship. They always seem to have a smile for us.

We were hurried along by the winds and the choppy seas which bore us swiftly eastwards on our way to Adelaide, until we came to the Cape Borda lighthouse at the western tip of Kangaroo Island. The lighthouse guided us inland and towards the wide river, and on towards the sheltered harbour where we have laid up for the night.

Some mariners get off the ship as soon as they can and head for the taverns but not I. I am tired, and there are plenty of mosquitoes buzzing under the trees on the shore which are keen to feast on the tender flesh of fresh white mariners. I am happy to avoid that insect ambush. Nor am I hungry for the taverns and their wenches, though plenty of our crew members are after the long voyage at sea. I prefer to sit comfortably here where I can enjoy my glass of grog and write a letter home. I have found some very smart-looking Royal Mail Steam Packet Company letter-headed paper to write on. That will surely impress Father and Mother to see how well I am doing. I will be able to catch the Mail back to Southampton from here.

In the next few days the "Egmont" will work its way along the coast to Sydney. I have spoken to others with whom I have previously sailed, and I believe I shall be able to secure my boarding there to take me into the Royal Mail Service in the Caribbean at last. Then I shall make some good money.

I shall also enjoy those charming desert islands that I have been dreaming of ever since I was a boy. The crystal clear blue waters, the wash of the waves on the fine white sands, the red and golden sunsets behind the spiky outline of palm trees, the warm evening sun and gentle sea breeze on my face, the aroma of a fresh cigar and the fire of rum from a sparkling cut glass tumbler as it burns my throat.

This is the life of a true mariner.

Royal Mail Steam Packet Company,
Provedore Department,
Southampton,   July 17th 18 69

Dear Father & Mother

I here enclose the order on the Company for £10 which you will forward to London about next Tuesday. I am quite well hoping you are all the same. My dearest parents I did not see Miss Purchase. I hope you will write me long letters and write every Mail hoping to find you all well when I return. I have not received my money yet for the Slops[1]. I am afraid I shall not get it until the next Mail. I got through last night all safe please to kiss little Georgie for me and tell him I shall be home in twelve months give my love to Fanny when you write to me. I must now say good bye and believe me to remain

your affectionate Son   Geo. Wm. Eastland

<u>Direct</u>
G. M. Lloyds Esq.
55 Moorgate Street   London E.C.

---

[1] Ready-made clothing and other furnishings from the ship's stores sold from the Purser's chest to the seamen. The cost of slops purchased were deducted from a sailor's pay, with a portion going to the Purser.

[Price, 3d.] St.499.   4926 — 4

A.9.

CERTIFICATE OF DISCHARGE

NAME OF SHIP.	Egmont
OFFICIAL NO.	50089
PORT OF REGISTRY.	London
REGISTERED TONNAGE.	809
DESCRIPTION OF VOYAGE OR EMPLOYMENT	Intercolonial
Name of Seaman.	Geo. Wm Eastland
Place of Birth.	Chichester
Date of Birth.	1844
Capacity.	Purser
Date of Entry.	16 July/69
Date of Discharge.	24 July/69
Place of Discharge.	Sydney

I CERTIFY that the above particulars are correct, and that the above Seaman was discharged accordingly.

DATED this 26 day of July 186 9

Witness N.M.B.Strorter (Signed) J.V.Mitchell

Master of the Ship.

Conduct   VG
Character   VG
Qualification   VG
Master declines as to _____

N.M.B.Strorter Shipping Master.

277

Friday 30th July 1869

St. Thomas Island, Caribbean

on the Royal Mail Ship "Tamar"

George William Eastland.

The contrast between the harbour at Sydney and that of St. Thomas Island could hardly be greater. Sydney is all noise, the bustle of trade and industry, and dust.
We steamed out of the harbour passing what remains of the last decaying black prison hulks that not so long ago were used to house convicts from England. These old wrecks rise like giant ghostly edifices from the water, still harbouring lost and miserable secrets from their wretched histories. Pieces of rotten timber and rusted metal jut out from the hulks, clinging on in defiance until their inevitable fall and splash into the watery depths below.
When the "Egmont" slipped into the harbour at St. Thomas it was like arriving in Paradise. Our ship entered through the narrow inlet from the sea into the large sheltered bay within. My eyes watered such is the beauty of this bay with its clear pale blue water surrounded by hills and mountains, and with the town at the far side of the bay, its single-storey white buildings gleaming in the sunlight. Rising behind the town are three pretty conical mountains.
To the left of the bay as we entered was a large hill with a fort upon it looking very grand. On the other side of the bay on more high hillsides are two more old fortresses.
Everything is here on this colourful tropical paradise island to make a young man happy. The lush trees are covered in bright pink and yellow flowers, and the sun shines all day out of the brilliant blue sky. The flat sea sparkles as far as my eyes can see.
Our ship anchored some half a mile from the landing places where all arriving ships have to wait to be visited by the harbour-master. His main concern is to ensure we are carrying no dangerous sickness on board. As soon as he was reassured on this account a flotilla of shore boats came to the "Egmont" to take passengers and crew members

wishing to go ashore, for the sum of one shilling and threepence each person.

As soon as my duties were completed upon our ship I took one of these shore boats to go and see what Paradise looked like for myself. When I got ashore I found St. Thomas is a hive of activity with much trade and commerce going on.

All manner of goods are available to buy here – silver and jewellery, liquor and tobacco. I was sorely tempted to buy some white attire as all the best dressed mariners and natives wear white to fend off the raging sun, but I dared not spend my savings. I will purchase a full set of whites when I return to the island after I am paid my next wage.

It is now the start of the hurricane season. It is still very hot – 90° in the shade. While I was on shore the rain suddenly came down. It is not like any rain you will ever see in Chichester. Just like the air, the rain is warm. From nowhere it comes down like a waterfall. Everybody dives into the nearest building for shelter, as you would be drenched in a second the rain falls so hard. Almost immediately the water runs down the streets like streams, and doorways are blocked with boards and other barriers to stop the streams running in. Then, as instantly as the waterfall started to pour it stops again, as if God has put a huge stopper into the rain hole in the sky. Ten minutes later the sun is shining brightly, everybody is back about their business and everything is dry so that you can hardly believe it ever rained.

Some of the ship's crew returned with all manner of exotic purchases. The antiquities and treasures look very striking and unusual, and will doubtless cause great intrigue and fascination when they are eventually taken home to families back in England. I will not be tempted to fritter my hard-earned cash on frivolous artefacts, for doing so will mean I shall have to risk my life in these hot and dangerous climates for longer. I will buy only what I need to survive, and will instead send all my savings home for Father and Mother to use, and to put in the bank for George and Henry. I will not stray from this purpose. I must get a safe to store my money and other valuables. I have little yet, but once I am paid I will need somewhere safe for my wages.

The ale on St. Thomas is cheap and the Caribbean ladies smile constantly, their white teeth gleaming from their brown faces, and they move with a becoming rhythm and sway. The bare pink soles of their feet seem to feel no stones. It is just how I imagined Paradise to be when I was a boy – only it is colourful so to dazzle my eyes almost to blindness. When I enter a dark tavern I can see nothing but blackness.

Yet I am restless and cannot settle my mind. I have left the "Egmont" and she has returned to Sydney. My pay from that passage means I have money now to stay in St. Thomas while I wait for my Caribbean Mail Steamer to arrive. It causes me angst to be spending money when I am unable to earn a wage until my ship arrives. I am resting up in the harbour on R.M.S. "Tamar" while I wait. I may have to wait a week or two yet.

I must remember that when my Steamer comes I will have work for a year, and I will then earn plenty of money to send to Father and Mother and for my boys. I must be patient. But I have waited so long to sail in the Caribbean that this new delay is bothersome.

A sea breeze blows into the cabin to keep me refreshingly cool. I leave the glass open all day, though the harbour is busy and noisy with loud voices of many tongues – English, Spanish, French and others.

When I was on the "Egmont" I was told there was Yellow Fever on St. Thomas Island. The people here look healthy enough to me. Every ship encounters some sickness, fever and belly ache. If I am careful I will stay healthy. I always use my mosquito net and shut the glass and cabin door at night when I sleep, despite the heat. I'd rather sweat than catch the Fever. I do not drink excessive ale though there is nothing else here safe to drink, and it is frightful thirsty weather. Some taverns collect rainwater to drink and there is plenty of ice shipped in from America, but I would not trust any of it. The ale is thankfully cheap.

I will be glad when my ship arrives and I can be off to sea where it is always much healthier.

I received a letter today in the Mail from Father. I am pained because he has not sent me a single newspaper or magazine, which I would have truly appreciated while I am wasting my time here waiting for my ship. When I write to Father I will remind him to send me papers next time for my entertainment, and so I can keep up with life in England.

Father's letter told me of things in Birdham that I would rather not have heard. It seems as if that common scullery-maid Miss Purchase has been spreading the muck about Mary and I, and what we did at the Harvest celebration. She has told stories that Mary and I were improper in public and that Mary bears my child.

That wretch always wanted me for herself. I knew she was trying to eye me and lure me with her low neckline at the dance. She was jealous of Mary and is now making trouble with her spiteful little untruths. If she were here now I would tell her she will entertain no man with her hateful scheming and deception. She will wrinkle with spite and age and remain a miserable spinster all the way to her grave if she doesn't mend her ways.

I do hope Mary is not with child as she is not the woman I want to marry. I do hope Father will tell me this. Father says that Mother is very upset by the gossip and that it has made her unwell. I hope Mother gets over it soon. That dreadful girl – I'd like to wring her neck.

I will use my time on St. Thomas Island to write letters and to explore this part of the island. I will write long letters to Father and Mother, and to Fanny. I cannot write to my sisters Mary or Martha as I forgot to bring their addresses. I must ask Father to send them to me along with my papers and magazines on the next Mail.

I must stop bothering about these little troubles that I can do nothing about. The still heat on this island fries my brain. It is cooler at sunset. I decide to go out and walk by the clear blue sea and watch the large orange sun sink down, before it turns the sky to a deep blood red.

As I watch the gentle waves wash upon the sandy beach I have plenty of time to think about the future, and to make my plans for myself and my boys. I look forward to being back on that ocean, feeling the waves under the ship and the pure sea air filling my lungs once more. I must make the most of my next twelve months of sailing, as soon I must settle down back home in England to look after George and Henry.

Soon I will sleep. Tomorrow will bring me another day nearer to the arrival of my ship.

St Thomas
West Indies
July 30th 1869

My dear Father & Mother

I now take great pleasure in writing a few lines to you to inform you I am quite well hoping you are all the same it is dreadfully hot here, my Ship has not arrived here yet. I shall stay here a fortnight for her. We had a very comfortable passage out here, the time seemed very long having nothing to do. When you write tell me all the news and all about Mary Clayton and what her father & Mother has to say about me. Dear parents when you write tell me if you have received my Money order from Southampton. I told them in the office to send you some Money that was owing me about two pounds. I think I shall be able to save some money out here because when I come home I want to take a place near South'ton and I must save £300 before I come home which will be about fifteen months time if please God my health is allright, there is not much sickness here at present. My dear parents please to send out by every Mail one News of the World, one Illustrated London News, West

Sussex, and Lloyds "Weekly paper besure and send those papers every Mail also a Punch.

When you write send me Patty's and Polly's directions so that I may write to them. I wrote to Nancy before leaving South'ton. I will write to Kitty next Mail give my love to them all and also Fanny. I will write to them all next Mail. I may write to Fanny this time perhaps. I suppose they have got my character flying at Purchases in a fine style but I would not have that Girl if she was hung in Gold. They are a proud good for Nothing set.

Dear parents I have not much news to tell you at present hoping you enjoy good health. The time will soon slip along for me to see you again. Kiss Georgie for me and please to accept my fondest love and believe me to remain your

     affectionate Son
     Geo. Wm. Eastland
     R.M.S. "Tamar"
      St Thomas West Indies

Tuesday 24th August 1869

Port of Spain, Trinidad

on the Royal Mail Ship "Conway"

George William Eastland.

My tongue is as if tied in knots.
This is not like me. Usually my words flow quite easily. But now I cannot find words to adequately describe the paradise that has dazzled my eyes, and assaulted all my senses this three weeks past.

I have had to pinch myself every morning to prove to myself that I am actually here and alive in these beautiful tropical islands, as it feels just like a dream – a bright colourful, incredible dream. The Caribbean is so unlike anywhere I have ever been before. Having seen these places I cannot imagine how anybody could ever want to be anywhere else.

My Steamer, the RMS "Eider" did not arrive at St. Thomas. It has a broken Port Paddle Wheel and is still being repaired. However, I managed to get myself work as Chief Steward on the RMS "Conway", and I could not have been happier when she slipped out of St. Thomas. I was so relieved to be back on the sea where the air is healthier, and able to at last earn some money. I sat around on St. Thomas Island far too long for my liking.

This voyage down the long chain of Caribbean islands has far exceeded my wildest boyhood dreams. Our ship has sailed upon a silver wake along the curve of these islands, across the translucent sapphire sea, broken only by the succession of sparkling emerald isles and the occasional whale. All the time the golden sun shines down upon the decks, and the splash of the waves on our bows and the flying spray rings like bells in the sea breeze.

After so many endless voyages across wild green oceans where you see nothing but the sea and the sky for weeks on end, this gorgeous chain of Caribbean gemstones has been like a wonder to me. We sailed out of Charlotte Amalie harbour from St. Thomas, and a few hours later were approaching our first Mail delivery at Basseterre Bay on St. Kitts Island.

The Vale of Basseterre on the western side of the island revealed itself as we steamed towards it. Soft, rich, lush cane fields covered the valley as well as the smooth slopes of Monkey Hill that rose up behind the town. Still higher peaks towered further to the north of the island, the highest peak of all being bare and black and protruding high above the blanket of clouds that clung to its lower slopes.

This summit is called Mount Misery. It seems a strange name to me for this beautiful peak, though I can imagine that to attempt to climb the impossible looking summit might inspire such a name.

The next morning we sailed again. This time we covered the three leagues south to Nevis, the sister island to St. Kitts, the two being separated only by a small shallow channel called the Narrows.

Nevis is completely green and as our ship approached it looked like an uninhabited desert island, such was the dense foliar carpet that draped over it. It was not until we got much closer that I could see any sign of human habitation. The capital Charlestown where our ship lay up, sits on the shore of a shallow curved beach called Gallows Bay on the west side of the island. Nevis is circular with its huge peak rising in the middle of the island, and because of its steep incline barely a quarter of the island is cultivable.

Charlestown is a very attractive town and many of our passengers landed there by taking one of the shore boats for the two shilling fee. Some passengers stay much longer than our steamer to sample the island's attractions, which include mineral springs, and the hot and warm baths. The climate favours many European plants, including sea-kale, turnips, carrots and strawberries, as well as the more exotic peaches and the delicious oranges.

And so our Mail deliveries and collections continued in this vein. We worked our way southwards along the curve of these magical islands that line the eastern extremity of the Caribbean Sea, all the way from St. Thomas in the north to Venezuela in the south.

It seems impossible that every island could appear even more beautiful to me than the last. But that is how it is. Each and every island has its own distinct character and stands in my memory - like a scattering of diamonds, all sparkling with the same impossible depth and yet each with it own unique and special attraction.

From Nevis we sailed to Antigua, and then to mountainous Montserrat where wild fertility and undergrowth drape the island in a vast tropical greenery. The original settlers here were Irish, and I have heard some of the negroes on the island pronounce their jargon with an Irish accent!

When we were there I was also told of the Soufriere – a green savannah that breaks free from the deep woods, and flows from the hills all the way to the sea and bursts with colourful flowers. But I had no chance to go and see it for myself on this trip. Our Steamer didn't stop for longer than to allow the exchange of Mails and unloading a few passengers.

Next came Guadaloupe – an irregular shaped island of two halves divided by a channel called the Riviere Salee, or Salt River. Our Steamer could not navigate it, but small boats and canoes ply the pleasant stretch of water which is about two leagues in length. The banks on each side of the river are packed with mangroves and palmettos.

The "Conway" stopped at the main port Basse Terre on the western half of the island, to exchange Mail and passengers. It is a pretty town but vulnerable to hurricanes due to there being no sheltered harbour. We steamed away from Guadaloupe, watching the great mountain La Souffriere puff out thick black smoke and sparks into the red sky at sunset.

Roseau, the capital of Dominica was our next stop. We arrived in warm rain which seemed to be making the plants and trees taller than anywhere else in the Caribbean. Ferns on the island grow to twenty-five feet high. Green coffee grows in huge plantations which scent the whole area in a most exotic way.

Next we made a short stop at Martinique. Our Steamers do not stay here and passengers disembark using shore boats. This is a French island, and the coloured women wear vivid crimson, green and saffron shawls over their heads bent back with jewels into a tiara. They are said to be outstandingly beautiful with their shiny cheeks, white teeth and vibrant headwear. Perhaps I may see for myself one day?

We continued on our southerly voyage to St. Lucia, then St. Vincent, followed by the one hundred mile detour east to Barbadoes, before returning west to Grenada. From there we steamed the final twenty-five leagues to Tobago where we were due to lay-up for two days, land our passengers and re-stock all our supplies. The "Conway" lay in Courland harbour where all the Steamers come, about two hundred yards from shore. The passengers were all landed using our Steamer's boats, and then the jobs of cleaning the ship and reloading provisions and coal were undertaken.

The first few hours at Tobago were very busy for me organising the deliveries of food and liquor for our ship. Later I had time to take in the beauty of this new destination.

This island is cooler than many of the others, benefiting from fresh sea breezes. The rainy season is upon us and the hot sunny interludes are regularly broken by torrential downpours. Lush tropical plant life of all shapes and colours grows in abundance here as do familiar European plants, all well watered by the rivulets which descend in their torrents from the higher ground down into the valleys and back into the sea.

While the passengers toured the island on mules some of the ship's crew got ready to go on a shooting expedition in the nearby forests.

Three days ago a few of the crew, including myself, each with our guns and a flask of drink left our Steamer at 6am on one of our boats, and we rowed to the shore where we met a local guide. He led us on foot out of the town and into the tropical undergrowth, all the time listening and pointing us in one direction or another.

Our guide's hearing must have been very well trained from years of local experience, as I could hear nothing beyond the constant buzzing and clicking and scraping of insects, and chirping, peeping and whooping of hundreds of birds, most of which were nowhere to be seen.

The small birds in Tobago are an astonishing mix of colours as bright as an artist's paint palette. Some are pale blue, I saw a blackbird with a dazzling yellow tail, and another was blue, green, yellow and grey, had an orange plume on its head and orange whiskers with black spots at the sides of its beak. Others have a kind of metallic green and blue sheen to them – the humming birds that hover for a moment then dive into the undergrowth faster than I can swallow, and there are red herons and parrots of every colour imaginable. The birds I like the best are small and vivid blue, almost navy with black feathers around their eyes, chin and wings, a long hooked blue beak and bright yellow legs and feet. I am told they are called Honeycreepers.

These birds all flock to the brilliant and colourful blossoms on the trees where they hover, hop and feed incessantly. The trees are not particularly high but most are very beautiful. One in particular has slender branches bending gracefully like a willow, with blossoms shaped like a tulip, some red and some white about the size of a liqueur glass. Its seeds are contained in pods that hang from its branches like French beans, and with long and narrow green leaves.

I would have hated to have shot one of the small birds as they are so pretty, but they were not what we were hunting. Even if we had been, our chances of shooting one of these tiny darting streaks from the rainbow would have been a thousand to one against us.

Our guide was on the trail of game, in particular Cocricos and Man-of-War birds, and possibly a partridge. These are all much bigger and a good deal slower in their movements, but still hard to find and even harder to shoot. The Cocrico is hard to see being rather like a grey and brown partridge, whilst the Man-of-War Bird looks like a huge black seagull. Our Captain was hoping to shoot a Man-of-War Bird without destroying it so that he could have it stuffed and mounted in a glass container and displayed in his cabin.

After a while we began to recognise the calls of our prey and many wayward shots were fired. Every now and again the humid dappled sunshine in the shady forest was interrupted by the deafening pounding of a new torrent of rain which would then stop as suddenly as it had started, just like a tap being turned on and off. Even the rainwater is hot here.

I was beginning to think that although this wild shooting in the jungle in the rain was a novel experience, our chances of shooting anything more than fresh air was as likely as finding a needle in a haystack. I contemplated that I could instead have been back in my dry cabin, writing my letters home and sipping a glass of ale.

Bang, Bang, Bang. It was like trying to shoot a flying owl by moonlight. We would hear the flap of a wing or get a glimpse of one of the larger fowl high above us amidst, or above the foliage. Even with a clear sighting of a flying bird most of our party would struggle to shoot it. We are ready and willing to shoot a pirate approaching our ship in a nearby boat, but I soon concluded that it was highly unlikely that any of our party had the shooting ability to hit a small flying creature which was for the most part out of sight.

But I was proved wrong.

Bang, Bang, Bang.

There was a loud shriek and a crashing of branches and leaves somewhere high in the trees behind me to my left. I spun on my feet to see something dark crashing through the canopy of branches, squawking and fluttering. Whether by chance or a good shot I will never be sure. One of the black Man-of-War birds fell earthwards, until its fall was interrupted by a dense bush eight feet above the ground. Although scrabbling and squawking in the branches of the bush the bird was mortally wounded, and after being hooked to the ground a sharp blow was delivered to the creature's skull to end its misery.

Once upon the ground and close up its size was truly astonishing. Its open wings must have measured all of seven feet from tip to tip, and it was about three feet from its beak to its tail. Our guide inspected the bird closely, and found an unusual sharp object pushing out of its bright red pouch just underneath its bill. It turned out to be a half swallowed flying fish measuring eleven inches that must have become stuck there.

The bird was presented to our Captain so he could have it duly stuffed as, apart from a broken wing that could be re-positioned, the bird was in a very good condition. Our party didn't get near to shooting any more birds that day, but despite the frequent downpours the shooting party did provide a welcome distraction from the daily routine on the Mail ship, and gave me the chance to see all those wonderful colourful birds. What a contrast to the sparrows and wrens of England.

Maybe I shall buy myself a parrot. I shall call him Friday – because we arrived at Tobago late on Friday.

The "Conway" arrived here in Trinidad yesterday evening. Coming from Tobago we approached from the north passing Monos Island and skirting the Gulf of Paria. This is a very beautiful approach with the wooded mountains of Trinidad to our port side, and the sea all around the purest ultramarine colour imaginable. The high mountains of Trinidad are covered to their peaks by gigantic trees which grow all the way down to the coast, where they merge with evergreen mangroves that dangle their looping branches into the water's soft waves.

Dusk was approaching as we neared the capital, Port of Spain. Its beautiful churches glowed in the last golden rays of the late evening sun, as it set to the west behind our Steamer. Many whales inhabit these waters, the huge beasts lifting out of the sea then dropping back again to create huge waves whilst shooting columns of silver foam high into the air.

A mile from shore our Steamer was met by a flotilla of boats all clamouring to take passengers ashore for around two shillings and sixpence. This island is more expensive than most but understandably so. I think Port of Spain is the finest town in all the West Indies. It has long, wide streets built in perfect straight lines. No wooden houses are allowed to be built any more that might become run-down and shabby.

Today we will reload the Steamer and fill up with coal also. I had some free time and decided to go ashore. I have been paid and I decided this would be the best place to buy the white clothing that I have been promising myself.

I went early to avoid the most ferocious heat and walked from the harbour into town. I have found that the busier and more developed towns in the Caribbean, as well as having banks, schools and churches of all faiths, often also have billiard-rooms and news rooms. Anyone can enter these news rooms, where they have books and newspapers and magazines from many European countries for travellers to read. I found one of these news rooms in Port of Spain and settled myself down for a little while in a comfortable high-backed chair with two English newspapers, and caught up with life back at home. The newspapers were about three weeks old, but life is slow out here and that news was quite recent enough for me. Still I would prefer it if Father would send me the papers and magazines that I have asked for so that I can read them on the high seas at idle times.

I struck up conversation with an old Irish mariner in the news room. He introduced himself as Captain Seamus, asked me my name and then told me much of interest about Trinidad. 'Trinidad is a wondrous oyland, so it is George. So'tiz clean an' much 'ealthier dan many av de others an' when yer are in port fer a few days oi recommend yer go an' see aroynd de oyland. Trinidad has beautiful lakes, hat springs, mud volcanoes an' on de oyland av Gasparie are amazing caves.

'Pitch Lake an de west coast is a unique natural wonder. It is ha'f a league in length an' breadth an' 'ome to beautiful shrubs an' flowers, wild pineapples an' aloes, swarms av colourful butterflies an' brilliant 'umming birds. Deep water-filled crevices conceal great quantities av mullet an' small fish. De lake repeatedly reveals an' den engulfs dees exotic gardens. Beware de saft muds, fer people 'av disappeared into dem never to be seen again.'

Seamus also told me about the ancient village of Savana Grande, deep inland where the Indians live. 'De village 'as two rows av well-spaced 'ouses built av bamboo an' thatched wi' palm. De Indians sit dare in de shade for 'ours in motionless silence, so they do. Yer shud go an' see de village sometime George. So'tiz a very peaceful place.

'Den dare are de Negroes. Dey are de future av dis island. Dey are full av life an' energy, quick ter learn an' good businessmen. Yer keep yer wits aboit yer George if yer are t'inking av buyin' t'ings in town. Dem Negro salesmen know dat mariners from Europe bring money wi' dem and dey will fair charm de coins roight out av yer pockets if yer let dem. Yer keep yer wits aboyt yer, George young man.'

I thank Seamus for all his interesting tips, and promise him that I will explore Trinidad when I come back in the New Year when the dry season returns. I am sure I will get plenty of time in spring to explore all the wonderful islands that the Mail Steamers visit so regularly.

I soon find myself in the busy thrumming market. There are rows and rows of stalls selling everything you can possibly imagine from jewellery and trinkets, fruit, and all sorts of wooden items, many with the most intricate carvings. And much more. The traders are all Negroes, as black as soot and all wearing white attire. The market throngs with European visitors, many mariners and even more local people.

The market seems full of Spanish and French women. The place is a frenzy of foreign tongues and bright costumes – it could easily be a merry French fair, except for the even more exotic array of goods for sale.

The Negro salesmen are just as Seamus suggested, energetic, animated, and full of chatter and life. They also seem to be having lots of fun judging by their beaming smiles and bright white teeth which flash when they laugh. I browse the market with no intention of buying these strange exotic goods, but it is fascinating to see what is for sale and just to experience this vibrant place bursting with spice and energy.

After a while I approach a stall displaying the most extensive array of clothing, mostly white, that I have ever seen. This is where I intend to spend some money. I remind myself of Seamus' tips and prepare myself to negotiate as hard as I can. The salesman, a tall Negro as black as the ace of spades sees me coming. He has a twinkle in his eye and a bounce in his step as he spreads his arms wide and says,

'Dese are da best wats ya will find anywheres ahn dis ahland Messa. De fahnest wats dat will keep ya cool as a coconut Messa.

'Ya can walk al ova de ahland to seek betta or cheapa Messa. An yo will sweat gallons Messa in yo search but ya will nat find betta. An ya will come back to me Messa, cos mine are de best wats in al of Trinidad.

'How lang ya got te walk in da sun Messa? Ya can tek as lang as ya like Messa. Mi nice cool wats will al be here for ya Messa. Unless some uddah mariner comes buys dem al while ya still decidin.

'Ah tink dat wud be a shame Messa cos dis sun be a frightful hat. Ya want a thin wat flannel next to ya skin Messa, some light linen jackets an some thin woollen socks. Ah sell ya a smart wat jacket at de best price on de ahland. Betta - ah can sell ya two jackets at a very special price Messa, special just for yoh Messa.'

Hard as I try to get him to budge on his prices it is like getting blood out of a stone. And all the time he has me feeling sorry for *him*? He rolls his eyes at my counter-offers, waves his arms, walks away and comes back again. He tells me the names of his eight daughters and sons who he has to feed.

Whatever I offer, the man sighs extravagantly, puffs his cheeks out and adds one more garment and a new price along with yet another 'Special Price, Messa'. He quite muddles my brain with new combinations of clothes and prices, and he also switches frequently between Spanish cents and English guineas. I am normally good at doing sums in my head, but such is the tangle of this Trinidadian salesman's continuous renegotiations it makes my brain feel dizzy, as if beset with sea-sickness.

I eventually agree the man's price and he folds up my pile of white clothes – shirts, two jackets, trousers, flannels, two caps and several pairs of thin white socks, and he packs them all into a neat brown paper parcel tied up with a string handle. He flashes me a wide smile revealing those great white teeth. I can't help but like the cheerful fellow.

Now I will be the best-dressed Chief Steward in all the Caribbean. I may have little use for these clothes back home in England but they will serve me very well for a year or two under the savage Caribbean sun, and will be well worth the money. My friendly salesman may have achieved a daylight robbery, yet to have acquired me such a wardrobe of clothes from the smart tailor on East Street in Chichester would have cost me ten times more than I have paid here!

Pleased with my purchases I return to my Steamer to find some shade from the sun before it gets any hotter.

I must write to Father and Mother before we weigh anchor again tonight. The "Conway" will exchange Mails with several other ships today at Port of Spain and then we will depart northwards once more. I will now rest awhile in my cabin and attend to my paperwork – the Tropical warmth has fair exhausted me.

~~Eider~~ Conway Trinadad
august 24th 1869

My dear Father & Mother
I now take the pleasure in writing you a few lines to let you know I am quite well thank God I was never in better health in my life. I think I shall do pretty well out here, it is a wretched place to stay in the weather is so dreadful hot. I have been all down the Islands since I arrived. I could not write to you by the last Mail as I did not meet it. I here enclose you an order on the West India Company for seven pound odd which you will please to forward to London to Change for me. I cashed it for the 2nd officer. My dear parents I shall be so glad when my time comes to come home as it seems so bad to be out here. I hope you are all quite well and getting along allright. I hope my health will remain good. I do not mind the hot weather, I think I can make some Money out here. I have bought myself about ten pounds worth of White Trousers, Shirts & etc since I arrived from England also some new flannel items a regular fit out for hot weather and saved twenty pounds besides this month. I shall forward some more money to you every Mail after this. I have had hardly time to look around yet, when you write

tell me all the News and besure and send the Papers. Kiss the Dear little Georgy for me I hope he is better tell Daddy to buy him something when he changes this order you can use the Money if you want to and next Month you can begin to put it in the Bank as I send it home to you. My dear Friends please to accept my fondest love and believe me to remain your

       affectionate Son
       Geo. Wm. Eastland

Dear Father direct to London for the order to be changed and send them your address and they will return you the Money.
    direct J. M. Lloyd Esq.
      55 Moorgate Street
       London E.C.

I have backed the order

P.S. I did not join the Ship I came out to, she has broken her Machinery. I have not been to St Thomas since I first arrived so I have not received my letters from home yet. I have been Shooting this last two days at Tobago we left there ~~last this morning~~ last evening and leave here again to night for Grenada, St Vincent, St Lucia & Barbados

Thursday 26th August 1869

Port of Castries, St. Lucia, 9.40pm

George William Eastland.

Our next island is St. Lucia where we have stopped for a couple of days to meet some other Mail steamers and exchange Mail and passengers. St. Lucia is a high and broken land with steep and lush mountains that no animal can climb.

St. Lucia may be my favourite of all the islands, for its beauty and its practical advantages. As we approach from the sea from the south the view that opens before me is stunning. Two columnar rocks, the Pitons or Sugar Loaves rise from the water to a great height to tower above our ship. These rocks appear like great Centurian guards where they stand at each side of the entrance to a small but deep and beautiful sheltered bay. A small and pretty village sits at the bottom of the cove and a sandy beach encircles the bay, and behind the beach lies a wide green belt of cane fields.

Behind the cane strip the mountains rise in majestic slopes and the clouds that cling to their peaks sometimes make them look dark. Then the sun lifts the cloud to unmask the green glory high above.

The Steamers mostly stop at Castries at the north-west of the island, which sits at the end of a deep harbour. This is one of the deepest and best harbours in the whole of the West Indies. Our Steamer unloaded its passengers here, and we have stayed a day to reload with coal and other provisions. This is always a very busy day for me, organising and recording the loading of new supplies of food, liquor and other items for the ongoing voyage.

I had a little time ashore at dusk and was astonished by a sight I have never seen before. I saw a million dancing and pulsing yellow lights that bathed the trees and undergrowth. It was as if all the stars had fallen out of the sky at the same time and landed upon the island of St. Lucia. Then I realised there were still a million more stars shining in the sky.

Fireflies.

Everywhere.

Before I go to sleep I will write Father a short note to catch the Mail Ship back to England now it has arrived here at Castries. He must send me a Safe for my valuables. I cannot continue to carry my wages around continually in my pockets.

St Lucia
Augt 26th 1869

Dear Parents

Please to send as soon as possible to Southampton my Iron Safe immediately you get this letter and tie the Key on to the Handle or put it inside the Chest and well lash it round. I sent you an order from Trinadad which I hope you will receive all safe. pay the train hire for the safe to Southampton it is dreadful hot here now. I am first Class. excuse the short note. I have no news to tell you. lots of love

I remain
your Affectionate Son
Geo Wm. Eastland

turn over

Direct the Safe
to
Mr Geo. Wm. Eastland
Care of Mr Simcocks
R. M. S. P. Provedore Stores
Southampton
He will forward it on to me

September 1869

St. Vincent Island

on the Royal Mail Ship "Conway"

George William Eastland.

Our Steamer continues its never-ending voyage from one sparkling green oasis to the next, across the vast watery blue plain that separates them.

The rainy season is to be observed carefully and afforded the utmost respect, for a warm sunny day can be transformed with unnerving rapidity by a tropical storm or hurricane.

Fortunately there is usually an island relatively close and if a storm rages or its arrival threatens, we lay our ship up in the nearest sheltered harbour whenever we can. To be caught upon the open sea amidst such watery catastrophe risks everything. To be on the ocean when a hurricane strikes is to place your soul onto a platter and to hand it to God for safe keeping, or not, as the fancy takes him.

Sometimes we are into a harbour and back out again with great haste, only staying long enough to exchange Mails and passengers. If we need to re-stock our supplies, or need to wait to meet another Mail Steamer, or if the weather is very bad we may stay for one, two or three days.

St. Vincent is a particularly sumptuous green island. Today's heavy rain showers separated by warm sunny interludes clearly feed this lush landscape. Unsurprisingly the island has its own botanical garden where, I am told, nutmeg, clove and cinnamon all grow particularly well.

St. Vincent is considered a healthy island as its temperature remains constant at 80-81° in the shade, and there is no marshland here to harbour those devilish mosquitoes. As a result more of our passengers choose to stay here for longer.

I can see Sulphur Hill – a large volcanic mountain three thousand feet high to the far north of the island. They say the last big eruption in 1812 brought flames and thunder, followed by earthquakes and lava flow down the north-west side into the sea. Barbadoes, twelve leagues away, was condemned to total darkness for four hours by the constant shower of favilla from the eruption.

We load plenty of coal today at St. Vincent ready for our next voyage to Barbadoes.

Barbados

When I first came to Barbados it was sunny and the sky was clear blue. I thought the "Conway" was in the middle of the ocean and wondered why our engines were slowing. I went up on deck to see and there was the Barbados shoreline, just a mile away.

Compared to the other islands Barbados is low and it cannot be seen until a ship is about eleven leagues off. It is pretty and well cultivated, and is similar in size and height to the Isle of Wight. Yet this tiny gem hidden amongst the sapphire waves deep in the Caribbean Sea is the most ancient colony of the British Empire.

Barbados was originally forested but most of the trees have been cut down to make space for sugar and other plantations. The highest part of the island is the north east quarter rising to a mere eight hundred feet, which is named Scotland. There is a hospital there where injured soldiers are taken to recuperate. Scotland is the healthiest place in all the West Indies.

Barbados is cooler than all the other islands. This must be because it is smaller and more level, and benefits from the north east trade winds which blow continuously across it, carrying all fevers and other ailments away to the big wide oceans to be dispersed and purified.

This cooler and healthier island is such a relief, yet we dare not stay here longer than necessary during the hurricane season as Barbados has no sheltered harbour to hide in. We will stay one day more to meet the Steamer that heads north, before we sail for Grenada.

I have come by shore boat for a dollar to Carlisle Bay, just south of the capital, Bridgetown. I enjoy a swim in the bay along with other tourists. Many local inhabitants also leap and play in the waters, their shrieks carrying upon the breeze, but they remain further along the beach. While swimming I can hear the banging of drums as well as gunshot coming from St. Anne's Garrison at the southern end of town. The sea is wonderful refreshing to my bones, to my hot skin and also to my head that throbs under the hot sun. I submerge myself again in the cool blue waters and enjoy the relief that flows over me.

I will not have time to venture far into Barbados on this visit but hope to on another occasion. The climate here seems more temperate, and more comfortable for an Englishman. As I lie in my cabin at dusk I hear the last post played on a bugle in the garrison, the tune wafting across the bay borne on the warm and gentle breeze.

My nose is starting to run. I notice that I am shivering and at the same time sweating profusely – like an old sow. I cannot believe that somehow, on this most healthy of islands I seem to have managed to pick up a cold. I retire early to bed.

Here I toss and turn for I cannot sleep. I am unable to breathe through my nose and so my throat becomes as coarse as tree bark and as sore as a nettle.

Perhaps I shall, after all be glad to leave this island.

Grenada

Why does the Caribbean have to be so treacherous to an Englishman's health? It appears at first sight to be the perfect climate – sunshine and blue sky and warmth. No frost and cold and sleet. Yet here am I with a febrile worse than any I can remember having in England.

The morning after I went swimming in Barbados I woke up feeling like death warmed up. My limbs ached, my nose and eyes were streaming, and my throat was as rough as sand. My voyage to Grenada was miserable and I feel little better now we are here. I cannot be sure if I sweat from the Caribbean heat or from the Fever. I have no strength. I want only to sleep, and I do just that whenever I can. But there is always much work to be done on this ship and I will not shirk my duties. If I do not work I will not be paid. I am caught between the Devil and the deep blue sea. I will work on.

The "Conway" may well stay in Grenada for a few days. I hope I will recover while we are here but I will not go onshore this visit. When I am not working I will sleep.

Grenada has become a regular meeting place and handover port for Steamers which can moor safely here in the deep sheltered bay. Steamers often stay here a few days, and stock up on coal and other supplies until all Mail and passengers can be exchanged. The ships will then all steam out of the bay together and depart with their cargoes to all the corners of the Caribbean.

I am feeling weary. Since I left Dell Quay in June I have heard little from Father and Mother and been sent no newspapers. When I, at last, get back to St. Thomas I dearly hope I shall find my Safe is there, and letters and magazines from England. I really miss having the papers to read. I also miss George and Henry. By the time I go home to England I expect they will have grown several inches taller.

This dreadful cold lays me low. I hope I will feel better soon. Every mariner fears illness in the Caribbean in case it turns into the dreaded Fever. Perhaps I should have stayed in England where the cooler climate suits me better?

Perhaps God is punishing me? Some days I feel so guilty that here I am sailing on the sparkling Caribbean, my skin turning browner under the tropical sun, enjoying juicy oranges and mangoes while my family struggle at home without me in the gloomy, grey damp of Sussex. Perhaps I have been selfish?

Maybe Father has not sent me any newspapers or magazines because he is fed up with me leaving him with all the responsibility of looking after Mother and my boys, while I please myself adventuring on the high seas, selfishly pursuing my boyhood dreams? Perhaps Father cannot afford to send me any papers? I must Mail him some more money – I don't need to spend much on myself here.

Being cut off from all that is happening at home may be the worst agony. My imagination is perhaps my cruellest enemy. How I hope I will find a letter from Father containing some good news when we return next to St. Thomas.

Soon we will sail to the west delivering the Mails to Cuba and on to Mexico. But first we must complete this Mail run aboard the

"Conway" which now heads north along the chain of islands back to St. Thomas. There will be much for me to do when we return to St. Thomas to ready my new Steamer, the RMS "Tamar" for the long voyage to Mexico. There will be supplies to purchase, inventories to check, and paperwork to be written. I must regain my strength somehow.

People tell me Havana is a wonderful old town so I am looking forward to seeing it for myself. I am also hoping to do some good business in Havana, so that I can save some more money for Father and Mother and for George and Henry.

Old Fogden at Dell Quay made Father promise that I would send him some of the finest Cuban cigars. That old man is like a walking chimney – always puffing on his pipe, his old head shrouded in a fog of smoke. His name is quite appropriate.

I think I shall make a good profit on cigars in Havana and I will mail them home to Father to sell. I will tell him to make sure Fogden pays before he hands over the cigars. If Fogden won't pay there are plenty of others in Chichester at The Lodge of Union who will pay Father a good price for the best cigars from Havana. This will give Father a good income for the winter.

Oh God, please forgive me for my selfishness and rid me of this awful Fever soon. It leaves me exhausted and miserable.

R. M. S. "Conway"
Grenada
9th Sept. 1869

My dear Father & Mother
    I now again take the fond pleasure in writing you a few lines hoping to find you all quite well at home. I have been very poorly since I wrote to you last. I am getting allright again now. I caught a heavy cold in Barbadoes when I was there. Dear Parents I have not received any letters since I have been out here. I have not been to St Thomas since I first arrived. I am going there this time and hope to receive all my letters there. I sent an order on the Company to you last Mail which I hope you received quite safe when you write please let me know if you had any trouble with it. I shall forward you some more next Mail. I am going to join my own Ship when I get to St Thomas the "Tamar" she will be repaired by that time. I shall then run to the Gulf of Florida if you see Fogden tell him I have not been to <u>Havanna</u> yet but am going down there this month. My dear Mother you will please to give my kind love to all my Sisters. hoping they are well and tell Fanny I will write next Mail. Kiss dear little Georgy for

me and tell him to be a good boy. My dearest Parents I have not much more to tell you hoping to hear from you soon do not forget my papers, please to accept my fondest love and believe me

to remain your affectionate Son
Geo. Wm. Eastland

Direct
    Geo. Wm. Eastland
    R.M.S "Tamar"
    St Thomas
    West Indies

Railway Cottage
Lewes
East Sussex
Sunday 12th September 1869

My Dearest George,

  I hope you are keeping well. I miss you so much, you being away for so long now. You know I am not one to stay gloomy for long, but at the moment I am finding it hard to feel any other way.

  I have been housekeeper here now since the summer and live just along the road in a small cottage. I was finding it hard to save any of my wages until I managed to find a lodger. Emma Houghton works at the inn just around the corner and now shares this cottage with me as well as the rent, which is a Godsend. She is very young and pretty. The inn doesn't pay her much, but she is a bright lass and does very well with tips from the customers. Emma is sixteen. You would like her George. She has deep hazel eyes and is a great mischief, but she is very kind to me.

  I thought working as a barmaid was hard but being a housekeeper is twice as hard on my body. My hands are as dry as toast and I can hardly kneel as my knees are so sore. I wrap up a cloth to kneel on when I wash the floors and at the end it is hard to get up again. There seems so much lifting involved in the work and my back is complaining even more than I am.

      I miss you so much, George. When we were small you were always there until Father sent you to Greenwich and got you wanting to be a mariner. I haven't seen you since the Christmas before last. I know that is partly because I am in Lewes. I wish all our sisters didn't live so far away. We occasionally see Matilda in Littlehampton, once in a blue moon Mary comes down from Petworth, and we hardly ever see Martha now she lives at Redhill. And you George, might as well be on the other side of the moon.

Mother and Father are getting really old now. I worry they will not be able to look after George for much longer. Thank God they have got Jane Glasspool to help them, as I don't think they could manage without her.

      I wish I could go over to see little George and Henry more often. I ride on the train from Lewes, which changes at Brighton and takes me all the way to Chichester. Father collects me with the small cart. It is hard for me to get a day off work as there is so much for me to do here. I have only managed to go back to Dell Quay once since I started working at this place. I am sure I will get another day off soon so I can visit Father and Mother and Georgy.

You would be proud of little George if you saw him. He is very lively and always playing pirate games. I sword fence with him and he always runs me through with his sword. I make a good pirate. I dress up with a scarf around my head and a patch over my eye. Father even found me a large hook that I pretend to have at the end of my arm instead of a hand. If I ever catch George he says, "I am not afraid of you nasty pirate. My Father will come back on his big ship and he will rescue me and lock you up in the pirate gaol."

I wish George and Henry could play together sometimes. Matilda brings Henry to Dell Quay when she can, but with Dick so ill she can scarce leave the tavern, what with serving the customers and tending to Dick. I do not know if he will recover and that will be hard for Matilda, and Henry.

I hope you can earn enough money to satisfy yourself and come home to George and Henry soon. Will you be able to come home this Christmas?

I can't help myself but I do worry about you, George. You are twenty-seven and no longer a young man. I wish you were back at home with your boys and I think you deserve a kindly wife to comfort you. I know there cannot be another Sarah, but there are some very nice ladies who could be a very good wife to a handsome mariner like you (Hellen asks after you), and I am sure George and Henry would dearly love to be together again.

I worry about you being so far away. I wish Father never told me of his own sea adventures, of the storms and injuries at sea as it makes me worry more about you. There seem to be so many perils — from pirates, and whales, and diseases and drowning. I wish you would come home where it is safer. I never used to worry this much.

Some parts of my cottage are damp. I cannot leave a fire burning when I am not there as it would not be safe, and in any case the fire would go out before I got home from work. This makes it hard to get the cottage warm and dry and I think the damp is making me unwell. I have had a cough for several weeks now and I just cannot seem to make it go away. One day I feel better, and then my throat becomes sore again and I start sneezing. Sometimes I think it is all the dusting that causes this. At least the house where I work is warmer, but at night I put lots of clothes on and two pairs of bed socks and I hug a hot water bottle to my chest underneath the bedcovers. In the winter there will be ice on the inside of my bedroom window in the morning, and my breath will appear like a cloud when I breathe out.

    Please do come home soon George. I think Mother and Father miss you more than they would ever tell you in a letter. George and Henry of course miss their Father, even if they don't understand it. I definitely miss you and so I shall tell you so, Big brother!

    Your ever loving sister,

Fanny

P.S. Emma told me that she was born in Greenwich in Kent in 1853. If you saw a baby being carried in a shawl when you were at your Mariner's School in Greenwich, it might have been Emma. Wouldn't that be a funny thing? I told you I don't like being gloomy for long. Come home to us George, so I don't have to be gloomy at all??

Tuesday 28th September 1869

St. Thomas, 10.00am

George William Eastland.

How much I love the ocean, and its thrilling heroic perils.

The infinite power of the wind and the waves, which can suck a huge Steamer down and yet further down, deep into a watery ravine where the walls of the sea tower above the ship ready to engulf it and plunge it to the very floor of the ocean.

Only then to lift us up through the sheets of salty spray like a volcano erupting, to spit our ship towards the clouds with such force that it seems our vessel must surely be hurled right out above the waves.

Yet she is not. She holds firmly to the crest of the sea and all aboard draw a deep breath of clear sea air, before the next green abyss opens beneath us and the inevitable plunge begins once more.

The sea and the wind do not frighten me. My ship and my crew know how to ride them.

Sometimes our ship will drop anchor and moor for a night if we are too late to enter a port, or if we seek refuge in a remote sheltered bay from a wild storm. In the dead of night a savage Pirate boat may attempt to steal upon our ship to catch us unawares.

These ruthless and desperate men will attempt to slip their craft silently alongside ours, climb barefoot and without a sound onto our ship to slit the throats of all crew and passengers from ear to ear, before claiming their bounty of the ship and all its cargo.

I do not fear these modern day pirates. Attacks in the Caribbean are not nearly as frequent as they were just twenty or thirty years ago, and these savages are less likely to attempt a big ship like ours. Our night watch would see them coming. My gun always stays close to me at night. The rest of our crew - the same. If pirates ever breached our decks two or three of them would die by my gun before they got near to me.

Wherever I go in the Caribbean islands white men must be outnumbered by African Negroes by one hundred to one. These men were slaves, former slaves, and sons or grandsons of former slaves. Slavery was abolished in the Caribbean some five years ago, but from what I see today Negroes working on the sugar and coffee plantations still endure great hardship. They work for long days under the burning sun for a pittance, and still live in simple houses with their large families. Their mostly white employers live in their grand white estate mansions, overlooking their plantations and the simple homesteads of their workers.

Most black men keep their distance from the whites or ignore them. Occasionally a large Negro will look you in the eye with a determined hatred. Slavery has ended but the scars are deep. I have heard some dreadful stories of violence and cruelty inflicted upon native slaves, and can understand why some Negroes despise fat white Europeans who seem to hold all the wealth on their islands.

I do not fear an angry Negro. He reminds me to be grateful for being born into such a comfortable life with such opportunities. But I am careful not to walk in deathly narrow alleyways in a harbour after dark, where I could be murdered in an instant by a silent shadow. In fact, I go onto the islands as little as possible now to avoid the danger of mosquitoes. Beyond my duties onshore as Chief Steward, and my business at the Bank I stay on our Steamer most of the time.

The merciless white sun beats down upon me to blister my skin and fuddle my brains. I cannot walk barefoot upon the wooden decks of our Steamer without scorching the very soles of my pink feet. The sun over the dazzling sea makes my cheeks ache from constantly squinting, and the lines next to my eyes and mouth grow deeper and browner every day. I look in my mirror and wonder who the brown and wrinkled old man looking back at me is?

The heat forces me to drink, or I risk turning into a dried up prune. Sometimes the water is safe to drink, but great care must always be taken. If I am not sure I will drink ale, but there is only so much ale a man can drink safely under this sun.

But the sun doesn't frighten me. My white clothes protect my skin, and my white cap saves my brains from becoming scrambled by the heat and shields my eyes. And while the sun shines the greater danger, mosquitoes, are kept away. To my mind this makes the sun a Mariner's friend.

There is one thing that does truly scare me. You cannot see it, and you cannot stop it. You cannot feel it – until it is too late. It is capricious in its choice of victim. The weak and sinful are frequently spared whilst a hearty, young and upright man may be struck down in an instant – like a great oak felled by an axe.

YELLOW FEVER. We know not whom, nor when it will strike next. But we know it will. This is my greatest fear.

I should pray.

Dearest God. Please look after George and Henry for me while I am at sea. Please keep them safe and guide them as they grow and learn. Please look after Father and Mother and give them strength to care for my sons. Please keep Mother and Father warm this winter as I know they feel the cold. Please look after all my sisters and their families, and especially Fanny who is on her own in Lewes. Please protect her from illness as she is not strong. Please protect my ship and deliver me safely back to England as soon as I have made enough money to be able to look after my boys and parents.

Please forgive me for all my selfishness. Please, please spare my ship from any more Yellow Fever. I will gladly suffer any storms and sickness, and any amount of hard work as penitence. Thank you God.

Amen.

Since the "Conway" returned to St. Thomas the time has been very slow and dull. My ship, the "Tamar" is still not repaired and instead I have been appointed to another Royal Mail Ship, the "Eider". She is a new ship and seems very comfortable but there is much to be done to prepare the crew, obtaining all supplies and equipment and everything else we need before she can sail. We will be stuck here in St. Thomas for weeks while everything is organised. This is bad news as with no passengers on board I cannot earn much money, and I do not think it is healthy sitting around in this port.

It is much healthier to be at sea. We have much sickness on board our ship at the moment and another of our crew has died of Yellow Fever. If it hadn't been for all the delays and repairs to our ships he should have been already on his way home to England. It is a very sad state of affairs. I have to calculate the wages he was due to the date of his death, and to arrange for the sale of all his possessions. Once all this is complete the statement of his true worth has to be sent to the Board of Trade in London so that his family in England can be reimbursed.

His 'true worth' was that he was a lively young man with his whole life ahead of him. Preparing these figures is a most wretched part of the duties of Chief Steward. The ship's Surgeon arranged for the very swift burial of the body at sea. A Yellow Fever-riddled corpse must be disposed of very rapidly and all bedding and clothing burnt immediately. There are no volunteers for this task but the Surgeon appoints men in turn for the jobs. Every man may be chosen in turn - they may not refuse the tasks without grave consequences.

When the "Conway" returned to St. Thomas I found a letter from Father had been waiting for me. My Iron Safe has not yet arrived. There were no newspapers or magazines with Father's letter either. If Father only knew how the hours stretch endlessly empty here laid up in this port waiting for our ship to be ready to sail; he would surely send me the Papers to read?

I will not entertain myself by going onshore to waste my money on drink and women like others do. I only go on land when absolutely necessary. Thousands of mosquitoes lurk on the island, especially at dusk when some men go to Charlotte Amalie town. Fewer of the deadly pests come onto our ship but when they do enter my cabin I squash them as soon as I can catch them. The generous smear of a mariner's red blood which appears as I crush one of these humming parasites tells me all I need to know. I always make sure my mosquito net is completely secure around me before I sleep at night. I do not want to perish from Yellow Fever.

Father's letter was not a long letter, but was long enough to concern me. All is not well at home.

Matilda's husband Richard sounds very unwell. He has not been well for some time now. He too was a mariner but is no longer strong enough to continue at sea. He has taken the easier life and stayed at home working in the White Hart tavern as Licensed Victualler there. But now Father says Richard is too unwell even to help in the tavern. It sounds like he is in a bad way, but he is no age to die – he must only be in his early forties. It must be a dreadful hardship for Matilda to run the busy tavern alone, with Dick unable to help. I hope she is managing with her daughter Ann and my Henry. This is another reason why I must go home before long to look after my boys.

I don't know what is wrong with my older sister Mary at Petworth. Father doesn't make much sense. It sounds like Mary is unhappy and she says something about the children being cold and unwell. It is all a bit strange. We do not see much of Mary since she went to live with that Professor of Education at his school in Petworth. William Pescod has all manner of fancy ideas about the world, but I never quite understood how any of them connect to daily life. Perhaps I shall get on a horse and go to Petworth to visit Mary and her family when I get home to England next year.

Mother has annoyed me very much. Sometimes she opens her mouth too wide, when she would cause much less trouble and unnecessary upset if she could just turn her cheek the other way and mind her own business.

When visiting Emsworth recently to visit her family she bumped into Mary Clayton and one of her brothers - I think it was John. I know it was my fault that Mary and I had our little bit of fun back in the summer, and it was not Mary's fault when that Farm Wench made such a bad stink about it with the local gossip, blowing it out of all proportion. I know Mother feels the family's reputation has been dragged through the gutter and she never really liked Mary Clayton. But the trouble caused was not Mary's fault, and Mother should not have poked her finger into Mary's face and insulted her outside the shops at Emsworth.

Being so far away from home and unable to do anything about these family troubles makes me feel helpless and very guilty that I am not there to help my family. I must write back to Father but I do not know what to say to him, my brain is in such a spin from all his unsettling news. I will not write anything at all until I can get my thoughts straight.

In the end I take myself off the ship and walk for a while along the shore. There are no mosquitoes here by the water at this time of day. It is close to noon and all mosquitoes are hiding in shady undergrowth waiting for their feeding time later when the sun goes down. I will be safely back on board ship by then. For now I walk, and let my brain unwind itself as the gentle waves lap against the shoreline, and the bustle and the shouting of the harbour recedes behind me.

When I return to the harbour I find a small crowd of people have gathered. I soon discover that in the middle of the crowd is a man with a small table displaying some photographs. One of them is a picture of the RMS "Eider". She looks a very proud ship and I think she would look even finer still in a frame on the wall of my living room in my cottage back home - when I buy myself one. The price for the photograph is very reasonable and I negotiate with the photograph seller to frame it for me. I am pleased with my purchase and carry it under my arm back on board ship and put it safe in my cabin. This fine picture will be a good memory when my sailing days are over.

I shall be so relieved when my Steamer is finally ready for the sea. Every day here is a fearful agony waiting for the day when we can at last sail out of this hot deathly port of boredom. I will come alive again once I can feel the sea beneath me and the salt wind in my face. With passengers aboard I will be able to earn good money to send home for George and Henry.

R.M.S.S. "Eider"
St Thomas
Sept. 29th 1869

My dear Father & Mother

I now take the greatest of pleasure in writing to you with very low spirits. I am sorry to tell you I have been worse since I wrote to you last than I ever have been since I have been to sea. I was very poorly for three days and never left my Cabin. I am appointed to the "Eider" you see she is a new Ship and every thing very nice but I am sorry to say we have a great deal of sickness on board. one young lad died yesterday with <u>Yellow Fever</u> he had been out here eighteen months and was going home by this Mail.

My dear Parents I here enclose you two orders on the Company one for £9.10/2 and the other for £6.17/2 you will please to forward them to

J.M. Lloyd Esq.
55 Moorgate Str.

London E.C. and he will return you the Money and please to pay Mr G. Smith that came home from New Zealand with me Ten pounds Sterling if he is not gone away. if he is do not signify but you must enquire directly you receive this letter as I owe him the Money. You can use what Money you want and the rest put away in the Bank in <u>My own</u> and <u>Fanny's Name</u>. I shall send you another order next fortnight for £15/-. My dear parents I hope I shall have my health and return home again to see you all, please God to spare me. I can save some Money out here.

My dear Parents I have been laying here a fortnight and am going to Stay here another month until the ship is ready for Sea. She is very pretty. I have a large Picture of her framed. I shall not make much money this next month while Staying here without any passengers on board. Dear Mother I am sorry you should have said what you did at Emsworth about Mary as she did not like you calling her a <u>dairy maid</u> which I think you might have kept to yourself. I am going to write to Patty next Mail you will please send her <u>two pounds</u> and tell her I wish her to buy herself and Children something warm Clothes for the Winter. I must write to Fanny to night. Kiss little Georgy for me and also Harry if you see him. I hope Dick is enjoying better health poor fellow.

My dear Parents you would not know me if you were to see me now. I have lost all my Colour from my Cheeks but I hope to get stronger again before long. Three or four days sickness in this Country does one as much harm as a months illness in England, now my dearest parents you must excuse my short note and please to accept my fondest love for you both. I never shall forget you and believe me to
Remain your affectionate Son
<u>direct</u>   Geo. Wm. Eastland
                R. M. S. "Eider"
                  St. Thomas
                  <u>West Indies</u>
Good bye lots of Kisses and heaps of love.
P. S. I hope you sent my safe allright.

Saturday 9th October 1869

St. Thomas

George William Eastland.

It feels like we are trapped on this Godforsaken island. It will be weeks before we are ready to sail. When we eventually voyage again I will probably be as sick as a parrot as this is too long to be off the sea.

When we sail it will be to Havana and Vera Cruz in the Gulf of Mexico. But for now our crew are all landlubbers. There is much to get ready on the "Eider". Being a new Steamer she has little damage or rot or damp to speak of. I have to go into Charlotte Amalie more than I would like to purchase food, ale and rum, china, bedding and all manner of other supplies for our passengers before we are ready for the sea. Deliveries have to be checked and stored and all paperwork recorded. All this activity has the benefit of making the days pass, but our return to the sea cannot arrive quickly enough for me.

I received no letters on the last Mail. I have been sent no newspapers or magazines. My iron Safe has still not arrived. It feels as if I am marooned on St. Thomas and cast-away by my family.

An Officer tells me that sometimes Mail is damaged at sea, or maybe stolen. He tells me the only way to be sure the Mail is received is to send it by Registered Mail. I will send all my money orders home in future by Registered Mail. Perhaps I should not blame Father. Perhaps he has sent me the Papers and they have been stolen before they reached me?

Thank God we have no new cases of Yellow Fever. It is still the rainy season here with heavy downpours. I hope all those mosquitoes have been hammered by torrents of rain and washed out of the sky. There have been reports of dangerous storms and hurricanes at sea which we have avoided by being here in St. Thomas. I suppose that is at least one good thing about being stuck here on this island. By the time we go to Mexico the worst winter storms might be all blown out.

My days are full and busy and leave me no time to think or worry. The nights are long and dark. I enjoy playing cards with other crew members but I will not gamble like they do. All my wages are to go home for George and Henry. Some men do not understand me, but I do not care. I refuse to embark on that slippery madness that leads some mariners into utter ruin. For some it is the gambling, for others it is drink, and for some the poison is women of lax virtue. Some mariners try all three. The sun, the sea, and the fear of sickness affect all men in different ways, and each man distracts himself from the perils in his own manner.

I prefer mostly to work hard. I will also have much time in the evenings this next month to write letters to Father and Mother and to all my sisters. I will send as much money to them as I can by Registered Mail. I can easily while away an hour playing a card game, or just playing Patience on my own.

You would think the Caribbean to be the most healthy place on this Earth. Yet, when I look in the mirror I do not recognise myself. I have lost much weight from my illness. My face looks thin and lined. When I was sick I did not have energy to shave, and now it is too much trouble to do anything with my large beard. It keeps the flies from my face.

Today I am in Charlotte Amalie ordering fruit for our Steamer, and having concluded this business I have found a barber. I will not trust him with a cut-throat razor on my chin, but I am tired of my long greasy hair that is itchy and gets in my eyes. I have it cut very short, and now it is very nice to feel the air on my forehead and on the back of my neck.

With my short hair and bushy beard it looks as if my head is turned upside-down, but I feel much tidier than before. As I stumble from the barber's back out into the bright sunshine I lurch into two very fine-looking young Spanish women who shriek and giggle. They walk quickly on, but cast a backward glance at me as they continue their giggling and chattering. With flashing dark eyes and shining long black hair their curvy brown legs glisten in the sun, and compel me to follow them, like sirens on a rock.

My body aches all over just at the sight of these two dusky beauties.

R.M.S. "Eider"
St. Thomas
Oct 12th 1869

My dearest Father & Mother
     I now take the greatest of pleasure in writing you a short note to inform you I am quite well hoping you are all the same. I was quite surprised you did not write to me by the last Mail. I also expected some papers to read as I asked you to send me some every Mail it is very dull laying up here nothing to amuse oneself. the weather is dreadful hot here, but thank God we have had no more cases of <u>Fever</u> on board since I wrote to you. I hope you have sent my Iron Safe to South'ton for me. we expect to be underway again in a month from this date. I shall be very glad when the time comes to get to Sea again. My dearest Parents I here enclose an order for £4.15.4 please to send it to London to get it Changed for me and place it in the Bank the same as the other. I cannot get any more orders this time. I must get some and send home next Mail. I want to buy a twenty pound one if I can get it. Please God to spare my health. I shall save some money out here. I registered my last letter to you I have also done the same with this one so

you mind and allways send to the Post Office every Mail and see if there are any letters from me as they keep the Registered letters allways at the Post Office it is the safest way to send the letters. _____

My dearest parents besure and use what money you want out of what I send home and make yourselves comfortable. the time will soon slip away for me to see you all again. I am going to write to Kitty to day and Fanny. I have been very busy since I have been in this new Ship. My dear Parents you would not know me hardly. I have let my beard grow, and have had my hair cut short it has made a great alteration in my appearance it makes me look much older, it is dreadful hot I am holding a fan in one hand and my pen in the other. My dearest Parents you must excuse my short note and please give my love to Fanny and Kiss dear little Georgy for me, and please to accept my fondest love and believe me to remain your
    affectionate Son
      Geo. Wm. Eastland

Direct

Mr. G.W. Eastland
R.M.S. "Eider"
St Thomas
West Indies

Friday 15th October 1869

Fishbourne Marshes, West Sussex, 4.30pm

George William Eastland (junior).

I am shipwrecked on this desert island.

Pirates are chasing me, but I can run fast. They will not catch me. I dive into the long grasses. I can see the beach from here. But the pirates cannot see me.

My heart thumps like a drum. I can feel it in my chest. I hope the pirates cannot hear it.

A sudden sound from the grass behind makes me jump. My knee sinks deeper into the mud as I twist sharply to face the pirate who has crept up behind me. To my relief there is no pirate. A dark feathery silhouette flies into the air flapping and squawking.

My heart is thumping even faster than before. I lie on my back for a moment and watch the bird fly towards the water, screeching all the way. I hope the pirates don't find me here. I lie on the ground and listen. Perhaps I should move?

After a few minutes I hear the pirates coming…and I can smell them. I can hear the clump of their heavy boots, and the clank of metal. This is probably chains they carry, or their sharp daggers or swords.

I cower in my damp hiding place. It stinks here. Is this the stink of the pirates coming, or just mud with the remains of dead rats in it? If I stay hidden and make sure I am not seen Father will come soon on his big ship, and he will make all the pirates walk the plank.

My knees feel wet and cold crouching in this long grass. The light is fading. Father has not come yet. He must still be fighting the pirates on another island.

I decide to grab my cutlass and surprise the pirates. I run out of the grass and swing my sharp blade stick from side to side as I run as fast as I can. I lunge and swing with my sword, to the left and to the right and I kill all the pirates I can see.

I continue to run on the path that goes along the Fishbourne Channel all the way back to Dell Quay, keeping an eye open for more pirate ships. Father's ship is not at the quay. Perhaps he will arrive back from sea tomorrow?

Darkness is on its way. I will go into the Crown and Anchor where Grandmother will give me some bread and a cup of milk before I go to bed. First I make sure there are no pirates drinking in the tavern.

But there are only farmers there, sitting, talking and drinking by the fireplace so I put my stick behind my bedroom door.

I will need it to fight more pirates tomorrow.

Friday 15th October 1869

Littlehampton beach, West Sussex, 4.45pm

Henry Eastland.

Not much warmth is left in the fast sinking autumn sun. It is getting cold.

I huddle next to Albert, as we rest our backs against the wooden beach groynes. We like to play ducks and drakes on our way home from school, but now we are tired.

'I don't know why we have to go to school, Henry. My father says it is a waste of time cos I will be a butcher when I am growed up, just like him. He will teach me all I needs to know to be a butcher.'

'What is it like to be a butcher, Albert?'

'It is good. Butchers cut up all sorts of dead aminals. I will help my father in his shop tomorrow. Sometimes I pull all the insides out of chickens – their hearts, livers, kidneys and gizzards.

'And there is also its testicles, and claws and its head – with the eyes looking at you.' Albert pulls a face.

'What are chicken tentacles, Albert?'

'They are just bits that hang. Underneath it. They look a bit like small eggs. But slimy. I wouldn't eat one, but Father does sometimes.

'I like getting my hands all covered in blood off the meat.' Albert waggles his fingers in front of my face as if pretending to smear blood on me.

I squeal and push his hands away.

We throw more stones into the sea. Plop. Splish.

'Are you going to be the same as your father, Henry? My father says your father must be very happy as he is surrounded all day by ale?'

'…that is Uncle Richard. He is not … well. He is in bed. I think he might die. I heard Aunt Matilda tell Isaac…he might die.'

We sit awhile in silence and throw more stones.

'Who is Isaac?'

'I dunno. He lives upstairs. I think he is a gas-engineer, or something like that. He helps in the tavern.'

'It would be … I don't know. Not very good not to have a father.' Albert stares hard at the stone in his hands.

'Maybe. I don't know,' I say.

Splosh, splash…

Thursday 21st October 1869

St. Thomas

George William Eastland.

So little seems to be within my control. I did not expect this. I like to be able to see a problem and to put things right.

I have been languishing here on St. Thomas Island for over a month. It is not that I miss the sea... though I do. After my illness in Barbados I thought a rest in a harbour might be a good thing, but it has not been. I have been unwell for weeks. We have missed some terrible storms – that cannot be denied. But there seems nothing I can do to get myself to sea. My work is all done, the stores and my records are very tidy, but we will not sail until the Steamer is all ready and the Captain decides to sail.

Sitting in this hot damp and overcrowded harbour feels like a game of chance. St. Thomas is the most unhealthy port in which to tarry. Every day someone on this island catches the Yellow Fever – it is a curse. More of our crew have succumbed. You never know who could be next. I would think the Captain would want to sail at the first opportunity so as not to lose any more of his crew, but there seems to be no urgency in taking this decision.

I am going to start sending home more money orders. I will keep with me only the smallest sum I need to survive, in case I am the next to be struck down with the Fever. It would be terrible if I died and my wages did not go to my family. To make sure I will send home all I have, before we sail to the Gulf.

My Safe has arrived. It has taken months to get here. This was something else over which I seemed to have no influence. Now I will send home all my money orders straight away by Registered Mail, so I will have little need for a Safe any more. Never mind. I will keep my gun and my letters in it, and perhaps some cigars if I bring some back from Havana?

I do as much work as possible. It helps the time pass, and makes me feel that I am doing all I can to hasten our Steamer's departure from this island.

The evenings are botheringly long. I have received letters recently from Father and from Fanny that fill me with concerns. I am bothered when I receive no letters, and now I am bothered when I do receive letters. I am conflicted when I hear my family are struggling at home, and tortured that I am unable to do anything about it. Perhaps I am the cause of their struggles? Perhaps I should be at home looking after my elder and younger family, instead of scuttling between exotic islands dodging tropical perils?

Father wrote and told me that Mother has been very unwell. After all the hardship she has been through I hate to think of her this way. He also told me there is some trouble with Mary. She seems not happy and I do not know what that Professor is about. It must be very hard for Mary and all those children.

As soon as I go back to England I will pay a visit to Nancy and George Cox as I want to talk to them about buying into their farm. I have money saved now, and I hope this could enable me to settle down and be close to little George and Henry.

I know from Fanny's letter that she is not well. She will not complain and give in, but I know my sister and I can tell that she is struggling away from home. She will not admit it. I wish she would go back to Dell Quay where she can keep an eye on Father and Mother and George – and where they can all keep an eye on her.

I will write to them all, but I am not sure my writings will persuade them to do anything that I suggest. Reading my family's letters is like watching a storm cloud gather from the west. I can see all the troubles that are brewing but I feel helpless and unable to do anything about them.

The only thing I can do is to earn as much money as I can out here quickly. The sea is quite safe and I can make a good wage. But the land is riddled with disease, and life here is a game of chance which I have played for long enough. I think I will give up tropical sailing and go home and farm. I think this should be my last year out here.

I must make the most of the Gulf of Mexico. I hope it will be safer for my health and be more profitable than the Virgin Islands.

I have heard that Havana is a very fine town.

R. M. S. "Eider"
St Thomas.
28th October 1869

My dear Father & Mother

I now take the greatest of pleasure in answering your very kind letter. I was very sorry to hear dear Mother had been so poorly but glad to find she was getting well again. I received a letter from dear Fanny she tells me she has been very poorly. I think she had best come home with you. I will send you plenty of money and make yourselves comfortable. I am happy to say I am very well indeed and please God I shall remain so. we have lost our 4th Engineer since I wrote to you he died with <u>Yellow</u> <u>Fever</u> only bad two days.

My dearest Parents I am sending home to you twelve pounds by the Chief Steward, Mr Bluikhorn of the "Shannon" he will send it from South'ton to you by Post Office order payable to George Eastland. when I sent the order on the company for my wages in the "Conway" I did not send the Certificate with it. I will send it next Mail. you cannot get it changed without that.

My dearest parents I hope you will make yourselves comfortable this winter and mind and have Fanny to take care of you, if she will not come home, get some good Girl to live with you so that you will not have to work so hard, I leave here the 17th of next month for the Gulf of Mexico. I shall be gone a month. I hope I shall not lay here again for a long time it is very unhealthy.

Dear Father let me ask you again to send me some Papers if you only knew how long the nights are to me you would send them. you must recollect I am not in <u>Australia</u> now to flit about, I never go out of the ship of a night at all, My dearest Parents I have been having a lot more white Clothes made. I bought one dozen and a half new shirts the other day and two doz socks and two doz Handkerchiefs. I have sent to South'ton for another doz of Shirts and 2 doz socks. I am getting a case Stock of white Clothes now.

My dearest parents give my love to Nancy & George and tell them I shall come to see them when I come home next time. I am going to write to Kitty to day also to dear Fanny. I am so sorry about poor Patty. I cannot think what she will do. he must be a Rascal to her poor Girl little did she think when she got Married it would come to this. I truly pity her and hope you will give her what I told you in my last letter.

My dearest Parents I think I have said all to you now and please to accept my fondest love and Kiss dear Georgy for me. I shall write again next Mail and send that Certificate to you hoping this will find you all well with many Kisses and believe me to remain your loving Son

Geo. Wm. Eastland

R.M.S. "Eider"

St Thomas

W.I.

P.S. I have not shaved since I have been out here. I will send you one of my Cards when I have one taken. I received the safe all safe.

Saturday 6th November 1869

Crown and Anchor, Dell Quay

'Granny, Granny – when will Henry and Aunt Matilda get here?'

'What is that George? Is Matilda here already? Oh gracious, I haven't even peeled the potatoes yet?'

'No Ann. They will not arrive for a while yet. It will take Matilda all morning to drive that cart up from Littlehampton. She said in her letter she will be in time for lunch. George has already peeled the potatoes and carrots. George – walk up the hill and along the lane to Birdham road. You will be able to meet them coming down from Stockbridge and get yourself a ride back on the cart. Put your hat on. It is bright but there is a cold wind out there today.'

'Why do they have to arrive so early on a Sunday? Am I to get no rest even on the Sabbath?'

'It is Saturday Ann. You remember we agreed that Matilda would come on a Saturday instead of a Sunday so that she could stay the night if the weather was bad, and Henry won't miss a school day?'

'I wish you wouldn't keep changing the arrangements all the time without telling me, George. It's all very well for you – you aren't the one having to cook the dinner and to be getting things ready are you?'

'All is fine Ann. Matilda won't be here just yet, and Jane has put the meat in the oven. Take your seat by the window and watch the river. You can warm yourself there in the sunshine behind the glass pane. The river looks lovely in the sunshine today.'

'Wake up Ann. I can hear George and Henry's voices in the yard.

'Come on in out of that cold wind, Matilda. Your cheeks look pink. Did you have a good ride up here?'

'Yes, thank you Father. It is a lovely bright morning. I came along the coast past Middleton and Bognor before turning inland along the Chichester road. It was lovely to watch the sea sparkle and to breathe that sea air. It refreshed my mind and blew away some of my troubles.'

'Look Ann. Here is our little grand-daughter Ann Barttelot, all wrapped up in warm blankets. And how is our special little girl today?'

'She is very well, Father - though a little shy. She will be happier when those two noisy boys go outside to play.'

'My, how she has grown since we last saw her. How old is she now, Matilda? I am losing count.'

'Ann is four and a half now, Father.'

'Ah, such a big girl now. And the 'half' makes all the difference, doesn't it? Come to the kitchen, Matilda. Our servant Jane will get you and Ann some nice hot drinks. Boys – go and give the horse some hay and plenty of water, then come back in for a drink. I am sure Henry must need warming up too.'

'How are you Mother?'

'What's that Kitty? Your brother? Your brother isn't here. He has gone to sea and we don't know when he is coming back. I thought you knew that Kitty? Surely Father told you that George is still away at sea?'

'Mother, come and say hello to your grand-daughter. Ann, come and see your grandmother. Her name is Ann too."

'Here are your drinks, Mr Eastland. Shall I put them on the table there?'

'Thank you Jane. How is the dinner coming on dear?'

'Very well Mr Eastland. The meat is cooked and tender and keeping warm on the hotplate. When Mrs Barttelot arrived I put the vegetables on and all will be ready in five minutes, if you are ready?'

'Is that lunch burning? I can smell the food. I suppose I had better come to the kitchen to dish the meal up.'

'Stay where you are Mother. Spend a bit of time with little Ann. I can go and help Jane to get the food ready. Father – go and round up those boys and tell them to wash their hands before they come to eat.'

'How are you keeping, Mother? Mother…'

'The first thing you will notice, Matilda is that your mother's hearing has become quite bad. Mother has not been very well this year, and she had a bad cold and cough through most of October that she struggled to shake off. I think her ears are blocked now. Thank goodness we have got Jane to help us with cooking, the housework and with little George.'

'I am big George now…'

'You are bigger than you were, my boy, but not nearly as big as you think you are. Now you two boys – make sure you eat all your food, waste not - want not. And remember your manners – do not speak until you are spoken to.'

'Is Mother better now?'

'She is over the cold but it seems to have affected her hearing as it is much worse than it used to be. And she sleeps much more now in the daytime. She has a nap every afternoon sitting propped up in her chair by the window looking at the river, or over there by the fire, often for one or two hours. I'm afraid we neither of us are getting any younger my dear.

'How are you and your family, Matilda?'

'Ann has started school now. Henry walks with her to the school – it is only a quarter of a mile away and she seems to like playing with the other little girls. Henry seems quite bright but I do think he could work a bit harder. I think he would rather play on Littlehampton beach than spend time reading a book or practising his sums - isn't that so, Henry?'

'You must always work hard at school, Henry - and you as well, young George. You need to learn to read and write well if you are to get on in this life. Your father learnt to write very well at his school in London, and it has earned him a well-paid job travelling the world. That is what good schooling does for you. Boys who don't try hard at school end up tilling the soil in a muddy field in the pouring rain until their backs give in, and then they have no money, and no roast beef! You mark my words.'

'Henry is a good boy, Father. All boys need to play as well as work.'

'I know, Matilda. But it does no harm to remind them every now and then, and so that is what I do – especially as their father is not here to do the reminding.'

'Why are you all whispering? I wish you would speak up so as I can hear what you are saying. Anyone would think you didn't want me to know. Has Fanny started going to school yet? She looks old enough to me to be going?'

'Fanny?'

'Mother means Ann. She gets confused with names sometimes, Matilda. She calls little George by the name Henry and our servant Jane can be called Fanny, Martha or even Matilda some days.'

'Yes Mother. Ann started school in the autumn and she seems to like it there.'

'How are you, Kitty. Is your tavern as busy as the Crown and Anchor?'

'The White Hart is very busy, Mother. Littlehampton is growing and the harbour is getting busier, and that brings many more people into the inn; which is good for business, but very hard work – especially with Dick being so unwell.'

'Is he able to help in the tavern?'

'No he is more or less bedridden. Annie, our servant is a very good nurse. She looks after Dick, feeding him and helping him with his toilet and everything. I, I could never cope without her. Dick is a pale shadow of the man I married. He has become frail so quickly. The Doctor seems unable to do anything. He brings different medicines of many colours but nothing makes any difference to Dick's pains and ailments. I think Dick is going to… to die.'

'Oh dear Matilda. We are very sorry to hear this news…'

'How would you manage the White Hart without Dick? There is always room here at the Crown and Anchor if you want to come back and live here. You could help in our tavern, and George and Henry could be together again? You know you would always be welcome here, Matilda.'

'Thank you Father. It is an idea. For now I must see what happens. Perhaps Dick will make a miraculous recovery. I am coping at present with the help of Annie. And Isaac Tompsett, my lodger is a Godsend. He does all the lifting in the tavern, and even though he works as a gasfitter in the daytime he always makes sure he is in the bar of the White Hart in the evening in case there is any trouble, and to help me throw out the drunks at closing time. I don't know how I would manage without Isaac now.'

'Good girl, Fanny. I always told you to get a Thomas. Every tavern needs a Thomas. When your Father was away at sea I always made sure I employed a Thomas in my tavern.'

'Please Grandfather, can I get down from the table?'

'Yes George, and you too Henry. Take your plates with you to the kitchen. Are you going outside?'

'Yes Grandfather. We would like to go down by the river.'

'Are you going to stay here tonight, Matilda?'

'I would like to if that is no trouble for you, Father. It gets dark so quickly now, and I don't want to be driving that cart in the dark with Ann.'

'In that case boys, you can go out to play for a while, but do not go too far, and make sure you are back before it gets dark. If you are good there will be fruit cake for tea. Jane makes a very good cake, and it will be fresh out of the oven.'

'Thank you Grandfather.'

'Have you spoken to Mary, Father? She wrote me a letter and seems beside herself with woe. Her children are unhappy and I just don't know what is going wrong in Petworth. Do you know what the trouble is, Mother?'

'I told Patty, 'tis no good. That scoundrel – I never understood why they went all the way to Petworth. I told your Father I'll have no more talk of it in this house. It makes me ill to think of all the trouble, and it is so unfair. Small children should not have to suffer such troubles. I'll hear no more of it. I need a glass of stout. Fanny… Jane – please fetch me some stout.'

'I also received a letter from George a while ago from Trinidad. Have you heard from him more recently Father?'

'Yes Matilda. He usually sends us a letter each month. We are worried about him. He has been quite ill and some of his crew have succumbed to the Yellow Fever. I wish he had not gone to the Caribbean. I think that sea is bad for your health. I wish he could have stayed in Australia and New Zealand. Those places are much healthier.'

'George told us the Panama, New Zealand and Australian Mail Company was dissolved earlier this year so I suppose that is why he had to go to the Caribbean?'

'I am sure they still have mail in Australia, so I don't see why George could not have carried on working for some other mail company. But George likes his Royal Mail – he thinks he is working for the Queen, and I expect the Company looks after English mariners better than some foreign mail service would. Trouble is, even the grand Royal Mail has no answers to the Yellow Jack.'

'It is only a fever isn't it Father. People in Chichester get the Fever, and although it is not very nice most people get better in the end, don't they?'

'I wish you were right, Matilda. But you are not. Yellow Fever is a vicious tropical type of the illness, which seems to be particularly dangerous for white men who are not used to the hot climate and the local diseases. Yellow Fever is almost always deadly and seems to pick its victims quite by chance. I wish George would come back and work the British or European waterways where we don't get the dreaded disease.'

'But does he want to? My brother was always so keen to explore the world on a ship and find his desert islands – would he want to come back now?'

'I don't know. But I do know I am worried he might become ill out in the West Indies, and more and more I think we need him back home. Your mother and I are getting too old to run the Crown and Anchor. And George and Henry need their father. Our whole family seems to be having a difficult time. There is you and poor Dick. Then Fanny - she seems to have been unwell ever since she went to Lewes, Martha is miles away in Surrey, and now there is poor old Patty.'

'Perhaps we should try to persuade George to come home to stay next time he is here, Father. Maybe, having been at sea for so long he has had his fill of it now and will be ready to come home? Can we talk to him at Christmas?'

'I don't think so, Matilda. His steamer is not due back from the West Indies until the spring. We shall not see George this Christmas.'

'What can we do? Spring is a long time to wait before we can talk to him. What if he gets the Yellow Fever before then?'

'I know, Matilda. That is why I am worried. Of course most mariners do not get the Fever but my worry is that some do. I know George does not go off his ship much, and he knows to use his mosquito net because it is those damned creatures that probably carry the disease. And George has been at sea now for a long time and been safe so far, so he must be doing something right. I should try not to worry too much, Matilda.'

Ann opens her eyes with a start. 'But us women do worry, don't we Kitty? It's all right for you brave adventuring fools to sail off into the sunset and drown all your sensible thoughts in ale at the nearest harbour inn. You forget we mothers carry our sons in our wombs for nine months, give birth to them, and then nurture them for years. Of course we are going to worry when they are in danger – it doesn't matter to mothers if our boys are seven months old, seven years or twenty-seven years. They are still our little boys, full of adventures and irresponsibility. Sometimes I think you boys never grow up at all. I think I need another stout. Fanny…can you bring me another.' Her eye-lids droop heavily, then slowly close once more as her chin lowers towards her chest.

'Perhaps we should write to George – tell him we are worried about his health and want him to come home?'

'You may be right, Matilda. But George might think he is taking all the precautions to avoid the Yellow Fever, and may not want to give up his sailing. I think we might have more chance of getting him to come home by telling him that we need him here, that Mother and I cannot manage for much longer without him, and that George and Henry are growing older and will soon forget they even have a father?'

'Can you write to him, Father? I think George will take more notice of you. He knows you understand the life at sea, and all it means to him, and I do not think he will go against you. Whereas a silly older sister who has never been on a boat...I don't think he would listen to me.

'Please Father, will you write to George and beg him to come home to his family, and in particular for his boys?'

Wednesday 10th November 1869

St. Thomas

George William Eastland.

Our Ship's Boy is called Chas. Never did you see such a rascal. Sharp as a knife, quick as a ferret, filthy dirty finger nails, tousled wavy fair hair and sparkling blue eyes. With a heart of gold. I can't help but like the boy.

His full name is Charles Johnson, but everyone just calls him Chas. He is tiny and about twelve I think, though he won't tell. He must be less than four feet tall. As Ship's Boy Chas' job is to be at the beck and call of the Captain, as well as the other Officers. He has to fetch and carry things, clear up mess, deliver messages, clean boots, do anything that needs doing for the Officers – and quickly. In exchange for this he is given food, drink and shelter, a few pennies for wages - and he gets to sail the world.

Chas told me his story a few weeks ago when idling away some time. He came from London. 'Me dad is a drunk and 'e 'its me - if 'e can catch me. But when 'e is groggy 'e can't even see me, let alone 'it me. 'e crawls 'ome at night covered in spew an' kips on the floor or on the stair. Me mam ain't there. She knows t' be aht at night and well aht of me dad's way. Anyways, me mam's a tart an' don't care 'bout nuffin'. She finds 'er entertainmint somewheres else. Me dad forces me mam t' give 'im money. 'e knows she's always got some. But wot can she do? She don't want no black eyes do she?

'I feels sorry for me older sisters bein' there, but I telled them to get aht like me. There ain't no food there. There ain't no fun at all. If me an' me sisters didn't work for pennies an' food in the markit we would starve, or just be theefs. I don't wanna be a waster an' drunk like me dad. 'e'll probly end up knifed t' death in some back-alley when 'e drinks more than 'e can pay for. Dyin' in yer own sick an' bein' chewed on by rats ain't how I wants t' end up me life. I ain't stayin' 'ere, I telled me sisters. I's goin' t' sea t' find a better life an' make me fortune.'

Chas hung around Chatham Dockyard pestering ships' crews until one of the ship's Masters agreed to take him on trial as a Ship's Boy. Chas has been at sea ever since.

Our ship has been stranded at St Thomas now for so long that my stores are all straight and I am just killing time until we set off to sea, and it can't come quickly enough for me. I am sitting on the deck of the "Eider" quietly playing patience.

Chas runs past carrying an arm-load of rolls of paper – probably maps or something that he is urgently taking somewhere for the Captain. He is holding on tight to make sure he doesn't drop any of the large bundle of scrolls. He sees me with my cards as he hurries past and says, 'Ello Mister George.'

'Hello Chas,' I reply and wave my hand at him.

A few minutes later Chas strolls up and stands next to me casting a shadow over my cards.

'Hello Chas. And what have you been up to today?' I ask him.

'Ah nuffin' much, Mr George. Jus' cleanin' the Captin's mess, polishin' all the Officer's boots, moppin' the fo'c'sle decks, cleanin' the gimbal an' glass, an' takin' lots o' maps from the Captin's quarters to the wardroom for they Officers to ponder on.'

'Ja wanna play cards, Mister? I bet I can beat yer. I'll betcha a sixpence that I can beat yer the best out o' five 'ands of any card game yer fancies.'

'Not a chance,' I tell him. 'It would be like taking a rattle from a baby.'

Quick as a flash Chas replies, 'I can't see yer rattle Mister? Where does you keep that then?'

And this is how he is – all the time. You can't help but smile at his bare-faced, but mostly harmless cheek.

'Right then Chas. We will play one game of poker to warm-up and then I will beat you over five more. I do not bet money as all my money is saved for my two boys, but I will instead wager you this penknife.' I pull a knife from my pocket. It is a nice piece with a white whalebone handle.

Chas' eyes light up. 'Don't get too excited,' I tell him, 'as very soon you are going to be sixpence poorer than you are now.'

I shuffle the pack and deal the cards, and Chas and I contemplate our hands as the 4th Officer, Mr Archer suns himself against the fiferail and watches on. 'You want to be careful, George,' Mr Archer says to me. 'That boy is as tricky as a barrel-load of monkeys.'

'Ah, he is just a kid. I shall teach him a thing or two about how to win at poker,' I reply.

We play our first practice game. Chas pulls some anguished faces and takes his time as he seems to struggle to work out his best combination of cards. I win the game easily enough with a full house comprising two jacks, and the sevens of hearts, diamonds and clubs. Chas looks a bit forlorn, and I begin to feel a little guilty about taking a sixpence off a young boy who probably has very little money in this world. Still a wager is a wager, and it was Chas who challenged me to the game, and not the other way round. So the boy will just have to learn the hard way.

The next game is different altogether. I struggle to make any sort of hand. In the end I just about manage to get two pairs – fives and tens. After pulling a face Chas produces three of a kind – three queens to win that one.

Chas seems to gain in confidence after that win. By the expressions on his face you would think I am beating him hands down, but in fact it is quite the opposite. In the third game when we are at one hand each I think I am home and dry when I hold a full house with three queens and two jacks. Then Chas lays his cards on the deck - four aces and a king.

In the end the boy has a runaway win beating me by four hands to one and I hand over the penknife which causes him to beam from ear to ear. 'Aint you gonna give me the rattle then, Mr George?' Chas says with a twinkle of his mischievous eyes.

Just then the Chief Officer, Mr Hampshire comes upon the deck and calls out, 'Boy. Where's the Boy?' Seeing Chas with me he carries on. 'Boy. Fetch some drinks. Go to the galley and fetch ten tankards and bring them to the wardroom - as quick as you can boy. Also, ask the Barman to bring the grog.'

'Yes Sir, Mr Hampshire sir,' Chas replies.

Chas tucks his new penknife into his pocket and says, 'Thank'e Mr George for the game o' cards. Any time you wants another you jus' lets me know.' With that he is gone in a flash in the direction of the galley.

The Chief Officer glances at Mr Archer. 'Be in the wardroom in ten minutes, Mr Archer. The officers will be looking at our maps in readiness for our departure in a couple of days.'

'Very good, Sir,' Archer replies.

Before he leaves for the officer's meeting Mr Archer strolls up to me. 'I think you've been had, George.'

'What do you mean, Mr Archer?'

'The poker. I think Chas may have been cheating.'

'Cheating? Surely not? But how could he…?'

'I saw he had some cards in his back pocket and I wondered what he was up to, so I watched him very carefully. I'll be damned if I could see him do anything but his fingers moved so fast, and it was uncanny how he produced so many aces and kings just when he needed them? I may be quite wrong but I would be very wary about betting anything valuable on a card game with that young lad.'

I chuckle. 'You may well be right, Mr Archer. I usually win at cards, and I couldn't quite believe how poor my hands were in that game. That penknife – I won it myself in a card game so I won't lose too much sleep over it.'

'That Chas – he is certainly bright as a button and cheeky with it. You can't help but laugh.'

Mr Archer goes off to his meeting and I check that there are still fifty-two cards in my pack. There are. I don't know exactly how that scallywag did it, but he certainly beat me hands down on this occasion.

Friday 12th November 1869

St. Thomas

George William Eastland.

I am happy.

Our Steamer is ready to leave St. Thomas and so am I. I am so thankful that we will be sailing in just a few days time on the fifteenth of November. It is so much healthier to be on the sea – too many of our crew have fallen to sickness while the "Eider" has lain idle in St. Thomas – it is dreadful. True mariners should always be sailing. Languishing in a port leads to idleness and mischief – neither of which ever profited a man.

I am past all my illnesses and have had my beard trimmed. I have also purchased some new white clothes – all in all I now look five years younger than I did when I was so ill in September.

I am looking forward to sailing to the Gulf. I have heard that Havana is a very fine place and I expect to buy cigars to enjoy. If I can get them at a favourable price I will send a box home for father to sell to make some money. He can use it to buy himself and Mother and Georgie something nice. Havana Cigars are renowned all over the world as being of the finest quality tobacco.

My stores are full of Wines, Port and Sherry, Spirits, and Ale and Porter, as well as all the foods we will need for our voyage. Everything is recorded in my stores books and all is tidy. We have a complete crew with no more illnesses, and the seas have grown calmer of late.

The other day I received letters on the Mail from home and I am pleased to hear that Mother and Father are both well. I wish I could share some of that lovely English autumn weather with them. How I would enjoy a brisk walk along the path beside the Fishbourne Channel on a clear sunny morning, with a crisp fresh breeze coming off the water to cool my cheeks. I can imagine the peewit swooping over the sparkling water caught by the low autumn sun, butcher's broom scratching my ankles, and the trees to my left burning red before they finally let go of their leaves ready for the winter.

Some days I am tired of this continuous heat in the West Indies. Always sweating and always thirsty. It is a good job that cheap white shirts are aplenty as they rot away in no time from the damp and the salt air. Sometimes the only relief is to swim in the sea, though the sea-water is warm like a bath.

I am going to miss being at home this Christmas. Father and Mother and George, and all the others will eat hot potatoes and beef for dinner, and they will roast nuts over the fire while the snow lies outside over the white fields of Sussex. George will probably slide on frozen ice at the edge of the Channel, or on nearby ponds dressed in a thick coat, scarf and hat.

I hope Fanny goes home at Christmas. I don't like the thought of her being on her own, working in some dark, damp house in Lewes. I must write and ask Father to try again to persuade her to return to Dell Quay. If I was at home I am sure I could make Fanny come back.

I must besure to make my fortune here in the West Indies this time round so that next Christmas I can be back in England with George and Henry. I do not think it conducive to good health and long life for an Englishman to stay in the Caribbean for too long.

This Christmas, if I am not working, I will spend the day watching a dazzling blue sky over my head with not one fluffy white cloud in sight, while I bathe in the clear waters of The Gulf or The Caribbean. One day I will describe the scene to my grandchildren – the white sands, the rustling palm trees, the bright red and green parrots with their loud squawking, and the beautiful black women with their gigantic colourful headwear.

They may not believe the tall tales of a wizened old mariner. I must keep a white hat or two, or some fat cigars when I get to Havana to prove it to them.

Father sent me some English Newspapers with his last letter, so now I have everything I could wish for on a long sea voyage. Our trip down the Gulf will take a month so I must write home to thank Father for the newspapers before we leave on Monday.

I am really looking forward to getting back on the Sea and for this change of scenery. From St. Thomas we will call at Jacmel in Haiti, and St. Jago de Cuba and Havana on the island of Cuba, before we head across the Gulf to Vera Cruz in Mexico. Finally we sail along the Mexican coast to Tampico.

The rainy season must soon end and all will be sunshine and blue sky. I look forward to drier air and much better health.

R.M.S. "Eider"
St Thomas
November 13th 1869

My Dear Father & Mother

I received your last letter & Newspapers all safe and am very glad to hear that you were better. I am happy to tell you I am enjoying first rate health and doing very well. I leave here on the 15th for the Gulf of Mexico. I shall be gone a month so you will not hear any more from me until this day month. I shall then send you home a large order hoping you received the one by the last Mail all safe. I am very busy getting ready for sea and hope you will excuse my short note give my kind love to all hoping to hear from you by the Next Mail on the 17th. I suppose it is cold in England now. I should like a little of it out here it would be a change it is dreadful hot here always the same night & day. I have had some more white waistcoats & Trousers made since I wrote last. I have now 8 White Coats, 15 New Waistcoats and 24 pairs of new Trousers this will last me now all the time I am out here. I should like to spend Christmas with you all at home give my love to Fanny and Kiss Georgy for me and please to accept my fondest love and believe me to Remain

   your ever affectionate son
     Geo. Wm. Eastland

Crown & Anchor
Dell Quay
Sussex
England
Sunday 14th November 1869

My Dear George
    Your Mother and I and all your Sisters hope you are very well. We all miss you especially George and Henry it seems such a long time since you were here with us all.
    You will be astonished when you see your boys they are growing so tall they will be taller soon than your Mother. Mother doesn't stand for long, mind you she has become very tired and quite stooped since her illness and sits and rests as much as she can she would like to be behind the bar but it is more than she can manage and she cannot hear what drinks people order in the noise of the tavern as her hearing is now much worse. You will imagine how much this pains Mother not to be in her bar.
    I have written to Fanny I am concerned about her ailments I do not think she is very happy at Lewes. You know how delicate her health can be. I have tried to

persuade her to come back home here to live but she was allways as stubborn as she was fragile Fanny would listen to you if you went to Lewes to speak to her — she always took notice of her big Brother. I am not sure I can convince her any more with my letters I cannot go to Lewes as Mother cannot be left on her own.

   Matilda came to stay for a night with Henry and Ann. It was good for Henry and George to see each other as they have not for some considerable time it is very hard for Matilda with Dick being ill it doesn't look good. Matilda is putting a brave face on the bad situation but she looks tired and I think she finds it hard with the White Hart and must be hard also for Henry and little Ann as Matilda must be upset I told her to come here when she can but she has to run the tavern and in the winter she will likely not be able to drive here I don't know about Christmas yet. I assume you will still be in the West Indies at Christmas so no change with regard to that?

   I must confess I am not getting any younger and your Mother is not as she was when you last saw her. I think if you could help us get Fanny back we could be much more comfortable. It feels as if the Eastland family has sailed into a choppy sea what with all of the above and poor Mary and that trouble in Petworth as well only Martha and George and their children in Reigate are doing well I don't know when we will see them. Martha writes about Robert, George and Alfred and she is with child again I think hoping for a little girl. She has three boys at the last count I think she is destined for a forth boy.

I appeal to you to come home as soon as you can and give the sea a rest, just for a while. I am sure Nancy and George Cox would welcome you to go into their farming business with them with the money you have done so well to earn at Sea and I would be very pleased to see you back altogether with George and Henry as I think they need to be with each other and their Father they will soon be grown up themselves and you can always go back to the sea when they are a little older.

Our creaking Family would love to have time with you now before we become too creaky especially your Mother and I. I spent years on the sea and never encountered any disease as vile as the YELLOW Fever. I will be very glad to receive you back home safe and would be much happier if you sailed round Britain or Europe as a

Captain of my many ships I always liked to see the perils the Sea, the storms, the pirates as I could deal with that which I could see. A vile foe like Yellow Jack which cannot be seen would unsettle me more than other dangers

I am sending some newspapers with this package I hope they reach you but they are bulky so I cannot send too many there are many more magazines and newspapers here which I will keep for you to read when you return home.

Georgie sends his love and Henry would if he was here I am not sure when we will see him next with all the trouble at Littlehampton. Besure to write and to look after yourself and please come home to be with us as soon as you can. Your Mother and sisters will also be very pleased to see you all well

Believe me to remain your loving Father

George Eastland

Tuesday 30th November 1869

The Gulf of Mexico

George William Eastland.

My Steamer, RMS "Eider" is on the Gulf run. The voyage from Havana to Vera Cruz in Mexico is trouble-free and relatively calm considering this is still the rainy season. We stock up our supplies at Vera Cruz and set off along the coast expecting an easy ride to Tampico. Up in the heavens God has other ideas.

As the day wears on the sky turns black and purple, and the wind sucks the sea into knots and tosses the "Eider" about with a vicious lurch. We have kept well away from the coast for fear of being blown upon rocks and coral reefs. We had thought to get to the port of Tampico, but the winds and the drag of the sea has slowed our progress and means we cannot get there. Now darkness has fallen. When we realise we cannot make Tampico before dark Captain Bruce decides the "Eider" should drop anchor and see out the gathering storm overnight. We find ourselves near to a small island. Our maps suggest this green patch to be the Isla de Lobos, but it might be another for all we can see in this dark wild storm.

Just before 6pm we tuck our Steamer as near to the island as we dare, knowing the sea near the shore will be shallow or rocky. We hope that the land will give us a little shelter. We drop anchor and pray that please God this storm does not turn into a Hurricane. The night is black as soot. There is nothing to see, no stars, no lights - just black rain and black spray.

Lanterns sway wildly, and card games make me giddy. There is little to do but eat, drink and sleep. The "Eider" has been through many such storms at night and I am not unduly concerned. The best thing to do is to sleep through them. The chances are that by the time I awake the sea will be flat, the wind gone and a huge golden sun will sit upon the rim of the horizon to welcome in the new day and light a watery pathway across the sea for the end of our voyage to Tampico.

I lie in my berth listening to the timbers creak, as our steamer lurches amidst the endless tons of water that brew in this salty cauldron. I drift into an uneasy sleep.

Wednesday 1st December 1869

Isla de Lobos, the Gulf of Mexico, 4.55am

George William Eastland.

I am hurled from my slumber and land on the floor of my cabin.

I slide backwards and hit my head against my Iron Safe and my elbow hits something else - hard.

I can see nothing - but sounds flood into my ears.

The sounds of a storm raging.

Roar of the wind.

The ship creaking and grinding.

Tumultuous crashing of water against timber.

Shouting. Screaming. Banging.

All muffled by the wind and the water.

The ship lurches and vibrates.

Are the engines running?

I can't tell.

I smell panic. My panic.

Is the ship even still afloat?

I feel for my boots and drag them on, as well as my jacket.

My cabin floor is dry so all cannot yet be lost.

I scramble from my cabin and head for the decks.

It is as if I am deaf.

I bump into crew and passengers.

Hard as we try to avoid each other in the gloom we are thrown by the lurching ship and smash into each other as if like drunken fools.

Faces of terror caught in the flickering light from a glim.

Eyes wide with fear.

Passengers huddle together, arms around each other.

One man wails as I pass – 'We will sink, we will drown, we are all done for.'

I shout back, 'We will be fine. Royal Mail ships love a good storm.'

As I make for the deck I am wondering, is the Steamer still anchored?

The ship must be freed or it will surely be wrecked?

Men run past with open mouths yet no sound comes from them.

I clamber up the manropes and emerge to the air where a few wild lanterns illuminate the "Eider", bucking and straining in the near dark.

A ton of water hits me full in the face and I cling on to a rail for dear life.

Rain and spray are one, flying horizontally to douse the ship like a giant sideways waterfall.

I can see only shadows through the blanket of water that buffets me in the gloom.

Men and ropes and all manner of things slide across the slippery deck colliding with each other on the perilous timbers.

One small figure flies straight over the side of the ship without even a cry.

Why did he jump?

The crew are fighting to raise the anchor.

I register this mercy for had they not, the "Eider" would be pulled apart like a sardine stripped to shreds by a hungry cormorant.

One Deck Hand loses his grip and slides helplessly on his back across the deck, frantically grasping for something to stop him being washed away by the merciless flood.

I am deafened by the thunderous gale blowing through my skull.

I feel the "Eider" judder and vibrate and she seems to spin as if snagged on a giant submerged rock.

As the "Eider" cants I am knocked from my feet and slither through a hatchway falling onto an officer who is trying to come up from the deck below. We fall together into a heap, our descent thankfully softened by a pile of damp discarded canvas sail.

'We are turning,' the officer screams. 'Make sure no passengers are on deck.'

I scramble back up the manropes to the deck but a wave across the sodden timbers almost sluices me back down the hatch once more.

I grip desperately onto a rail with all my strength.

As I emerge again a dreadful crashing noise rises even above the gale.

I turn my head to see the steam winch give way and the capstan spin like a top, the heavy bars shearing off in all directions right at the men who have been heaving for all they are worth.

A man hurtles through my legs knocking me from my feet once more.

My indignant shouts are drowned by the water flying across the deck and into my mouth. As we collide with the side of the paddle-wheel casing I grab the man by the arm.

As his body turns to face me I see – he has no face.

Where his face should be is a bloody pulp.

His left eye hangs upon what remains of his cheek.

I too am covered in blood, spattered all over my front.

Until another wave of water washes over me to once again separate me from my crewmate.

His body washes and slithers alongside the railing, where it comes to a contorted resting position.

The body's face is unrecognisable.

Yet I recognise it.

Its mouth screams.

At least – it opens. I can hear nothing but wild wind and water and the pounding of my heart in my skull.

It is William. William Percival - my Storekeeper, his face smashed. Yet he lives?

Hauling him by his arms like a sack of potatoes I scramble on my hands and knees back to the hatch to return to the Main Deck.

I slide the poor man into a cluster of willing hands that reach up from below.

Before I can think, the ship's Surgeon, Charles Oxley grabs my arm.

He is shouting something?

I cannot hear.

I am deafened by the storm, or is it my fear?

I feel paralysed.

He shakes me.

'George, George.'

He looks terrified.

Charles is a good man.

'George. You must help. There are more than I can manage on my own.

'The men. They are hit by the Capstan bars. Please help bring them below deck before they wash overboard. I can treat them down here.

'Quickly George. Leave the dead ones. Just find those that still live.'

I will help.

I must help.

I am alive.

I must be grateful.

I am a lucky one.

Charles needs help.

I have never seen him look so terrified.

These thoughts fly through my head in an instant.

I see men lying around the broken remains of the Capstan, some oozing with blood. Some have obviously broken arms and legs, their limbs protruding from their bodies at unearthly angles.

Some scream silently in this wretched roaring gale. Others lie in a waterlogged tangled mass of hair, ragged limbs, timber and foam. All these broken bodies are dragged back and forth by the floods of seawater that breach the decks, as our ship bucks and heaves and strains in the wicked storm.

I quickly realise I must attend to the muted screamers first despite their seeping blood, ripped skin, smashed faces, and hanging limbs. Their wide mouths tell me they still have life.

The others may be, if nothing else, beyond pain.

I support a man whose arm hangs limp and bloody. Clutching him under his armpit we stumble across the deck to the hatch where those helping the doctor carry him below.

I return across the deck where two more men seem tangled together. The first has a deep channel cut across his forehead and is not conscious. Is he alive?

The other is not moving either. His legs face the wrong way.

I retch.

I turn and see screams behind me. Another Able Seaman is trying to crawl towards me. He cannot walk. His legs are broken. Then I recognise him. It is Joseph Lloyd – the Captain's servant.

A heavy rope has broken free above the man and swings wildly from a mast like a Devil's whip. It lurches then suddenly flicks, like twine in the gale, eager to decapitate any man who strays within its range.

I watch for a moment and judge its reach carefully before crawling along the edge of the rail to fetch the bloodied mariner.

He screams at the wind as I push and drag him, crawling low beneath the deathly rope back to shelter. I am grateful the wind drowns out his anguished cries.

I go back and forth. Time passes.

I fall and slither on this slimy deck. Towards yet another body.

Not knowing if he be alive or dead until I roll him to take a look at his face.

After recovering all the injured men we gather the broken corpses and take them down to the main deck for the Surgeon to identify them and confirm them dead or otherwise.

Charles and his helpers work frantically to treat the living wounded.

I check the upper decks one final time. The bodies are all gone. Either rescued, or washed overboard.

A pale daylight now begins to glimmer in the sky. The deck turns red.
So do my hands.

I return wearily to the main deck and gratefully retreat from the searing wind. I put my fingers under my armpits to bring back the feeling that I have lost to the cold and the wet.

I slump down for a moment and close my eyes to gather myself. The swollen and battered faces of the men I have attended, contorted with agony and terror and dripping with blood will haunt my dreams forever more.

I quickly re-open my eyes.

I help the Surgeon to drag the corpses into a broken wretched pile in a dark corner of a cable-tier where we cover them with a heavy tarpaulin for now. Sea burial will follow as soon as it is calm enough.

With our anchor up and all men safely below deck the "Eider" rides the remainder of the storm facing into the gale, its paddle wheels turning steadily.

As the gale drops to a moderate easterly wind so my heartbeat drops to the pace of a moderately steaming engine. The "Eider" smells of shock as we resume our passage to Tampico. I am shivering uncontrollably. I make my way to the stores where I manage to find a tot of rum. I have two.

My stores are wrecked. I have never seen such a mess of smashed food and broken bottles and casks, and now I have no Storeman to help me clean up the mess. Poor bugger. I hope he lives. If his injuries are too bad I hope he dies – soon.

I will, however be eternally grateful that I have somehow avoided serious injury in this storm, unlike my unlucky shipmates. Captain Bruce says this was a storm like no other.

I am told the Captain gave the order to turn the "Eider" astern, which is what caused the Steam Winch to give way and led to the catastrophe.

I have never felt so frightened at sea before.

God has spared me from this watery grave, and with the hurricane season soon to conclude I can surely look forward to blue skies and my return to England in the spring.

Thank God for this mercy.

The "Eider" limps towards Tampico with its cargo of casualties and corpses, and with our sad tale to tell. It occurs to me that news of the disaster may travel back to England where my family will hear of it.

I must write a letter to reassure Father that I am all well, and make sure it catches the first Mail to England.

A little later I return to my cabin to put on some dry clothing. I remove all my drenched and torn rags and look in the mirror. A wretch with hopelessly matted hair, a red swelling on his cheek and blood dripping from his ears and nose stares back at me.

My body aches all over. My elbows and knees are cut. The nail on my right thumb has been tore clean off. I cannot count my bruises.

I can count my blessings.

Royal Mail Ship "Eider" 50163 – Official Log Book

<u>1869</u> 1st December at 5am Lobos Isl

On weighing Anchor off Lobos Island the Spindle of Steam Winch carried away causing the Capstan to revolve violently backward, the pad's of which had been lifted to slack cable to clear chackle off the starboard Pipe which could not be cleared without so doing. The Engines had been moved astern to clear the Chackle.

J. Bruce
Commander

S. Hampshire
Chief Officer

Royal Mail Ship "Eider" 50163 – Official Log Book

1st December   Lobos Isl

The undermentioned Crew were injured by the Capstan Bars.

C. W. Archer 4th Off – Killed from blow on Chest, Right Temple + back of Head.

Edwin Coates Butcher Fracture of Forearm.

Joseph Lloyd Capt Servant - Do- Left Femur.

John Craddock A.B - Do- Right-Do.

Wm Percival Storekeeper Do- Bones of Face and Lower Jaw + Blinded + loss of left eye.

Thomas Osborne Boots Incised wound under the Left Jaw + Blinded.

Thomas Marshall A.B. Severe contusions of Right Foot.

Stanley Hampshire Chf Off – Sprained Feet.

Chas Johnson S. Boy Knocked overboard.

Royal Mail Ship "Eider" 50163 – Official Log Book

1st December 1869 Lobos Island

Hope 11/6

Found in Forecastle one box – locked – belonging to Charles Johnson – S. Boy – Sealed up the same. Put it away – to be handed to Consul on arrival in St Thomas

J. Bruce   Arthur Green
Commander   2nd Off

Royal Mail Ship "Eider" 50163 – Official Log Book

2nd December   At anchor off Tampico Bay

Committed the body of C.W. Archer to the deep with the usual ceremonies

Southampton
4th Jany 1870

Capt Eastland
Dear Sir,
 Herewith I forward
Bank Notes £30.
P.O. £3. 14. 6.
forwarded by G.W.
Eastland West Indies
trusting it will come
safe to hand.
 I remain
  Yours etc
   A Ian Sartin

Saturday 15th January 1870

Dell Quay, Chichester

Ann Eastland.

It is morning.

Nancy is here. She has not been well, so she was allowed a little time off work and came up on the train from Hermitage to stay with us for a few days to rest.

It is pleasant for this time of year for the weather is dry, crisp and cold. The sky is blue and the water in the Fishbourne Channel is calm. I am sitting behind the bar in the Crown polishing a few potatoes, daydreaming about when my son will come home from the sea this spring. And then I see Nancy through the tavern window coming back to the inn from the quayside. She seems anything but calm.

I shout, 'George, George what is the matter with Nancy? She is running up from the quay, red in the face and howling. What on earth can be up with her?'

George emerges from the cellar. He says, 'Fanny. You mean Fanny. Nancy is not here. She lives in the New Forest.' My husband goes outside to meet Nancy where she fairly runs into him almost knocking him off his feet.

'Whoa whoa Fanny,' he cries. 'What is the matter? You look like you have seen a ghost or something. Tell me, what is it?'

Fanny is gasping for breath, bright red in the face, her eyes wild with fright and seemingly unable to string together any intelligible words.

George leads her by the arm back into the bar where I am sitting. 'Come and sit down Fanny. Mother – put some rum into that glass you have just cleaned. It will help to calm your nerves, Fanny. Then you can tell us what has happened to you. Have you been attacked out on the quay? Surely no mariner would attack my daughter on Dell Quay? If so I'll have his guts for garters.'

George and I sit, one each side of Fanny as her body, shuddering with sobs and tears slowly subsides into relative calm. It takes a few minutes – I don't recall ever seeing her this shaken up. She begins to speak but she is stammering and I can feel her body trembling as I hold my arm around her shoulders.

'He he might be injured or or dead, or drowned. Lots of men have been. Terrible, horrible storm and and lots of injured – they, they don't say how many. I wish he didn't go to sea. I wish he would come home and be safe. I wish you hadn't sent him to sea Father. I always thought you were wrong to send him away. If anything has happened to George I will always blame you Father.'

Fanny starts sobbing again.

It is then that I notice. A newspaper is sticking out from under Fanny's skirt where she is sitting. I pull it out and look at the page where Fanny has opened it and I start reading. It is today's edition of The Hampshire Advertiser which Fanny must have got from one of the boats at the quayside. The headline reads, 'SHOCKING ACCIDENT IN THE WEST INDIES.' I read on. My own heart is now pounding in my chest as my eyes race over the smudged newsprint, made more so by Fanny's tears.

'There was a storm at daylight, all hands called to the deck, a winch broke and there were lots injured and killed. Oh God George, why do they make this damned print so small nowadays? They just do it so as I cannot read it!! What if our son has been hurt…or worse?'

George grabs the newspaper from me and reads the article for himself, straining his eyes to read the small print. He reads it several times, then finally puts the paper down with what almost appears like a grin.

'What the hell are you grinning about George?' I glare at him. If I had more strength I would punch him. I feel my nails digging into the palms of my hands, first with fear and now anger.

'Do not worry ladies as I believe our son, and your brother, dear Fanny to be well and uninjured by this terrible incident. And this is why I believe this to be the case…

'Firstly any self-respecting Chief Steward would probably have been slumbering cosily in his bunk at dawn. Secondly, when all Able Seamen were called to the deck to heave anchor, that would not have included George. He is not a 'Hand' and he would have had many

373

other important duties to attend to. And finally... who else but the Chief Steward would have provided the information for this newspaper article? George keeps much of the ship's paperwork and is probably their best penman. I even recognise one or two of the phrases in the newspaper article as being George's words, like the one about a man's boot being 'pared off' as with a knife.

'Furthermore, the newspaper article tells of the injuries to a boy, a storekeeper, the butcher, and a cabin steward. As sure as eggs are eggs, if the Chief Steward had been injured the newspaper would have said so.

'Rest assured ladies, as I believe that we will soon receive confirmation one way or another that our George has survived this very unpleasant episode all safe and well.'

Please God, I hope my husband is right this time. I will not relax until we receive word to confirm George is safe.

Now, what was I doing before all this dreadful commotion with Nancy? Damn nuisance. Is there never any peace?!

Saturday 15th January 1870

Dell Quay, Chichester, 3.58pm

George Eastland.

I sit in my chair by the fire and watch the flickering flames.

I have read that article in the Hampshire Advertiser over and over again looking for clues to my son's fate. The damned article doesn't say when the Accident happened, only that it occurred on board the "Eider" when it was on the Gulf of Mexico route, and that it happened a few days before the "Seine" left St. Thomas for Southampton.

I have also read the letter George sent dated 13th November, which arrived here early in December – I can't remember exactly when now. In it he said the "Eider" would be gone a month to the Gulf and that he was due to embark on the 15th November.

Surely if the Accident had happened on that voyage I should have had a letter from my son by now? He always writes each month, yet we have received no letter since the one he wrote on 13th November. 'Thirteen, unlucky for some' – tries to push its way into my mind. I must not give in to silly superstitions. I received a note dated 4th January along with £30 just the other day from the Southampton Office. But George might have sent that money weeks ago, before the accident. Surely the Southampton Office would know if George had been hurt, and they would have told me?

Perhaps the "Eider" returned to the Gulf in mid-December and George missed the Mail between the sailings? I am sure the Accident must have happened before Christmas as it would take at least a fortnight for the story to get back to England and to be printed in the Advertiser?

My hope hangs on the clues I find in the newspaper article. It names the fourth Officer who died, Mr Archer as well as the butcher, the captain's servant, the storekeeper, and even a boy who was washed overboard. I am sure if anything had happened to the Chief Steward it would have been included in the newspaper?

Thank goodness I have managed to allay the anxieties of Ann and Fanny. But I will only still my own racing mind when I receive some confirmation that my son lives. If the "Eider" sailed again to the Gulf from the middle of December for a month we may not receive a letter from George until the end of January. This could be the longest January in my life. I will check the post every day for a Mail from the West Indies. Oh heavens - tomorrow is Sunday and there is no mail delivery. Curses.

I stare into the fire and pray…

'Dear God, please deliver my son from that dreadful Accident at sea, please give George time to write home to us very soon to let his Mother and I know that he is allright and please blow the wind in the right direction to speed the mail carrying his letter back to Southampton with the greatest of haste. My poor old heart cannot cope with much more of this strain. I am getting too old for it. Ann and I will be eternally grateful for George's deliverance from that dreadful storm. Amen.'

I wonder if George has even received the last letter I sent to him when I asked him to come home as soon as he is able? This is the trouble with George being on the other side of the World. News only travels as fast as the quickest mail ship. And only then if a letter has been written.

I watch the flames lick around the coals and try not to drift off to sleep as I fear the nightmares. It is hopeless.

Monday 17th January 1870

Letter received in the mail at Dell Quay today

The amount of orders are £33. 14 - 6

"Eider"

St Thomas

Dec. 16th 1869

My dear Father & Mother

I now take great pleasure in writing you a few lines to inform you I am quite well hoping you are all the same.

I have a very sad tale to tell you. we had very bad weather down the Gulf of Mexico this time and between Vera Cruz and Tampico we took shelter during the Gale under an Island called Lobos. we anchored there at 6 p.m. The next morning at 4 a.m. all hands were called to get up anchor it blowing then a Strong Gale from N.N.W. and heavy sea setting in over the Coral Reef. while getting up the anchor the Captain gave orders for the Engine to turn astern. the Ship got stern way on her and tightened the Cable. the Steam Capstan gave way and consequently the Main Capstan took charge and flew round backwards knocking the men right & left. the 4th Officer was Killed and a Deck Boy & my Store-Keeper had his face all smashed also his nose & Jaw Bones broken his left eye Knocked out. it was wonderful how he lived his teeth and all was gone he looked a dreadful sight. He is left in Havana Hospital. The Butcher got his left arm broken in two places. The Captain's Servant had his leg broken in two places between the Knee and the Hip. A Bedroom Steward got his jaw and face cut open and his back hurt, and about seven more wounded one of the Sailors got his leg Broken. The Doctor and myself served them up in the bad places. you cannot imagine what it was like when the wounded and dead were brought down on the Main Deck after the accident occurred. The scene of the dead Bodies and the cries of the wounded were something dreadful. My dear Parents I am sending home to you some money but I will put a Slip in the letter when I close it as I do not know how much it will be. I am sending Mr. Gorham 1000 Cigars. I shall tell him to send you the Cheque or wait until I come home. If he should pay you the amount will be £20.0.0. I have cleared seventy pounds this month what money I send home you will please to put in Guiggen & Company Bank for me. Havana is a very nice City indeed. I bought 6000 Cigars there. I have sold them all.

I have a very pretty Bird I bought in Vera Cruz. I shall Keep it until I come home if I can. it is something the same Kind as the one Fanny has got only it is a bright red all over with a Black topicar.

My dear parents I hope you will make yourself comfortable and enjoy a nice Christmas. I shall be home next Christmas with you please god. I hope poor old Dad is quite well give my love to Dick and Kitty and George and Nancy & also to poor Patty. you can send her a Christmas present for the Children if you like, and give Fanny a new dress. What you receive from me put down in a book and what you use put down also but besure and use what you want for yourselves, also write always and tell me if you receive the Money all safe that I send you. I shall send the Money home rather fast now I hope for the next ten months and then I shall come home to stay for a time with you all. I am enjoying very good health now thank God if I can keep so fit will do very well. I suppose things are very dull at home. when you write send me some late papers. Kiss little Georgy for me. I hope his leg is getting better. It will be a terrible trouble to me for life.

I here enclose a brief letter for Fanny hoping she is quite well. I must now end my epistle & hoping you will enjoy a Merry C-mas and a happy new year. us poor Sailors we have to put up with any thing but never mind it will not be for ever. please to accept my fondest love and believe me to remain your affectionate Boy

                    Geo. Wm. Eastland

R.M.S. "Eider"
St Thomas
January 13th 1870

My dear Father & Mother
 I now take the greatest of pleasure in writing to you to inform you I am quite well and hope you are all the same. I missed the Mail last month and so I did not send the letters to you. I sent you a month ago £3.14.6 which I hope you got all safe and £20 worth of Cigars for Mr Gorham. I send by this Mail an order of the Company you will please to send to the <u>London Office</u> to be Changed with the Certificate pinned on as you receive it.

By the last Mail I also sent to you the Money orders payable to George Eastland making £23. 6-10 alltogether which I hope you will receive all safe. I leave here on the 17th for the Gulf of Mexico. I have been very busy lately since the 16th of December I have had to Superintend two Ships the <u>"Eider"</u> and <u>"Mersey"</u>. The Store Keeper of the "Mersey" died last week with Yellow Fever. he had only been out here a month. Dear Parents do not be surprised if I come home in April. I think it very likely I may. It is dreadful being out here so long I shall be so glad when my time comes to go home please God I will spend two or three months with you then. Whatever you do you must not let Hellen know I will be home in April. I do not know how long the Trial will be in London, nor do I yet know how long I will be off the sea.

I do not want to think about that pretty Girl until I know I am finished with the sea. It would not be fair to her, nor to my heart. When you write to me do not stir my longing by telling me anything about her as any woman would be but of little use to me while I continue the Sea. If I have time I shall write to Fanny if not you must give my love to her hoping she is well and enjoying better health. I have not much news to tell you at Present I do not like being here at St Thoma's much it is very unhealthy but I never go on shore only on business. I have got a case Stock of Clothes now.

Dear Parents Please to give my love to all my Sisters and kiss the Boys for me hoping to see you all again soon and believe me ever to remain

your affectionate Son
Geo. Wm. Eastland

Wednesday 19th January 1870

R.M.S. "Eider", Captain J Bruce's quarters

'Good morning gentlemen.'

'Good morning Captain.'

'I have summoned you all here to update you on matters relating to that most unfortunate Accident that befell our Steamer, the "Eider" in the Gulf last month. I wish to ensure that all you Officers fully understand the consequences. It was, of course a most regrettable Accident which incurred the Company some considerable expense...'

'It wasn't entirely an accident was it Captain? Changing the steamer's course...'

'Silence! I have not yet bid you to speak.

'As I was saying, the Royal Mail Steam Package Company has taken note of my initial report of the Accident. The Company is understandably grieved about the cost of the damage to the structure of the "Eider" and the destruction of fittings, fixtures and perishables, as well as the possible damage to the reputation of the Company in the eyes of potential future passengers.

'Which is why I have called you all here now. I have received this letter from the Company's Court of Directors in London. The Company is to conduct a Trial at the London Office to ascertain fully what happened in the Gulf. Myself, and all the Officers serving on the "Eider" are to be summoned to attend the Trial to provide their accounts of the Accident.'

''Tis a grave pity the Fourth Officer, Mr Archer is no longer here to give his account. God Rest His Soul.'

'Quite right, sir. Quite right. A most promising young Officer he was, of course. Now, as I was saying...we will therefore be taking the "Eider" back to Southampton a little earlier than previously planned – probably in April. I trust you are all clear so far?'

'What will we be asked at the Trial, Captain?'

'We will doubtless be asked all manner of questions by those pen-men who reside in their fancy offices in London, sitting at their leather-clad desks with their overflowing drinks cabinets and cut-glass tumblers.'

'How should we explain the damage to the Steam Capstan and all the injuries and deaths among the crew?'

'And how should we explain the orders to turn the ship which led to the disaster?'

'I suggest you each think very carefully about what story you will tell at the Trial. I also suggest you only state what you saw with your own bare eyes and what you heard with your own ears. Do not repeat tittle-tattle untruths that others may have told you based on their own misunderstandings.

'Remember, we were battling against a ferocious hurricane fighting to prevent the ship being smashed onto the nearby island. Steering a Steamer in such weather is nigh on impossible for any crew.'

'It wasn't classified as a hurricane, Captain?'

'Semantics! Were we to know that at the time? It felt like a hurricane.'

'But an order was given to turn the "Eider" astern?'

'I would respectfully repeat what I said earlier, gentlemen. Think very carefully before you open your mouths. Remember, you all make a very fine living on the sea under my command and I would very much like my loyal crew to continue to sail with me in the future. It is much to the advantage of all of you to continue in our fine service. You will all doubtless have to place your hands and swear on the Bible to tell only the truth. You must only say what you yourselves personally witnessed. There was much water and noise on the night of the hurricane. What you thought you heard over the din of that hurricane may be far from the truth. What you cannot be absolutely sure of you cannot report at the Trial.

'You should also bear in mind that those stiff-collared buffoons in London wouldn't be able to tell between a storm and a storm in a teacup. Some of them may have been on a rowing boat on Hyde Park Lake of a Sunday afternoon, but likely none of them have any idea about hurricanes. We Merchant Seamen risk our lives every day on the high seas to make a fortune of profit for the Royal Mail Steam

Packet Company. Those men in London should be eternally grateful to us mariners.

'The sea is a dangerous place. Accidents happen. I believe this crew should be praised for keeping the "Eider" afloat in such a hurricane, and for looking after all the Company's passengers and ensuring none of them suffered anything more than the most trivial of injuries. Now, before you all get back to work do any of you have any further questions?'

'Captain...since the 'accident' there seems to have been great indiscipline amongst the crew. The ship's log is littered with reports of 'wilful disobedience of orders', 'mariner drunk and incapable of taking the wheel', 'asleep whilst on lookout', 'men going ashore without leave', and just the other day 'fighting and creating a disturbance in Saloon during dinner hour'?'

'What is your point, Second Officer?'

'I think this poor discipline should be stamped upon – an example now needs to be set to dissuade others from such insolence and disrespect to our ship.'

'I agree with you Sir. Of course the penalties for such offences are set out in the Company's rules and I cannot deviate from them in ordinary circumstances. I do, however ultimately decide which offence has been committed and the severity of the fine, and the length of the incarceration varies accordingly. For the time being I want all offenders to be sent to myself and Mr Hampshire. We will award the appropriate penalty, or find other means to show these miscreants the error of their ways.

'So, can we now get on gentlemen? Do any of you have any more questions?'

'No Captain Bruce.'

'Very well, my good men. Now, will somebody fetch me Surgeon Oxley and Chief Steward Eastland. I need to talk to them. They will also be summoned to the Trials in London and questioned because they dealt with the injured.

'Dismissed.'

Wednesday 19th January 1870

R.M.S. "Eider"

George William Eastland

Tap, tap, tap.
'Eastland? Captain Bruce wants to see you in the wardroom. Now.'
'Yes Sir. Is something up?'
'Not for me to say, Eastland. Don't delay.'

Tap, tap, tap.
'Enter.
'Ah…Eastland. Come. Take a seat next to the Surgeon. Brandy?'
'No, thank you Captain.'
'I wish to talk to the two of you about the hurricane last month. I firstly wish to commend you both for your very considerable bravery and devotion to duty on the day of that dreadful Accident.
'Fortunately such a dreadful Hurricane is a rare occurrence, and our fine Royal Mail Steamers can usually cope with all the rough weather thrown at them. But that Hurricane was exceptionally severe causing the most unfortunate casualties.
'It was so unusual that the Company's Court of Directors have sent me a letter informing me that a Trial is to take place at the London Office, probably in April to establish all the facts of the Accident. The two of you will be summoned to attend the Trial as you most immediately attended to the casualties.'
'Sir, the "Eider" has sailed unscathed through many rough storms. Were not the injuries and deaths caused because the "Eider" changed course causing the Capstan to break into the faces of all those poor Deck Hands?'
'Were you there Eastland, when the order was given? Or were you still asleep in your cabin?'
'Well…I was told an order was given…'
'You will both do very well not to repeat second-hand untruths at the Trial. As in any Court of Law you may only give as evidence at

the Trial things which you yourselves have seen and heard and not idle gossip and lies. Mark my words, to repeat things you yourselves did not witness would be viewed most unfavourably upon your own Judgement Day.

'I understand that you, Eastland saw much sea-water, rain, blood and horrific casualties. And I believe the Surgeon had many severe injuries to deal with, as well as the unfortunate corpses. Eastland - you must tell the Trial all about your brave efforts to rescue those poor unfortunate victims of the Accident. And you Oxley, must tell of your valiant work in saving the lives of those injured men.

'I am truly grateful for the brave efforts of you both on the day of the storm, and will be most appreciative of your factual statements about the casualties at the Trial. I would be obliged if you will leave reports about mechanical matters, weather conditions, navigation and passenger safety to those who were at the helm – myself and the other Officers.

'Furthermore, I wish to demonstrate my gratitude to you both in tangible fashion. Eastland – you will be given an additional sum of money in your next pay for assisting the Surgeon with the casualties. I am told you showed great bravery in the most highly unusual circumstances of the Accident in that vicious Hurricane that would not normally befall a Chief Steward.

'You Oxley, are well used to sickness and misfortune. But you did your profession proud by dealing with so many serious injuries so well, with such skill and with such a steady manner. I will gladly direct one or two of my finest bottles of brandy to your quarters.'

'Thank you Captain. You forget that I am teetotal. Nevertheless, I shall be pleased to accept your kind gifts. I shall give a bottle to my brother in England who is most partial to a good brandy, and the other will be of great benefit to my patients. A small measure works wonders for the alleviation of toothache, as well as other wounds and infections.

'Is that all, Captain?'

'You may go. I know I can rely on you both.'

Life has been very hard since that bloody storm. The "Eider" took a fearful battering and much damage had to be repaired. My stores were a frightful mess, and the cleaning and replacement of perishable and non-perishable stocks has taken me days to complete. The paperwork is also as great a task.

As if that isn't enough the Storekeeper of R.M.S. "Mersey" died of Yellow Fever early in January, and I have had to superintend that Steamer in addition to the "Eider". My own Storekeeper, William Percival died in Havana of his injuries following that night of Hell.

Captain Bruce is correct. He can most certainly rely upon me to tell all that I saw and heard when I attend the trial in London.

I will not invite God's wrath by failing to account for anything to do with that dreadful day. I will tell what I saw, what I heard, what I did, what I was told by others, and of how many storms I have previously sailed through without such a calamity of deaths and bloody injuries.

When I reach my final Judgement Day I want to hear God say, 'George, you told the truth, and omitted nothing.'

If errors of judgement were made in that storm which cost the lives of our crew they must be discovered so that they might be avoided in future. I do not want my poor Storeman to have died in vain, nor others to follow in future in the same way due to the same mistakes repeated.

All the more reason for me to give up the Sea. I will bite my tongue for now but at the trial I will tell all that I know. I have had my fill of the West Indies. It appears like a turquoise Paradise, and for a young mariner with no ties and responsibilities it may well be for a time.

I have now seen too many men die out here in these bad places and I have my family to think of. The only good thing to come from that storm is that I will go back to England in April. I will count the days until I can go home to look after George and Henry and Father and Mother.

I will send home to Father all the money I can. I do not want to keep much out here in the West Indies in case we have any more storms.

I have also sent home two parrots – one for Fanny and the other for Father to look after for me until I get home. I got them in Havana. When I am back in England they will remind me of the colour of the West Indies. The parrots have the most amazing bright feathers you can imagine – red, yellow, green and blue. I think 'Fanny' would be a good name for a parrot.

R. M. S. "Eider"
Havana
January 24th 1870

Dearest Father & Mother

I now take great pleasure in writing to inform you I am quite well hoping you are all the same. I am happy to inform you I shall be home in April if all goes well. I am going home on a trial at the London Office about the Accident down the Gulf last month so I shall be at home for two or three months in the Summer which will be a great treat for me. It is very unhealthy out in the West now. I don't think if I once get home again Safe I shall ever come back to the West Indies again that is if I can do without. My dearest Parents I sent home to you per "Shannon" fifteen pounds (sterling) and an order on the Company for the Surgeon for £8.6.10 which I hope you will receive all safe in all £23-6-10 please to place it in Guiggen & Company Bank for me. My dearest Parents that Affair on board last month has caused a great deal of disturbance. The Captain will no doubt get into trouble about it.

My dearest Parents I hope to spend a pleasant Summer at home with you all when I get home. I expect to be in England in April. It is all very well to be out here. I can make plenty of money and also have very good living; but the risk you run of one's life is worth double the Money and when you go to bed at night you do not know if you will get up in the morning without fever.

My dearest Parents I think when I come home I shall try a healthier route if I get less money as I do not like the West Indies. Please to Remember me to all my Sisters and Brothers hoping they are all well give my love to Fanny and Kiss little Georgy for me. we leave here to day for Vera Cruz & Tampico then back to Havana & St Thomas.

My dearest Father & Mother I have no more to tell you at present hoping to see you soon and now please to accept my fondest love and believe me to remain

      your affectionate Son
       Geo. Wm. Eastland
       R.M.S. "Eider"

R. M. S. "Eider"
Havana
Feby 5th 1870

My dearest Father & Mother

I now take great pleasure in writing to you to inform you I am quite well hoping you are all the same and wishing you all a happy new year.

We arrived here to day at Noon and leave here to morrow (Sunday) at 4p.m. The last six Sundays we have been working all day. we have either been going into Harbour or coming out it is very hard work here in the West Indies and the climate is very oppressive. I shall be so glad to come home again thank God I have been very well lately and hope to remain so while I am out here. I expect to be home the Middle of April. I am very pleased to inform you I have made a good month this month again. I shall clear between Sixty and Seventy pounds and hope to next month the same after. Then I shall be in England for a time. I will write and let you know when I am coming and when to expect me. we have had a very pleasant trip up the Gulf of Mexico this time. I have not heard from you now for six weeks. I hope you received the Money all safe the last two months. I shall not send any this time as I have no English Gold. I am sending by the "Neva" from St Thomas a Box to you containing 1 Box of Chocolate for your breakfast of a morning some nice sponges and some Jelly so if you get this letter please to send to the Railway at Chichester for it as soon as you get the letters by the "Neva". This letter I am writing now goes by way of New York.

My dearest parents please to remember me to Nancy and George Cox and tell them I will advance them Fifty or a Hundred pounds on their Stock on the Farm if they like at the Rate of 10 per cent per annum, or if not I will advance one hundred pounds and become a partner in the farm and business and if they want more than one hundred I can advance as much as they want. And if they do not want the Money if you can see a nice Cottage for sale any where for about two hundred pounds let me know. I should prefer it with about an acre or so of ground to it. Dear Parents when you go to town please buy two nice easy Chairs for me and use them for yourselves also a nice Sofa to cost about (three guineas) and the Chairs about (two guineas) each and any thing else you see to make you comfortable and besure and use what money you want for yourselves to make you happy as you are all my trouble now. I shall be so glad to see you.

I took a diamond Ring from a man the other day for seventeen pounds he owed me the Money. It is worth thirty guineas at the least. My dear Mother I have a beautiful Bird on board like the one I gave Fanny it is really a beauty and I have two Parrots one talks very nice. I hope you have taken care of my dog for me.

My dearest Parents you will please pay Mrs Barttelot for Harry. Give my Kind regards to all my relations and kiss the Children for me. I have got some very pretty Pictures for my Bedroom it will make the young Ladies Blush when they look at them.

Dear parents when I get this next letter from London I shall Know if I am to come home in April or not and if I do not come home in April it will be October or November before I am in England but I will let you know as soon as I hear which way it will be hoping this will find you all quite well and please to accept my fondest love and believe me to remain your affectionate Son
                              Geo. Wm. Eastland.

Sunday 6th February 1870

R.M.S. "Eider", Havana, 6.00am

George William Eastland.

I toss and turn. I cannot sleep even though it will not be light for another hour yet. It is not my usual stormy nightmares – other things, choices, trouble my brain.

The "Eider" arrived here mid-day yesterday. There is no time to enjoy this fine town on this occasion as we have spent all our time unloading passengers and cargo, and re-stocking with coal and other goods. We are due to set sail once more at 4pm today on our way back to St. Thomas.

In all the time I have been in the West Indies I don't think I have felt so well as I do now. I think the Gulf of Mexico is a better place than the islands of the Caribbean. I hope our stay in St. Thomas will be brief, and that we will steam back to Havana and on to the Gulf with the greatest of haste. I will not disembark from the "Eider" any more than absolutely necessary at St. Thomas.

I have learnt many ways to stay healthy in the West Indies. The climate is frightful dangerous to all Europeans, especially when they first arrive in these places. These cooler winter months from November to February are by far the most healthy months, with the temperature nearer 60-70°F. Europeans arriving new in the hot season are burned to a cinder, or near drowned and catching chills during the rainy months. February is as healthy as it can ever be out here.

At this time of year one of the biggest dangers are the heavy night dews which seem to cause Deck Hands no end of illness and misery. I avoid going on deck until the sun has been up for an hour and dried all the moisture. If it cannot be avoided I take care to wear my strongest boots and cover my skin to avoid contact with the dews.

Havana is a truly wonderful port. Although I only made a short visit to the town yesterday I have been here several times before to look around and marvel at the place. The entrance to Havana is very striking. Ships pass through a wide channel with the Morro Castle and the imposing fortifications of Las Cabanas on the left. While on the right-hand side rises the Fort of La Punta – a collection of great buildings including the large prisons and other buildings and houses.

The channel then opens up into the magnificent deep bay where a thousand ships can comfortably anchor, and even the largest ships can moor at the quays due to the great depths of the bay. All vessels are safe here, protected from the worst of the seas.

The old streets of Havana are narrow and full of colour and life, while behind them wider more spacious avenues and larger buildings open up. There is money in Havana and very many wealthy people. It is a good place to do business and there are many fine things to be purchased in the shops. The port is constantly crammed with vessels of all types, the main exports including sugar, tobacco, coffee and cigars.

The town is so unlike Chichester in England that it could be in a different world. There are grand ornate hotels. La Fonda de los Americanos in the Calle de Obra pia is the hotel most frequented by English and American visitors. It has a huge dining room and its main corridor is over two hundred feet in length.

I sat there, in the hotel lobby one hot afternoon. With a cool beer in my hands I marvelled at the endless long passage, the gleaming reflections on the stone floor and the constant pitter-patter of busy footsteps that echo down the long hallway.

Many of the large buildings have both windows and doors that reach to the ground, and are frequently not glazed. Instead they are secured by vertical bars made of wood or metal which give the buildings the appearance of prisons, but let in much very welcome air. Shops open right onto the street and many of them are filled with Birmingham ware. Almost anything can be purchased in the shops of Havana, including jewellery, wooden carvings, and paintings quite unlike anything you will find in England. I bought some colourful paintings of the very comely Spanish girls, which puts a smile on the faces of every man who sees them.

The people and the streets are bright and gay – there is life and colour everywhere. The most impressive street of all is the grand Paseo de Tacon where all the rich and fashionable people come in their two-wheeled carriages called volantes to congregate and mix and court.

By contrast with this over-exuberance of dress and architecture the cathedral in Havana seems very plain outside. Three huge doors open into the lofty interior. The Cathedral is, however a special place for all mariners as it is the resting place for the greatest adventurer – Christopher Columbus. I spent some very peaceful minutes there when I first visited Havana.

Whilst we have steamed back and forth between St. Thomas and Tampico these last few months there has been little rest. There have been constant passengers and Mail to deliver to Havana and Vera Cruz in particular, and with all the passengers on board the "Eider" I have been earning very good money. I have accumulated plenty enough to buy a share in Nancy and George's business, and to buy myself a place to live with George and Henry. When I go back to England in April I will have earned enough to never need to come back to the West Indies with all its perils to my health.

I have not received any letters from home now for several weeks which always unsettles me. I worry what is going on back there and it is such a delay before I can find out. I will be so pleased when I get back to England in April – it is not too long now. I must be patient. It is a funny thing that the nearer you get to something good, the harder it is to remain patient.

It will be a wonderful thing to be back in England and away from the dangers of the sea. I have asked Father to buy me some furniture and I hope to invest in Nancy and George's business. My brain tells me I should now settle in Sussex or Hampshire. It is safer and I should be there to look after my family.

But I know my troublesome heart will always yearn for the sea, and I am tortured by this conflict.

Friday 11th February 1870

R.M.S. "Eider" during Havana to St. Thomas passage

George William Eastland.

Life is such an infernal paradox.

One day it is comfortable with good health and good fortune, and the next the sky falls in with the arrival of some unforeseeable disaster. You then become reconciled with a life of misery and helplessness (the right and just situation for all sinners) when, out of the blue and when you least expect it another quite unexpected turn of good fortune presents itself.

I have concluded that God's will is always to remain unfathomable.

I suppose the only thing a man can do is to be grateful when those times of happiness occur, and to cherish them to the utmost for as long as they last. For they will come to an end as surely as every summer comes to an end.

My Caribbean dreams have turned to nightmares. I toss and turn and dream at night of storms and smashed and bloodied faces flying towards me, dripping blood all over my clean white clothes; until I wake with a jolt, all dripping in sweat.

By day fear of the Fever grips our crew. I have seen too many mariners perish from this vile affliction. I only go ashore now when absolutely necessary. There are far fewer mosquitoes on our Steamer than on the land, and whenever we arrive at a harbour I do all in my power to get our ship away from the shore and out to sea again as quickly as possible.

We have spent this last three months plying between St. Thomas, Havana, Vera Cruz and Tampico. The rains have passed and the sea in the Gulf is altogether calmer. On the sea it seems much healthier now than in the oven of the Caribbean summer.

I spend as little time as I can in St. Thomas – that stinking over-populated rat-hole and meeting place for all the world's mariners and diseases.

We stop at Havana for coal and cigars. This place I like. At Tampico in Mexico we exchange both Passengers and Mail but rarely do we pause there for long.

Vera Cruz has presented me with a mighty and highly unexpected headache. My last visit there is imprinted vividly upon my brain and now leaves my mind in a turmoil.

On this visit to Vera Cruz we are caught by the Norte wind as we cross the Bay of Mexico. The first sign of its approach is a gentle cat's paw across the surface of the sea from the north. Five minutes later the Norte hits us hard to starboard. The sky turns black and sand flies in the air to whip our faces and make it hard to keep our eyes open. Which seems odd - for all I can see is the sea. Where does the sand come from?

With Mexico in sight the Norte expires as suddenly as when it arrived, the sky clears and our ship is joined by an abundance of merry wildlife. The colourful accompaniment includes majestic plunging whales, leaping dolphins, shoals of silver flying fish hanging in the breeze with no apparent need to be in the sea at all, huge blue-tinted bonitos, shoals of pink Finny Tribe fish and assorted sea birds flying above us.

From a long way off-shore I can see the Peak of Orizava, the Star Mountain. Its snow-capped summit emerges gloriously out of lush cedar and pine forests. Some time later the coast of Mexico appears at Point Delgado, and steering south along the coast we eventually pass the light-house and the Castle of San Juan de Ulua.

Soon after comes the first glimpse of Vera Cruz as it reveals itself in front of the "Eider". A breathtaking panorama emerges before us of countless red and white cupolas, and an endless array of domes, towers and battlements gleaming imperiously in the afternoon sun.

We enter the great harbour passing through a narrow channel between sunken coral reefs, out of which rises the great Castle of San Juan as if straight out of the water. The "Eider" anchors under the western wall of the castle, a mile from the Mole – the city landing place. Shore boats immediately come alongside to take passengers onshore. However, passengers cannot land at Vera Cruz without a passport and some say the city is full of disease. Some choose to stay on board the "Eider", preferring to wait till we arrive at Tampico to disembark.

At sunrise the next morning I go ashore to order supplies for our Steamer. In the half-light there is something trist and gloomy about Vera Cruz. Above the shadowy buildings hundreds of black Zopilotes swoop – their loud rasping cries echoing all around the city. More of the vultures walk the streets along with the wild dogs ripping and fighting over garbage.

They seem little bothered by men and only a direct kick is ever likely to distract them from their feeding. Having eaten their fill the cloud of black beasts take to the skies, and circle the rooftops showering the church towers and other buildings generously with the product of their feasting.

I do not hesitate to pass beyond this grim quarter as rapidly as I can into some wider and more pleasant streets. Some of the larger houses bear flat roofs, thick enough to withstand the heaviest rains and the most merciless sun. Some still have cannon-balls lodged in their walls from the French attack on the Castle of San Juan in 1838.

When I reach the old market I find it swarms with Indian traders wearing all manner of strange and colourful costumes. I negotiate, shoulder to shoulder with other local buyers, many from the large hotels in Vera Cruz.

The produce on offer at the market varies considerably in quality and it requires much concentration to acquire a fair price. The vegetables are of poor quality and few in number, and the meat is very strange. It is cut into thin ribbons, having been dried in the sun without salt and tastes foul.

The fish, on the other hand is exceptionally fine. I recognise little of it, apart from the mullet, but it is colourful, moist and tasty. I also purchase well from a selection of water fowl, tortoise, armadillo and some deer. Our passengers and crew dine well in the Gulf of Mexico.

I speak Spanish very well now and always use the native tongue in Mexico when bargaining for coal, food and other supplies. I am watching the tortoises swim in a large tank and considering how many to bid for when one of the Mexican traders starts talking to me.

He can tell I am English and reveals that he has some measure of the language himself. Having each ordered our tortoise and deer we continue our conversation. The man is short, like all Mexicans, thick-set and swarthy. He appears middle-aged, his black hair showing hints of grey at the edges. His black and lively eyes bear a twinkle.

'Ello sir. My name Arturo. Welcome to great city of Vera Cruz. And you sir...?'

'Pleased to meet you, Arturo. I am George Eastland. Chief Steward on the Royal Mail Ship "Eider".'

'You draw good deal with Indian. You choose fishes and vegetables good too. Arturo see you good trader.'

'Thank you Arturo. Honoured, I am sure.'

'I not know on ord? Arturo, Manager at grandest hotel Vera Cruz. Casa de Diligencias. Hotel grow much. Much European visitor more. Hotel need new Manager, understand European. I show you grand Mexican hotel?'

'Honoured means proud. But Arturo, I have to return to my Steamer. If you insist I can come and see your hotel this afternoon. Perhaps two o'clock? I have some free time before my Mail Ship leaves tonight.'

'Si Si, two o'clock. You ask for Arturo. I come show world best hotel Casa de Diligencias. Come to Zocalo. Main plaza. Good meet you Senor George.'

Just before two o'clock I find my way to the Zocalo. The plaza is dominated by the massive hotel – a vast array of curved arches and pillars of two storeys built of gleaming white stone. People bustle across the plaza, this way and that going about their business.

I enter the hotel through a gigantic door in one of the archways and find myself in an even grander and more luxuriant lobby. It is a huge white space of marble and stone with windows all along the front of the hotel. Light floods in across the gleaming patterned floor tiles and lights up the massive paintings that adorn the walls of the lobby. The lobby contains heavy chairs and marble tables and numerous doors, as well as a wide sweeping staircase which rises up from the huge entrance area.

I approach a tiny Mexican at the reception desk who is dressed all in white including a smart cap.

'I have come to meet Arturo?'

'Ah, Senor Eastland. Arturo expecting you. I fetch.'

The Mexican scurries away, and almost immediately scurries back again carrying a silver tray holding two ornate cut glasses of icy lemonade which he places on the marble table in front of me. Next to the tray he also sets down a silver dish holding small pieces of mazapan.

'Drink please, Senor Eastland. Arturo here coming.'

The generously iced lemonade is most refreshing. A moment later Arturo approaches, a wide grin upon his face and shakes my hand enthusiastically before sitting down to sip at his drink.

'Welcome my hotel, Senor George. Casa de Diligencias. Biggest hotel in Vera Cruz. Best hotel in all Mexico. Hotel grow. More Europeans. I need new Manager. Manager who know business. Manager who know European as well as tropics. Tell me George, about you work.'

I tell Arturo of my work as Barman and Pantryman, Purser and now Chief Steward managing food and drink and all manner of ship's supplies. I tell him of England, of Europe, of Australia and New Zealand and of my time in the West Indies. I also tell him about life in an English Tavern.

Arturo raises his arm and clicks his fingers. In an instant two more glasses of iced lemonade appear before us on the cool marble table. Arturo's dark eyes dart and twinkle as I speak. When I finish talking he takes a deep breath and pauses, as if thinking deeply.

'Senor George. Ship like floating hotel. You know kitchen. You speak European and Mexican. You make very good Manager in best hotel in Mexico. Come – I show you.'

Arturo leads me through the vast hotel. He shows me the dining room with its high vaulted ceiling, the tables all laid out in rows with crisp white tablecloths and silver cutlery neatly lined up. All is very quiet there. Unlike the kitchens which are a hive of activity and noise.

Although the next meal time is not yet imminent the large chaotic kitchen is alive with Mexicans, scurrying here and scurrying there carrying pots and saucepans of water and food. Others are preparing vegetables and fruits, and steam rises from various pots on large stoves. All manner of aromas mingle and circulate in the air. Knives and other utensils are wielded and glint brightly, and the continuous babble of urgent Mexican voices fills the air.

Arturo guides me through countless lounges where guests talk, play games, or simply doze in their chairs. He shows me the huge tanks filled with rainwater which the hotel uses. Throughout his tour he tells me of all the many advantages of life in Mexico. He tells me of the gold and silver riches of the country. Arturo tells me that Vera Cruz is very healthy thanks to the Norte winds and the wild dogs and Zopilotes, which are the scavengers that protect the city from malaria.

'Zopilote protected by law. George no kick Zopilote!'

Arturo also tells me Vera Cruz has a theatre, Exchange Rooms where travellers can read the foreign papers and play billiards, that the doctors are very competent, and that the town is very safe – having a garrison of some four thousand men.

'Temperature in Vera Cruz never below 60°. No like England – rain rain rain.' A wide beam crosses Arturo's face reaching from one ear to the other.

At the end of the tour we sit in a lobby on plush divans. 'Senor George. Vera Cruz three hundred thousand people. Growing all time. Good for hotel. You good man. You no want to be sick on sea any more. You deserve comfortable life in hotel. I like offer you job of Hotel Manager. Senor George say yes?'

I am almost speechless. I never thought Arturo had been serious. I didn't expect this offer. I can, however see how my life on the sea gives me many skills for this job, but I would never in my wildest dreams have imagined such a life for me.

'Arturo – I am most astonished by your offer, and honoured.'

'Ah, Senor George. Arturo now know 'hon-ord'. Is good. Senor George accept position of Manager, si?'

'It is very sudden Arturo. I need some time to think.'

Arturo screws up his face, then...

'Arturo fool. Of course, Senor George. I no tell Pay. I hon-ord to offer George many hundreds of Mexican Gold Doubloons for new Hotel Manager.'

I cannot stop myself laughing out loud at Arturo, who for once loses that permanent grin to look instead quite confounded.

'Gold Doubloons sound very intriguing, Arturo. But how much is that in English pounds or guineas?'

The smile returns once more to his face, and he concentrates for a moment.

'I told Arturo – fool. Senor George pay five hundred English Guineas each year. What you say? Good job? Senor George Say yes?'

'Thank you Arturo. That is a very fine offer. I need some time to consider before I decide.'

'Of course Senor George. I show you more of Hotel Casa de Diligencias. Best hotel. Hotel Manager sleep in best room. Senor George decide.'

Arturo clicks his fingers again and the same Mexican as before hurries over to where we sit. Arturo speaks urgently to the man.

'Fetch Leticia. Straight away. Leticia show Senor George rest of hotel. Leticia very handsome. Senor George say yes after Leticia show best rooms.'

Five minutes later Leticia approaches our table.

'Senor George, this Leticia. Leticia show Senor George best rooms in Casa de Diligencias. Finest hotel, finest rooms, finest wife.'

Arturo leaves me with his wife. Leticia is petite, and very pretty with long jet black hair down to her very slim waist. She wears a long silky yellow dress tied at the waist. The fine material clings tightly to every nook and cranny of her curvaceous brown body, which glistens with a light sheen of perspiration and leaves little to my imagination. She wears a large yellow flower in her hair and walks barefoot on the cold stone floor. She has the whitest teeth I have ever seen, and an even wider smile than Arturo which sets off deep dimples in her cheeks. Leticia cannot be more than twenty years old. I think to myself, Arturo is very fortunate to have a wife so young and beautiful.

'Come Senor George.' Leticia takes me by the hand and leads me up the grand marble staircase to the wide landing upstairs. She leads me along the impressive corridor, and as we walk across huge and brightly coloured rugs we pass statues of people and animals displayed on elaborate stone and marble stands. These stone corridors are kept wonderfully fresh and airy by the breeze that blows in through the succession of arched windows on both sides. We turn left along another passage, and at the end Leticia turns a door handle and opens a massive white wooden door.

The most sumptuous bed-chamber I have ever seen opens before my eyes. Leticia closes the heavy door behind us and watches as I admire the ornate white and gold furniture, the high decorative ceilings and the large glittering mirror hanging on the wall. I stroll to the window where I get a view of a wonderful garden with neat symmetrical paths, hedges and statues.

As I turn back towards Leticia she sits down on the side of the bed and smiles at me.

'Senor George. You like? Best room, best wife?'

Leticia reclines back onto the silky crimson linen upon the large bed, and as she does so loosens the tie around her waist. Her yellow dress parts at the front and slides from her body to reveal silken brown skin all the way up the inside of her slim thighs, and between them a lush tropical vegetation of dense black hair shrouding a glistening ripe red fruit.

'I thought you were Arturo's wife?'

'No, no. No Arturo wife. I be your wife, Senor George. You come lie with me. This best room. This best bed. Make very good room. Leticia make Senor George very happy man?'

I realise now Arturo's ploy to persuade me to agree to his proposal. I will not be bribed this way. Leticia is very beautiful but this is not the way. Now I am about to return to England... or maybe instead to become Manager of the best hotel in Vera Cruz – now is not the time to muddle my brain just for a few minutes of lust.

'You are very handsome woman Leticia. Senor George must leave now and return to ship. Ship leave Vera Cruz soon. Thank you for showing me the hotel.'

I tear my eyes from the puzzled-looking beauty lying on the silk bed, exit the bedroom and make my way back along the corridor and down the grand staircase. Arturo sees me coming.

'Senor George – you European very quick. You like wife? She make happy?'

'Leticia is a very beautiful lady. I must return to the "Eider" before dark. Thank you for your kind offer. I will let you know my decision when my Steamer returns to Vera Cruz, in two or three weeks I think. Goodbye Arturo.'

'Goodbye Senor George. Remember, good job and good Wife. If Senor George no like this wife Arturo find other Wifes? Make Senor George very happy man.'

I now face this highly unexpected dilemma. I have had enough of the sea and was reconciled to go home to England where I could live a healthy life and look after Father and Mother and my boys.

Now, quite astonishingly, I have this new alternative offer of a job and a life away from the sea where I could earn a fortune of Mexican gold and sit in the sunny gardens and drink lemonade all the year round.

The "Eider" slipped quietly out of Vera Cruz harbour at dusk nearly two weeks ago. I gazed ahead of the Steamer, mesmerised by the luminous orange and red fire-ball of the moon as it rose perceptibly into the darkening sky. Its face was split by a horizontal whisp of a cloud. This fiery red orb seems ten times bigger than ever it does in the northern hemisphere.

Watching its two halves glow I pondered in which hemisphere my future might lie?

R. M. S. "Eider"
St Thomas
Feby 12th 1870

Dear Father & Mother

I now take the pleasure to inform you we arrived here this morning at 4 a.m. after a fine passage and all well on board. I do not know until the 14th where we go next but I expect to go the Gulf again as we have made a quick passage this time. The West Indies is rather healthy now it is the coldest season of the year. I wrote to you from Havana on the 5th by way of New York thinking you would like to hear how I was. I am sending you a Box per the "Neva" and as soon as you get this letter you send to the Railway Station for it contains fourteen pounds of chocolate, five sponges & 2 doz of Guava Jelly. I think you will like it very much. you can slice up the Chocolate in a Cup and pour Boiled Water on it and it is made ready to drink. It is very nice indeed and very Strengthening.

I expect to be in England in April and then I shall stay a Month or two with you hoping you are all quite well at home. I wrote in my letter by way of New York to offer to lend

Nancy & George one hundred pounds at the rate of ten per cent interest providing they will give me a Bill of sale on the Business & stock on Farm for a Security, or to let me go in partner in the farming Stock & c.

My dearest parents I have had five Hundred a year offered me to go to Mexico to be Manager of the largest Hotel in Mexico it belongs to a Company it is a very large place and the town is pretty healthy. I have to settle next week whether to go or not if I go I shall come to England again before I go to Mexico for if I can see any thing to suit me I shall leave off the Sea as early as I can. I am getting Sick and tired of it but of course I must not complain. I am not sending any money this time. I have no English Sovereigns.

I hope my parrot and Dog is all right. I am getting a regular old Batchelor. The West Indies has put about five years on to my looks since I left England. I shall soon be an old Man. I have lost a great deal of Hair off the top of my head since I was home. The climate plays the Devil with any one. I have been wonderful careful of myself since I have been in the West Indies. I have seen lots of poor fellows turned up since I first came out here.

I was in Havana last Sunday. It is a very large town indeed and some fine Building in it. Tell Father I speak Spanish now like a Native. The Spanish Girls are very handsome indeed and very charming in their manner.

Please give my love to Fanny for me and tell her I have not heard from her for a long time. also to all my Sisters and Kiss the Boys for me and please to accept my fondest love and believe me to remain

your affectionate Son
Geo. Wm. Eastland

Dearest parents I have enclosed in the Box a Box of Cigars for Father they are the finest Cigars made in Havana tell him I hope he will enjoy them I have nothing else to send him this time.

Sunday 27th February 1870

Martinique

George William Eastland.

Today I have no life. This is not like me.

My stomach grips and I have a head pain to split my skull. If there was a golden guinea on the floor of my cabin I would be too pained to fall out of bed to pick it up. I must have drunk some bad water or eaten some rotten piece of food yesterday? I am fortunate that as Chief Steward I am allocated my own cabin. Most of the crew, outside of the officers, share four or more to a cabin. I am thankful that I can at least be ill in my own privacy, in comfort.

I sleep.

I cannot remember which place we are near? I think the "Eider" is working its way northwards along the chain of islands back up towards St. Thomas. By the middle of next week she will be loaded with the Mail and other cargoes and we will be bound once more for Vera Cruz in Mexico stopping at many islands on the way. I have an important decision to make but I am too tired to think about it now.

The seasons scarce change here being hot and dry all year round. February and March are often the driest months and some rain now would be a blessing, but not expected. We sometimes get a little rain early in the morning or at night, but you scarce notice it as the ground is dry as a bone and like a furnace by day. Is it night or day?

I sleep.

I wake again. Sweating. Our ship is frightful hot and airless and it is best for a man's health to get some fresh air when he can. The "Eider" is still – perhaps we have reached St. Thomas?

Many mariners shelter from the long hot hours of sunshine spending their wages in the taverns on beer and wenching. As punishment for injudicious plunging of their intromittent organs many men, to their regret, grow spectacular genital sores, or develop gumma or lupus all over their bodies accompanied by other pains. Sometimes these pass of their own accord, or the ship's doctor will try to treat the most severe with mercury, which sometimes proves successful. Other times the poor miserable patient dies, from the disease or the remedy I would not like to venture.

I would rather head for the best shady bars by the sea where I can walk awhile under the avenues of trees. There are all manner of exotic trees on St. Thomas the like of which you never saw in England. The most are palm trees and coconut palms also, but I like the seagrape that grows freely near the coast and produces very tasty purple fruit, very like normal grapes but easy and abundant to pick while strolling. The huge red turpentine tree is most impressive with its massive straight trunk rising maybe two hundred feet into the sky.

When I have strolled enough I would sit in a bar sipping my ale, read the newspapers and doze in my chair with the sound of the sea in my ear.

However, today I regret I cannot leave the ship. Indeed I cannot leave my bed for I am not well. I would be mightily annoyed about this if I didn't indeed feel so out of sorts. I think today is Sunday? I keep falling in and out of sleep and I have lost track of the time?

If it is still Sunday I can pray in thankfulness to God for delivering me from all the terrible storms that I have sailed through, including a couple of near wrecks, as well as my remarkable avoidance of injury and the calenture that befalls so many mariners sailing in the tropics.

Thank God this is to be my last such voyage and in April I will be back in Sussex and settling myself on a piece of land and property to make roots, and having made my money whilst surviving the hazards of the sea to settle into an easy life with my sons. I will then be able to look after Father and Mother and my Dear Fanny, and perhaps find myself a servant girl to help me look after my boys and to milk my cow, and perform other such necessary services that fit the position of servant.

This dreadful heat has exhausted my body today. I just need to sleep a while longer.

I reach for my glass of water and drink the last of it before lying back in my damp bunk.

I sleep.

Sunday 27th February 1870

R.M.S. "Eider", Martinique

Charles Oxley - Ship's Surgeon.

Our Steamer has paused at Martinique to load and unload passengers and Mail. We will not stop here long. I haven't seen George, the Chief Steward and would have thought nothing of it but that the Captain says he hasn't either. This is untypical because George is often to be seen checking the ship's stores of food, liquor and other supplies against his stock inventories especially when we arrive in a harbour, such is his very dutiful attention to detail.

So I have come to George's cabin and find the door is closed, which is also unusual as all doors are mostly left open by day to allow what air there is to flow and to freshen the cabins. I pause. Perhaps he is resting?

I knock on his cabin door and listen.

Nothing.

So I knock again, a little louder this time and listen.

Still nothing.

Perhaps he is not here? But I am concerned because a man can fall overboard and drown in an instant, and I feel it is my responsibility having now missed him to try to be sure to confirm his location and safety.

So I turn the door handle and find the door is not locked and I gently push it open.

I can see nothing at first in the gloom but my nostrils tell me the story. I retreat quickly from the cabin and close the door. I hurry to the sick-bay to fetch a bucket of cool water, some clean cloths and also a flagon of drinking water. I mix some Peruvian Bark into the drinking water to help George fight the fever, before returning to him with haste.

Before entering George's cabin I pick up an oil lamp from the passage and tie a large white handkerchief around the back of my head to cover my nose and mouth. I enter the cabin where I quickly light

George's own oil lamp to cast some light around the place. I can see the shape of George curled up on his bunk almost naked. The cabin is very hot and reeks of sweat and vomit, which I can see lies in a large puddle on the floor next to the bunk. I can also see George's body moving up and down with his breath, so all is not lost.

I open the small scuttle-hatch to the cabin to get some fresh air in and call out, 'George – I have brought you water. You must drink to help you to get better.' I touch George's arm. He is wet with sweat and as I fear is hot as an oven. He stirs at my touch and swings his arm wildly, but I stay out of reach as I have seen many mariners with a tropical fever and am very well used to how it affects their moods and movements.

'George,' I say again, 'I have opened your scuttle to get some fresh air and I will clean your floor to clear the smell. You have a fever and must drink. I have brought you a large jug of water and will leave it in your cabin here on the table.' I place it there near to him with his glass.

George has now awoken but is struggling to open his eyes and complains about the bright light and says his head is in terrible pain. I put the oil lamp down on the floor in the corner of the cabin so the light is much dimmed, and George takes his hands from over his eyes.

'How long are we in St. Thomas? I haven't ordered any supplies yet?'

'Just rest George. We are in Martinique today and there are no supplies for you to be concerned with. We will not get to St. Thomas for a day or two yet. Just rest.'

'I am so hot, and then cold from my sweat and my head feels like it is split into two. I don't know how long I have slept. What day is it?' George asks me.

As I clean the vomit from the cabin floor using the bucket and water I brought with me I reply, 'It is Sunday, George. I think you have slept for some time, which is a good thing and the sweat is your body's way of flushing out the fever. I have cleaned your floor and brought you dry sheets. The most important thing is that you drink as much water as you can and continue to sleep.'

It is good to see that George is not delirious with the fever, but he is animated and understandably panicked by it. 'Oh my God,' he says, 'Why has God given me the dreaded Fever on this my last voyage? Whatever have I done to deserve this demise? I have two young boys at home that depend on my safe return from the terrible seas and where is the justice in allowing me to die to leave my boys abandoned?'

I do my best to calm George for I know that panic will divert his scant energy away from the giant task of fighting the fever, which is a severe enough battle alone for any man to fight. I do pray that George will overcome this dreadful fever because as well as being one of the most thorough and sober Chief Stewards I have ever worked with, he is above all a God-fearing man and friend whom I do not wish to lose. So I will do all I can to help him overcome the sickness.

At the same time I know I must not loiter in his cabin any longer than necessary as I have responsibility as the ship's surgeon to all of the crew, and infection is so easy to spread on a ship. So before I leave I tell George, 'You are an experienced mariner and know the way the fever works. You have a good supply of water now which you must keep drinking from every hour to drown the fever and to fight your headache. We must starve any infection so I will give you no food yet. The fever must run its course. You are lucky – you have your own cabin, and we must make sure the infection does not spread anywhere else on board the ship, so you must be confined here until the fever passes. I will visit you, day and night to ensure you have water and to check your progress. After you have slept I will bring you a warm caudle to drink. You know I must also lock your cabin to ensure you remain in it, in case you have a fit.'

George nods and thanks me for my assistance. We both know that the tropical fever is serious. Like all experienced mariners George has always draped his mosquito nets over his bunk to guard against the infected insects, but sometimes the devils find a way of getting in. And if they do, being trapped inside the net with their unsuspecting victim asleep they can often bite several times before being discovered, or may be just rolled over and crushed without the poor mariner ever being aware of the thing.

Sometimes a mariner will recover from the fever after a bout of the sweating and sickness and pains in the head and back of the neck. Unfortunately by far the greater majority of those falling ill do not recover, especially those whose skin begins to turn yellow from the jaundice, those who start severe nosebleeds, and those who become delirious or descend into catalepsy, often injuring themselves physically.

After closing George's cabin door I order the carpenter to straight away fix two sturdy bolts to the outside just in case George goes on a rampage, as we cannot risk the infection spreading through the ship. All that remains is for me to pray to God for George's deliverance from this terrible illness that claims so many innocent mariners in the tropics.

George, of all people does not deserve such a miserable fate as to die of the Yellow Jack.

Royal Mail Ship "Eider" 50163 – Official Log Book

Feb 27 1870   At Martinique

George W Eastland Chief Steward — sick and off duty.

C. J. Oxley

Surgeon

Monday 28th February 1870

The "Eider", 5.32pm

Charles Oxley.

As I promised George, I have continued to attend him in his cabin at regular intervals through the night and again this morning. I always cover my face with a clean handkerchief when entering the cabin, and am diligent in washing myself thoroughly and all over with soap as soon as I come back out.

George has not spoken to me since last evening. He has stopped vomiting since the night – he can have nothing left in him to produce apart from water. He looks thin and his skin grey, but not yellow as far as I can tell. I know not what other symptoms he has today as he continues to sleep, but still his fever is fearsome and his body continues to pour sweat.

He drinks some of the water I leave so he must awaken from time to time. With sadness I must keep his cabin bolted until I am sure the calenture has passed.

Royal Mail Ship "Eider" 50163 – Official Log Book

Feb 28

Lat 16°.26

Long 63°.16

George W Eastland Ch Steward sick and off duty.

Tuesday 1st March 1870

The "Eider", 5.00am

George William Eastland.

As I awake in this prison cell I try to open my eyes to see what is about in this world. But I cannot open them properly as the light is too dazzling. I must have been hit on the head with a wooden club as my head hurts like it has been all smashed in and this hurt goes all down the back of my neck in agony. Yet when I touch my head with my hand I find no blood as I would expect there to be?

Also my legs feel as if they are broken – it is excruciating pain if I try to move any of my body. I am drowned in my sweat and never have I smelt such a rancid stench as this – the pirates must have put boiled rats under my bunk to add to my misery.

***

Worse than the pirates I am beaten in by the fact that Man Friday, my constant companion on my desert island for years has treacherously handed me to the pirates because I laughed at his comical way when he became intoxicated with rum.

***

I cry out for Father and Mother as I cannot understand why I cannot move. Everybody must be downstairs in the bar of the Bull's Head drinking. Perhaps someone will come and give me some medicine if I make enough noise. I throw myself off my bed with a crash and land in something slippery that smells like sick. My hip now hurts. I pass out.

***

I am lying on my bunk looking at the ceiling of my cabin where rays of sun reflect in a watery pattern like there are yellow waves above my head. Have I been swimming in the sea with Sarah? I am so wet that I must have been, but why go to bed when I am still wet? Then I remember Sarah died – my sweet Sarah. We had barely been married and had our two boys George and Henry and then Sarah got

coughing and couldn't survive the winter, dying so painfully from consumption. How could God rob me of my gorgeous Sarah while we were both still children ourselves? I might as well have died then too - I miss her so much.
Damn you God!

***

Please God do not take me yet. I do not care for myself but I worry about the others.

I truly repent for all my sins. I know I shouldn't have run away when Sarah died and should have stayed and looked after my boys, but my mind was gone and I couldn't get over the grief of losing my Sarah when we had hardly been together. The sea has helped occupy my crazed mind and to see the things I should be thankful for once more.

I know I shouldn't have charmed Mary Clayton when I am gone to sea and no hope of seeing her again.

I know I should be more grateful to Father and Mother for looking after little Georgie, and to Matilda and Dick for looking after Henry for me. Mother and Father should be resting at their age - not looking after children all day.

I do not fear death but please do not punish others for the sins I have committed. I have always worked hard and tried my best. I should not die before my parents and with my boys so young – they have all suffered more than enough.

Please let me beat this dreadful fever and come home to England as planned after this last voyage so I can look after my boys and let my parents rest as they deserve.

***

What hateful fate do these invisible pirates have for me keeping me locked in this dirty cabin? Why do they not come and show their faces rather than starving me to death in this stinking hole. I would rather walk their plank into an ocean infested with sharks than lie rotting here in my own carcass.

I'll not drink their water for I know they have added poison to it, and with that I kick the table across the cabin sending the pitcher of water crashing to the floor where it smashes to pieces and the water washes out under the cabin door.

'I wish hurricanes, lightning and Yellow Fever upon all flea-infested pirates,' I scream as I fall from my bunk, unable to hold myself up with my back and legs now locked in some sort of spasm.

Royal Mail Ship "Eider" 50163 – Official Log Book

1st March   St Thomas

George W Eastland Ch Steward sick and off duty.

Tuesday 1st March 1870

The "Eider", St. Thomas Island, 2.30pm

Charles Oxley.

George's fever has continued today unabated – and I have continued to attend him regularly, but I am unable to keep changing his bed-linen as he sweats continually. George has been restless, mumbling words and curses, only some of which can I make out, and throwing his head about. More worrying he has not been drinking much water today and I fear he needs the fluid urgently in his body. This morning I tried to pour a little into his mouth but he just choked and spat it out in my face, shouting something unintelligible.

George has had the fever now for nearly three days. If he is to beat this dire affliction I am most likely to see an improvement in his condition today or tomorrow. I have come to his cabin just now as there were reports of a commotion and breaking glass or crockery from inside. I can see water has poured from under his cabin door, but all is quiet now.

I unbolt the door and look in carefully holding my oil lamp in front of me. The flagon holding his water is in pieces on the floor just behind the door, and George is lying on the floor looking up at me. It looks as though he has had a nosebleed as there is blood on his left cheek and around his eye. I go to help him back onto the bed but with wild eyes he thrusts his fist at me and says, 'Keep your filthy hands to yourself, you dirty pirate!'

I realise I have to leave George alone in his delirium. I right the small table which has been knocked over, and replace the broken flagon with another filled with fresh water which I hope George might drink when I have gone. 'God bless you George – I pray with all my heart that the fever will leave you,' I say, as I back out from the cabin and close and bolt the door again.

As I leave George's cabin I consider my options. There is one more thing I could do to help him. Now our Steamer has returned to Charlotte Amalie I could take him off the ship and to the Hospital? He may have a better chance to beat the Fever there under the constant watch of the medical officers, and in cooler conditions than are possible on the "Eider". I think I must give George this final chance.

If I can get George to the Hospital it will also help reduce the risk of the Fever spreading to other crewmen on board the "Eider." As ship's Surgeon I must do my best for the health of all the crew.

Royal Mail Ship "Eider" 50163 – Official Log Book

1st March 4pm

Sent G.W. Eastland Ch Steward + Henry StEwbury (2nd Waiter) to the hospital.

C. J. Oxley + J. Bruce + S. Hampshire

Wednesday 2nd March 1870

7.00am

George William Eastland.

To my great relief I awaken from that terrible nightmare. I thought I was to die of fever in that dark stuffy cabin or drown in my own sweat.

I now find myself lying face down. I am hot as a furnace and I struggle to open my eyes which sting from my salty sweat. My eyelashes are caked, and I realise I must be lying on a beach as my fingers dig into the sand. I can feel a seashell between the forefinger and thumb of my right hand.

My back is burning. How long have I lain here since the shipwreck on this desert island beach? I roll over to relieve the burning pain on my back and am immediately blinded by the fiery orb above my head, and flick more sand into my eyes as I try to shield my face from the heat and dazzle.

I lie in this state for some minutes whilst trying to summon the strength to move. My lips are cracked to blood and my mouth parched dry as a desert as the hot salty sea breeze whips over me relentlessly. I become aware of the waves breaking at my feet and realise my legs are cool as they lie in the water's edge.

I continue to shield my eyes as I make a giant effort to raise my head to look at the sea. Through my sand-caked eye-lids I squint at the white heat-haze above the turquoise sea which seems to merge with the sky – an endless blue inferno. I splash some sea-water over my face with my left hand but the water is boiling and the salt stings my chafed lips.

Besides the wind and the waves there is no sound. I am alone. There is no-one else. I see no wreckage.

By some miracle I have been tossed up on this remote shore by the savage sea which has for some reason spared me from a watery grave. I know not why. I know not which sea I am in. I remember something of a large paddle-steamer and a dingy brown cabin with no light and no hope.

I try to stand but have no strength, so I must crawl up this beach to find shelter from the sun and the sea. Turning again onto my front I press my hands into the sand and edge forward, inch by inch. Every few yards I rest for my strength is quite gone. And all the time I can feel my sweat oozing and my back burning – I will surely become a brittle twig of charcoal if I do not get out of this fearful heat. I can see the yellow sand rises gently to a line of lush greenery, perhaps two hundred yards in front of me, which I pray will be my salvation.

To my utter despair it seems that no matter how far I crawl my arms remain on dry sand, yet my legs stay in the water. The tide must be coming in – I must keep crawling or I will certainly drown. I renew my efforts and despite my sore and now bleeding finger-nails I dig them into the sand and push faster with my feet to get me up this beach. It seems no matter how fast I crawl I cannot get my feet out of the sea, and the line of trees comes no nearer. But continue with this toil I certainly must or I shall surely perish. I cannot tell if I sweat from the heat, or from fear.

The next time I look up I see my green and red parrot on the shore and he is calling to me – 'Run George run, the cannibals are coming; run George run, the cannibals are coming.'

And then I hear their bloodcurdling cries and screams approaching upon the sea behind me. They must be coming in their canoes with spears to kill and then eat me.

I hurl every ounce of my remaining strength into crawling faster up this merciless beach, and yet the harder I try the slower I move. I cannot understand this as normally I can move very quickly – why, at this time of my greatest peril can I not move faster than a beached whale?

My parrot beseeches me, 'Come faster George, come faster George.'

I can now hear the splash of the cannibals' oars quite clearly and I can picture them – dark naked bodies all paddling like fury with white eyes and teeth all a gleaming ready to devour me, each with a human bone sticking through his nose as a trophy.

I know this time I am all done in. I look to the beach to see my parrot for the last time but he is gone.

Instead, at the water's edge is my sweet Sarah. The dark ringlets of her hair fall onto her shoulders. Her skin is so white and smooth, I know not how under this fearful sun. She looks sadly at me as I thrash hopelessly at the shallow water's edge.

'Sarah, Sarah you must run away and hide from these cannibals for they will surely eat you,' I implore her. She doesn't seem to hear me so I cry again louder this time and more frantic, 'Sarah, Sarah please run. You cannot save me. Run and save yourself.'

With the waves washing over my back and to my chin and with the cannibals in their canoes nearly upon me, their paddles splashing viciously in the foaming waters, I see into Sarah's deep hazel eyes and in that instant I see into her soul.

Sarah smiles to me and reaches her hand towards mine, and I stretch my hand out to hers…

Royal Mail Ship "Eider" 50163 – Official Log Book

March 2nd at 7am

St. Thomas Hospital

George W. Eastland Chief Steward departed this life from Yellow Fever in St Thos Hospital

C. J. Oxley
Surgeon

S. F. Hampshire
Chief Off

John Bruce
Commander

Royal Mail Ship "Eider" 50163 – Official Log Book

March 3rd 10am St. Thomas Hospital
The Remains of George W Eastland were interred in this Country took an inventory of his Effects + found as follows.

       John Bruce   S.J.Hampshire
       Commander   C. Off

Wages	55.6.8	Cash	37.10 -	Cash in possession of the deceased		12	12	8
Money in poss	12.12.8	Fees	- 3 -	One Trunk containing viz	1 Garrie Bag			
Sale of effects	22.10.1	Funeral expenses	9.10 -	1 Stick	1 box containing viz			
	90.9.5		47.3.0	1 Felt Hat	7 Coats			
Deductions	47.3.0			2 Clothes Brushes	9 Prs Trousers			
Balance	£43.6.5			14 Waistcoats	8 Vests			
				21 Shirts	1 Albusan			
				6 Colored ditto	4 Books			
				19 Trousers	3 Prs Pajammas			
				31 Pairs Socks	1 Hat Cover			
				23 Sailors Collars	1 Coat			
				14 Ties	3 Vests			
				9 Hat Covers	1 Life Belt			
				1 Handkerchief	1 Pr Leggings			
				1 Black Cap	1 Comb Brush Bag			
				1 Comforter	1 Razor & Stand			
				2 White Coats	1 Pr Slippers			
				8 Pipes	1 Box Handkerchiefs			
				3 Shot Flasks	1 Cashbox containing viz			
				13+/o open collars	1 Masons Certificate			
				1 Spirit Flask	5 Intercolonial Service			
				1 Boot Jack	3 Discharge 1 Large Seal			
				1 Tobacco Pouch	1 Pearl Ring 1 Diamond Ring			
				1 Pocket Book	1 Gold Watch 1 Gold Locket			
				1 Pr Nifopins	1 Ornamental Watch 1 diary			
				1 Card Plate	1 Small Nugget 1 Spade			
				1 Screw driver	1 Silver Coin 1 Broken Brooch			
				Snuff 13oz	1 Gold Watch Key 2 Gold			
				2 Pictures	1 Breast Pin 3 Shirts Stands			
				One Bag Containing	1 Signet Ring 1 Hasp Ring			
				7 Shirts	1 Pr Earings 3 Portraits			
				3 pr Trousers	6 Copper Coins 1 Stores knife			
				3 Pajammas	The undermentioned articles sold before this made			
				3 Coats		£	s	d
				20 Singlets	18 Boxes of Cigars	12	16	6
				3 drawers	24 Single ditto	"	5	"
				5 Waistcoats	3 Pictures	1	11	5
				7 Prs Socks	10 Seamans Caps	"	7	"
				9 Handkerchiefs	1 Mosquito Curtain	"	2	"
				11 Collars	3 Guernseys	"	5	"
				4 Prs Boots	1 Cigar Holder	"	14	"
				1 " Leggings	1 Iron Chest	"	8	"
					1 Gun	1	19	7
					1 Boat	2	18	4
					1 Parrot in cage	**1**	**2**	**11**
						22	10	1
					Total Amount	£35	02	09

Postscript

1 Parrot in cage is the true-life story of my great-great-grandfather, George William Eastland. Yet, until now, it has never been told.

In 2004 I stumbled upon my ancestor's handwritten letters and other documents. The papers were worn and the handwriting loopy and hard to read, but when I persevered the documents began to reveal his maritime life. After a few years of further research, including in Sussex archives, The National Archive and the Greenwich Maritime Museum much more was revealed.

The story thus emerged, like an old ship reluctantly given up by the sea and washed up on the shore, one hundred and fifty years later.

After his death his name and details were added to the gravestone of his beloved wife Sarah at the Church of St. Mary the Virgin at Appledram. In 1872 his Father and Mother, George and Ann both died: they had probably had enough of this world. They were buried in the grave next to that of George and Sarah. The two graves with their headstones remain tucked away under the shady canopy of trees immediately behind the Church. The ancient church today stands quite isolated at the end of a long pathway surrounded by countryside.

You can stand next to those two graves under the trees on a warm summer's day and look up to see glimpses of blue sky between the leaves as they rustle in the wind above your head. It is very peaceful there now.

If you close your eyes and listen hard you might just hear, upon the breeze, the distant flapping of canvas sails billowing high upon a mast, the whistling cry of an albatross, or the faint ringing of a ship's bell.

SHOCKING ACCIDENT IN THE WEST INDIES.—News has reached Southampton of a shocking accident having occurred on board the Royal Mail Company's steamship *Eider*, Captain Bruce, a few days before the *Seine* left St. Thomas for Southampton. The *Eider* is one of the inter-colonial ships, and it seems that she was on the Gulf of Mexico route when the fatal occurrence took place. It had been blowing hard, and the vessel was laid to for the night under the lee of an island called Lobos, between Vera Cruz and Tampico. At daylight next morning all hands were piped to heave anchor, and whilst the men were at work orders were given to turn astern. This so much strained the steam winch that it gave way, and the capstan being unable to bear the additional pull, and the falls, or ratchet claws, not being down, it flew round, the bars being scattered in all directions. Mr. Archer, the fourth officer, was struck by one of these at the back of the head, and instantaneously killed; a boy was knocked overboard, and nothing was seen of him afterwards. It is also stated that the storekeeper's face was almost entirely smashed, both jaws and his nose being broken, and his left eye knocked out. The poor fellow was left at Havanna, and was not expected to live. The butcher's arm was broken in two places; the captain's servant's leg was broken in two places; a fore cabin steward's jaw was badly cut, and his back hurt; a seaman's leg was broken; while some sailors were more or less injured. Mr. Hampshire, the chief officer, was struck in the leg, but he suffered no harm. However, he had a narrow escape, as the sole of his boot was pared off as with a knife from heel to toe. Mr. Archer was a smart and promising young officer, very much liked by those engaged with him, and much sorrow has been expressed at his shocking death. When the accident occurred he was on his first intercolonial voyage, he having gone out from Southampton in the *Seine* to join the *Eider*.

The Eastlands

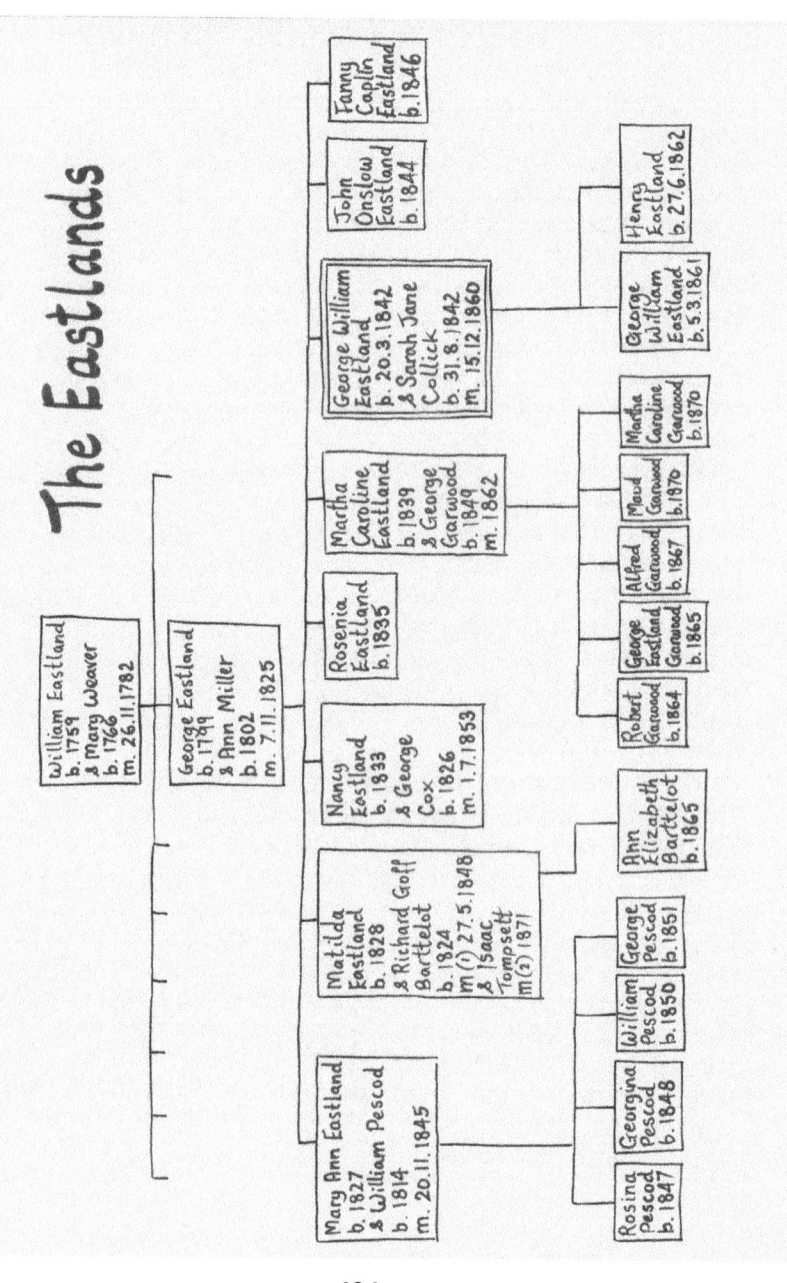

- William Eastland b. 1759 & Mary Weaver b. 1766 m. 26.11.1782
  - George Eastland b. 1799 & Ann Miller b. 1802 m. 7.11.1825
    - Mary Ann Eastland b. 1827 & William Pescod b. 1814 m. 20.11.1845
      - Rosina Pescod b. 1847
      - Georgyna Pescod b. 1848
      - William Pescod b. 1850
      - George Pescod b. 1851
    - Matilda Eastland b. 1828 & Richard Goff Bartelot b. 1824 m.(1) 27.5.1848 & Isaac Tompsett m.(2) 1871
      - Ann Elizabeth Bartelot b. 1865
    - Nancy Eastland b. 1833 & George Cox b. 1826 m. 1.7.1853
    - Rosenia Eastland b. 1835
    - Martha Caroline Eastland b. 1839 & George Garwood b. 1849 m. 1862
      - Robert Garwood b. 1864
      - George Eastland Garwood b. 1865
      - Alfred Garwood b. 1867
      - Maud Garwood b. 1870
      - Martha Caroline Garwood b. 1870
    - George William Eastland b. 20.3.1842 & Sarah Jane Collick b. 31.8.1842 m. 15.12.1860
      - George William Eastland b. 5.3.1861
      - Henry Eastland b. 27.6.1862
    - John Onslow Eastland b. 1844
    - Fanny Caplin Eastland b. 1846

The Collicks

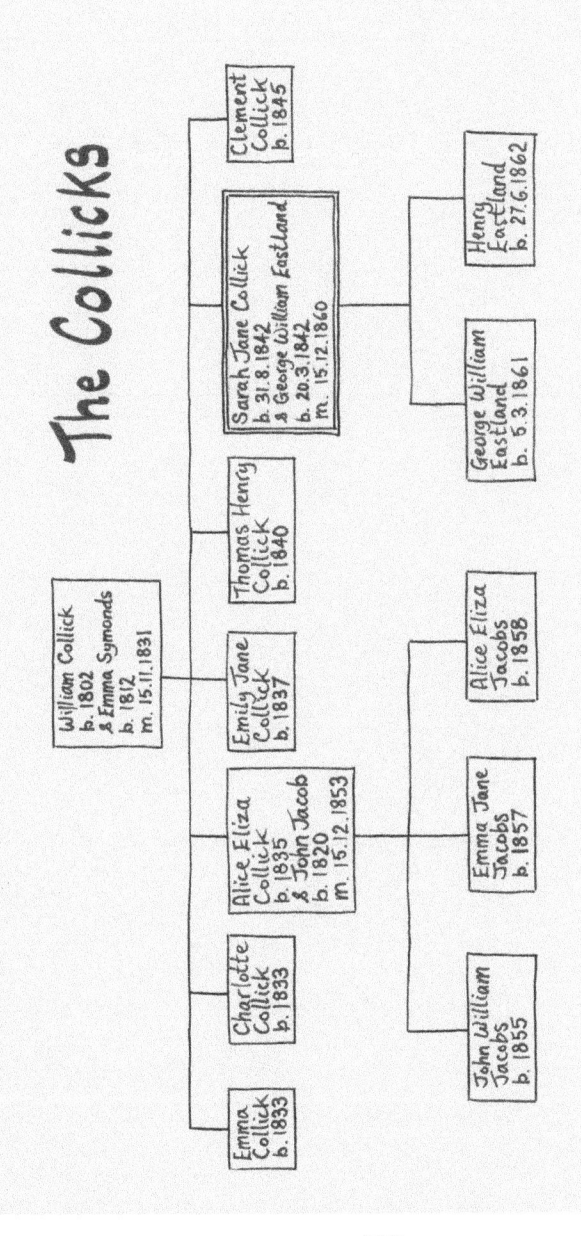

- William Collick b. 1802 & Emma Symonds b. 1812 m. 15.11.1831
  - Emma Collick b. 1833
  - Charlotte Collick b. 1833
  - Alice Eliza Collick b. 1835 & John Jacob b. 1820 m. 15.12.1853
    - John William Jacobs b. 1855
    - Emma Jane Jacobs b. 1857
    - Alice Eliza Jacobs b. 1858
  - Emily Jane Collick b. 1837
  - Thomas Henry Collick b. 1840
  - Sarah Jane Collick b. 31.8.1842 & George William Eastland b. 20.3.1842 m. 15.12.1860
    - George William Eastland b. 5.3.1861
    - Henry Eastland b. 27.6.1862
  - Clement Collick b. 1845